THORNS OF THE MESQUITE

THORNS OF THE MESQUITE

BY PATRICIA LEE LEWIS

Published by Levellers Press, Florence, Massachusetts

Printed in the United States of America

ISBN 978-1-965664-23-0

For my cherished grandchildren,

Zoe, Oliver, Grace, Georgia and Benjamin,
who will sing the songs, paint the images,
write the poems and stories of these days,
and change their world.

Author's Note

I was born and raised in Austin, Texas, and though I moved to New England with my family many years ago, the spirit of the Lone Star State—as they say—has never left me. My early childhood was marked by visits to my grandparents' ranch in West Texas, and the powerful images from that landscape and life have infused my writing for decades.

It was while I was leading a writing retreat in Ireland that the seed for Thorns of the Mesquite was planted. An image of my great-aunt Dona, whom I'd met only briefly at age five (but I remember to this day how she called the chickens), appeared to me, walking a dirt road on that very ranch. I was compelled to follow. What resulted, years later, is a novel born of deep personal roots.

Disclaimer

While *Thorns of the Mesquite* is set in a carefully researched part of West Texas of 1938, drawing on period newspapers, historical society reports, and firsthand accounts, this novel is a work of fiction. A wild west story told from a feminist point of view, it includes challenging topics and emotions concerning racial, sexual and domestic violence and may not be suitable for some readers. All characters, their names, dialogue, and the events and places depicted are entirely imaginary and are not intended to represent specific historical individuals or actual occurrences. Any resemblance to real persons, living or dead, or to actual events, is purely coincidental.

In the dark times
Will there also be singing?
Yes, there will also be singing
About the dark times.

Bertolt Brecht from "Motto" 1938

CHAPTER ONE

DONA ROSE WILLIS LOVED TO WALK, especially on the first day of April, when all the living things on the ranch sang out, exultant in the sun. She felt proud to have been born at the start of a new century, thirty-eight years before, and on this day, the air coming down from the Panhandle swirled around her like river water, cool and clear and running light. As she walked, her old cotton dress, the same color as the dried-up road, grew feather-light and soft. A dust-brown bird with buttons up its breast floated along the dusty road toward the high pastures.

The trembling came inside her neck, the wind of her body moving. It happened like that. A voice hummed, and it was not her voice. Alongside the road, live oak trees and cedar scrub echoed the gentle sun. Jackrabbits darted between clumps of cactus, searching for safety. Pods of the mesquite, dried at the end of last summer, rattled against each other like castanets. What else to do in such beauty but let the voice open.

I come to the garden alone, while the dew is still on the roses. And the voice I hear falling on my ear the Son of God discloses. And he walks with me and he talks with me and he tells me I am his own. And the joy we share as we tarry there none other has ever known.

Why would this old hymn come to her in the lightness of an afternoon? Roses did not thrive on dry, hot ranch land. It was hard enough to raise winter wheat and maize. And she was pretty sure she didn't belong to Jesus. But still, there was joy to share. No denying it.

It was a rare day. Noontime's dinner was over, dishes put away, the wash hung to dry in the sun, and she had swept the kitchen and porches extra well. Nobody could fault her for stretching her legs a little.

Her husband, Roy, and brother, Luke, had gone to town to meet Roy's son, Joe Bob, at the feed store. The men never walked if they could help it. They rode in trucks or on horses nearly everywhere. According to them, walking was for sissies and poor people — the Negroes and Mexicans. Well, she was merely a woman, which didn't count for much either, as far as she could tell. And she worried for the colored folks, some being her friends, hearing of the troubles that seemed to hang always over their heads.

She walked uphill, toward the only high ridge on the ranch, auburn curls escaping the shade of her straw hat, and her long legs reaching. The road carved through cactus and rabbit brush, and rose into the limestone flank of First Butte, tough and sharp under the heels of her boots. As a child she'd found fossils of sea creatures, pictures made by the fairies. That the plateau was once an ocean — that the dry, rough, sun-bleached home of her heart had been a watery land — well, that gave her hope. Everything changes. Including people.

She left the trail and made her way across limestone ledges toward a thicket of live oaks.

Lots of creatures sought shade from the sun on a ranch in West Texas. Some were not a person's friends, like scorpions and rattlesnakes; and some were, like centipedes and horny toads and jackrabbits. Horses and sheep and people and cattle sheltered under trees and inside tangles of cedar and oak and mesquite. It took a careful person to navigate the territory and not get in somebody's way. Like in the way of a bull's long horns, or a Tom turkey fleeing his ground, or a momma buzzard on the nest.

And Dona was careful. She grew up on her pony, helping her daddy and his brothers round up the calves for branding and the steers for market. She'd paid attention to how they found shade to eat their dinners and take a swig from their canteens. She'd flushed doves and tanagers from the cedar brakes and taken their place in the cool, tangy shadows. In the high pasture, where trees grew in patches, holding on to dry rocky ground by main force, the sun cast mirrors in her brain, and, as she took refuge under the live oaks, Dona said, thank you. Though she had no real notion whom she thanked, on an afternoon like this.

She had reached the place on the ranch she loved best, the old Sheepherder's Hut. She depended on its rough limestone walls and chimney, and the view from the low front door, where to the east, flat lands bristled with cactus and mesquite. From their pens on the main ranch road rippled the baying of Luke's Blue Tick hounds; and the lowing of Roy's Angus cattle came to her across the pastures, where they grazed among the thorns.

It had been a long time since Dona had fled to the Hut, like a fugitive. When she was little, and her mother allowed her to ride her pony as far as the buttes, she had pretended the Hut belonged to her. At the ranch house, she shared a room with her sisters, and she loved them just fine. But there was no place in the whole house where she could hide and read books as long as she wanted, or play all by herself.

As a girl, she'd loved to read and tell stories. Much better to be good at sewing and cooking for twelve, like her grandmother, and being thrifty with the egg money, like her great-aunts. But Dona had graduated from the junior college in town; and to this day, whenever she could, she'd go to the county library and bring home the latest *National Geographic,* and whatever book might "expand the mind," as Mrs. Monahan, the librarian, put it.

Roy didn't like that. He didn't read anything, except about ranching or hunting or war. And of course, there had been one war; and now there looked to be another one coming. So mostly he favored listening to the six o'clock news on the radio, and what he did read was purely useful, according to him.

All in all, her own life disappointed her. No children of her own, and never would have. A husband who drank enough to get mad and scare her to pieces. Dona stopped. She'd meant to come there and feel better. And now, she needed to escape her own, angry self.

She perched on the great boulder beside the Hut. The plains to the east, the red and black cattle, the deep greens and blacks of wild brush, the yellows and rusts of dirt and rocks, they seemed to sing out, like a great choir, *Arise, Arise, Arise!*

And she begged of the live oak trees, "How on earth, can a woman like me rise up?"

After she walked back to the ranch house and washed up at the trough, after she changed her walking boots for scuffs, put the pot on for coffee, stirred up the cook stove and started supper, she opened the letter lying on the kitchen table. The envelope smelled of saddle soap and leather mixed with stale tobacco. Her brother, Luke, had brought the mail in from the box by the main road from town. A sign that the clouds often darkening Luke's spirits had lifted, for a spell.

In wavering handwriting, on paper as pale and pink as her soft cheeks, the letter from Dona's Aunt Jeanette read, "*Dear Dona, On Annalou's birthday you always sent presents. She is thirteen. I have done my best to care for her this past year. I am getting old. You have no children. She can be on the train from Dallas on April 15. Please, will you take her in?*"

Annalou Rose Willis was the only child of Dona's younger brother, Lon, and his wife, Sugar, killed almost a year ago in a car crash. Dona had not seen her since the funeral. It frightened her to think about caring for a girl. So much could happen to her. So much had already happened. But, of course, she would say yes.

IF ONLY SHE HADN'T SAID YES TO ROY TEN YEARS AGO. The weather had been partly to blame. Rain in early spring on a ranch like hers in the almost-desert of West Texas brought riches greater than any diamonds. Scrawny weeds that hadn't bloomed in fifty years were out there busting their britches, breaking loose with yellow and red and orange blossoms bigger than the plants. Anything would grow, with a little rain.

"Time to rejoice," Reverend Andrew MacMurray had said to his congregation. "Time to give thanks for the beauty of the earth, for the beauty of the skies."

And they sang that familiar hymn. When they got to the end, where everybody, from moody Luke, to crotchety Mrs. Simpkins, sang a little louder than usual, *Lord of all, to Thee we raise, this our hymn of grateful praise*, why, Dona thought she might have to run out of the church and stand under the live oak tree by the graveyard and cry for happiness. But instead, Roy Fergus Turn, sitting so handsome and straight beside her in the pew, reached over and squeezed her hand. She held her breath as something new and thrilling moved between them. In that moment almost ten years ago, she gave in to the life of a rancher's wife, instead of the life of a rancher.

After her mother and daddy had moved into San Angelo, the county seat ten miles away, and her sister, Daisy, had died of pneumonia, and nobody in her family had wanted to take over, this had been her ranch. At least, before she married. Now Roy had taken charge, Texas ways being what they were.

She had liked running the ranch herself. She was good with cattle and pigs and chickens, and she liked being with the sheep and goats. She looked forward to working with the men and women from Mexico, who would appear one day at her back door and disappear another, months later, as silently. And when Negro men and women would catch her eye on the street in town in front of the general store, she would ask if they would like to help her out with the haying or the plowing, and they would. Some, she got to know pretty well.

But even after her brother, Luke, had said, "I'll stay and help you, Dona, but I ain't gonna be in charge a nothin';" even when she could count on Luke's help, she had not been so good at selling the cattle off to the stock yards in Fort Worth, or the horses or pigs at auction, or making sure the crops of maize and oats brought the best price, or knowing how to fix the wagon shafts, or the tractor when things went wrong.

Since grade school, Roy had had a crush on her. She liked him because he was smart and polite and sweet. But in high school Dona wasn't interested in boys so much as in books and horses, and she'd gone on to college. So, after a few years, Roy married another girl. Their son, Joe Bob, was no more than five when Lucille, Roy's wife, up and died of pneumonia and for the next two years, little Joe Bob was raised mostly by Josie Mendez, the Mexican woman who took care of Roy's house, and sister to Juan Carlos, Roy's top ranch hand.

Roy had a head for business and handled machines and cattle better than most. He'd been raised on a ranch before his daddy died from drinking and gambling and who knows what, and little Roy and his momma went to work for other ranchers. Maybe they would be a good pair. Maybe they could make the ranch green again, like it had been when her daddy bought it, before the drought set in—when peaches ripened on trees irrigated by the river, when there was more grass than cactus, more pecan and oak trees than mesquite and cedar.

They were married in the First Presbyterian Church in June, 1928, with little seven-year-old Joe Bob; Dona's grandmother, Myrtle Rose Cunningham; her mother, Ophelia Cunningham Willis; her sisters, Myrtle Sue and Unity Ann; her brothers, Luke and Lon; her Uncle James, sheriff of Comanche County; her second cousin, Edward, the lawyer; and everybody else, on both sides, present. Ranch families from Mertzon, with their fierce blue eyes, cattle raisers and cotton growers from Lipan Flat, east of town, and their towheaded children; hardware store owners, farmers, doctors and seamstresses from San Angelo, Comanche and Brownwood, squeezed onto straight-backed wooden pews and fanned themselves with their hats or scripture-embossed fans, provided especially for the occasion.

In the back of the church, in the last pew, sat six people, the likes of whom had never been allowed to worship in that fine establishment—Josie Mendez and her brother, Juan Carlos Hernandez, members of the Santa Lucia Catholic Church; and Samuel and Maisie Washington and their two little boys, members of the African Methodist Church on the edge of town. All had been specially invited by the bride. And since this was a wedding and not a regular church service, why, nobody could say a thing against it, much as they might want to.

CHAPTER TWO

SUNDAY, APRIL 3RD, DAWNED HOT. To a restless congregation in the church where Dona married Roy ten years before, Reverend Andrew MacMurray preached about honesty. "It is an eye, Brothers and Sisters," he said, using his holier-than-thou voice, "and it never has to close. I exhort you to make it your guide in life."

Dona was itching to get back to the ranch for a long ride on Duke. Josie would have dinner ready and Juan Carlos would have finished the morning chores, so she'd be free. But when the Reverend preached about being honest, she sat still and closed her eyes.

Lord knows, she tried to tell the truth, but lots of times she wasn't sure what it was. She didn't really mean what she said, not entirely, like when she said she loved Roy. Well, she did, of course; he was her husband. But sometimes, when he'd been at the whiskey a bit too much and his temper flared; or when it had been a month since they made love; when every night he came back from the cattle so tired he could barely shovel in the supper she'd kept for him on back of the stove; when he stunk like a bull or worse and didn't take a bath even on Saturdays; when he yelled at her because the bacon wasn't crisp or the coffee wasn't strong; or the sow's eyes were oozing and Dona should have noticed when she slopped her and the piglets; or when he seemed not to see her at all, but only what she did for him and the ranch, and then that wasn't good enough, either—well, whatever love was supposed to feel like, she didn't feel that.

Really, she didn't have any stronger feelings for him than she did for her brother, Luke, with his unpredictable ways. Or for her brother, Lon, bless his departed soul. Or for Melvar Sinclair, her childhood friend. Why, she'd lots rather spend a morning with Josie Mendez, hanging heavy work britches on the clothesline, than ride to town with Roy in his truck with nobody saying a word the whole way—in case it should cause him to find fault. Why on earth did he get mad at her so much?

Sure, she wandered off from time to time, riding Duke up the high pasture to the Sheepherder's Hut, where she could look out over the ranch all the way to Jesus. And what on earth did she mean by that? Jesus. Well, she wished she had known him. The one who had saved the prostitute from getting stoned to death. She didn't like what her church had done to him. Like making him the only savior of the world, and if you didn't sit in that hard pew and listen to Reverend MacMurray turn his face scarlet over "all you sinners who thought there might be another way to believe..." Oh, how on earth had she gotten herself off on that subject again?

Her conscience, that's what hurt, and Dona felt it, right between her ribs. A snake that lived coiled up in her stomach, asleep most of the time; but disturbed, like now, it flicked its tongue and muscled its way up her chest, through her throat and stared from her eyes. It didn't like what it saw, and sometimes it would strike when she was the one at fault. That's when she turned on other people, with venom. And why? Because she was afraid. Afraid to look at how awful she really was, a liar and a false witness. So, she lashed out at the nearest person, usually somebody weaker.

And even though she loved him, and raised him like her own, her temper made young Joe Bob wary of her, and maybe it was even why her own brother avoided her when she was upset. Maybe that's what happened to Roy, too. Maybe he felt bad about himself. She could see how a guilty conscience could have fangs, how it could strike back, and sometimes she imagined how its bite could be fatal.

Dona opened her eyes and her stomach tightened. She was in church. Reverend MacMurray had ended his sermon and the deacons were walking down the aisles with collection plates in their hands. Time to pay up.

Chapter Three

THEY CAME GLADLY FROM THE barn the next morning, the hens, queens and princesses, the old king, Buster. They waddled and scurried, they pecked and squawked; younger ones held back a little, so not to be overrun by their betters.

Dona loved that moment best, to stand in the dust of the barnyard, to hold her apron, heavy with feed, by its two corners. To call, "here chick, here chick, here chick chick chick." To dip and fling, to dip and fling, the circle reaching wider and wider, hens' frantic scratching growing steady with the plenty; and Buster, tail feathers high, chest gleaming emerald, copper, bronze, strutting the perimeter of his subjects, too proud to grovel with the rest.

On mornings when the last star rose over the ranch at dawn, Dona came there. In that sanctuary, those were her holy ones. From beneath the live oak tree, their beauty rose divine.

She sighed and whistled for her horse. In one week, the girl, Annalou, would come. And would the mornings ever be the same as this bright one?

A long way off gleamed the white faces of Hereford cattle. Dona clucked to Duke and they slipped and slid down rock ledges toward the cedar brake at the edge of the river pasture. The breeze blew cooler there, and what with the kingfisher diving from willow limbs, pairs of mallards passing through, and the stately green heron, it was probably lots more interesting for the cows, too. They could mosey over to the river to drink, and how many times had she seen their cloven hoof prints in the mud, and cow pies on the shore.

Dona admired cows, their eyes like deep pools, the way they chewed side to side, as though they had all the time in the world for eating. And they were nearing their death. Not the heifers, not yet; but the mommas, after a few years of bearing their calves, with other cows as witnesses, they wouldn't be far from being shipped to Fort Worth to the slaughterhouse. Like Dona's brother, Lon, and his wife, the beautiful Sugar, no one was ever far from the slaughterhouse.

"Let's take a walk through here, old boy; take a look at those mommas and babies."

Dona counted on Duke's understanding. How he seemed to know her mood, her will, her opinions; and he was not like his name. Not haughty, not too serious. She stroked his withers. "Why, Duke," she said, "you are plumb wonderful."

Ahead at the edge of the cedar trees, early Indian paintbrush blossoms had found enough soil on that dry, rocky ranchland, to make a carpet woven like a Chinese tapestry; like something she would stare at in her *National Geographic* magazines.

"Look here, Duke. I haven't told you yet, but my niece Annalou is coming to live with us next week. Let's come back to this place with her. There's so much we can do with a child at this ranch, besides work. Like what we used to do with Joe Bob, when he was little. Why, we can lie down and take a nap. We can squint and see a school of salmon flashing between the sun and those clouds. We can pretend we see elephants and ostriches. We can say we don't have any worries in the world."

Duke snorted and Dona laughed. "Too silly for you, old boy? Okay, let's see what's happening out here on the real ranch, where we will not see elephants, but maybe we'll come upon an armadillo with ruby eyes."

They trotted along the sheep fence between the river pasture and the McGregor ranch, and Dona, watching the graceful flight of a scissor-tailed flycatcher, felt light as a girl. But when she turned toward the earth, there hung a fawn with its front leg twisted between strands of barbed wire, its eyes infested with maggots.

"Oh, Duke. We are not to feel too much joy, are we?" She dismounted and knelt by the fawn and released its legs. "This poor little baby, following its mother, trying to jump the terrible fence." Dona's grief for the fawn and for her brother's child rose from the well which has no bottom. "How can young Annalou bear it?"

"Duke, the buzzards are already gathering and they have to live, too. But we can do something. See these figures in the rocks? These are the bodies of creatures who lived in the sea that covered this whole ranch and all the ranches between the hills. They died, like this little fawn, and this land is their graveyard. It will never end, this dying."

She circled the tiny, speckled body with limestone rocks to tell its place, for later there would be no sign it had ever lived.

Chapter Four

Two days later, the jingle of the peddler's cart filled the barnyard. Dona dried her hands, flung the dish towel on its hook over the drain board and fairly ran to the back porch.

Sure enough, hailing the house from his wagon, with Molly his mule leading the way as she had when they headed off last November, Melvar Sinclair, the peddler all the ranch women waited for — perhaps because of his wagon-load of fabrics and household goods, perhaps because of his exotic good looks — was making his first springtime round of the ranches.

"Melvar," she called as she pushed open the screen door. "I'll be right out."

Dona pulled on her barnyard boots and skittered down the steps. She stroked Molly's long ears and found the place under her chin where she loved to be scratched.

Melvar climbed slowly from the wagon's seat. How like a mountain lion he seemed, graceful in his power.

She swallowed and remembered herself. "Molly will want a drink, I reckon. I drew fresh water this morning from the windmill tank into the trough."

Molly thrust her muzzle into the mossy water and drank like she'd been thirsty for days, which she probably had. Melvar sat on his haunches under the old mesquite tree, leaning into its shade.

"I have coffee from breakfast. May I bring you a cup?"

"Yes, ma'am, that would be fine."

She ran back to the kitchen and before she grabbed one of the big speckled cups, she wrapped her arms about herself and hugged from side to side. "A new dress," she said to Josie, who added kindling to the cook stove, "I am going to make a new dress."

As she pulled tops off the biscuits, slathered some of her fresh butter over the bottoms and spooned a pile of peach jam onto a tin plate, she sang a song she'd learned during the war. "*How ya gonna keep'em down on the farm, after they've seen Paree? la la la la....*"

Josie grinned and Dona chuckled. "Maybe I'm the gal on the farm, and the cotton calico I'm hoping Melvar has in his wagon is Paris." She whistled the tune again. "Well, a new dress would be good enough to dream in, surely."

Melvar stood as Dona came around the house. His life must not have been easy, brought to West Texas from Persia as a boy of thirteen by a missionary, Reverend Arthur Sinclair, nearly thirty years ago. She saw how he shone, with his deep brown hair and eyes, and skin the color of pecans. Sinclair had said that the young boy was an orphan begging his living on the streets of Tehran when he spotted him. And that he had something God-given about him, as though a light fell on him from above, as he sat cross-legged before a table of wooden wares.

But most people in the congregation had shunned the child whom they called simply "Sinclair's boy." He looked like a Mexican to them; the kind of boy who would have lice and ribs that showed through. He arrived with a language they couldn't understand any more than most people in her church could understand Spanish. And of course, everyone knew you couldn't trust a Mexican.

"After you've had your coffee, maybe you'd show me whatever yardage of calico you brought."

"I think I have something you will like very much. It will make a beautiful dress. Let us look at what I can offer from my wagon."

"Thank you, Melvar. I've long admired the formal way you speak your perfect English. You're a blessing. It's your calico to be sure, but it's also your kindness. I mean, you take time to have coffee and visit. Would you please tell me something I've wondered about?"

"I will try."

"When the Reverend Sinclair asked you to leave your country and come to Texas with him, why'd you say yes?"

"Oh, my, that is not a hard question. He did not ask my permission."

"What?"

"No, he did not. He asked if I would like to go and see my mother. You see, I was not an orphan, but my family, though loving, had been made poor by war and lived in another part of Persia. When I was ten, and strong for my age, my grandfather brought me to Tehran, our big and magical city, to learn a trade. To help my family, back in the country. It was many years before I saw my family again."

"But Reverend Sinclair said you were begging on the streets when he found you."

"I was not. I sold small tables on the street, things I had made as I learned my trade. I was by then thirteen years old and had taken with joy to woodworking and the lessons of my teacher."

"But why on earth would Reverend Sinclair lie?"

"I think to make a sympathetic story. He wanted me to return to the United States for reasons of his own."

"Oh, Melvar. I'm so sorry. And your family? Did they find out what happened to you?"

"I returned to Persia after Reverend Sinclair died. I found my family, but that is perhaps a story for another time."

"I'm sorry to pry, but I've known so little about you all these years. You were away for a long time." Dona observed her hands folded in her lap and said, "Is Melvar your real name?"

He took in a breath. "My name is long. My family called me Melvar, the name you know."

"It's a beautiful name and the fullness of it is perfect. And now, how about we find the perfect calico for my dress?"

"The bolt of fabric I have in mind is wrapped in a quilt from my mother's hand, and it is waiting for you on the seat of my wagon."

Dona lifted each edge of the quilt and thrust her fingers into the folds of calico. "It's soft and light as air, and the colors splash like flowers. I feel like dancing."

Accepting the money Dona offered, and from the seat of his cart, Melvar smiled and reached to shake her hand. "Dona, I have missed coming here, and I am in your debt."

She kept her hand in his for a moment before pulling it away.

"I miss seeing you, too, and I'm so happy you're making your rounds again. Also, I forgot to tell you that my niece is coming to live with us on the ranch. She is thirteen, and perhaps she'll also need a dress."

"That is good news for you, Dona. Of course, I will have something for her to look at."

"I wonder. Do you still make things of wood?"

"When I find a pine log, or stump of pecan, over time perhaps a bowl or a simple chair will come from my hands. I keep my saw and chisel sharpened. It is work I love very much. Especially if it is for a friend I care about, such as you."

"The next time you come, would you bring something you made?"

"I will be honored. And I will bring sufficient gingham to make an apron for your dress. For special occasions, and graceful enough, I think, for dancing; even in the kitchen."

After supper, a few days after she'd bought the gingham off of Melvar's cart, Dona stood in front of the old place they called the shacks, near the river. Through cracked panes, she peered into the dank front room where she had danced once with her Uncle Baugh; Bob Wills and His Texas Playboys cranking out the music from her grandmother's wind-up Victrola. It had been years since she had danced, so why did she want to twirl a skirt and pound her feet?

Maybe because of Melvar? He had jingled up to the ranch house again this morning, and true to his promise, he had brought something he had made of wood. Before his rounds to all the other ranches, all those miles of dust and cactus, he had returned to her.

"That beautiful, golden violin. You made that?" she had said. "And, you play it, too?"

"I do." Putting it under his chin, he drew a bow across the strings. The tune was unfamiliar to her, but it lilted like a lily, unfurling toward the clouds.

"Is that lovely tune from your country?"

"It is, and I am glad you like it. Here is one I believe you know." He tapped his boot on the wagon's floor in time to 'Turkey in the Straw.'

As the last notes faded, she said, "Great heavens. Is there no end to your talents?"

"That is the end," he laughed. "And now I must make my rounds."

A gust of wind rattled the dried mesquite pods above their heads as if to close the conversation. They smiled at the flourish and Melvar moved Dona's hand from its hold on Molly's bridle into his own. Opening her hand and tracing the lines of her palm with his finger, he said, "You have a very long lifeline, my friend. I hope for you great happiness."

He bowed again, climbed aboard and clucked for Molly to begin their journey.

Dona waved until they were out of sight, and with a sigh, ran the tip of her tongue across her palm.

MELVAR SETTLED DOWN under the mesquite tree by the ranch house early the next morning. His wooden wagon and Molly the mule rested in the shade of the barn, and Dona had her hands in the wash tub.

"Leave the familiar for a while," he said, "and come walk with me."

"The familiar would be a good thing to leave." She stood and rubbed the small of her back. "But, Melvar, I have to get my chores done. Josie's been called to Mexico for a little while, to take care of her mother. Who else'll finish this laundry? Who else'll make dinner for the men? Who else will get everything ready for Annalou. She arrives in two days."

"I can help with the laundry," Melvar said.

"You?"

"Yes, why not? My bolts of material become dusty. I've done much laundry in my life."

Dona felt his eyes the way she felt a barn cat's, that he knew everything. She turned back to scrubbing a shirt collar.

"Your tiredness, is that from pain in the body?"

"No, and I believe you know it isn't. No, it's in my heart, or something close to my heart. Maybe in my belly."

"You have not had children?"

"No."

"And is that a sadness for you?"

"It's part of it, I suppose."

"And the rest?"

"I don't know for sure. And I don't want to talk about it right now. There are so many shirts and I haven't begun on the britches."

"Would it be permissible to help you?"

"You want to help with the wash?"

"Yes, of course. I am strong."

Melvar had been sitting on his haunches, his accustomed position. When Dona asked about it during one of their talks, he said he must have sat like that as a child in Persia, that he couldn't remember many things about his earliest childhood there, but that squatting felt natural and easy. He had laughed then and said that it made a good change from riding on the wooden seat of his wagon over roads of dirt and stones.

But now he stood, and walking to Dona's side, he rolled up the sleeves of his blue cotton shirt. The insides of his arms, dusky and smooth, so different from her milky ones. His were luscious.

"I am quite serious, Dona. Please let me help. Perhaps you might hang the ones you have finished on the line while I take care of these things?"

"But what if the men return from town to find you doing their wash? What'll they think?"

"What will they think of me? Or of you."

Dona turned her back to him and picking up the basket of wet clothes, she walked to the clothesline without answering. Why, she wondered, did she worry so? It wasn't worry. The clenching in her stomach. The sour taste in her mouth. That was not worry. That was fear.

She did not want to lose Melvar. She did not want Roy to see her with him, doing the wash. He would know; surely, he would know that this was no ordinary friendship. But was it ordinary? A traveling merchant and a ranch wife doing the wash together—no, that was not ordinary and Roy, anyone, would see that.

She shook out one of Roy's work shirts and fixed its hem to the line with wooden pegs. Upside down. Upside down every one of those fifteen shirts. Everything, upside down.

Luke had whittled the pegs. Every mid-winter night for years it seemed that Luke had whittled something useful for her. The clothes pegs, the curved soup ladle, the handle on her mop, a pecan-wood coffee cup which she kept on a special shelf. Said it helped him get through those long nights. What would Luke think of his little sister, that when she heard the jingle of bells on Melvar's cart and the steady clop of Molly's hooves, her whole body felt like skipping. That she wanted to run through barnyard dust, laughing like a child?

She was a grown woman, a married woman respected in her county and by her own family. She could not think of what would happen if they found out.

These past few days, she would smooth her apron over her everyday dress or dust off her riding britches and keep on with whatever she was doing until Melvar called out, "Is anybody home?" And she would say, "Over here," if she was doing the wash below the windmill; or "I'm in here," if she was frying chicken and couldn't leave the stove; or "Around back,' if she was working in the garden. And he would always find her there.

That garden. Was it the one in the hymn that had trembled from her throat on the dusty walk to Sheepherder's Hut only two weeks back? And Melvar. He was the one who walked with her and talked with her, like no one had ever done. Could it be that she was also his own?

He finished the wash and moved to the basket. "I will hang these on the line, if you give permission."

Dona laughed. "All right. I give permission."

Fifteen shirts, nine pairs of blue jeans, fifteen pairs of socks and a dozen undershirts hung on the line in neat rows when she and Melvar walked across the caliche road and into the shining green of the hay field. The sun sat low in the morning sky. They would have an hour.

They made their way to the far edge of the field and sat on a flat rock, wide enough for two slender people. The hay topped off at the height of their eyes, and the world was pierced through with emerald shafts. They were careful with each other. But something had arisen shining and unsayable between them.

"Dona, if it is not too personal, I would like to know, what are your favorite things?"

Dona grinned. "Too personal? Well, let's see. I love to watch green turtles piled on a log in the green water of the river. That's one. And then, the way a scissor-tailed fly catcher soars like an angel, its tail feathers shining in the sun. And you know the fossils from the ancient lake that used to be here, the limestone rocks filled with sea creatures—I love those. Now, you tell me."

He cocked his head at her and smiled under the shadow of his big hat. "I will say my favorite things, but what I love best I cannot speak about at this time. In nature, it is to watch the sun moving down the sky behind the big oak trees. They are black and the sky is red and purple and gold. So much like what I remember from my childhood."

"Do you miss them terribly?"

"Whom do you mean?"

"Your mother and your father, and the rest."

"It is strange, but I no longer miss them."

"It must've been so hard when Reverend Sinclair took you away."

"It was an abomination of feeling, but I have learned to feed myself with those feelings. My memories are bitter and they are sweet and they are food for my life."

"I think you have a very large heart."

"I do not know how large it is, but it connects me with Persia and West Texas and you and my family equally. It's long since I tasted the bitter. Meeting you when we were children, Dona, that began to restore the sweet."

"Truly?"

"Your kindness was from the beginning. Reverend Sinclair took me to attend the church and you were there in the choir for children. Perhaps you were nine years old. And after church I stood behind Reverend Sinclair and you came up to me and said, hello."

"I remember."

"You asked my name and when I whispered, Melvar, and Reverend Sinclair told me not to speak, you did not laugh. You said, 'I am glad to meet you, Melvar.'"

"And you said, my English no good," Dona smiled.

"I wanted to sit down then, under the big elm tree, and ask you to teach me."

"And why didn't you?"

"Because Reverend Sinclair did not wish me to talk with a pretty little girl. He was very strict and it was not strange for me to feel the sharp buckle of his belt."

"It's terrible for any child to be beaten. But you grew silent and strong, like a tree, and kept to yourself."

"It is important to eat from the past and to grow from it. That is the way of my people. Our culture is perhaps the oldest in the world, and without the past we would know very little."

"So, then, may I ask you a question about your family? It's a hard one."

"Yes, of course, anything you wish."

"Did your uncle sell you to Reverend Sinclair?"

Melvar looked down. His hands rested over his knees and he turned the palms to face the sky. "Sinclair did not buy me."

"He stole you?"

"Yes, apparently he did so."

"How do you know?"

"I may have mentioned before that when I became grown, and after Reverend Sinclair died, I travelled back to Persia and members of my family. It was difficult to find them because of the war, but they did not give me up at all. In fact, they mourned me for a long time. My mother declined and it is said that she died of a heart sickened by my loss."

Dona saw how some people, no matter how hard the life becomes, rise like butterflies from death. Clouds covered his birth in a village in Persia, but he remembered well his mother and his father.

"They found tutors for me and a nurse for Bita, my baby sister," Melvar said. "I applied myself to my studies like a fledgling preparing to leave the nest. There came a war. Our family lost our home and land to new leaders, and we ran into hiding. We were by then very poor and as I have said, at ten, I was sent into the great city of Tehran to learn woodworking from an uncle, who was kind. The roots of that work became for me a life."

"So that is how you learned to make beautiful things, and you still do."

"Reverend Sinclair was a Baptist missionary. He seemed to like me and my wooden things, and was friendly. But one day, he turned into a creature unrecognizable to me. And though I was strong for my age, he was stronger and succeeded in abducting me from Tehran, tied and gagged. I was many days kept in the hold of a ship, headed for Galveston, Texas."

"Great heavens. Because you were a beautiful boy?"

"Apparently, yes. He adopted me, and his church praised him for saving a wretched child. But, in the hold of that dark ship, he took me to be his slave, in body. Which, out of fear, I became. But never his slave in mind or spirit. Attending church, yes, a wretched child, a slave with my master. But it is how I first saw you. And, Dona, at that moment, a freshet of clear water broke the dam in my heart."

Tears made their way down the cheeks of this man, whose spirit filled her own.

"After that, little by little, I picked up the peddler's trade, not a threat to anyone, and learned to listen. When I turned eighteen, the Reverend died of unknown causes. I took what I needed of his belongings and what he had bequeathed me, and left the town. I made my way back to Persia. When I returned many years later, bringing with me my little sister, I had become this, a man of the shadows, who knows how to turn what he learns to his advantage."

Dona reached across the rock where they sat and put her hand in his.

When Melvar left in his wagon and Duke and Paint had whinnied their last goodbyes to Molly from the corral, Dona had barely time to get dinner ready before the men returned from the fields. Thank heavens she had already fried the chicken in the cool of early morning; the potatoes were done and ready to be mashed; and she had two jars of her own green beans to open and stir up fast with some bacon in an iron skillet. Biscuits of course took no time at all and as soon as the oven burned good and hot, she put them in to bake and turned to making cream gravy.

It was hard not to think of Melvar, his lean, noble face, his fingers spread long on his knees, eyes green and gold and dark as the river, as gentle as Molly's. So, he had thought of her all these years, noticed her growing up, known of her marriage, and perhaps of her struggle to keep this ranch from belonging only to her husband.

"Just think about dinner," she said aloud. "Get that gravy made and set the table. Tell Josie how much you missed her, whenever she gets back."

She had fixed five glasses of tea when the rattle and grind of Roy's truck reached the barnyard. In three minutes, he and Juan Carlos and Luke and Joe Bob would be washing up at the windmill pump and in two more minutes they would be in the kitchen, blowing and hawking and stomping their big boots and saying all the things they always said about being mighty hungry, about how good it smelled, and could they have a mite more sugar in their tea. And never once would any of them say, "How are you, Dona? What kind of morning did you have?" And they would never thank her for all her work to keep them clean and fed.

She thought of Melvar, and how he used his hurt feelings to grow strong, and she said, "Have a seat, boys, lots of good food today. And I want to thank you for working so hard on the ranch this morning. And every morning. Thank you for taking such good care."

Roy said, "Is something the matter?"

"Why no." She handed him the bowl of gravy. "I'm just glad to see y'all."

The men seemed to be eating faster than usual, their eyes cast down, hats on the backs of their chairs. Dona liked the feeling that came with saying the good things.

"And remember, boys, little Annalou arrives tomorrow, so let's all be nice."

Chapter Five

At the first sign of dust rising out by the cattle guard at the main ranch gate, Luke, Joe Bob and Dona gathered in the mesquite tree's shade by the barn. Their grins made shy by curiosity, they waited for Roy's truck and a sight of Annalou.

Dona hoped a girl of thirteen would not notice that her best yellow housedress had thinned with wear. Perhaps she wouldn't think it too doughty, covered with a kitchen apron, its tiny brown and white checks. And what shoes to wear for this first moment in over a year between the orphaned child and her childless aunt? Even for the barnyard, she had chosen her better leather pumps, almost good enough for church. Dressed and waiting, she was as nervous as a hummingbird. How could she ever talk with Annalou about her dead parents? Even harder, how could she raise a girl? What if Annalou had turned angry, a child who would never like her aunt?

But when at last she saw the girl who emerged from the old truck, pale and tall and frowning faintly, she gathered her in her arms as though she had been waiting for this moment for years. Which, in a way, she had.

Annalou rested her head on Dona's shoulder and said, "Oh, Aunt Doney, Aunt Doney," before she stumbled to her Uncle Luke, who looked pleased to get a hug.

"Howdy, Joe Bob," she said, looking up at him and putting out her hand, "you sure did grow."

Joe Bob's face reddened. "Yep, guess I did, and I'm mighty glad you're here, Annalou. Awful sorry about your momma and daddy."

Annalou nodded and folded her arms around her chest. She shuffled to the edge of the barnyard and bowed low. It looked as if she might throw up, but instead she called out.

"Aunt Doney, all of y'all, come look. This beautiful flower."

They came closer, and saw the way her long braid reached for the ground, how in the late sun her hair shone like new corn. Annalou knelt and stroked the tiny flower.

"Why Annalou," Dona said, "I believe you've found the finest buttercup of the spring. Look, the yellow comes off on your fingers. They say if you put it to your nose and it leaves a yellow spot, you will soon find the one you love."

"I'm a little young for that," said Annalou, her mouth curling to a grin. "But will there be more?"

"Oh my, child, every year this whole ranch is yellow, and this year, with the rain we just had, it will be like a painting; we'll show you where to look. Didn't you have these in Mertzon?"

"Well, maybe we did. But you know, I wasn't on a ranch, or outside so much."

"These little flowers do best on poor soil, Annalou, and most of the soil around this ranch is pretty poor. Lots of wildflowers, all colors, thrive here."

"I believe I am going to like poor soil," said Annalou, glancing up, her eyes squinted. "Might I pick just this one for my pocket?"

ANNALOU SLAMMED THE SCREEN DOOR and scurried down stone steps to the door yard. She'd been at the ranch for two weeks, and on this morning, she'd waked up to the sound of Aunt Doney banging away on the washboard over by the windmill. She stood close to the water trough for a moment, without speaking.

Across the edge of the river pasture, a bird she had never seen before swooped for its breakfast, catching the sun like the blade of a sword. And in the brake of mesquite at the river's edge, Tom turkeys chortled and called, perhaps to her. Annalou took a breath deep into her belly.

All this time since her parents were killed something dark and heavy had sat in her chest. It woke her up in the middle of the night; it slowed her down when she ran late for school; it tied up her throat when she tried to eat. Aunt Doney and Uncle Roy had done their best to make her welcome, and though the school year was almost over when she arrived, the other students and the teachers had been nice to her. She tried, she really did, to smile and be friendly and polite and grateful. It made her nearly sick to her stomach.

But this morning, after yesterday's brief rain, the air had cleared and Aunt Doney worked in sunshine. She hummed as she slung the heavy work clothes from tub to tub.

Today, with hens running around her feet, like she belonged there, and with the windmill creaking in the small breeze, yes, perhaps she was happy. But could she be good enough so they'd let her stay? What if she was too much trouble to have around, who would take her in? I'm like the piglet we kept under the wood stove last week, she thought, the one the other piglets shoved out of the litter. That little fellow had nothing going for him but us, and what if we decided one morning that he was too much trouble. What if when he squealed and kept us awake at night, we had put a pillow over his head or thrown him outside for the coyotes to find? It was a good thing he was cute and grew fast, or Uncle Roy might have done just that.

"Aunt Doney," she said, "can I give you a hand?"

"Sure, honey. Really glad you're here. Wanna learn how to hang khaki pants on the line?"

A WEEK INTO MAY, winds out of the north blowing across the maize stubble turned the kitchen cold. Luke hadn't been around to buck up mesquite for firewood, so Dona was being stingy with the fire. Come to think of it, where'd he been?

"Aunt Doney, "Annalou asked, breaking Dona's thoughts, "does it ever snow around here?"

"You bet, honey, in winter. This is a late storm. In the old days, it would rain real hard and fill up the wells and rivers. Of course, we had a goodly amount of rain last month. But usually, the big clouds come and we hope for rain; and we're disappointed most of the time.

"Your great-grandmother, Myrtle Rose Cunningham—your Nanna—when she was your age, so the story goes, saw a blue norther dump five feet of snow on her family ranch, over toward Comanche. The people who'd lived there all their lives, why, they couldn't believe it."

Annalou and Dona finished picking stones out of the dried pinto beans spread on the kitchen table. Dona rinsed them in the sink with water from the windmill tank and put them in the deep soup pot. She threw in a piece of salt pork and a little chili pepper, slid the pot onto the back burner and stirred. The beans would cook for a while and soak until morning.

Annalou washed the table clean and sat down. "So, what happened when the blue norther hit?"

"Lots of people died," Dona wiped her hands on her apron. "Horses and cattle. Sheep did better than most, what with their wool coats, and they'll eat almost anything; but it took a long time for the sun to get hot enough to melt that much snow. Then, wagons got stuck up to their axles in mud. Crops spoiled in the fields. And the sickness came. The epizootie, they called it then. The Great Influenza. Children and old folks dropping in their tracks. Nobody knew how to cure it. Still don't, really."

"Your momma, she was all right?"

"She was. She's always been strong, but she lost her littlest sister and brother and she says she liked to never got over it. I believe her."

"I've never seen much snow, Aunt Doney, just little dustings, but I dream about it some. I'm under the snow and I know it's blistering cold, but I never feel it."

"Well, that is peculiar. What's it mean, do you reckon?"

"I think it's about losing my mother and daddy in that accident. When the sheriff came and told me, the cold came into my body and I couldn't cry. I couldn't feel sad. That is an awful thing to admit, isn't it."

"Not awful, honey. You had all the stuffing knocked out of you for a long time."

Annalou crossed her arms around her chest and sighed. "I miss my momma's apron. I miss my daddy's blue eyes. But I don't miss the yelling. Or the drinking. Or momma crying in the middle of the night."

They sat in the quiet for a moment.

Dona said, "Did you ever try writing things down? I mean, your dreams and all that?"

"I did try, once. I had the little diary you sent me for my eleventh birthday, remember? And I wrote about being lonely. And how I was sometimes afraid of my daddy when he'd been out on a tear and even of my momma. One day while I was at school, Mother found my diary." Annalou shut her eyes. "And she read it, every word, and she got really mad and she grabbed me by the arm." Annalou bowed her chin almost to her chest. "She made me watch her throw it in the cook stove and she poked it 'til it burned right up."

The mockingbird sang down at them through the stove chimney as though there were no cares in the world.

Dona cleared her throat. "How about if I get you another diary, honey? Tomorrow, when I go to the general store."

Annalou looked toward the chimney. Her voice trembled. "Do you think they might have a red one?"

In two days, Annalou was off at school. Bells on the cart and the clop of Molly's hooves in the barnyard dust announced that Melvar had arrived, and before she could quite dry her hands on the dish towel and smooth her apron down over her skirt, Dona was out the door and at the wagon. An animal heat, like nothing she had known, rose to her face, her neck, her hair. She stared at Melvar, astonished, and could not speak.

"Hello, Dona," he said. He pulled his hat off his head and placed it over his heart. "I have found the gingham for a fine apron to go over your beautiful new dress."

"The new dress. Oh yes, the beautiful new dress. I haven't made it quite yet, but I'm glad to see you."

"And you would still want the gingham for the apron?"

"Oh, yes, and I would like...I'm not myself right now. Forgive me. Welcome, Melvar, it's good of you to come by."

He climbed down from the wagon on the side opposite Dona to lead Molly and the cart to the water trough. He stood where he had stood to take Dona's hand in his and remark on her long life line. It was a spot she had visited every day since, to remember his gentleness.

"I'll fetch a cup for water. Or would you like coffee? And how about some sweet potato pie?"

As she poured the coffee into the same two cups they had used before, the cups she had set aside so no one else would find them, she thought, *Dona, you are acting like a silly girl, which you are not. Calm down. This is your friend. Surely, he cares only for selling the cloth.* But still her hand shook as she poured the cream and stirred in the sugar.

He stood by the big mesquite, his back to the porch. "Dona," he said, as she came up behind him.

"Melvar." It was a moment only. She leaned down and balanced the tray on the edge of the watering trough. "I forgot my purse," and she turned to go.

She could hear him move toward her, his boots cracking last year's dried pods of mesquite, each slow step like sparks snapping.

She paused, her arms rising into air of their own will; rising to hold something she could not see but only pull into her chest, something so precious it would take a lifetime to love it enough.

"The sun feels good this morning, bright as it is," Dona's voice wavered.

"Sometimes," Melvar said, "I close my eyes so I can see better."

"You mean, see into your memories? Or do you magically know when nobody is at the ranch house but me? Like now?"

They turned to sit on the back steps of the ranch house, in mid-morning sun.

"Now, looking at you, your hair, brown and gold and red and shining, I am distracted from this moment."

Dona shoved her Stetson hat over her curls. "This better?"

Melvar laughed. "That's not quite what I meant, but maybe. In Persia, my family was accustomed to sitting quietly with our eyelids almost closed, and attending to the world inside ourselves. It is a habit I have kept."

Dona wrapped her arms around her knees and sighed, drawing the skirt of her housedress tight around her ankles. "That kind of stillness. I often yearn for it. We are moving around that sun as fast as can be and most of the time I am struck dumb by all there is to do." Dona bowed her head toward Melvar. "But you," she pushed her hat away from her forehead and gazed into the amber-green of his eyes, "you're always, well, here."

Melvar grinned, the lines in his cheeks like rivers through a golden desert. "Being here? It is the only way I can live. Being alive by being wherever I am, right now. Do you know what I mean?"

Dona nodded and stretched herself to standing. "I want to be like you. A peddler with a mule and a cart who sees everything."

"And I want to be more like you," he said, rising next to her. "You have much to love. I would like to be a rancher who cares about sharp-needled trees and the horns of bulls and loves her niece—and befriends a poor peddler."

"You must go, Melvar. It is important that no one mistake our friendship."

"The costume I wear, that of a peddler, with nothing but trinkets on his mind, is to you no disguise. You have seen me from our first meeting, without fear of my dark skin, or my words, odd and halting as they are."

He turned to Molly and rubbed her ears. With his voice almost a whisper, he said, "Only when I am with you, and when I am alone with Molly, do I not play a part."

He frowned and reached for Dona's arm. "You will not run away if I tell you of another part?"

"Something I won't like?"

"It is possible. I am close to a lawyer in town, your cousin, Edward Cunningham, and to the judge, Angus Cameron. Powerful men."

"How do you mean, close?"

"I know things about them that would bring them down."

"Why're you telling me at all?" Dona's voice, as she whispered, was sharp.

"Trouble is coming in our county. A rising up, again, of hatred by white men, especially toward the Negroes. Perhaps what I know will be of help to others you care for."

"You're scaring me."

"There is reason to be afraid."

"You have to tell me what trouble."

"I cannot say any in particular, at this time. But be on your guard. And remember that I am on your side. No matter what."

"What do you mean?"

Melvar glanced toward the ranch house. "It is time. I must climb onto the bench of my wagon and become once again the peddler. Molly and I will raise little dust as we leave. And we will come again."

Chapter Six

"You have to do it, Dona. That dang steer got into the cows again and gored one of the calves. I ain't got time to catch up with the accounts tonight and the tax fellow comes early tomorrow morning."

"But Roy, I don't know how you've been keeping the accounts. You insisted on doing them your own way when we got married."

"Don't care, Doney. Cain't lose that bull calf. He's out of my best cow, and I gotta stay with him. Worth at least $50. Do your best. Whatever else, you're not stupid."

It took Dona all night. She pulled out Roy's boxes and ledger sheets. He'd written each figure in his careful hand; every one with a decimal carried to two places; and from the looks of the pencil marks top and bottom, each column added twice.

She examined the payday ledger; she studied the small pieces of paper from the feed store, receipts for grain for chickens and horses, medicine for horses and cows, sheep, mules and pigs, oil for the truck, hinges for the worming chute and shearing pens. From the general store, she found receipts for her dried pinto beans, corn meal and salt. It had been a busy month, what with having to feed the ranch hands and her family.

Some things did not show up in the pile of papers, a few things Dona bought for herself with her own egg money. Calico and gingham from Melvar Sinclair, for instance. Thinking of the day she bought that calico made her blush. She would not mention her extravagance to Roy.

And then there were the receipts for money coming into the ranch. Pigs sold two weeks ago, which still made her sad; cattle sold up river as breeding stock for the new ranch some big business had started; wool from the sheep; mohair from the goats Roy was trying out; precious spring lambs slaughtered for Easter dinner all over the county.

As the sky over the machinery barn lightened, Dona straightened her back, stiff from the night of working by lantern, and made a fresh pot of coffee for herself and whoever might be waking up soon. A neat stack of the ledgers sat ready for the tax man, and she wondered why on earth Roy had insisted on keeping them to himself for all these years. Maybe he had something like egg money, too. Someone like her peddler in his life, who brought color to his cheeks as she swished her skirts at the auction. Well, tomorrow, or as soon as she could, Dona would find a way to convince Roy to turn the accounts back over to her. When her daddy entrusted the ranch to her keeping, before she married Roy, she was in the catbird seat because she controlled the money. She'd prefer by a long shot to be that one.

After supper, as the dark deepened and the others had gone to their rooms, Roy came in from the barn and said, "For God's sake, get Josie to help with the dishes and come to bed."

"Roy, you know Josie is still in Mexico, and after I finish the dishes, I have to read a little while most every day."

"What's more important than coming to bed when I do?"

"Lots of things. Learning about the world."

"Why do you need to know so much? You cook pinto beans, collards and cornbread better than any ranch wife around, and you and that quarter horse of yours even win at the barrel races."

"It's what you said, Roy, ranch wife. You and everybody else thinks of me as married to this ranch."

"Naw," he grinned. "You are married to me and I am the ranch."

"See what I mean?" she was not grinning at all. "I am nothing but a barnyard servant."

Roy lowered his head, narrowed his eyes, and glared at her from under his eyebrows. Which meant he was angry. Which meant that she should obey him and come to bed. But tonight, she would not. She was exhausted, with no sleep last night, but she was bound and determined to stay up and read her new *National Geographic*.

"Sorry, Roy, it's not that I don't care about you, but you've been drinking, and I need to do this." She turned back to the sink to dry the dishes. She felt the heat of him before she felt his hands, but not soon enough to dodge.

"Maybe I had a snort or two, but I'll hog-tie you and put you in that bed if it's the last thing I do." He lifted her into the air and threw her whole body onto the linoleum floor. She tried to scramble up, but he was the fastest calf roper in the county and had wrapped her ankles with the rawhide string he always carried in his pocket. She pulled herself along the linoleum floor by her arms, trying to get to the kitchen table.

"At least you give the calves a running start. What kind of cowboy are you?" She came to her knees and clutched the edge of the table, pushing up to her hobbled feet. She grabbed her grandmother's yellow vase filled with purple asters from the center of the table and held it ready.

But Roy was spent. His hands shook as he knelt to untie the rawhide and free her ankles. "Here," he said, pulling out a chair, "here." He filled a glass from the water pitcher next to the towel rack and handed it to her, moving to take her hand in his. He could have been a rattlesnake, as fast as Dona drew her hand into her chest.

"Don't touch me, Roy."

He stepped back, hands out. "I am sorry, Dona. I am so sorry."

Dona supported her weight on the table and tried to catch her breath. "Get out of here."

He didn't move.

"Go to bed," she said, her voice softer. "I will sleep in the living room." She lowered her voice still more. "Do not come near me ever again."

"No, honey," his eyes opened in surprise, "you don't mean that. I said I am sorry."

"Yes, you are sorry, Roy. And that is not the man I thought I married. This is the last time you will hurt me."

He breathed faster, heavier. Her neck tightened, but she did not look at him.

Annalou spoke from the hall doorway, "Aunt Doney, is everything okay? I heard somebody hollering in here."

"Everything is fine. Your Uncle Roy is on his way to bed. I have a few things to finish up. See you in the morning, okay?"

"Okay," Annalou said. She waited for a moment before she turned down the hall to her room.

When her door closed, Dona said, "Roy, there is nothing else tonight. Please go to bed, I know you are worn out. We'll talk in the morning when we're feeling better."

Roy stood as a man under sentence. His big shoulders drooped, his head dropped forward on his neck, his hands hung limp at his sides. He turned away from her and walked down the hall.

Dona shuffled across the screened porch, down into the barnyard to the horse trough, which the windmill had filled with fresh water that afternoon, and buried her head in it. She blew air from her mouth, came up dripping over her housedress, and bent, head to knees, stuffing the apron in her mouth.

If Annalou hadn't come in, Roy would not have stopped.

THEY SAT, THE NEXT MORNING EARLY, Dona and Roy, finishing their coffee, fingering the table's oilcloth.

Roy said, "How about we take a look at that new little stallion?"

In a few minutes, they stood by the roping pen in the light of the early sun. Above the collar of Roy's blue work shirt, the freckles on his neck shone pink and gold.

"What did we know of love, Roy, when we married?"

"What are you talking about now?"

"I mean, you lost your daddy when you were so little."

"Yep, eight and a half."

"And your momma was mean as a rattler."

"Meaner."

"And you married Lucille when you were awful young."

"Yep, eighteen."

"And you had Joe Bob after a spell."

"He came along when I was 24. We lost the first little one."

"Right, and then you lost Lucille when Joe Bob was still a tyke."

"Yep, he was five." Roy shoved his hands in the front pockets of his pants, hunched his shoulders and faced the ground. "Why are you doing this?"

Dona leaned her arms on the splintered timbers of the corral and peered up into his face. "Honey, what chance did we have? We got married after you lost everything except Joe Bob. I'd never been married, never had a child, and I didn't have a ghost of an idea what I was doing with you or with him."

"You didn't love me, I guess." Roy turned toward the center of the ring.

"I sure thought I did. I always liked you. You were like a window into another world for me, dropping out to help your mother when your daddy died. I wanted to stay home, too, to be with chickens and horses and cattle all day long. I thought I'd like it, but Mother said I had to stay in school. You were a kind of hero, taking on all of that work when you were so little."

"Not much fun, now you remind me."

Dona put her hand on his arm, "I know that now. But I was a girl with a big imagination."

"You still are. I always, well, loved you for it."

"But, Roy, neither one of us had a real idea of who we were, or who each other was."

"Guess not."

"And the little bit of safety we grew around us in the beginning, that's pretty well shattered now."

"Guess you're right, Dona. Guess you are always right." He slammed the top rail with the side of his fist and turned away. "So why don't you get yourself another life. Quit your griping and leave."

"But it's my ranch, Roy." Dona's voice was low and tight. "And the only place I'm going right now is to the kitchen to make breakfast for you and everybody else." She clutched her elbows, to hide the shaking in her hands.

Chapter Seven

Dona had finished up the breakfast cleaning and was almost through making dinner for the noontime meal. She stabbed a drumstick with a long-handled fork, threw it on top of the mound of fried chicken and with a screech, slid the skillet to a cooler spot on the stove. She untied her apron, hung it on its hook on the wall, walked down the hall and knocked on the door to Annalou's room.

"You can come with me, if you want to, Annalou. I'm going out for a spell. Got to find myself a better attitude."

"I'll get ready right quick, Aunt Doney."

In the bedroom she had shared with Roy for all of their married years, Dona exchanged her housedress for a pair of khakis and a tan work shirt, pulled her canvas coat from the closet, shook off her slippers and pushed her feet into her boots. She was mad at Roy, but really, she was worried about what Melvar had said about some kind of trouble coming in the county. And right now, she was more worried about Joe Bob's attentions to Annalou. She'd caught him looking, that certain way, sidling up to her real close, saying things to her that made Annalou blush.

Gathering a few warm things to stuff in her saddle bags, Dona went to the kitchen for cornbread and chicken and a canteen of water. She did not look at Roy and Joe Bob and Juan Carlos, who were seating themselves at the table.

Roy said, "Just where do you think you're going, Dona? We ain't had our dinner."

"Chicken's fried, cornbread's made, mashed potatoes and cream gravy on the back of the stove. Annalou and I are going out for some clean air."

"Why in tarnation?"

"Just doing what you suggested. Gonna think about how to get inside another life, isn't that what you said? It's too close in here for me right now, like maybe I'll suffocate if I stay another minute. You and Joe Bob can have a fine time talking about what big men you are, owning a 10,000 acre ranch you didn't do one thing to deserve, except be born boys and be lucky enough to marry into my family."

By now Annalou was close beside Dona and reached for her hand. The two of them walked out the kitchen door, across the screened porch, down the steps and into the barnyard. They did not look back, but when they reached the horse paddock, Roy bellowed about how they'd better get on back here and put some food on this darn table, and Dona said, "okay we can breathe. He's not coming after us now."

"How do you know, Aunt Doney? He still sounds really mad."

"I can just tell, honey, it's instinct. And besides that, he's hungry."

Shadows were growing behind the Sheepherder's Hut when Dona and Annalou rode to the front of the one-room limestone building and dismounted. They set Duke and Paint to graze on the meager pickings around high pasture's stones and pushed the door open. Over the weeks since they had been coming up to the Hut they had made some improvements.

First of all, they had swept it to within an inch of its long history, finding every cobweb, black widow and otherwise, every bat dwelling, every nest of swallow or mouse. They had found holes in the walls where porcupines had made a habit of coming in, eating edges of the door, and small branches of charred mesquite left behind years ago in the fireplace. Every time they came back, they did a little more. And last time, they had finished fixing the wooden mullions of both windows and puttied clear glass into every space. That had taken a lot of doing, hiding the glass from Roy, getting it up the mountain on horseback, figuring out how to repair the splintered and scarred wood, but now the afternoon light shone in as through clear water, turning the stone walls peach and gold.

"Let's have a little picnic, Annalou, and pretend we don't have a worry in the world."

They sat side by side at a window, gazing across scrub oak trees, out as far away as a person could see, to the edge of the earth, to the Twin Buttes that poked their squat bodies into the air when all about them was flat and serious.

Annalou put her hand on Dona's arm. "Aunt Doney, couldn't we live here? Couldn't we plant a garden up here and bring a couple of the cows and the chickens and all of our books?"

"I know what you mean, but we have work to do down there. What about Pansy, the new momma pig? Who would take care of her when she has her little ones next week? And all the rest of the critters that depend on us. Mostly, what we have to do is get those men to shape up."

Annalou was by now sitting on the floor with her back against a wall. "Uncle Luke is cold to me some of the time and warm some of the time. And most of the time Uncle Roy is okay." She stopped and folded one hand inside the other on top of her knees. "It's Joe Bob I'm scared of, Aunt Doney, and Uncle Roy has got to get him in line or I don't know what will happen to me."

"I've noticed some worrisome things, too. Tell you what. I'll talk to Roy on Saturday after they get home from the rodeo. Joe Bob usually goes to bed real early after calf-roping. It's been hard to find any time alone with Roy when he's not dead asleep, himself. We've been having a bit of trouble between us, you know, and I've heard a rumor from one of my neighbors about him spending time with a pretty Mexican girl named Rosa. But I'll do my best."

"Thanks, Aunt Doney. I hope the rumors aren't true."

"Don't you worry. I was thinking about us having a slumber party tonight—you and me and the horses. What do you think?"

Almost dawn, and Roy was fit to be tied. Dona had not slept on the sofa. Not out in the barn feeding the hens, or gathering the eggs, not making the coffee, not getting the wash ready to soak.

Not in the outhouse, not in the kitchen or on the back or front porch. Not out by the windmill hauling water. The truck was in the barn; the wagon was in its shed. She hadn't been there all night and neither had Annalou.

All of the horses were accounted for except Duke and Paint. Two sets of horse tracks, large and smaller, both well-shod, led from the barn paddock across the dusty road to the river pasture and south toward the limestone hills, and none returned.

"Why in tarnation didn't she tell me, when she was heading out all mad, that she wouldn't be back?" Roy's forehead beaded with sweat under his broad hat.

He walked up the back porch steps, through the screen door without slamming it, across the porch and into the kitchen. By the time Luke and Joe Bob came in, the coffee was boiling and three speckled cups were laid out on the counter.

"Well, lads," he said, "I ain't happy about this one bit, but I reckon Dona knows how to handle herself and Annalou. No way am I going after her. I think we know why our women folk left, and you heard the ruckus yesterday. I guess it's my fault. But it'll go better if we've helped out a little, especially for me."

"Yep, you and Dona have been a mite testy here of late. Maybe she needs a little time off," said Luke, who rarely had so much to say,

"Well, she's your sister, Luke," Joe Bob said. "You ought to know her mind."

"No man knows the mind of a woman, son," said Roy. "And don't you forget that. But Dona left and took Annalou and that's all we know for sure. Except, they didn't take the truck, and that's a sign they might be back. So, who wants to slop the pigs and feed the chickens, and who wants to gather the eggs? I'll get breakfast. Ham and eggs and leftover biscuits sound pretty good to me."

"I'll milk Mehitabel right quick," Joe Bob said.

"And I'll tell those hens who's boss today," Luke said and went out through the back door. Joe Bob followed him across the yard to the barn and chuckled. Luke's voice was breaking as he yodeled, *Here chick, here chick, here chick chick chick.*

Roy and Luke and Joe Bob and Juan Carlos had finished the barnyard chores and the supper dishes, when Dona and Annalou unsaddled their horses, let them out in the paddock with their oat bags, walked up the front porch steps, took off their boots and stepped into the kitchen.

They said a polite good evening to the men, who said nothing. They lifted the cup towel on the back of the stove to find the leftovers. Sure enough, cornbread and cabbage were still warm. Dona filled plates for Annalou and herself; they sat down at their places and Annalou said, "Thank you, good Lord, for the food."

Luke walked out to the porch and disappeared to wherever he went, these nights. Juan Carlos tipped his hat, said *buenas noches*, and slipped out the door. Joe Bob turned on his boot heel and stomped down the hall to his room. As his door slammed shut, Roy, with his arms folded tight against his chest, cleared his throat, but said nothing. He pulled out his chair and sat at his place at the table, staring at Dona under his thick eyebrows, and then at Annalou. Neither looked at him. But they glanced at each other, and smiled.

Roy said, "Okay, girls, that's about enough of that. What the hell's going on!"

"What do you mean, Roy?" Dona said. "We've had a lovely day and night in the hills, is all. A person kind of forgets how beautiful this ranch is, stuck around the barnyard all the time. And thank you for doing the chores, and making supper. Your cornbread is delicious."

"You know exactly what I mean, Dona. You left without telling nobody where you was going or when you'd be back. We had to do all your work, and Annalou's. And besides that, we was worried."

"Worried? Why Roy, I wasn't sure you'd care."

Annalou pushed back her chair and stood up. "Please excuse me. I'm going to my room."

"Take a walk with me, right now, Dona," said Roy.

"A walk? How lovely. We haven't taken a walk, in years. Let me get a lantern."

Roy humphed, his forehead wrinkled to his scalp. "I'll meet you at the barn."

The light from Joe Bob's room shone on the pecan tree outside his window. But Annalou's window was already dark when Dona walked across the barnyard. Roy moved from the door of the wagon shed and came toward her.

She was tired, but still she tingled with the thrill of escaping with Annalou. For a little while, she had rebelled; she had left behind everything that sapped her hope for the life she'd dreamed about as a child. And there was Roy, coming to meet her in the dark. Despite how angry he could be, how it felt to be slammed against a wall when she disobeyed his wishes, tonight she was not afraid.

They stood face to face in the night, with only the sound of their breath to guide them. Her voice came as soft as a dove's. "Tell me about her, Roy. The other woman."

His shoulders tensed and he turned from her, mumbling, "Ain't none of your damn business."

Chapter Eight

Dona loved to make biscuits. Something about working the white flour and soft sweet butter between her fingers soothed her. Today, as she poured a cup of Mehitabel's buttermilk into the dry mixture, she thought about her grandmother. That was her way of making biscuits and for how many generations had women before her made them, just so. And how, with all the work of a ranch, had she kept up with twelve children, a husband and all the various relatives and ranch hands it must have taken to build their spread?

And her own mother. Raising five children, tending to a husband who was a doctor and away from the ranch to help his patients most of the time. How had these women done it? It was a question she'd asked herself, and her mother, many times. The only thing that ever came clear was that they had to.

She laid the biscuits in rows on the baking sheet, slid it into the oven and closed the door. She arranged the slabs of smoked ham in a cold skillet and stirred the fire. She put another skillet on to heat. Ten minutes. She went into the dark of the living room, felt her way to the piano and moved her hands over the surface until they rested against the cold metal and glass of a picture frame. Yes, this was the one she looked at over and over. She carried it back to the warm kitchen and sat again at the table.

Dona's mother, Ophelia Lafayette Cunningham, at about thirteen, stood on the front porch of a wide, wooden house. She was taller than the other eleven children, as tall as her mother, and looked straight at the eye of the camera. She was the oldest girl. Like Dona. The bossy one. The one you could count on. Like Dona.

Fourteen people, some standing, some sitting on the stoop, two in arms, and no one was smiling. Maybe they were afraid of the camera. Maybe Ophelia's father had been angry that day and yelled at their mother the way he did most of his life. They had known each other after all since they were children. But Myrtle Rose, Ophelia's mother, did not look upset. She looked straight ahead. That was the way to bear it, all of these children, that stern husband, the life of a ranch woman in West Texas.

Maybe Myrtle Rose had known the Comanche raids, the settlers taking the land, maybe she had seen things too awful to talk about, ever.

Dona held the frame to her cheek. Her face was wet with tears that dropped onto the glass. Why was this sad? She bowed her head into her hands, the photograph between them, and closed her eyes. It was about losing the past, the ones you loved, whom you would have loved, if you had known them.

She had no time for this nonsense. Biscuits were golden. Ham sizzled, and the pan for the eggs was nearly hot. She had to get up now; she had to get a move on.

Chapter Nine

On the first day of June, Annalou dangled her legs over the dam and stared at the crack for a while. While the river piled against the old dam, she thought about Joe Bob, and what scared her. The crack ran all the way down the dam, from the top on the dry side where you could walk if you were careful, to the bottom where rocks stuck out of the water. She was peering down, her fingers grasping the edge, when a horse whinnied from up river. That was not Paint's whinny. She scooted back to land and ran to the pecan tree where she had left Paint, with his reins hanging. But he was gone.

Annalou whistled the signal she'd agreed upon with Paint. It was a risk, for what if the person on the horse was up to no good? What if it was Joe Bob? But Joe Bob was with Uncle Roy at the upper corral, cutting the bull calves out of the herd. Wasn't he?

Annalou pushed herself between the trunk of a pecan tree and the brushy side of a river willow, grateful for the horse's warning. She hunkered down, not letting herself think of the snakes and spiders who also find safety in places like that, and peered out. In a minute, a rider on a big sorrel mare trotted into the clearing next to the dam and dismounted. It was a girl. Annalou stopped herself from crying out with relief. She'd best watch for a while.

The girl dropped the mare's reins and walked with her to the edge of the river above the dam. She knelt and scooped water in both hands, splashing her face and neck. The mare pushed her muzzle in the water to drink. "That's better ain't it, old gal," the girl said to her horse.

Annalou crawled out from the willow brush and as she stood, she called out, "Hello, there."

The girl looked to be a little older than Annalou. Tall, too, with bright red hair peeking beneath a well-worn felt hat; and she was a little bow-legged. A good sign she'd sat a horse for a long time. She turned toward Annalou and said, "I thought somebody was around. Saw a Paint gelding grazing over yonder, all saddled up."

"That's mine," said Annalou, feeling foolish for losing track of her horse, who trotted toward them as they spoke. "I'm Annalou. Who are you?"

"I'm Merrybelles," said the girl, lifting her hat. "Merrybelles from the Richards Ranch over to Knickerbocker."

"You come all that way this morning?"

"Yep, Sheba and me, we started out early, after chores. It's only thirty miles, give or take."

"Where you headed?"

"Brownwood. It's a ways from here."

"You are welcome to rest a day or two, if you like. There's room out in our barn."

"Whose ranch is this?" Merrybelles asked. She untied her saddle bag and pulled out a map.

"It's the old Willis Ranch, called Willis-Turn Ranch, nowadays." Annalou walked over to look at the map which Merrybelles had spread on the ground next to Sheba. "Here, on the Middle Concho River. Right here where it shows the dam."

"Your family own this spread?"

"My Aunt Doney's family owns it. I live here now. You want to ride back to the ranch house with me? My aunt's gone to town and I've got to help get dinner on for the men. I'd be glad to have you, Merrybelles. And Sheba, too."

"Well, thank you kindly, Annalou. Sheba and I could use some grub and a little siesta in the shade."

IT DIDN'T TAKE LONG to get dinner on the table. Dona had been called to town to take care of her sister, Myrtle Sue, who was having one of her spells, and no telling when she'd be home. She had fried the steak and thickened the cream gravy before she left at dawn that morning. Annalou slid a batch of biscuits in the oven to bake and when Merrybelles had washed up and asked what could she do to help, Annalou sent her out to the garden to pick six big tomatoes. "Slice them thick, please Merrybelles, and then put some of this Miracle Whip on top."

"Like my momma used to make," said Merrybelles, a small smile on her face. Without her hat, her hair tumbled in curls around a face as pretty as Annalou had ever seen. It was so much like her own mother's face, with its clear, lightly freckled skin, small straight nose and bluebonnet-blue eyes.

"Mine, too," said Annalou, working hard at the cream gravy, stirring until it bubbled just right.

"Your momma here, Annalou?"

Annalou turned toward the porch. Dust rose out by the first cattle guard. "Looks to be Luke's truck. Be here in a minute. We'd best set that table."

"I can do it. I'll wipe the oilcloth first."

"Thank you, Merrybelles. Set for six today. I'm real glad you're here."

The men washed up at the windmill trough, stomped their boots against the stone steps of the porch and ambled into the kitchen, single file. Roy, Luke, Joe Bob and Juan Carlos.

"Gentlemen," said Annalou with a bit of pride in her voice, "this here is Merrybelles from the Richards Ranch over to Knickerbocker. She and her mare are staying for dinner."

"Good to meet ya, Merrybelles," said Roy in a low grunt and tipping his hat. "Saw your mare out there in the shade. Nice animal."

"Howdy," said Luke, his hat against his chest.

"Well, hello," said Joe Bob, grinning at Merrybelles and running the tips of his fingers around the brim of his Stetson. He grinned toward Annalou, who was busy pouring the coffee.

"*Mucho gusto*," said Juan Carlos, nodding in the direction of Merrybelles and placing his hat on the rack next to the back door.

Merrybelles said, "glad to meet all y'all." She paused as if thinking what else would be proper to say, and then, looking at Roy, said "thank you for having me," and waited with her hands behind her.

"Oh, sorry, Merrybelles. You sit here in Aunt Doney's place. And Uncle Roy will say the blessing."

"Dear God, bless this food, Amen," said Roy.

It was the custom at dinner to eat in silence, and usually it was an easy silence with hungry, hard-working people reaching and slicing and filling their stomachs as fast as possible. Today Dona's absence and this new, very pretty girl at the table unsettled the silence, making it hard for Annalou to swallow her food.

That evening, Annalou and Merrybelles had finished most of the supper dishes when the phone on the wall sounded out three rings.

"That's for us," Annalou said. She dried her hands as she hurried to the hall doorway and lifted the receiver out of its holder. Stretching close to the mouthpiece she said a loud, "Hello? Yes, this is Annalou Willis. Yes, I'm Dona's niece. Who is this? Sorry, Bertie, I can't hear too well. Would you please say that again?" She pushed the receiver against her ear, stretched on her tiptoes, and held on to the door jamb.

She turned toward Merrybelles. "Bertie's the telephone operator, and she says that Aunt Doney's calling from the hospital."

"Thank you Bertie. Yes? Is that you, Aunt Doney? Oh, no. I am so sorry. Merrybelles, can you go find Uncle Roy? In the tractor barn. Aunt Doney? Yes, I'm here. It's Aunt Myrtle Sue? Oh dear, no. I am so sorry. It was so sudden, not one of her spells? Are you all right? No, we are fine. I can take care of things just fine. Don't you worry one bit. Here comes Uncle Roy. Please take care of yourself and Mamaw. It must be so hard for Mamaw. Yes. I will. Goodbye, Aunt Doney, I love you. Tell Mamaw I love her. Here's Uncle Roy."

Roy's hand swallowed the receiver as he bent toward the mouth piece. "Dona," he said, "what happened?"

Merrybelles scrubbed the iron skillet clean and was hanging it on its hook to dry when Annalou walked to her side. "Merrybelles, think I'll go outside for a little air. You want to come?"

"Sure, but I'd like to finish sweeping the linoleum first."

"Thank you. Feels like you've been a friend for a spell."

"I know, and I'm glad to be here. You go on and I'll be out in a shake of a lamb's tail."

"That's what my momma always said."

"Must be we're from the same part of Texas," said Merrybelles, with a smile.

Annalou was sitting on the stone steps of the back porch when Merrybelles pushed open the screen door.

"Pretty nice out here," she said, taking her place next to Annalou. "I'm real sorry about your Aunt Myrtle Sue. My momma died unexpected-like, too. Not long ago. It's awful hard to accept."

"Oh, your momma? It's the saddest thing. What happened to her?"

"She had the TB and we thought she was getting well and then one morning she didn't wake up."

"She didn't wake up?"

"She'd strangled in the night and nobody heard her."

"Nobody?"

"Nope. My lousy good for nothing daddy was in the bed right next to her, but he was drunk as a skunk and he never woke up when she died."

"That is awful."

"Awful is right. And I can't stay home no more."

"That's why you're on your way to Brownwood? Merrybelles, maybe you could stay with us, at least for a while. We could use some help around here and I'd sure be glad of the company of a girl around my age."

"Where is your momma, Annalou, if you don't mind my asking?"

Annalou looked at the sky, black as slate and glittering. "Sometimes I wish on that star over there, the really bright one. And I sing the twinkle-twinkle song so I can make a wish."

"Me, too," Merrybelles folded her hands behind her head and pointed her face up. "What do you wish for?"

"I used to wish for my mother and my daddy to be alive again."

"Oh, they're gone, too."

"In a car wreck. A year ago. Drunk, like your daddy. At first, I wished for them to be alive and to not be drunk."

"At first? So, what do you wish for now?"

"I wish Aunt Doney could be my mother."

"She's your momma's sister?"

"My daddy's. She takes care of everybody she can."

"You're pretty lucky, then."

"Yes. I guess so. Compared."

"To me," said Merrybelles.

Lifting her face to the sky, Annalou sang. *Twinkle twinkle little star, how I wonder what you are. Up above the world so high like a diamond in the sky...* Merrybelles joined in, her voice deeper, hoarser, cracking. Annalou thought that maybe some of those stars were tears.

The girls sat quietly then, listening to the night calls of creatures who had their own lives to live and in a little while Merrybelles said, "I can't stay but a day or two, what with being expected out there, in Brownwood. But maybe I can come back, if your family says so."

"We'll talk with Aunt Doney when she gets home tomorrow, but I can pretty much guarantee she'll want you to stay here. Tell you the truth, I could use the help of a brave girl like you."

"Why, especially?"

"I may need a little protection from Joe Bob."

"Don't that beat all. I thought that today at dinner. The way he looked at you. You all right?"

"I'm okay now. But it sure would be good to have a roommate, if you see what I mean."

"Yep, I do. And if Aunt Doney says yes, I'll be back in two shakes..."

"...of a lamb's tail," said Annalou and they both laughed. "Now let's go inside and make up a pallet for you on the floor of my room, just for a night or two."

Chapter Ten

In Dona's kitchen that Sunday, after Merrybelles left for Brownwood, Myrtle Rose Cunningham, Dona's mother's mother, waited. The table stood unadorned and sturdy under its oilcloth. A lantern hung from the stamped tin ceiling, and five chairs, wooden and scarred, stood empty around its edges. In the sixth chair, Nanna sat, her hands curled in her lap like kittens, sleeping. Her black shoes tied tightly around her feet, small as her hands, pointed toward each other like an arrow's head.

"Nanna," Dona said, turning to her, "the beans are nearly ready. Surely, you'll stay and eat with us?"

Nanna put a hand over her mouth and moved it to straighten the net over her white hair. "Not this time, Dona. I am not feeling so well as I might and I only came for a morning visit. I don't want to be a burden. Perhaps Luke can drive me home?"

"You've never been a burden in your life, my dear Nanna. You are always welcome here. You know that don't you? How does a fresh cup of coffee sound?"

"Don't go to any bother, honey."

"No bother at all. I'll have one myself. And maybe a piece of this custard pie?"

"Oh, well, custard pie." Nanna folded her hands again in her lap. "Perhaps a little pie and coffee would taste right good."

"Thank heavens, Nanna. I thought we were going to lose you there for a minute."

"Lose me?"

"I mean, that you might be leaving for home. And I worry about you living on your farm all by yourself." Dona carried the pie plate and a cup of coffee to Nanna and set it in front of her. "We want you to stay here with us. Will you please think about that?"

"Your mother asked me to stay with her, too, but I said, not right now. Honestly, I don't much like being in town. But, why would you want me?"

"Because I love you. You have cared for our family for so long; you were there when I and all of my sisters and brothers were sick or unhappy. You've been the one we could tell anything and you would love us. And you wouldn't go tattling to mother or daddy. Nanna, you mean everything to me."

Nanna straightened her skirt over her knees, pulled a white handkerchief from her dress sleeve, lifted her glasses to wipe her eyes and settled her feet exactly side by side. Her thin voice wavered as she raised her chin and said, "You wouldn't mind having an old fossil who is nearly 100 years old in your home?"

Dona laughed, "we'd be so happy, Nanna. And I promise, we will make sure your peach wine is always in the cupboard, right over there."

Dona found Roy in the wooden barn and drew a breath for courage before saying to him, "I'm sorry not to have talked with you about this before, but Nanna took a fall last week and it's not safe for her to live alone at her farm. For the time being, she will have to live with us."

"For Pete's sake, can't she live with your mother?"

"She doesn't want to live with Mother; you know she doesn't like it in town."

"Dadgummit, Dona, we barely got room for us. And with Josie gone, you've got more to do than you can handle."

"Where would you have her go?"

"I don't give a rat's tail where she goes."

"Roy, I am not going to argue about this. Nanna is staying here for her birthday, at least." Dona closed her fists and turned to the bin of oats.

"Duke and I are going to the river. I'll grain him when we get back. Would you at least check on Nanna for me? She's napping in Annalou's room."

"No," Roy said, mounting his horse, "my gelding and me, we're going to the Keyhole pasture. You want your ole granny here, you stay."

He was gone.

"WHEN I RISE UP, HALLELUJAH, I thank the morning." Nanna lay flat in the bed and thrust her hands toward the ceiling, fingers splayed as far as her arthritis would allow.

Dona peered into the room. "Nanna, you feeling well?"

"I'm feeling like a million bucks." She clapped her hands together. "I'm feeling like my old self. These past two days here with you, good as gold. And, I slept the whole night long. That chamber pot there? See? It's empty. Cain't remember when that happened. Oh, but I guess I will need to visit it right quick now. Shut the door on your way out, honey."

"You don't need help?"

"Never did, never will."

"All right. I'll be right out here when you're done."

Dona scooted to the kitchen and moved the skillet to a cooler spot on the stove so as not to burn the bacon. She poured coffee in Nanna's favorite cup, splashed in some cream and scurried back down the hall to Nanna's room.

But Nanna and the chamber pot were gone.

"Nanna." Dona whirled toward the drawn-drape darkness of the front room across the hall. "Nanna, are you in here?" The tick tock of the old clock was the only sound.

She rushed down the hall toward the front porch; the rarely used front door stood open, the screen door, open, and there, under the live oak tree, sitting on the chamber pot like a pigeon on its roost, was Nanna. Her white nightgown and her white hair, thin and long, rippled in the slight breeze. She gazed across the maize field to the clouds, her hands folded to her chest.

Dona halted. It was as though a tornado had passed, had lifted an old and fragile woman, the hall, porch, limbs of the giant oak, and set them down without raising a speck of dust.

Maybe she has died. Dona's thoughts tumbled. *Maybe this is heaven for her, the fields, the tree, the clouds.* She folded onto the limestone stoop, its stones holding fossils so much older than this small bird of a grandmother, and she said, "Bless you, Nanna."

"Did you say something, dear?" Nanna turned. "Oh, good that you are here. I can't seem to get off of this thing."

Dona's ribs shook with laughter, as she reached down and under Nanna's arms. "Up you go."

Nanna's gown, cloud-like, settled around her hips and fell to her bare feet.

"Nanna, you haven't got your shoes on; shall I carry you inside?"

"Oh, no, honey. I been barefoot all my life, don't you know? Hooves for feet." She laughed like a girl, as though any minute she might twirl away with a dust devil.

"Let's go back on the porch, at least, okay? And I'll tend to the chamber pot."

"I almost forgot. It's ever so much nicer to use it outside under a tree, don't you think?"

"Yes, of course, but Nanna, you did put a bit of a scare into me."

"Sorry for that. When I woke up this morning, I felt so free and young again. Like I could run barefooted and climb a tree or sit by the river with my cane pole and fish for crappie with my gran."

"Like I used to do with you?"

"You?" She stared for a moment. "Dona. Yes, yes, like you did with me."

"What happened just now, Nanna. Did you forget who I was?"

"I am a little tired, now, honey. That rocking chair on the front porch, right yonder. Maybe I could sit there a spell?"

"Do you remember what tomorrow is?"

"It's June 7, 1938. How could I forget."

"What is that?"

"It's the day I will turn one hundred years old. It's a mighty good day. And Dona, will Luke be here?"

"We'll all be here, Nanna. You bet."

ON NANNA'S BIRTHDAY her tiredness had deepened, and after Dona helped her into her new dress, she sat propped on pillows in Annalou's bed. As for most of her life, Nanna was at the center of her family. Ophelia sat beside her, holding one of her mother's spidery hands.

"I want to remember us this way," Nanna said. Her voice cracked like old shoe leather, the strain of breath taking something to itself. "You, Ophelia, my darling only living daughter, you have never failed me, or anyone. Dona, my oldest granddaughter, you are the heart of this family now, the wise one. And I thank you kindly for inviting me to stay with you."

She put her hand on her chest and coughed. It seemed to strengthen her and she said, "You, Roy, my grandson-in-law, you have the good sense of a man with ranching in his blood. And your young stallion of a son, Joe Bob, has promise in his eyes. Luke, my only remaining grandson, grown as gritty as the stone you peddle against hard steel, I knew you best as a young boy. Whip-thin, unpredictable and wily as a goat. You still are."

Luke covered his mouth to hide his grin.

Nanna rubbed her chin with fingers like twigs. "I want to remember you, my best family." Her eyes closed against tears.

Dona folded Nanna's hands over her stomach, letting them rest on a pink swirl of the dress Nanna had asked for. A present for this one-hundredth birthday. It was the dress she did not have when she was fifteen, the dress that would have made her feel pretty, that would have caused her to smile when Oscar Johnson picked her up for the church supper dance, and would have made her hold her head high. Instead, she had worn a cousin's outgrown dress, gray and blue and baggy at the waist.

Nanna had described it perfectly, this dress: made of sky-pink Dotted Swiss, its sleeves puffed, its skirt gathered full, with dots that shimmered like stars. And by a miracle, Ophelia had found the material in town and made it for her.

"After all these years," said Nanna, opening her eyes. "I am beautiful."

Joe Bob and Luke were in the kitchen with Roy when Dona and Annalou came in from the hall. "She's sleeping and Mother will stay with her for a while. Thank you, boys," Dona said to Joe Bob and Luke, "for making room for her to stay with us. You've both got a lot to do and living in that bunkhouse can't be easy."

"It's not so bad," Joe Bob said, grabbing a cold biscuit from the back of the stove.

"She was my favorite," Luke said. "Still is. I'll try and make her happy." He ran his hand across the back of his neck, in the way he did when he had something hard to say.

Dona poured him a cup of coffee from the speckled pot on the stove.

Taking a sip of his coffee, Luke said, "When I was a boy I was thin, like she said, and not very brave. Being small, I had a lot to prove to the bigger boys. She gave me something I never forgot and I'll use it 'til I die, I guess."

"What's that, Uncle Luke?" Annalou said.

"When I was young, I couldn't hardly talk at all. I stuttered awful bad. You'll remember that, Dona."

"I do."

"I had so much to say I couldn't get it out. It made me real mad, and sad. I felt bad about myself. Kind of like Nanna in that old dress of her cousin's."

"You talk real good now, Luke. What happened?"

"It was Nanna. I did what she said. I went ever day before light and stood at the side of the river and I talked to it. I told it everything that was hurting me. Sometimes I shouted it. Sometimes nothing came out. But after a while, I could talk and not just to the river. She's the reason. She believed in me. She gave me a way."

Dona sat for a moment. She had never in all their lives together, brother and sister, ranch hands, allies, heard that story, or known him to cry. When he was a small boy, that time he got kicked in the back by his pony, he pushed his fists into his cheeks without a sound and not a tear came from him. But now, this man, contained like the bole of a tree, was weeping.

"Luke, why don't you go and tell that to Nanna? I know she's pretty tired, but some place in her will hear how much she means to you."

Luke gathered his elbows into his middle, wiped his cheeks with hands that had broken and mended so many times they were like roots, pushed his chair back and stood up from the table. "I'll do it, and I thank you kindly for listening."

Luke tiptoed down the hall and into the bedroom where Nanna lay resting. Dona heard the squeak of bedsprings. Perhaps Nanna had turned toward him, or tried to sit up; perhaps he had laid himself beside her on the narrow bed. It was like a prayer, this quiet air filled with the longing of a boy.

"I guess I'd best see to the chores," Roy said, setting his empty mug on the oilcloth. "Annalou, you want to come with me?"

"Sure, Uncle Roy, I need a drink of water first. I'll be right on out."

Roy let the screen door slam as he made his way down the steps to the barnyard.

Dona sighed. "Can't ever remember to be quiet, that man."

"That story, Aunt Doney, I used to think Uncle Luke was maybe a little slow. You know? But he's not at all, and now I want to ask him a lot of questions. Do you think he'd mind?"

"I don't expect he'd mind. In fact, maybe he'd be a lot less lonesome if you asked him things. But don't expect much at first, okay? He can get in a pretty bad mood if you push him. Now go on out to help your Uncle Roy. He might have some good stories, too."

Dona cleared the table, washed and dried the dishes, swept the crumbs from the linoleum and set out the makings for the next morning's breakfast. Luke's wail sounded like wind through cracks in the barn, like the rattle of tin rusted away from its moorings on the roof. It sounded like someone mourning the dead.

"*Luke's told her his story*," Dona whispered to herself, wiping tears from her cheeks. "*After one hundred years, this was surely the happiest day of Nanna's life*."

Chapter Eleven

Dona heard the clatter in her dream. Which in her dream was her baby sister, Unity Ann, at three, throwing her breakfast dishes onto the kitchen floor and laughing.

The laughter woke her up. Mornings in the ranch house were always quiet. Before light, the rooster, yes, and inside the house, perhaps a creak of bedspring, a cough, only that. But this morning, somebody laughing, somebody banging around in the kitchen. And then she remembered. It was indeed her baby sister, grown up, who had arrived yesterday afternoon with no warning at all, not even a telephone call that she was sorry to have missed Nanna's birthday.

"What an awful way to start the day," Dona said aloud to Roy, who was still asleep, as he should be at 3:00 am. "She's in there already. She's already making a mess." He didn't blink or make a sound, except that aggravating, soft breath.

Because Roy did not respond, and because Dona was the older sister and had some rights, and besides that, this was her house, she got up, pushed her feet into slippers and her arms through the sleeves of her robe and opened the bedroom door.

Oil lamps were on, everywhere. The hall, the bathroom, the kitchen, over the kitchen table. And Unity Ann was at the stove. She was laughing and humming something that sounded an awful lot like *She'll be coming around the mountain*, like she was on stage.

She was always on stage as far as Dona was concerned. Couldn't the woman ever relax and be normal? But this morning, Dona did not want to fight with her sister. She wanted this to be a lovely, enjoyable day of family and talk around the table. She wanted to feel good about Unity Ann, and she mainly wanted to find out why she had appeared out of the blue.

She clasped her hands in front of her chest and said, "Good morning, Bright Eyes," which had been their father's name for Unity Ann, his favorite daughter.

Unity Ann's elbows flew out like wings as she tried to turn toward Dona and at the same time not spill the coffee she was at that moment pouring into her cup. The coffee splashed onto the stove, onto the floor, leapt onto Dona's best robe—and instead of stopping and saying, oh I am so sorry, did I burn you, or any of the other things their own mother might have said, Unity Ann laughed again, more gaily, put down the coffee pot and cup and threw out her arms for a hug, which Dona pretended, in her rush to dab the coffee off of her robe with the nearest cup towel, not to notice.

Annalou stumbled in from the hallway, half asleep, and said, "What's going on Aunt Doney?"

And Unity Ann started to laugh again. This time she went for Annalou, arms outstretched, with her good morning sunshine, thanks for giving me your bed, and managed at last to give somebody a real hug.

Whereupon Dona took her place at the stove, not to cook but to mop up the coffee, gain her composure and wonder why it was always so hard for her to be with this sister, whom she meant to adore.

By now, Unity Ann had sat down next to Annalou at the table and was telling her in what Dona thought was a remarkably loud whisper how beautiful she was becoming, and asking how it felt to be thirteen now, a teenager, and almost grown. And what did she want to do with her life?

"Unity Ann," said Dona, "we are not quite awake on this ranch until 4:00 or 4:30. Would you mind keeping your voice down for a little while?"

"I wasn't being loud, was I, Annalou? You always tell me to be quiet, Dona, you have always tried to make me be quiet. And I'm sorry, but I am who I am and you will have to accept me or ask me to leave."

"Oh, dear," said Dona, and turned back to the stove. "I guess I'd better make some more coffee. And who wants bacon, eggs and grits this morning?"

"There'd better be something to make up for this noise," said a deep voice, and there was Roy, in the doorway. "Good morning, Unity Ann."

"Good morning, Roy, my darling. I don't know how you live with my sister, year after year. She has no sense of humor, at all. I couldn't sleep a wink. The bed is awful, one sprung spring after the other. And that stupid rooster crowed all night long."

"Glad you liked it," Roy said.

Annalou laughed, then, and Unity Ann, and finally Dona. It was funny, this way of beginning a morning, a family visit. Everybody being who they were, which was sometimes terrible and sometimes ridiculous.

"Sorry I spilled coffee on you, Dona," Unity Ann said, "but I was so excited to see anybody, really."

"It'll come out, don't worry, and now that we're all wide awake, well, everybody but Nanna, who claims to be deaf as a post. I hope we have a good day."

"Could you smile at me just a little, like you mean it?" said Unity Ann, sounding like a charming child.

"Yes, of course," said Dona, and smiled. It was almost a real smile. She did feel better, especially now that Roy was there. He didn't take to heart anything Unity Ann said and never had. Dona needed to learn that, too, and this was the hundredth time she had thought that in her life.

"Maybe a little later, Unity Ann, we could take a walk. It's been a long time since you and I have had time together."

"I would love that, big sister. I'm about to have a little visit with Nanna, right now. I'm going to tell her I love her even if I missed her birthday. But how about after we finish the chores?"

"You're going to help?"

"I sure am. I'm dying to help."

In the middle of the afternoon, the sisters donned their straw hats and coolest blouses, and strolled along the dirt road toward the river.

"Are our feet exactly the same size, Dona?" Unity Ann placed her boots into the prints of Dona's.

Dona halted. "Mine may be bigger, what do you think?"

"It's true," Unity Ann sighed. "Everything about you is bigger."

"Like what?"

"Like your brain, especially."

"I doubt that. You are one sharp gal. Why, you used to beat all the rest of us at checkers, remember that?"

"But I've always been really dumb when it comes to love." Unity Ann stopped, pulled up her blouse and pointed to her ribs. "Take a look."

"Great heavens, that's awful. Were you in an accident?"

"Yes, I accidentally ran into my big, brave husband's fists."

"My dear." Dona lowered the blouse and patted it into place as gently as she might soothe a foal. "He beat you up pretty bad. How long ago?"

"It's been a couple of weeks. I wanted to come here right away, but it hurt too much to drive. And I sure didn't want to ask him to bring me. Sorry I didn't call. Honestly, I didn't want anybody knowing that I was coming here. And you know how the party lines are in the country, with every person possible listening in on every conversation."

"Where is he now?"

"He took off. Last time he did this, I said I'd call the sheriff, if it ever happened again. And I did."

"And did the sheriff arrest him?"

"No, Jim blasted out of there in his new red pickup, and hasn't been back since. But really, Dona, that sheriff couldn't have done much. It's not against the law to hit your wife, not in this state. You can always say she was unfaithful, or didn't obey the way she should. Or some other bull. I've got a really smart, rich friend who tried to win a case of assault against her husband, and you know what?"

"What?"

"She got laughed out of court for not living up to her wifely duties, which were numerous and actually all about sex. Of course. The judge was a man, the lawyers were men, everybody in that court room was a man, except for the stenographer, and as far as I know, she never speaks."

"Unity Ann, honey, how can I help?"

"You just did. You listened. You didn't say that maybe it was my fault that he beat me up, again." Her voice broke. "And isn't it funny? It makes me tear up. I've been strong. I haven't let anybody see me cry. But now..."

She buried her face in Dona's neck, whose own shoulders were heaving.

They stood together, arms around each other, their hats crooked on their heads, Dona crooning, "There, there, sweet sister. It will be all right. There, there..."

AT ALMOST DUSK, they returned to the ranch house to put supper on, and found Annalou curled up on the porch swing.

In a sleepy voice, she said, "Where have the two of you been for so long?"

"Oh, Annalou," Unity Ann said, squatting beside the swing, "I'm so sad to say goodbye to you."

"Do you really have to go?"

"I do, honey. We have an awful lot of work to do at the ranch, and right now it's up to me and my cowhands. Gotta get back there tonight. Maybe you'll come to see me pretty soon?"

"I'd like that a lot, thank you. Could we, Aunt Doney?"

"You bet. We'll figure out a time. Okay, Unity Ann? I'll call you on our party line, so everybody in the county will know our plans. But you call me, too. I need to keep up with my baby sister a lot better than I've been doing."

Chapter Twelve

"Where's Uncle Roy, Aunt Doney?" Annalou eased herself barefooted into the kitchen.

"Good morning, sleepyhead. He took your Uncle Luke and they went hunting about three o'clock this morning. Thought I'd make us some bread while the house is cool."

"Anything I can do to help?"

"How about some breakfast. I put back some bacon and biscuits for you and Joe Bob, and it's easy to scramble a few eggs."

"Joe Bob's still asleep?"

"No, he went down to the river right before sunup to check his trot lines. Thought some mean old catfish might taste good for dinner."

"Any coffee left?"

"I put on some fresh when I heard you stirring in there. Grab a cup."

"Aunt Doney, ah, this is kind of a hard question and I'd take it kindly if you would keep it to yourself?"

Dona turned from the stove and looked at Annalou for the first time that morning. The sweet face squeezed toward the middle like a rag. She sat with Annalou at the kitchen table and held out her hand.

"Why are you crying, dear heart? Whatever it is, I'll never tell. And you can probably count on it being something that's happened to me, too."

"Remember the other night, when you and Aunt Unity Ann came back from your walk and I was out on the porch swing?"

"Sure."

"Well, I went out there because when nobody else was in the house except Nanna, I heard Joe Bob singing right through the wall of my room. And it wasn't a regular old song. It was about me, and it was about, it was about—- how pretty I would be without my clothes on."

She peeked at Dona through large eyes that were at this moment dull and gray and as troubled as thunder. "He's big and he's really strong."

"I can talk to his daddy. And if his daddy won't do something about it, I'll talk to Joe Bob, myself. Come here and let me give you a hug. And when this bread is done, let's take a walk over to the mesquite grove. It's real private there."

"AUNT DONEY, HOW DID YOU GET SO BRAVE?"

They had sauntered in silence to the young mesquites and stood side by side in their shade.

Dona chuckled. "It's funny you should ask that. I've been thinking of how brave you are. You know, I used to be so timid, I was scared of jack-rabbits; but now I look for them. Their ears are beautiful.

"I decided one day. I was maybe your age. I got tired of being scared. I thought about my Nanna, how she had lived through so much danger growing up, and she looked everything hard in the eye. And I wanted to be her. I wanted her inside of me. And somehow, it worked. I got braver. Even walked different, straighter, shoulders back, head up."

"That's how you walk now."

"That's how it started. Maybe you could try it, too."

"Would you mind if I try to be you?"

"Why, I wouldn't mind it at all. Could be fun, seeing myself at thirteen again."

ANNALOU HAD HEARD EVERYTHING. The walls of the old ranch house were sturdy but thin and though she'd put her pillow over her head, she couldn't escape Joe Bob's big voice, or what Aunt Doney said about Dolly's foal coming. She got out of bed, pulled on her jeans and the denim shirt from yesterday, and went out into the hall.

It was nearly light. Dona was sitting at the kitchen table, her hands around her coffee cup, looking off into the distance. Annalou whispered, "Good morning, Aunt Doney."

Dona turned. "Oh, child, you startled me. I'm just waiting to put breakfast on the table. Want some coffee?"

"I'll get it. I heard something about Dolly and a foal. Do you think I can help?"

"I don't know. I heated some water. Joe Bob hauled it to the barn. Uncle Luke is out there with Roy. There's probably enough help."

"Do you think they'd mind if I came on out?"

"I don't think so. Just stay out of the way and learn what you can. You never know when you might need to help something have a baby. Finish your coffee."

Annalou sat in her chair, across from Dona. "You doing okay, Aunt Doney?"

"I'm all right." Dona smiled a little. "Are you?"

"Pretty good. I'm glad it's Sunday. Do you think I could take some time to ride up to the Sheepherder's Hut today? After I split the kindling, I mean?"

"What if I went with you?"

"I'd really like that. Maybe after dinner? When Uncle Roy and Uncle Luke and Nanna are taking their Sunday naps?" She scuffed her feet under the table. "But, would it be okay if we don't tell Joe Bob? I mean, I really don't want him to know that we go to the Hut."

"Fine with me."

"Sounds like the men are coming back," Annalou said.

"Oh gracious." Dona pushed back her chair. "Will you crack those eggs into the big skillet? I've got the bacon ready, and the grits. I'll quick stir up the biscuits and get them in the oven. It's hot. Won't take a minute."

Dona had this awful feeling as she did the dishes that it was time to begin again, that nothing she had been doing was leading to a good end, except for maybe with Annalou. But, how could Annalou ever learn to be a strong, independent woman, if she saw Dona bowing before the will of her husband and afraid of her stepson? But, isn't that how a woman was supposed to act? In West Texas, where only a few years back, women were counted as chattel, right under the horses.

Dona was wringing her hands and walking back and forth between the kitchen and the porch, when Annalou, who had been splitting kindling for the wood stove, hollered from the chicken yard, "Aunt Doney, Aunt Doney, help!"

"Oh, lands sake, what now?" Dona said under her breath. But she called out, "Coming," left the kitchen and ran down the porch steps.

Facing Annalou across the barnyard fence was the biggest coyote Dona had ever seen. It was as tall as a wolf, and its eyes, devil-wild, locked on Annalou.

Dona backed up slowly. "Be still as a stone." She felt her own ghost pass through her body, shivering. "Please," she said to it, "let me get to that rifle."

Dona had always liked coyotes, and usually it was hard to get one to stand still so you could get a good look. But this one. This one was crazy. Maybe rabid.

She felt her heel reach the porch steps, turned and eased open the screen door. Her rifle was in the corner of the porch where Roy had been cleaning his guns the night before. What if it wasn't loaded. She picked up the rifle, pulled back the loading chamber. There was one bullet. Well, that would have to be enough. She cocked the hammer and turned at the moment Annalou flung her hatchet at the coyote's head. The hatchet glanced off his shoulder and he leapt over the fence. Dona took aim, seeing nothing but his eye. She squeezed the trigger and the coyote dropped like a sack of chicken feed.

"Don't know why he was after you, Annalou," Dona shouted, "but maybe we'd best give you some target practice with that hatchet." The laughter that fell between them was phony, but it calmed the trembling and beat the dickens out of tears.

"Come look at this big fellow, Annalou. A mighty fine specimen of a male coyote."

"A shame," said Annalou, leaning close to the coyote's face.

After Dona called the sheriff to come get the coyote so it could be tested for rabies, they saddled up Duke and Paint and headed for the high pasture and the Sheepherder's Hut. They were back at the ranch house in time to make Sunday supper of pancakes, sausage and molasses, and nobody had missed them.

ANNALOU SCARED THE LIVING DAYLIGHTS out of Dona, carrying on in the middle of the horse pens, howling under what Dona had to admit was a perfectly round moon, but Dona paid attention. She understood. What was a thirteen-year-old girl going to do on a dusty ranch with mostly old folks around for company? It was her time, her sickness had come, she fell off the roof, or whatever it was Nanna had always said about menstruation. Why couldn't people just say it outright?

Terrible things could happen to a young girl, sure enough. When that schoolmaster had pushed himself inside her, and there she was, like always on a Friday after school, when she was on all fours and scrubbing the floor as hard as she could, to get through and get on home, he was watching. Maybe she was taking too long. She hurried up so he wouldn't scold her. But when he fell over her shoulders and hitched her skirt over her waist, big and strong as she was, she could not get out from under. She was thirteen. The baby did not live. Dona could not have another.

Oh yes, now that she was half along her natural life, she wished she could tell the world what could happen, even when the girl had no idea — especially then.

It was last week that she and Annalou had a talk. Dona had found a pamphlet in the library called "The Blessing of Being a Woman," and wondered what on earth might be on the author's mind. It was written by a doctor who was of course a man. And it turned out to be about menstruation and how women got pregnant and the thrill of having a baby and how a baby is always the product of two people who love one another and other nonsense. But at least there was the part about menstruation, and she read it carefully. So much about her own body was a mystery to her. She surely did not love that schoolmaster, and she had gotten pregnant. Other couples who had loads of children didn't seem to give a hoot about each other; in fact, the husband treated the wife like a dog about half the time.

Dona had driven back to the ranch from the library vowing to talk with Annalou as soon as possible. And the talk had gone pretty well. Annalou, it turned out, had learned a few things before her mother and daddy were killed. Her mother's brother's wife, Johnnie White Crow, who said she was from the Sioux nation, had told Annalou stories. Like the moon had something to do with her body; like, when she was old enough, every month her body would bleed; that the blood was a sign of her connection to White Buffalo Woman, who was someone in the sky that women could count on; and that Annalou should find a way to talk with her, when the time came.

It seemed to Dona that Johnnie White Crow was on to something more helpful to Annalou than what Dona had read in the pamphlet; at least it made her feel less alone. But nevertheless, as they made supper together last Thursday, she recounted what she had learned in the library; and Annalou repeated the story her Aunt Johnnie had told her. And that had been all the time they had to talk in private. The men were washing up at the windmill pump and in a few minutes they were at the kitchen table looking for their supper.

So tonight, with Annalou out in the horse pen under that brighter than bright moon, Dona slipped through barn shadows to be close by.

Joe Bob was perched like a buzzard on the corral fence next to the tack shed. His body, black against the moon, fairly stretched toward Annalou, whirling as she was in the moonlight.

"Yoo-hoo," Dona yelled, in her best time-to-come-inside voice. "Annalou, where are you?"

She was sorry to see Annalou stop dead still, but it could not be helped. And she was not sorry to see Joe Bob slide off the top railing and disappear inside the tack shed.

"Too bad to stop your dancing," she said as she climbed over the corral fence and dropped to the ground.

"Right now?"

"Yes, honey. Right now. Come on, let's sit on the old hay wagon and look at the moon together. It's mighty special tonight. There's something I need to tell you."

They settled on the wagon and in the moon's light their eyes held shadows. Dona said, "When I was your age, I was on my knees scrubbing the schoolroom floor..."

Things were better after that, Dona thought. Joe Bob quit hanging around when Annalou was taking a bath, and it had been quite a while since he'd called for her through the bedroom window to come for a walk. What was it with seventeen-year-old boys? No brains but between their legs? Annalou had understood what Dona had to say that night. She had been frightened by Joe Bob, already, but something had taken her over, the moon, maybe, out there in the corral, and she'd plumb forgotten herself. She'd be lots more careful now, she'd said, putting both arms around Dona, so as not to be a worry, and yes, not to get herself in trouble.

SUNDAY MORNING, after Annalou had finished her chores and breakfast and Aunt Doney had said she could go out for a while but don't go far, Annalou put a bridle on Paint, climbed on his back, and headed for the river. It was one of those mornings when sadness followed her, and she missed her momma and her daddy, but especially her momma, so much.

The river was what made those pecan trees tall, all that water behind the dam. All that good dirt in the river pasture, what remained after the terrible dust storms these past years, was what settled at the bottom of a giant lake, a long time ago. Aunt Doney had told her that. And that granddaddy had loved being a country doctor and he loved having a ranch before he and Mamaw built their house in town, but in his heart, he was a farmer. He wanted to grow crops that people could eat, and had planted these pecan trees by the river.

When she rode Paint away from the ranch house, that morning, past the barn, through the gate alongside the cattle guard where she'd found the rattler's skin in April, beyond the windmill's steady creak and moan, the cluck of hens, the grunt of hogs, and the mournful voice of coonhounds baying far down the dusty road toward town, Annalou let loose the weight inside her chest that had been there right along, and she wept.

The river pulled at Paint, too, with its cool green and quiet. And while Annalou lay with her arms around his neck, not guiding, not speaking to him, he made his way there and stood with hardly a snort or a shake of his head until she roused herself and slipped off his back. "Thank you, Paint," she said, and led him to the river to drink.

The pecans towered above them, a grove of deeply grooved trunks reaching through thick canopies to a sky that was as clear and blue as her mother's eyes. A gray squirrel sped up and down the trunks, checking on the readiness of the crop. A farmer-squirrel, no doubt. And at this, she smiled. Which felt better than sobbing.

She hitched Paint to a small pecan sapling in the middle of a patch of grass near the dam, and walked to the center of the grove. She bent to the ground at the base of one especially large tree and pressed her back against it. "I'd like to talk to all of y'all beautiful trees."

She took courage from the soft shushing of leaves in a faint, hot wind that had risen from the pasture, and said, "I need your help."

The mockingbird, who had been singing with all its might to proclaim its right to this place, became quiet; Tom turkeys, who had called to each other through the brambles upriver ever since she'd arrived, settled down; and Black Angus cows, lined up across the river on the other side, their necks extended over the water, their split hooves deep in mud, stopped mooing their objections and turned their ears toward Annalou.

"Thank you," she said, pressing her back more firmly against the tree. "Maybe you remember your parents. Or maybe you don't need parents anymore. Mine were killed in a car wreck and it was my daddy's fault. But they were both drunk. Maybe they didn't suffer that way, I don't know. Momma was thrown onto a barbed wire fence. They found most of her scalp hanging on it. She had red hair, like fire, so thick and wavy and she would let me brush it sometimes. Daddy was killed; instantly, is what they said. The thing that holds up the steering wheel went right through his heart. They hit a cow on a dirt road. And it was night, and the cow had gotten loose and she was not killed instantly. The sheriff had to shoot her. I think about her enormous eyes, rolling around in her face, so afraid."

Annalou stopped speaking and lifted her head from her knees. Five Black Angus cows in a line, hides gleaming like oil, stood with their feet in the river and their ears toward the trees. They looked at her with their calm, huge eyes.

"Oh, I see," said Annalou. "You knew already. Maybe you always know everything. Our friend, Melvar, he says everybody always knows everything. That must include cows. And trees."

She stood up, turned to face the trunk of the tree, and put her arms around it. The wide grooves made room for her nose; she rested her forehead and chin flush with the bark, and breathed in the rains of spring, the winds of winter, the constant sun, the community of molds. "Will you be my momma?" she whispered into the dark heart of the tree. "Will you be my daddy?"

The tree's gray bark took Annalou's tears into itself. On a West Texas ranch, water was always precious.

Along toward evening, Annalou rode Paint back to the ranch house corral. She felt a little better, the trees having done their part. Josie was back from Mexico, thank heavens, so she hoped she hadn't been needed to help Aunt Doney with supper.

The voice came low and deep from inside the tack shed.

"Joe Bob?" The skin around her ribs crawled to her stomach and she gripped the pommel of Paint's saddle like a shield. Joe Bob didn't answer. There was no sound at all from the shed.

"Come in here." It was Joe Bob, but his voice was funny. Kind of soft and maybe, why, could Joe Bob be crying?

"Hey," she said. "Ever thing all right in there?"

"No."

"Can you come on out? Maybe I can help?"

She moved closer and as her eyes adjusted to the dim light, she could see Joe Bob's wide back, the pale denim shirt he always wore. His head was bare and resting on the rack right where she'd planned to put Paint's saddle.

"Where's your hat?" She had never seen Joe Bob outside without at least his old working Stetson. Something was wrong, for sure, but Annalou didn't want to go inside any place with that boy and nobody else around.

"I got hurt, Annalou. Crazy Jim spooked at a jackrabbit and throwed me clear to Sunday. Daddy's gonna kill me. He taught me better than to get throwed."

"How bad you hurt? And how on earth did you get back here?"

"On Crazy Jim by hook and crook and an old cedar stump, but I can't move my left arm without it hurting something terrible."

"I'll go get Aunt Doney."

"No," Joe Bob raised up his head. "You gotta help me."

"I don't know what to do to help. Aunt Doney will and I'm going to get her right now."

"Annalou, please. She'll tell Daddy for sure."

"Sorry. I'll be right back."

Annalou ran as fast as she could to the rock house. "Aunt Doney," she panted. "Come quick. It's Joe Bob."

As Dona pushed open the screen door of the back porch she was already pulling on her boots and telling Annalou to run get Josie to help out in case Nanna needed anything. And in two shakes she had Joe Bob in Roy's truck and they were headed for the medical clinic in town.

"The arm is broken but the bone is going to heal right well," Dona told Roy that night at supper. "And don't you be yelling at that boy for falling off his horse. He feels bad enough. Go in there and help him feel better. He's the only boy you got."

Roy wiped his mouth on his sleeve and pushed back his chair. "Thanks for supper," he said. He walked toward the hall door. "And thanks for taking good care of him today." He didn't look at her. "You are a mighty fine woman, that's for sure."

"Why, Roy Turn, that's the nicest thing you've said to me in a spell. Not quite worth a boy's broken arm, but I'm glad to hear it. Now, get in there and be a good daddy."

Chapter Thirteen

The next day, in the back of the tack room by the horse corrals, Joe Bob sat on a sawhorse. He was rubbing the nosepiece of a bridle, that being something he could do with one good arm, and besides he liked cleaning tack when he had a problem on his mind. He was thinking about his mother's eyes. Her eyes had been sad even when she smiled. Were all mothers like that?

Joe Bob hated pink. It wasn't hard to think why, but he didn't like to say. Talking about his mother made his stomach hurt. He was five when anybody would have seen that she'd be dying any day now; but the funny thing was, her mouth was pink as a petunia. He'd asked her was she all right, and why was her mouth so pink and she had smiled. And she told him about her Brightly Pink lipstick and a cowboy named Max Factor who made it for ladies to look pretty. And she hoped he liked it. Which he did, but not because it smeared on his cheek when she kissed him before she fell asleep. Every night.

One day he climbed on the chair next to her dresser when his daddy had walked to the front porch for some air. He opened the Brightly Pink the way she did, and colored his mouth. When he made himself smile in her mirror, his eyes sparkled almost like hers did. But it was a lie. His eyes would never look happy again. And the grease on his mouth wasn't anything like the bacon grease he tasted from the can on the stove. It was something you had to be careful of. Because maybe it made you die. The skin of her face was yellow and shriveled like a dead cactus, but his mother's lips were pink as his pony's tongue. Pink was a color you could never trust.

Dona wasn't a mother, was she. Just a barren, scrawny ranch wife, that was his opinion, but still he liked her all right. She fed him good, and dang, could she ride a horse. That was what he admired. She wasn't afraid. She'd get mad at him sometimes, and maybe he had it coming, and sure enough she didn't mind telling him how to do things. Like the other day when he was practicing for the calf roping at the West Texas Rodeo competition, she hollered, "Sharpen that shoulder, Joe Bob, you'll never make it into the finals like that."

He hung the bridle on its peg and started in on his roping saddle. It was true in anybody's mind that Dona liked to have her way more than was seemly in a woman. And he was sure she liked Annalou better than him. Still, when there was something come up between them, Dona sided with him as often as with Annalou.

Joe Bob didn't know what he wanted to do with his life. He thought he might like to be an animal doctor, but that would take a lot of years in college. His daddy expected him to stay on and help run the ranch when he finished high school. Dona had asked if he might think of going to junior college there in town where he could learn a lot about ranching and animal medicine. He'd been thinking about joining the Army when he turned eighteen. The Army didn't draft ranchers or farmers, so he'd never get the chance to see the world, if he didn't enlist. What would his daddy think of that, enlisting? Why couldn't he just ask him outright?

Joe Bob finished up the saddle. He'd cleaned and polished the leather until it was soft, even where it cracked. It was a job he liked and nobody bothered him. Maybe the Army wasn't such a good place for that. Did people bother animal doctors? Probably.

On the first day of summer, there on the flank and scree of the high pasture, Annalou was on foot and afraid she was lost. Afraid that night would come and scorpions would slither into the tops of her boots, or screech owls would settle on a nearby oak branch and scream until she died of fright.

Aunt Doney told her not to walk around the hills when it was getting dark. This was the first time; really, the first time it made a difference. But she was bothered about Joe Bob and she'd needed some room. And there had been something in the afternoon light, the cloud-mountains with their flattened bottoms, floating across the hot country as though they had puffed like biscuits. She had to get to higher ground, closer and closer until maybe she could see the gods who, according to her books, lived inside the red-gold light.

A bit of the late afternoon light was left, enough to look out at the horizon and pick out glints off the river, if she could find a lookout in the right direction. Live oak trees stretched their limbs toward the clouds, like sentinels standing guard against her seeing.

Annalou tried to speak and found that she could not. Her throat was the rain-ruined leather of old saddlebags, parched and unyielding. She had thought surely there would be a stock tank someplace near the high pasture's old windmill, but in the dusk, she could not find the windmill, tall as it must be. And she had no idea where the Sheepherder's Hut lay, where she and Aunt Doney had left a jar of water, just in case.

Why hadn't she ridden Paint up there? Why take out on foot like a fool? Annalou imagined all the questions Uncle Roy would throw at her and all the looks of disgust she'd get from Joe Bob at supper. But, wait, there wouldn't be any supper, if she couldn't find her way to the road. Even on this longest day of the year, there wouldn't be anything but the sounds of the night.

A family of quail ran across the clearing, rustling dry sage and bobbing their heads like mechanical toys. Annalou laughed and rubbed her face with both hands. "It's only getting to be night. Time for the animals and birds to wake up or go to sleep, and me, too. But I don't have the sense God gave a frog to stay calm and cut out the nonsense in my head and find my way. Stand still," she said to her own self, "take a deep breath, and close your eyes. When you open them, you will see a sign."

These were instructions her mother had given her when she was very little, in case she got lost. She had almost forgotten them but there they were, as if her mother had spoken. She sat down on the nearest flat rock, sighed and closed her eyes.

"Annalou," someone called. "Yoo-hoo, Annalou."

"Yoo-hoo," she yelled back. The shod hooves of horses slipped on loose stone, heading her way. Through the lace of mesquite branches, lights danced over the crest of the hill. Beams of lanterns ran across cactus patches, up trunks of oaks, over limestone outcroppings with their ancient fossil treasures, searching.

"I'm here," Annalou hollered, waving her arms and jumping up and down until the lights found her, when Aunt Doney held her in her arms and hugged her as though she were precious, and when Uncle Roy said, "thank God, young'un, let's get you home."

At full dark, they returned to the ranch house, with most of the chores still needing to be done. Roy unsaddled the horses and gave each one a bag of oats, checked the water troughs by lantern light, and drove the truck into its place in the shed. Luke threw some feed to the chickens in their pen inside the barn and secured the barn doors. That would do against the coyotes but he'd tried every which a way to keep out those other varmints, those pesky raccoons, snakes, possums and skunks who liked a taste of fresh chicken eggs more than was polite. The best he could do was to shut the hens behind wire and keep it mended. Wasn't near good enough, of course, but he kept trying.

Dona took up her place at the stove and had biscuits, eggs and beans going in nothing flat. She carried a plate of biscuits and jam to Nanna, who was already asleep. And Annalou, head bowed, went straight down the hall to the bathroom and washed up as good as she could, though it wasn't Saturday night. All the trouble she'd caused, it made her feel downright dirty. But Joe Bob had met them at the corral and said he'd allow that anybody could get lost up there. He'd smiled at her when they got to the kitchen. Smiled like a real brother might and said he was right glad she was doing fine.

Chapter Fourteen

"That church service was awful," Joe Bob said, dropping into a kitchen chair.

"I didn't see you during the sermon," Dona said, frowning at the skillet she was drying. "Thought you'd left."

"I was in the shadows in the back. It was the only place I could stand it, to listen to that lying preacher preach."

"Why, I'm surprised at you. What do you have against Reverend MacMurray?" Dona turned from drying the dishes and sat at the table across from Joe Bob. It was so long since they had really talked, and with all that had happened between him and Annalou, she wanted to hear anything he had to say.

Joe Bob twisted in his seat and crossed one ankle over the other knee. "I don't know exactly what I mean, Dona, and don't you go judging me. But what I know about that preacher makes me really mad and then to hear him be so sweet and smarmy with his holier-than-thou words on Sunday, well it stinks, that's all."

"I have my own notion of what you mean about that preacher, but I'd like you to tell me, if you don't mind."

Joe Bob glanced around the kitchen. The room was quiet and cool for this time of afternoon. Sunday dinner had been more peaceful than usual, and Dona's fried pork chops were especially delicious, at least she thought so.

"I saw him at the chicken ranch last night," he said.

"The chicken ranch? Oh, the *chicken ranch*. Oh, my. That really is shocking. No wonder you are upset."

"I mean," said Joe Bob, turning to her, "sure I was there, too, or I wouldn't have seen him, but I'm seventeen and I'm not a minister; and I'm not even a good boy."

"True," said Dona, and they laughed. "I see what you mean about Reverend MacMurray, though. He's a married man, right? What's he doing at a house of prostitution? And then what's he doing preaching to us on the Thou Shalt Not Commit Adultery commandment the very next day?"

"I don't know what to do, Doney." Joe Bob rubbed his face with his large hands. "Should I go and talk with him and tell him what I saw? Or should I tell other folks in the congregation?"

"Did he see you?"

"No. He went in the back door and he was wearing a funny kind of hat, pulled down over his forehead. I wouldn't have recognized him myself, except that hat caused me to take a better look for who was under it."

"What were you doing in the back?"

"I was watching out for someone. Please don't ask me."

"Okay, I won't ask, but if you ever want to tell me I won't tell your daddy, or anybody else. Promise."

"Thanks, Doney. I'm really sorry for how hard I am to live with sometimes, I just want you to know that."

"Well, it can't be easy having your daddy marry somebody like me."

"Why do you say that?"

"I'm not a regular wife, you know. I mean I stand up for myself a lot more than some think I ought. And I really don't like for anybody to treat a woman or a girl disrespectfully." Dona looked squarely at Joe Bob then.

His face had reddened, and tears welled in his eyes. "I really like Annalou. I know she's young. And I don't know how to control myself sometimes, and I get so mad when I act like an animal around her. My whole body twists me around."

"So, what Reverend MacMurray was doing at the chicken ranch isn't so different from what you want to do with Annalou. Am I right?"

Joe Bob pushed his chair back, his eyes hot.

"Okay, calm down, Joe Bob. I want to help. But we've got to be honest with each other. You are a powerful young fellow, and you are a lot smarter than I sometimes give you credit for. There are things you can do with what you feel toward girls, good things, things that can make a difference in the world."

"Like what, Dona, like what?" Joe Bob stood up and headed toward the back door.

"Not quite so fast, honey. Maybe I have an idea for how you might find out."

Joe Bob lowered his shoulders and turned to face her. "I'm listening."

"You've got the idea, already. Go outside, but not to be mad. Go someplace you don't usually go, like down to the Kelly Hole at the river where nobody will bother you. Get real quiet and still. Pretend that everything you see and hear has some kind of meaning, that everything is speaking to you."

"What?"

"I know, but give it a chance. Let yourself ask whatever question is most important and listen for the answer. You can do this as often as you like, but you have to trust what you learn. That's the secret. okay?"

"Okay. So, I go to the deepest place in the river and I sit on the bank and I ask questions and I listen?"

"Yes."

"And what if I don't hear anything?"

"Pretend like everything you see and hear means something for your life. See what happens."

"It's gonna feel loco."

"But believe me, it works. Enjoy yourself."

IT WAS NEARLY SUPPERTIME when Joe Bob got back. Crazy Jim whinnied and Duke answered. Dona was thinking how all living things seem to talk to each other, when Joe Bob walked into the kitchen.

"Your daddy came looking for you earlier. Needed you in the East Lee pasture; but I told him I'd asked you to do me a favor down at the river, that I wanted another one of those big freshwater clam shells we've been finding."

"But I didn't bring one back."

"Right." Dona smiled at him, "here is the one you found." She handed him a large shell from the several she had hidden in her underwear drawer so Roy wouldn't take them for his collection.

"Thanks, Dona, and thanks for sending me off to the Kelly Hole."

"Worked, did it?"

"In a manner of saying, it did." Joe Bob lifted a cup from the shelf and filled it with coffee from the pot. He sat at the table and grabbed the sugar bowl, dumping some sugar in the cup and stirring with his forefinger.

"Joe Bob, please remember to use a spoon."

"Sorry, I forgot. I'd like to tell you what happened. Crazy Jim and I got down there right quick and I'm pretty sure nobody noticed where we was going. I set him to grazing and went to the edge of the river below the dam, you know, where the big flat stones stick out. I sat with my boots off so I could hunker down and be still. And right away, my question came. It wasn't about girls at all. It was about me. What am I going to do with my life that will amount to anything."

"Good question."

"And right away, a bull frog started to croak and the red tail hawk hollered and before you know it, a Tom turkey called from the brush. Not loud, you know, like to another Tom, but more like he was talking to me.

"Seemed like ever thing wanted to answer my questions, and I kept listening. I kind of floated in my mind with my eyes closed and let all the voices float too, like they was inside me and they was my voice. Strange, but okay. And they told me mainly to keep listening, to keep asking, because the river was talking all this time, or maybe singing more like, and it was saying he's one of us, he's one of us and so I thought that maybe I have a calling."

"Yes, I expect you do, and what do you think that calling could be?"

"I think—it's with nature."

Joe Bob drained his coffee and stared into the bottom of the cup. "I don't know what for sure, but something about looking real deep and hearing real careful and maybe studying in books about the critters."

"That seems like a good thing."

"And it was like the river, well, it was like the river is the blood of the rest and it was asking me to know it too and learn how to keep it strong. And, I thought of how we irrigate the crops from the river and how maybe that's not the best thing to do because we're going to use it up one of these days and then where will any of us be? And that's crazy to think that way, ain't it?"

"I wouldn't say crazy at all, Joe Bob, I would say wise. And I would say you have received a message from really deep inside of you, and that you are one lucky fellow."

"Lucky?"

"I've known you since you were born." Dona reached for his hand and squeezed his broad fingers. "Your momma and daddy wanted a big family and you were the first, so they were really happy. And you were exactly the baby your daddy could be proud of from the start, a big, strong boy with a wide grin who right away loved to ride in front of him on a horse. And your momma, why she doted on you like you were the only child in the world. After she got so sick with the cancer, you'd run in from the barn to see her and it was like something inside of her would light up.

"She knew she was dying. She was going to miss you so much and she hated the thought of you being without a momma. She loved you more than anything. She hoped I would marry your daddy after she died so

I could take care of both of you, and I've never told another soul about that, including your daddy."

"That's why you married him?"

"Partly. I loved him, too, and I guess he loved me. And I couldn't have any babies of my own because of something that happened to me when I was really young. Well, you and your daddy, you needed somebody like me. And I needed you. So, in a couple of years, we were a family."

"And we still are." Joe Bob pushed his chair back and stood up. "Doney, I'm right glad you told me about all this. There is some luck in that, and it's a lot for me to think about."

"It is, honey, but now you know you can go to the river or anyplace else and talk with all those parts of yourself. You'll learn to trust what you already know, believe me. You have the makings of a fine man, Joe Bob, and a powerful man, and it's up to you, which way you lean.

"Don't worry about the preacher and what he does. He'll get his just rewards. You follow your own best self and you really will amount to something. Now go do your chores and let your daddy know you're back."

"Do you need Joe Bob this afternoon?" Dona asked after dinner the next day.

"I suppose Luke and I could handle the mowing," Roy said. "Why?"

"I was thinking that Joe Bob and I might look over a paper for the junior college together. Just to see what it says. What do you think?"

Roy shuffled his hat in his hands and turned to Joe Bob, listening from the hall. "Ah, I well, Joe Bob, would you like to do that?"

Joe Bob nodded. "Guess this would be as good a time as any, if you don't need me for the mowing."

"Okay, then, I'll count on you for the grinding. Tomorrow, pretty much all day."

"Yep, I'll be ready first thing in the morning."

When Roy and Luke had cleared the porch and she could hear them stomping off across the barnyard toward the tractor shed, Dona said, "I hope you don't mind. I'd really like to see you do what you want, Joe Bob, and I don't get the sense that you want to be a rancher all your life."

"What makes you say that, Doney? What else would Daddy let me do?"

"Honey, remember what you learned down at the river yesterday. How about sitting with me here at the table for a spell and let's look at that paper."

Joe Bob turned down the hall and rustled about in the living room. Soon he emerged, holding not a paper but a book.

"Oh, you have the catalogue. That's better. What have you found in there?"

Joe Bob sat at his place at the table and opened the catalogue at a page marked with a torn piece of paper. Dona sat beside him in what was usually Luke's chair. She leaned over to read.

"This is the engineering section," she said, looking up at him.

"You were expecting the animal science section," he said, flatly.

"Well, kind of. Engineering is what interests you?"

"Yes. I mean, I love the animals, too, but maybe not as much as machines." He grinned.

Dona smiled back at him. "I'm pretty ignorant about engineering. What is it?"

"It's learning how things work. It's making things that work. It's figuring out how to take a good idea and make it work."

"Like what?"

"A better mowing machine. Better hay baler. And, after listening to the river, I know there's a better way to find water in this dry West Texas, and lots better ways to use the water we have. It's the future, and I want to be part of it."

"What about oil engineering? A big future there, too."

"Yep, for sure, it's called petroleum engineering. I'd maybe want to design oil rigs that don't fall over or explode and kill the men, and drill bits that don't break under pressure. And maybe that's what I'll end up doing. But the river told me something different." He drew his fingers through his thick hair. "We can't drink oil, but we can't live without water."

Dona's eyes softened from hazel to green as she cocked her head toward Joe Bob and grinned. "Let's take a look at what that catalogue says about water engineering, then. Sounds like a darn good idea to me."

Dona was not the kind of woman who hated other people. But, at church, where you'd think Christians would practice what the Bible said about everybody being God's children, she had to hold her tongue.

Why only two Sundays ago, Reverend MacMurray preached on how white people were better than the other races. He said, "Well, look at us. We're the ones in charge and the 'niggrahs,' everybody knows their grandparents were slaves. Why, Wetbacks can't speak English, let alone get to be citizens of these United States. Goes to show you who the Lord loves best."

Dona had to go home right away after church that day, telling Luke she didn't feel so good. Luke was looking a little peaked, too, so the two of them rattled back to the ranch in Luke's old Chevy truck. It was such a rare thing, to talk with Luke without anybody being around. She missed their talks, their little brother and sister jokes, his strange ways.

"So, Luke, what did you think about the pastor's sermon this morning?"

Luke scratched under his best cowboy hat. "I think Reverend MacMurray done read a different Bible from the one we read when we was little." He paused and took in a breath.

Dona waited, but he said nothing more. She chuckled. Leave it to Luke to put the right spin on it.

"I got really mad at him, myself," she said. "And I know not to speak up in church. Thanks for bringing me home right away. I might have made a fool of myself, if I'd a stayed to shake his hand."

Luke said, "we got some awful good men working for us who have dark skin, black and brown, and some don't talk English. I'm right messed up about it. I don't know much about the world, except what I get on the radio about the war that's maybe coming, and that's real bad news about this here Hitler; and I hear things around the feed store."

"Like what?"

"Like that there's been some niggers hanged up north of Dallas."

"Luke, please do not say that word."

"Sorry, Sis. I mean some Negroes. Two or three Negro men. A bunch of white men in those white robes and hoods hanged them up and I don't really want to mention what else they did. The whole town came out."

"Had to be the Klan did that."

"Yep, and we got the Klan right here. The fellas at the feed store made jokes about it just yesterday, and said they'd like to see some darkies hung around here."

"Roy, did he know about this?"

"Yep, he was right there, sitting on a sack of maize seed."

"You men," Dona said, looking toward the wooden gate she was about to jump out and open. "Don't you care when people are murdered right here? You only worry when there's a war coming from someplace else?"

"Hold on a minute, Sis. I don't know what to think. It's probably not right, but this county has had plenty of hangings and whatnot against the colored, and it's what's bound to happen again. I don't have a crippled calf's clue what to do about it. And I didn't want to get you all riled up, either."

"Well, you have." Dona pushed open the cab door, ignoring the creak and groan of metal on metal. "You go on to the house. I'll get the gate and walk on back. I expect Josie's got dinner almost ready, anyhow."

When the dust from Luke's truck had settled, Dona climbed on the open gate and swung. It didn't clear the ground like it had when she was a little girl, when she weighed almost nothing. But with lifting and scooting, she managed to stay on and close the latch.

"Things change," she said to the gate, "when you are a grown-up. You can't hear about hate and torture and treating other people worse than you treat your cattle, and not say something. You have to hang on to what you believe and make things better."

But she was afraid. A woman on a ranch in West Texas, even a white woman, wasn't worth much beyond her labor, in some books. So, what would happen if she made trouble. And what kind of trouble could she possibly make all by herself?

Chapter Fifteen

Two weeks after she and Luke sat through MacMurray's hateful sermon, as the hens grew quiet on their nests and Dona and Annalou closed the barn doors for the night, a man whispered from the tool shed, "Miz Willis."

Dona turned fast to get in front of Annalou.

"Miz Willis, don't be afeard. It's just me, Samuel." And the man stepped out of the shadows, holding up his hands.

"Samuel Washington," Dona said. "My friend. I am not scared of you, but what on earth is happening?"

"I need a place to hide."

"What from?"

"A lynch mob."

"Oh, my lord, Samuel. I heard the Klan is riled up again. Let's get you out of sight. Here, you go into the wooden barn for now. Roy and the other men are off moving cattle to the railroad pens at Barnhart, but other hands are around the place, so be careful. I've got to think what to do. Bet you're thirsty. Hungry. How about some supper?"

"Much obliged, Miz Willis," Samuel said, and disappeared into the barn.

Dona and Annalou ran to the ranch house and gathered up all the leftover fried chicken, corn pone, coffee and red beans they could, and filled a jug with water. They hurried back out to Samuel and settled on bales of hay.

Dona said, "Samuel, might you tell us what has happened?"

Samuel cleaned his plate, drained the coffee cup and water jug and set them aside. "I wanted to learn to read."

"Read?"

"Yes'm, and I'd been working for Reverend and Missus MacMurray for a few years. You might know that."

Dona nodded. Samuel was not only a tall, well-built man, and known to her to be a hard worker, he was smart, with a good head for figures. He had solved problems with water drainage at the shacks when nobody else could; had told other workers how to get something done right; had spoken up for more books at the school for Negro children where his little boys went. And he couldn't read. She should have realized. When Samuel was a child, Negroes were not encouraged to learn.

"And one day, Missus MacMurray said, 'Samuel, do you know how to read?' I said I can read somewhat, but not too good, and I always wanted to read books. She said she'd teach me. I said I'd be much obliged and it'd be after work hours and she said how about Saturday after work when the Reverend was at the church to write his sermon, and I said my wife and little boys'd bring my supper and wait for me to walk home with them, and it was all settled."

"So, what happened then?"

"Two Saturdays, we'd had our lessons and was working on number three at Missus MacMurray's kitchen table, and we was careful to keep the blinds up and the lights bright, against any misunderstanding." Samuel halted and cleared his throat.

"But I guess Missus MacMurray didn't tell the Reverend about keeping on with the lessons and somebody saw us through the windows and ran to tell the Reverend. And the Reverend, he went to his brother, you know, the deputy sheriff, and turned me in. Said I was seeking the attention of a white woman, which I was not. But the deputy sheriff, he stopped in at the Longhorn Saloon and rustled up a posse to find me and string me up."

"How did you escape?"

"My cousin, Abraham, he was working at the saloon, cleaning behind the bar, and right away he ran to the MacMurray kitchen to say I'd better get out of there. Which I did. And I begged Missus MacMurray to watch after my family, who was waiting in the bushes for me to finish my lesson. I felt my arms go around them all, and said get home quick; but I wasn't quick enough for myself. The men in that posse, they was wearing the white hoods, and they was the Klan and they busted into the kitchen, thinking I was there, and I took off running for my life."

Samuel stopped to catch his breath, which had gotten faster with the telling. "And Missus Turn, I was headed here."

They sat for a moment in silence. "Thank you, Samuel, and thank heavens you've made it this far. Reverend MacMurray's sermon should have warned me about something horrible, like this. We'll do our best to help." She wiped her eyes.

"Annalou, please go to the hall closet and grab a couple of wool blankets; and oh, yes, a tin cup and plate from the cupboard and a dish towel, some matches and a candle. And any flashlights you can find. And please tell Nanna we are going out for a night ride, so she won't worry."

Dona saddled up Duke and Paint and by the time she led them to the barn, Samuel was ready to go.

They packed up the vittles and other things in blanket rolls and tied them behind the two saddles. Dona handed Samuel her own .38 pistol, loaded, which, at first, he did not want.

"Samuel, we're riding a piece up into the hills, but you never know who might figure out where you are these next few days while we find a safer place for you. We've got to keep this a secret and I can't count on Roy or Luke to protect you. Here. Four extra bullets."

Samuel tucked the pistol in his belt and plunked the bullets into his pants pocket.

"You ride Paint. Annalou and I will double up on Duke. Where we're going, it's gonna be a mite steep and rough."

It was around eight o'clock when they headed out toward the limestone butte. In an hour they reached the high pasture windmill and water tank. They let the horses drink from the cattle trough and to rest their legs. The moon was rising about half full over East Lee pasture.

Annalou said in her quietest voice, "Samuel, I am sorry for your troubles."

"Thank you, Miss Annalou."

"You don't have to call me Miss, Samuel. I'm just plain Annalou, if you don't mind. Unless you want me to call you Mr. Samuel."

"Samuel is just fine, Annalou." He grinned. "I guess we settled that."

"But Samuel, did you run through the thickets, the whole ten miles from town?"

"I guess I did."

"Were they chasing you in trucks?"

"They was. Glad they wasn't on horses. Couldn't a lost them near as easy. Had to hide out during daylight today, so I snuck into your shacks, Miz Turn, to wait for evening. Got a bit of a rest, and a drink outa the river."

Dona walked around the base of the butte, stopping to listen to the night. A barred owl hooted from the cactus field and crickets rasped their tunes.

"Time to head up this bluff, we're not too far," she said.

For about twenty minutes, they rode uphill on a road they could barely see. Rounding a sharp bend, shining in the moonlight, stood the white limestone Sheepherder's Hut.

"Quiet as the moon, itself," Dona said. "Thank heavens."

"I COULDN'T SLEEP MUCH, Aunt Doney," Annalou said, wiping crumbs from the table's oilcloth. "So, I wrote in the red diary you gave me."

"I'm glad you're using that diary."

"I plan to write in it every night, now that I've gotten started. Before, it was so pretty and new, I felt unworthy. But about when Samuel arrived here last night, I had to write it down."

"As soon as we can this afternoon, we need to get on up there to see about him."

Annalou hid her diary away under the mattress in her room and came back into the kitchen. Dona was fixing to cook pinto beans for that night's supper, spreading the dry beans on the kitchen table and sorting out stones and clots of dirt.

"These beans, they're real good for you," Dona said, "and usually I cook up a double mess, to have leftovers for later in the week. But, with making sure Samuel has enough at the Hut, I figured I'd better use the really big pot."

"I would say we used to eat pinto beans and cornbread, mostly, when I was little," said Annalou. "And cabbage, too, in winter."

"Your momma could buy everything for that whole supper for about 50 cents, tops."

"Really?"

"Yep. It's a good thing to know how to feed folks with not much money. It's come in mighty handy these past years, what with the Drought and the terrible Depression. I think we would have starved to death, if we had counted on having cash money. Why, in my momma's day, they grew nearly everything they ate. Or they traded for it. Did you know that? That your ancestors didn't have much money either?"

"No, I thought they were rich, owning ranches and all. Like you."

"Throw the pickings outside, will you, honey? I'll wash these beans in the bucket. And please grab a nice piece of salt pork from the larder."

The beans were cooking on the back of the stove, pungent with garlic, pork fat and chilies, when Dona and Annalou sat down at the table with cups of breakfast coffee.

"About my forebears, nope, they weren't all rich, and neither are we, by the way. You've seen the photograph of Mamaw's whole family, haven't you, in there on the piano?"

"I've seen a photograph of lots of people on the front porch of a wooden ranch house, is that the one?"

“That’s it. I look at it often, myself. If you want to bring it in here, I’ll tell you what I can, about the family.

Annalou returned in seconds and sat the ornate frame between them.

“Let’s see,” Dona said, “here in the middle is my momma’s momma, your Nanna, Myrtle Rose Dillard, and her husband, James Joseph Cunningham, the real tall, boney one in the big hat. Right now, your Nanna sleeps most of the time, but back then, she must have been a champion work horse.”

“And is that Mamaw?” Annalou asked, pointing to a girl about her own age.

“Yep, that’s my mother, Ophelia, tall and broad shouldered like her daddy. And these are her brothers all in a row, who mostly became sheriffs in one county or another between here and Brownwood and up to Lubbock. Seven of them. Here are her sisters. Dona, and Daisy, and Unity Ann, and Myrtle Rose. Your aunts have those same names. We carry names on for a long time in our family.”

“I never met some of those uncles and aunts.”

“They died off before you were born, mostly to tuberculosis, but there are lots of second cousins and cousins once-removed living around here.”

“But Aunt Doney, where’d your family get so much ranch land?”

“My great-grandparents, the generation before this photograph, got it mostly from the Republic of Texas, hundreds of acres. For fighting Mexicans for the Republic, and mostly for fighting the Comanche Indians.”

“How come the government had that land to give away?”

Dona peered out the window above the kitchen sink and sighed. “Well, truth to tell, they stole it.”

“Stole it? Who from?” Annalou’s eyebrows raised.

“From the Indians, who had hunted on it for hundreds, maybe thousands of years.”

"That sounds awful."

"I think so, too. There was plenty of blame to go around, of course. The Comanche warriors were about as fierce as they come, but you know, if I had been one of them and these white settlers laid claim to the land my people had been part of for so long, I might have done some pretty awful things to defend it, too."

"So, our family didn't have a right to it?"

"Doesn't seem so to me, but it depends on who you talk to, I guess."

"And how did they eat, I mean your great-grandmother, in the beginning? Beans and cornbread like us?"

"Maybe so, because they could bring dried beans and corn with them in the wagons and they wouldn't spoil. But remember, there were buffalo herds and prairie dogs, jackrabbits and quail and fish and lots of deer, and if you were a good hunter or trapper and especially if you had horses, you could do all right."

Dona carried the coffee pot from the stove to the table and filled their cups.

"And what about vegetables, Aunt Doney, what about fruit?"

"As I remember the stories, the women in settler families always tucked seeds in their clothes and bedding, and hung herbs to dry from the cover on their wagon, no matter where they hailed from. Even so, lots of babies died and lots of families liked to have starved to death, especially when they were caught in a Blue Norther. Temperatures could drop from 100 degrees hot to 20 degrees cold in minutes. It was a mighty hard life.

"Later on, our ancestors brought their slaves from the deep south, South Carolina, Tennessee and the like, to work the cotton fields. Samuel's ancestors, no doubt, among 'em."

Annalou pushed her chair back from the table, picked up the photograph in its fancy frame and walked into the hall.

"Aunt Doney, how do you stand it sometimes?"

"Stand what, honey?"

"Knowing so much and not being able to do anything about it."

"Oh, which do you mean? Our government stealing the land? Our family killing Comanche families, or bringing slaves to work the cotton?"

"All. And other things."

"Like Samuel?"

"Like what happened to Samuel. I mean, I know you've hidden him from the posse, and from everybody but me, but it's so awful, what they want to do to him."

"You're right, and I don't know what to do about it anymore than what happened with the Indians. Or about this Europe war, with this terrible Hitler fellow, and all the killing. But with Samuel, you helped me."

"I didn't help much."

"I don't know if I could have been brave enough to hide him up at the Sheepherder's Hut if you hadn't been with me. And I sure couldn't have snuck that much food up to him without riling somebody."

"But I'm just a kid. I did what you told me to do."

"You are a kid, but you are smart and you really care about things." Dona folded her arms on the table.

Annalou leaned over from her chair and hugged Dona's shoulders. "Aunt Doney, I love you so much and I think you can do anything. So, isn't there something more we can do to help Samuel? And, you know, other people in danger, like him?"

Dona lifted her head and squinted at Annalou. "You will get us in trouble sure as shootin', young lady. I don't know. It's dangerous to think it, but maybe there is something we can do."

"Like what?"

"Like I don't know, quite yet. But a while back, before you came here, I was sitting up at the Hut, feeling sorry for myself, and useless. Believe it or not, I heard the land singing. It said, 'Arise!' And now, with you giving me a kick in the flanks, I'm not gonna sit back down, at least that."

"Aunt Doney, I need to tell you. I had a dream last night and it really scared me."

Dona raised her eyebrows and leaned closer.

"It was about Samuel." Annalou pulled her knees to her chest. "He was running barefoot across a pasture full of cactus and his clothes were half torn off. He wasn't making any noise at all. And behind him, not far behind, there were big hounds like Uncle Roy's Blue Ticks on his trail, baying like the dickens and their tongues were hanging out, but instead of the tongues being pink and long and dripping, they were on fire. I started screaming, NO, NO, NO, and trying to run toward them, but I couldn't run, something was holding me back."

She dropped her forehead to her knees and squeezed her eyes shut. "I woke up and my throat hurt like I really had been screaming. Those dogs were going to catch Samuel. He didn't have a chance."

As Annalou told her dream, Dona had felt it. She felt the sting of cactus needles in her feet, and the heat of dogs at her back.

Annalou wiped her eyes on her shirt sleeves and stood up.

"Don't worry, Annalou, I'll ride on up to the hut and check on Samuel right now. If anybody asks, say I've had to take Duke out for a ride and I'll be back real soon."

Dona took off then at a gallop, heading toward the high pasture. It was a cool, high-blue day, the kind of day when it seems like nothing in the world could be wrong. Maybe those hound dogs hadn't found their way to the hut. Maybe they never would. And when she reached the little rock hut and called her loudest yoo hoo, and when Samuel appeared from behind the clump of cedar trees looking hale and standing tall, she jumped down from Duke's back, and tried through her tears to tell Samuel why she was laughing.

That evening after supper, Dona and Annalou were alone long enough to talk.

"I'll wash if you'll dry and put away," Annalou said, as they pushed back from the kitchen table.

Josie and Juan Carlos had gone to their cabin for the night. The men had gone to the barn to put the animals to bed, Roy to the horses, Luke to the Longhorn steer he was trying to settle, and Joe Bob to the chickens and pigs. They would be back soon.

"I'll have to go tomorrow morning to see about Samuel," Dona whispered, "and take those beans and some more corn pone. I'm worried he doesn't have enough to eat, and a regular bedroll would be a comfort."

"What I am worried about is that somebody is going to find him," Annalou said. "I wish you'd let me go with you."

"I need you to stay here and help Josie with the meals, and Nanna, so the boys don't start asking questions. You can pack some more supplies, though. Tomorrow is a good time to go, since all the men will have their hands full, rounding up sheep from the pastures to check them for worms."

"Aunt Doney, what made you believe Samuel?"

"I've known him for years. He's part of a big family of aunts and uncles and cousins and I've noticed that people in his family and other colored people in town turn to him for help and advice; and he's good at minding his own business. He's always been honest with me, and, I can't put my finger on it, but there's something about him that you know you can count on. I'm sure it's a problem, in a way, that he's so well-known in town. Kind of a target, you might say.

"It's against the law in Texas, you know, to lynch a person, and it doesn't happen so often anymore, at least not around here. But I have to admit, there's something that always scares me about a bunch of white men. Like they'll do things together they never would do by themselves. And when you have a posse of them who have hatred in their hearts for anybody that's different, and they call themselves the Ku Klux Klan, I wouldn't put a thing past them. Not one thing."

Annalou wiped the sink with the dishrag, wrung it out and stretched it on the stove rack to dry. Dona hung her dish towel next to the rag and leaned both hands on the counter.

"I am white and married and was raised a Southern Baptist, and even I am scared to death of those men. I can't help thinking about Samuel and how terrified he must be; and yet, he thanked the Lord that he's alive. He's got everything against him and why on earth he trusts me enough to come here, I don't know. But it seems like a chance to do some good, and there aren't many chances like that come my way."

"Or mine, either," Annalou said.

After supper was usually Dona's time for reading. But the next evening, she could not settle down. Samuel was fine again this morning, and at least he had more vittles, but nothing was really fine. She eased through the porch doorway to the barnyard, as the sun, low on the horizon, set giant clouds into a crescendo of colors. She put her palms together in prayer.

"Oh, magnificent star in the west, our light and our life. Protect Samuel from harm. Let him find his way to safety; let him be with his wife and little children. Let all people be free and without fear." Her face shining with tears, Dona threw open her arms and said, 'Oh, great setting sun, what can I do?"

The light faded from crimson and gold to peach to that all-night blue gray she loved. Across the caliche road by the metal barn a whippoorwill called. It nested in waist-high oats, its baby chicks hidden and endlessly hunted by foxes, raccoons and who knows what all. Like Samuel. She shivered.

With the men off to their work in the pastures the next morning, and the sky barely gray, Dona rode bareback on Duke down to the dam. A sliver of light moved into the river from the far side. A water moccasin. The snake was not alone, but led a line of three smaller snakes, one-third its size. In all her years at the ranch, in the decades of fishing from this very spot, she had never seen a grown moccasin swim the river with little ones—like a mother. And as much as she feared their venom and had stayed out of that slow green water above the dam most of her life because of them, she marveled that while their bodies curved from side to side, their triangular heads shot through the water in perfectly straight lines.

It was a sign. Of course, she thought, that is the way of it. That's how we can change the minds of the men behind that lynching posse. Her mother was the one person who would know what she meant. It was time to go to town.

Chapter Sixteen

On Thursday afternoons, come hell or high water, four men on top of the dung heap of the county, including the one Dona was bound and determined to see, played a game of Texas 42 at the general store in San Angelo, the county seat.

She drove the old Chevy truck right up to the edge of the store's wooden steps and turned off the engine. Her mother had agreed, when she'd told her of the plan. She had to get to the ones who were behind the Klan, and she couldn't care how powerful and respectable they were.

Clenching her white-gloved hands, Dona stepped through the doorway to the store's back room. Four men in their Stetson hats sat in wooden chairs around a square wooden table, each with a line of dominoes in front. Another leaned in a chair against the wall, paring his nails with a pocket knife.

The men glanced at each other, at the dominoes they held close to their chests, and played their hands in silence.

"Good afternoon to you, Judge Angus Cameron, and you, Reverend Andrew MacMurray, and you, Attorney Edward Cunningham, and you, Banker James Llewellyn, and you," Dona turned toward the man sitting in the chair against the wall, "Mr. Butch Dillingham, proud owner of this general store. You're the ones who think you run this county."

Edward Cunningham glanced at her and back to his hand. No one else acknowledged her, but the hunch of his shoulders told her that he was embarrassed. She was about to bring him and his cronies to task.

She stepped further into the room and bent toward the table. "I've known you all my life. I know your mothers and daddies, your children.

And for most of these years, I've been proud to be your friend. But, boys, after what's happened in this town, I am ashamed."

Not one man turned his head toward her.

"Your turn to shuffle, Angus," Andrew MacMurray said.

"It's way past time for lynch mobs to keep folks in line—and as you well know, it's not legal. So, what do you do when you don't like the way a Negro man is acting? Do you bother to speak to him? Do you think to ask the white woman who is his friend and teacher what is going on? No, you stir up the local bucks. You make those boys do your dirty work."

She walked to the table and stood between Angus, The Judge, and Andrew, The Reverend. "You are all bullies. You can't even look me square in the face."

The men drew their dominoes from the newly shuffled pile and arranged their hands.

"And it makes me sick to look at you."

Dona moved around the table, her low-heeled pumps swishing the worn wood. "Butch, I'd like to sit a spell. That looks like a good chair and maybe you've finished with your fingernails. Don't you have business to tend to inside?"

Butch, his face flushing redder than usual, out of an old habit tipped his hat to Dona and stood.

"Sit down, Butch," Edward Cunningham said. "She is my cousin. She can have my seat. How are you at 42, Dona? What kind of stakes can we raise?"

"What do you mean by stakes, Edward? And when you say, 'we,' are you and I partners in this game?"

"Well maybe not partners, but shall we say allies?"

"I'd like to say allies, depending on what you mean by that. Will you stand behind me while I play? Will you offer advice and counsel, Counselor?"

Edward's mouth twitched into a smile. "Perhaps, Cousin, if you will listen."

"I'm in," Dona said, taking off her gloves. "Let us shake on it, Edward. But let us pick up the game at another time. I've got a mess of chores back at the ranch and Mother is waiting for me at her house. Shall we set a time?"

"Shall we say tomorrow, Friday afternoon, 5:00 o'clock, my office?"

"Agreed."

Dona turned to the table of players. "Gentlemen, thank you for your time and attention. It seems the game has changed and we will let you know how it goes. I want to win fair and square. May I have your blessing, as a worthy opponent?"

No one moved or spoke until Edward said, "Boys, the lady has asked for our blessing. She has mine." He pulled his hat off his head and put it over his heart.

The judge, the reverend, the banker and the owner of the general store took off their hats, and, watching Edward, held them over their chests and nodded. No one except for Edward looked Dona in the eye, but several throats were cleared. She smoothed on her short, white gloves, nodded to each lowered hat, and left the room.

FRIDAY AFTERNOON AT 5:00 O'CLOCK, Dona arrived with her mother at the door of Edward James Cunningham, Esq., Attorney at Law. The august Mr. Cunningham, himself, ushered them into his private office and shut the door.

"Ophelia, it is so good to see you," he said, taking her hand in both of his and smiling into her face. "And Dona, you are looking lovely today."

Dona stood at least six inches taller than Edward Cunningham in her pumps, and she would normally be glad of the advantage of height in the conversation they were about to have, but on the other hand, they had come to ask a favor.

The women settled themselves in the two leather chairs arranged in front of an expansive desk of dark mahogany. From his chair behind the desk, Edward Cunningham leaned toward them; his eyebrows, thick as hedges, raised expectantly.

Ophelia said, "Edward, you and my dearly departed husband, Gordon, were friends all of your life. You and I are more than friends, we are first cousins."

He nodded.

"And truly, that is the only reason I feel that we might impose on you."

"Go on, please, Ophelia," said Edward with a hint of impatience. "You know I will do whatever I can."'

"A short while ago, right here in our own town, a posse of vigilante men tried to capture a Negro man with the intent to kill him."

Edward Cunningham's mouth tightened and he clasped his hands together. "How do you know about that, Ophelia?"

"I am not at liberty to say, quite yet, but he is in mortal danger and for no good reason in the world." She cocked her head and peered out of one eye, examining him, like a crow might.

Edward blinked his eyes, hooded from years of secrets he'd been made to keep, and stood from his desk. "I am ashamed to say it, but someone I know well was one of the men. And in case someone presses charges, I have agreed to take him as my client."

"Of course," said Ophelia, lengthening her already straight back. "You are sworn, if he is your client. But Edward, how can you take the side of anyone who would lynch another human being?"

"I think these men did not mean to lynch Samuel. But rather to scare him."

"But why on earth?"

"Because he was spending time alone with a white woman after dark. Why do you think?"

"I think that is stupid. Why, Samuel was there to learn to improve his reading. It was his third lesson. The windows were open. There was nothing to hide. They were sitting at Mrs. MacMurray's kitchen table under a light. Samuel's wife and children had brought his supper."

"What I mean, Ophelia," Edward leaned closer, "is that there is no cause ever, and surely you and I and others of our generation know this, for a Negro and a white woman to be alone together after dark. Except for one thing."

"One thing?" Dona said.

With a sigh, Edward leaned back in his leather chair, and, over fingertips pressed together in front of his chest, he forced a smile at Dona. "My dear, don't pretend you don't know what I'm talking about. It is against the law in Texas for a Negro and a white to have relations. That is what I mean."

"But what is the evidence in this case?"

"As I said, they were together, alone, after dark."

"Edward," Ophelia interrupted quietly, "if you believe they were breaking the law, why not have them arrested? Why protect someone in the Klan?"

"Did I say anything about the Klan?" Edward smiled. "No, the problem is that for the men in that posse, the law is too slow. I don't agree with them, but I see their point of view."

Edward Cunningham glanced down at his pocket watch. "As you both must surely know, the Klan is not illegal. It is protected by the Constitution of the United States of America. Members have the right to assemble and the right of free speech."

"The right to take the law into their own hands?"

"Of course not, and I would be happy to further our discussion, but I'm afraid we are almost out of time. What exactly can I do for you?"

Dona pressed her notebook to her chest and glanced at her mother. Ophelia gave the smallest nod and Dona said, "Cousin Edward, what we hope from you is that you'll help us spread the word among those men who were after him, that Samuel wishes to reunite with his family and live peaceably in this community. And that what they did was unchristian and wrong. Can you help us with that?"

Mr. Cunningham sat perfectly still.

She waited and when Edward did not respond, she went on. "You have a reputation for fairness and honesty. Why, you are an upstanding member of the First Presbyterian Church, as I am, as my husband is, as many of our family members are. But surely Jesus would not have been part of a lynching mob. Come to think of it, he was the victim of just this kind of mob, filled with fear and hatred."

Except for her father, whom Dona had adored without thought, Edward represented the highest level of professional achievement and integrity of anyone in the family. He was a man of influence in this county; got things done; brought order to their world. And it was rarely clear, at least to her, how he did this.

But sitting in his office, under his scrutiny, she was certain that Edward was lying to her, that when he had smiled at her as a child, he had been lying. He did not stand against cruelty of person against person; he did not question the racist laws that the State of Texas still upheld. The crack in her trust of Cousin Edward deepened and she would have to be as careful with him as she was with any poisonous creature.

But it remained that he could help Samuel if he wished and she could think of no one else to turn to.

"We beg of you," Dona said, "to consider helping to smooth the troubled waters. Your client does not have to suffer. Samuel will not bring charges against anyone, if he can be assured of the safety of his family and himself. Cousin Edward, please use your influence and your good heart to bring peace to our beautiful county. You know what we ask, and I believe that after some reflection and prayer, you will take our side in this matter."

The two women stood, and put out their gloved hands to shake his. Edward Cunningham stood and extended his hand to them. "You are courageous women. I cannot agree with you on everything, but you are right that our county cannot stand unlawful bloodshed, even if in the minds of many it is deserved."

As Ophelia and Dona prepared to leave, he said, "One more thing. I often think of Gordie. When we were growing up he was my best friend and the one person I would listen to; maybe because he listened to me. He always reminded me of what was right. So, when he married you, my own cousin, Ophelia, I could see it was a good match. Now that I am old, it seems that he is here with you."

He paused to check the calendar on his desk. "Today is Friday. Perhaps you could visit me again tomorrow afternoon at about this same time? I will try to have some news."

"I AM SORRY TO SAY THIS, MOTHER, but I don't trust Cousin Edward."

Ophelia backed out of her parking place into the town's busy traffic and pointed the Cadillac sedan west on Beauregard toward her home. "Let's roll down the windows to let in that lovely air," she said.

"Mother, could we please talk about this before we get to your house? I am really upset by that meeting."

Ophelia sat forward, hugging the steering wheel in both hands. "I have to concentrate on driving, honey. It's not my strong suit. Why don't you do the talking."

"Okay, I will. Cousin Edward knows exactly who those men are. I believe the leaders are the men he plays dominoes with on Thursdays, plus however many more, and maybe he is one of them."

"Wait a minute, let me get past this intersection and I'll get over into the park. There's lots of shade under the trees."

Neither woman spoke until the car was fully stopped and Ophelia had pulled the emergency brake.

Dona said, "You are worried, too? About Cousin Edward, I mean?"

"I am, indeed. All those years when he was so close to your daddy, I guess I never paid him much mind. I mean, he is my cousin, but he was Gordie's friend. They were the busiest men in town, so probably they saw each other only at Masonic Lodge meetings and the country club. And now that I think about it, they would go off by themselves, usually into the men's smoking rooms, and I didn't hear what they talked about."

"Daddy was on the side of the Negro and the Mexican, wasn't he?"

"Land sakes, yes. And maybe some of those talks were your daddy trying to get Edward to change his mind about the races. I don't know. Your daddy didn't tell me things like that. I agreed with him and I suppose that was enough for both of us."

"Do you think Cousin Edward has guessed that Samuel is at the ranch?"

"I think that's very likely."

"I've got to get home and warn Samuel, then. Annalou had a dream that people were coming for him, and she's a lot like you that way."

"What way do you mean?"

"Knowing things like that. Dreams, strong feelings about what's going to happen. She's got the gift, I think."

"Then we'd best listen to Annalou."

"We've got to find another place for him to hide. But Mother, he can't hide out forever. He has his family, those two little boys. We've got to change the minds of those men, even if Cousin Edward won't help us."

"He may after all. I'd sure like to think he will. But meanwhile, you are right. We must do what we can. Let us close our eyes and ask for help."

They sat in the car with the doors cracked open to let the cool air from the live oak tree enter with whatever blessings it had. A mockingbird high above them began to sing. It seemed to Dona that it sang every song it had ever heard, and she wondered how on earth it decided which one to sing next.

In a few minutes Ophelia said, "Here is what I must do, Dona. On Sunday, I will pray for those men in the middle of the First Baptist Church. Samuel and every other colored person around here is in terrible trouble if we don't find a way to reach those men. Whoever they are, they are as bullheaded as children. I will pray aloud for them. When the minister asks who wishes to come forward to testify, I'll go forward to the foot of the pulpit, face the congregation and pray as loud as I can. I'll pray for their souls, for their minds, for their hearts and let them know that I know what they have done. I'll ask the Lord to remind them of the words of Christ. I'll quote Corinthians 13, the greatest of all things is love. And pray to the Lord that his love and forgiveness will heal the wounds of racism and bigotry in our hearts and in our community."

"Oh, Mother," Dona said, rubbing her forehead, "you would do that? That would be the best thing." She folded her hands in her lap.

"I'll be like that mockingbird, honey. Didn't you listen? Sing from my heart the songs I have learned all my life."

Dona raised her head, pulled back her shoulders and squinted like a mischievous girl. "All right, but do you think those men will know what 'bigotry' means?"

Ophelia chuckled. "Sorry, I guess I got carried away by my own preachiness. I will be scared. But there is nothing more powerful than prayer—and a woman speaking her mind."

THAT NIGHT, DONA'S THOUGHTS WERE WILD. Samuel was in the Hut. Was Samuel in the Hut? Who will call on the angels for sustenance? It is raining fire and brimstone somewhere. To the ends of the earth, are all dark-skinned people persecuted? The world is mean with light-eyed men.

The next day and the one after that, she rode Duke to the Hut. She carried food and water and whatever Samuel needed. He worried about his family, and wanted to get back, hoping that things in town had cooled down. But she asked him to wait, until she could talk with another friend, someone she trusted to know what went on in town.

HOW MELVAR KNEW that she needed to talk with him about Samuel, Dona didn't ask. But the next morning, there he was. Every blessed time she heard the bells on his wagon, her heart beat so loudly, she was afraid anybody could hear it. Even with worrying about Samuel, when Melvar arrived, she felt like a silly, thoughtless girl.

"Yoo-hoo, Melvar," she called, as though he were any other friend.

She loved the way he raised his hat and dipped his head toward her. Blue jays did that, and they called, too, the way he did. "And a good day to you, Missus Dona." Formal-like, in case, in the middle of a weekday morning, someone besides hens and barn cats listened in.

She stood near the house and waited for him to unhitch Molly.

"She's in good spirits today, eh?" Dona said, turning to him. His naturally olive skin had darkened in the strong sun of summer and his hazel-amber eyes glowed in contrast. To Dona he was beautiful in the way that the crowns of live oak trees are beautiful in the shining first rays of morning sun, and it was hard not to stare.

"You are looking well," Melvar said.

"And you, too. You seem especially happy today."

"I am always happy to come to your ranch. I only wish I could be here more often. I also hope I have something among my wares that will please you today."

"Now that Molly's settled with her grain bag, how about a glass of water or some coffee?"

"Thank you, Missus Dona, coffee would be most welcome."

He took his usual place in the shade of the big mesquite.

When Dona returned, she said, "I made this with sugar and milk. That is how you like it, yes?"

Dona knew perfectly well how Melvar liked his coffee. She could never forget anything about him, but she didn't want him to know how she noticed the least thing, how she thought over every detail of him and their conversation after he left on his rounds.

He did seem to admire her. Why else would he appear so often at her doorstep when she was sure he did not visit the other ranches but every month or two. Why else would he stay for an hour when she could not always afford to buy the least thing from him? And why did it mean so much to her to spend this brief time with him, when no other man had ever pulled at her like this?

"I want to tell you of a very special person who needs your help," she said.

Melvar peered into Dona's eyes for a moment. "It is possible I know this friend, and of course I will try to do what you wish."

A half-hour later, Dona stood up from where she and Melvar had been sitting, and stretched her arms over her head. "Can you ride a horse, Melvar?"

"I am a fair rider."

"Well then, let's take a ride to the Shacks and get some work done. We've got to make another place for Samuel to hide."

Chapter Seventeen

"Annalou, Melvar tells me that Samuel is still in great danger. I must get back up to the Hut today. What an awful mess this is. Watching those water moccasins curve across the top of the river; and this whole idea of going to Cousin Edward. Trying to make things right by using his influence behind the scenes—going in sideways toward the law, you might say. But he really is a snake. I mean he is one dangerous man to have on our side. If he is on our side. And I've got to go to Samuel right now and warn him to stay out of the Hut in case Cousin Edward and his cronies remember there is a hut, which I am very much afraid they will."

"Can't I go, too?"

"I wish you could, but one of us has to stay behind to get dinner ready for the men. They're with the crew from Mexico, shearing sheep all morning and then again this afternoon. Josie's helping out with my morning chores and some laundry that needs doing for Nanna. I should go ahead to make sure Samuel's all right, if you feel okay about the cooking."

"Of course," said Annalou. "But what if something happens to you?"

"It won't.

Dona could still feel the breath on her neck of those hounds in Annalou's dream, and that, with what Melvar had told her, was a bad sign.

Duke fairly pranced up the side of the hill toward high pasture, slowing only at the scree line and lunging forward with good will. He wanted to go faster but at about the halfway mark up the hill Dona reined him in. He stood, in the way of a good quarter horse, with not a flick of his tail to call attention. His ears were alert and pointed forward. Blue jays rasped their warning call. Someone or something was up ahead.

She clucked Duke to a slow walk along the side of the hill. She had tied her rifle to her saddle and now she held it close to her side. They were almost directly below the Sheepherder's Hut but it was still quite a way around and up the rough trail before it would come in sight. Maybe the jays were fussing at Samuel. Maybe that's all it was. Dona loosened the reins a bit.

A blue jay screeched and a rifle blasted, once. A pistol fired, twice. A man ran down the hill ahead of her, slipping on scree, rifle over his head for balance, one arm tucked against his chest. He had not seen her. She pulled the reins tight, and sat the saddle as still as a tree. She'd seen his hat, his clothes, and that he was young and injured and white. Her only hope was that he wouldn't turn her way.

The man veered off and ran between two cedar brakes toward the road. Loose rocks crunched under his boots, slipping, sliding; and a motor revved up. An old truck, maybe older than Luke's, and from the way it clattered down the road toward the river pasture, it was in pretty bad shape. She let Duke have his head, then, let him plow uphill as steeply and fast as he wanted, until they came within sight of the Hut's limestone chimney. Duke's nostrils flared and his ears lay back on his head.

"Whoa," she whispered, "easy boy."

There was no sound now. Not even the cry of jays. Buzzards circled over the rim of the hill, two and then three. Dona dismounted below a live oak grove and dropped Duke's reins on the ground. "Stand, boy," she said, and crouching low, moved toward the chimney at the back of the hut where there were no windows.

"Hello?" she called. If Samuel was in there, he was hurt, or worse. If someone else was in there, he'd have a gun. She couldn't leave Samuel, no matter that he had a pistol, no matter what.

The sound was harsh and soft at once, primal with pain and caution. The hair on her neck stood up.

"I'm coming in," she called. "Whoever you are, I'm a friend. This is Dona Willis Turn, and I live here."

She ducked under the two windows in the side wall of the Hut and crept toward the door. It was open wide. She peered around the door jam, prepared to pull back or be shot. Samuel.

He lay on his side in the far corner next to the fireplace, facing the door. Curled into himself, his hand covered in blood, he pressed the pistol against his chest.

"Samuel, it's me. It's Dona." She crawled to him and said again, "Samuel."

He was alive. His shoulder moved with his breath, and he shuddered.

"Missus," he said.

"You're going to be all right, Samuel," she said into his ear. "Can you talk?"

Samuel grunted.

"Where did he get you?"

Samuel's breath was forced as he said, "Back."

"I'm taking the pistol, Samuel, so I can see."

He released the pistol and again pressed his hand into his chest below the shoulder.

"Can you move your hand away?"

"No."

"I need to find where the bullet went in. Think you can roll toward me a bit?"

"Uh huh."

"Got it. That lowdown coward shot you in the back, but you got him, too.'

"Maybe." His breath came in gasps.

"I see where the bullet went in, Samuel. Please move your hand so I can see if it came out." Samuel moved his hand away, sticky with blood.

"Bullet went through. Don't worry. Happened to one of our hunting dogs, and we saved him. I've got to close up the holes right now."

Samuel grunted again. His breath harder and shallower.

From the cotton cup towels she'd folded around the vittles, Dona made two square bandages. She ripped pieces of cloth from her shirt into narrow strips.

Samuel could hardly breathe. Dona pressed plugs of cloth into the bullet holes, as hard as she dared.

"It's not an artery, Samuel. But the bullet got one lung. Try not to panic. Can you hold this bandage over the hole?" And as Samuel lay there, eyes closed, his calloused hand holding firm, Dona ran strips of cotton around the shoulder and chest of the man before her who was making no sound at all.

"Samuel, can you hear me?"

He made a low humming noise in his throat.

"Alright, then, let's see if you can sit. Hold on to me."

A fallen hero rose in an act of will beyond anything she had witnessed. Slowly, methodically, he shifted his weight, balanced his body, and slumped against the cabin wall. Blood soaked the bandages, and his breath was harsh and quick.

"Keep your hand there, Samuel. Got to keep pressure on those bandages. I've got a canteen in my saddle bags. You need water."

Only at Duke's side did she think of the danger. What if the gunman had returned? She unbuckled a saddlebag, grabbed a canteen and ran back into the Hut. There had been no sound outside to alarm her, but also there was no time to dawdle.

Samuel drained the canteen.

Dona said, "Samuel, like when our hunting dog was shot, your lung's collapsed. It's got to seal where the bullet went through. Can you ride?"

Samuel made an effort to get up.

"Wait," she said, and he lay back against the wall.

In a moment, his breath changed, and he said, "Now."

Dona offered both of her hands to his good one. She bent her knees as he rose, and leaned back to balance his weight with hers. They made their way to the door of the Hut and stopped. Whippoorwills chanted from the cedar brake, but no beings called out in warning. Duke's nostrils flared, and his ears flicked forward and back. He was ready.

Dona had never had to decide whether to kill a human being. Jackrabbits, yes, when she was growing up; hawks above the chicken yard, the rabid coyote the other day that was going for Annalou. She didn't like shooting anything alive, and certainly not a person. But she would. She felt it in her spine. Somebody was driving that truck for the gunman. She'd bet the ranch that the lousy cowards had headed back to town to rustle up their cronies, make sure Samuel was dead. They'd be back like a pack of coonhounds, hot on the trail. No time to think about it.

If Samuel had not been strong in the legs, and the heart; if Duke, had not stood as still as a stone for Samuel to mount; and if Dona had hesitated one moment in her resolve to get Samuel to a safe place, they might not have made it out with Samuel alive. There was a long journey ahead.

"Samuel, don't go to sleep. Duke's gonna want to take our usual road, but I'm thinking the men might be coming back that way."

Samuel nodded. He sat straight in the saddle, one hand over the bullet hole, and stared ahead.

"We'll ride to the edge of the butte. I think we could see riders coming pretty well."

Blood seeped through the rags she'd tied around his shoulder, but it was darker. And his breathing was shallow but regular.

She untied her other canteen. "Here's a little more water, Samuel, it will help you."

"Thanks."

"You can thank me when we're out of danger."

Samuel's faint smile reassured Dona and as she swung herself onto Duke's haunches, pulled the reins around Samuel and clucked Duke into a walk; she could feel the pain in Samuel's chest through the insides of her arms.

She let Duke have his head on the loose scree, wishing for a lightness to come into their bodies, for an ease to enter and bear them. She wished they might become invisible, soundless, and more than in any time in her life she wished for someone to pray to.

Samuel's shoulders trembled. Sweat coursed down his face and arms. He did not waiver in the saddle as he clutched the saddle horn with one hand, nor did Duke falter, though the way was difficult and unaccustomed. The straight line of Dona's back did not give. They were three parts of an arrow shot from a righteous bow, aimed for a room at the back of a stone house under a wide oak tree—and, with luck, arms strong enough to lift Samuel to safety.

She'd have to tell Roy. Melvar would help, he said he would, and she could trust him. But it was Roy who could intervene with the men in town. They respected him as a champion calf roper, bull rider, and lasso-throwing cowboy. And he was as mean as they were when he had to be. It was also Roy who could get the doctor out there in a hurry. If only she could convince him to help, and not turn Samuel in to the deputy sheriff.

Huge in the afternoon light, the windmill swung its triangular arms and pulled them home. Samuel slumped across the pommel, his head and shoulder heavy against Duke's neck, his cheek cushioned by the stubby mane. And Dona, holding him around the waist, her legs a vise clamping Duke's belly, called out as they rode beneath the windmill, as they pushed into the shadows of the big oak. She called for help to Roy, to Luke, to Annalou, to whatever god might listen, whatever angel might hover waiting for the time when Dona should at last bow her head in supplication. And when her horse stopped by the familiar steps, and when she slid her body off her horse and reached for Samuel, and with arms as bloody as a butcher's, she held him as he lurched up two stone steps, then three, across the porch and through the kitchen door, and when they staggered down the hall and into Joe Bob's bedroom, Samuel had done the most that he could do. Together, they laid his body down.

Dona washed the wounds, plugged the vile bullet holes with iodine and fresh cotton cloths, and Samuel slept.

Where was everyone? Nanna was inside, surely, but deaf and probably asleep. Why wasn't someone there to help her? Had they heard a truck roar away through the gate? Had they gone after the men? And then she remembered. Every man on the place would be at the sheep shearing. They would not be back until dark.

"Here I am, Aunt Doney. And Josie, too." Annalou slammed the screen door, ran the length of the kitchen, the hallway, and hesitated at the doorway of the bedroom, with Josie right behind her. "We were in the barn and thought I heard you holler. Oh, no," she said, and lowered her voice. "Samuel."

DONA FLEXED HER HANDS; she rubbed her neck with them. So tired. She sat on the porch swing, and wrapped her arms around her ribs where sensations from the past few hours caught and burned.

Samuel must need more water. His bandages would need changing. Josie and she could only do so much. She must call her mother. Ask her to get a doctor to come for Samuel. Someone they could trust. Do not call her cousin, Edward. Melvar had no telephone. Where could they go that was safe? What would it mean to be safe? She was so tired. What if more gunmen came? Her rifle was tied to her saddle. Get it. No. Call her mother, right now. Her mother would make things better. Nobody would hurt Ophelia Cunningham Willis. Nobody in his right mind. Dona pushed herself to standing and went into the house.

She pulled the receiver off its hook on the wall telephone, and stretched toward the mouthpiece. "Bertie, can you hear me? Bertie, this is Dona. Please connect me to my mother...please. Number 087 Yes, Bertie, an emergency."

She stood on one foot, resting against the doorjamb like a broom that had done its work. "Oh, please," she whispered, "please be home, please Mother." She lifted her head, pushing her mouth closer. "Hello, Mother, is that you? Mother, I need a doctor right now. A good doctor. You know what I mean. Please. To the ranch house. Right away, yes. Thank you, Mother, and thank you, too, Bertie."

"Oh, Lord," she thought, *"what if Bertie calls somebody in that mob. Samuel is not safe here. Annalou and I are not safe here."* She put her head in her hands and covered her eyes. Samuel's groans echoed down the hall.

"We're coming, Samuel." And she scurried with Josie to help him.

The clock in the kitchen was the one Dona's daddy had given her for a wedding present. *'May you have the time of your life,'* his card had read, and surely, she thought, with a twist of her mouth, she was. It was almost four o'clock.

Maybe she and Samuel could get to the Shacks where Melvar had helped her make a hiding place.

SAMUEL'S ARMS AND CHEST stretched Roy's plaid shirt, and the denim britches were a little short in the legs, but all in all they would do. Dona had changed the bandage over Samuel's shoulder wound and found no new bleeding. He had rested for a few hours and his breath had deepened a little, but his lung would take much longer to heal, so she dabbed iodine over the wounds, plugged the bullet holes with clean bandages and taped his shoulder to hold them in place.

"Samuel, do you think you can make it back to the kitchen?"

"I do."

"We are trapped here. I suppose you know that."

She helped him along the hall.

Samuel bowed his head and whispered, his breath coming hard. "Thank you, Jesus, for my family, and for Dona. Amen." He tried to straighten. Blood seeped from his wounds.

"I hoped to get you to the shacks, Samuel, but you aren't ready. We're going to have to wait for the doctor." She walked back and forth across the kitchen floor to the porch. "I don't know if my mother reached him. I can't get through to anybody on the telephone. Even the operator, that helpful Bertie, she can't get through the party line, five women trying to talk every afternoon at exactly this time. Those men wouldn't stop at hurting a doctor or a schoolgirl, would they?"

"I believe you are right. I believe sure enough they wouldn't stop at nothing." He slumped against the table, his eyes closed.

"Samuel, you've got to wake up." Dona put a wet rag on his neck and pulled up his shirt to redress the bullet hole.

She had not heard the bells, but Molly nickered. Paint answered from the corral, and Duke. Like whisperers they spoke. There was danger in noise.

In a moment, Melvar crossed the screened porch and stood before them. His eyes on hers were clear and warm, and his hands as he reached toward Samuel were steady.

"Is he alive, Dona?"

"Yes, but suffering. The bullet collapsed his lung, but it went clear through. The lung can only fill again with air, if the holes are completely plugged to make a vacuum."

"This I know. But men have been at the shacks. They tore them apart. They must be around here somewhere. They have a truck. I have a wagon, and it is ready for our friend."

"How did you know to be here?"

"Bertie is a very old friend of mine, and she hears what goes on everywhere. She knows you let me help with the shacks."

"The telephone operator, Bertie? So she called you?"

"Something like that, yes, but now, we must help Samuel into the wagon. And if you have water and food to spare. And any bandages."

Annalou and Josie, who had stood at the edge of the kitchen, arms full of blood-soaked sheets, dropped them to the floor. They ran to fill canteens from the well, and packed up every leftover morsel of food from the icebox and more from the pantry. Dona filled a sack with gauze and iodine and tape.

"The wagon, Samuel," Dona said, sponging his face with cold water. "Melvar has made you a bed. He will cover you and keep you safe until he can find a doctor. And dear Samuel, try and relax when your breathing gets hard. Your lung is trying its best to heal and fill with your breath."

Together Dona and Melvar eased Samuel onto the narrow, cotton mattress, packed heavy cloths around his wounds and made a pillow for his head. They covered his body with lengths of calico and gingham, with flour sack dresses and cup towels, and around the sides, they piled small tools and harness rings and all the wares a traveling peddler carries. His face they left open until the very last.

Dona put her hand on his forehead. "Samuel, I will see to your family. You can trust Melvar."

"Yes," Samuel said, moving his eyes over Melvar's face.

"We must go. And you will be well, Dona?" Melvar said.

"I'll be well. I don't want to know where you are taking him, so I can't tell anyone. If there is some way to let me know how he's doing, I'd be grateful."

"He will be safe and I will find a doctor."

"You know the back way out of the ranch?"

"I do, it's slower than the main road, but we will not be seen."

Dona held out her hand to him, and he took it in both of his.

As quietly as a mule can pull a loaded wagon along a dusty ranch road, so did Melvar and his wagon disappear. Even the bells were silent.

Chapter Eighteen

Dona tried to imagine what Samuel felt, buried under bolts of fabric and tools. She trusted Melvar. But nothing would matter if the gunmen guessed that Samuel was in that wagon. And where was Melvar going to take him?

She did the two things she could, at that moment. She trotted Duke over the wagon tracks, and grabbed her rifle from the saddle.

Down by the river, someone revved the engine of a truck, its rusty cough familiar. Were they coming or going? Duke halted and his ears, alert, received signals ahead, behind. He was wary, but his ears said he was not afraid.

She led Duke back to the paddock and into his stall, speaking in a low voice to the other horses.

The chug of the old tractor broke the quiet as it rounded the back of the wooden barn and headed for the machine shed.

"Luke," Dona shouted, running to his side. "Bring your gun and come on in the house, quick. Where are Roy and Joe Bob?"

"Problem with the windmill out the east Lee pasture. Found it while we was at the shearing. The boys took the truck to town for supplies and I rode my horse back to pick up this here tractor."

"Somebody's coming to make trouble, Luke. And I'm going to need your help."

"When?"

"Right now."

Annalou held open the screen door to the porch and in a moment all three were inside the kitchen.

"Think I saw 'em," Luke said. "Three fellas, old Dodge pickup, moving fast out of the main gate toward the river pasture. Maybe an hour ago."

"Did they see you?"

"Nope. I was heading back this way on my horse, but I went aside to check a couple fences. Came back here for the tractor to lift a post. Lucky to miss 'em, I reckon. Why do you say they're trouble?"

"They want to lynch Samuel Washington. And they think he is here."

"Samuel's here?"

"No, thank heavens. A friend took him away to try and find a doctor. One of those tough guys shot Samuel in the back. Bullet went clear through his lung and out the front. Maybe he'll make it, maybe he won't. The thing is, Luke, when they find out Samuel isn't here, they'll be after me to tell them."

"But why in tarnation do they want Samuel? And, Doney, why was he here?"

"Because a lynch mob was chasing him and he escaped. Ran here, on foot, clear from town, and asked me to help him. So, I did."

"Holy smoke, you sure do know how to get us in trouble."

"You'd have done the same. You'd never let a lynch mob string up an innocent man because he was colored, now would you?"

Luke was quiet. His breath was ragged.

"Don't know," he said, "probably not."

"That's what I thought. And our momma's helping, too."

"So, what'd you do?"

"I took him up to the Sheepherder's Hut, along with some grub and water and a pistol. About a week ago."

"Oh, God, Doney. Didn't tell me? Or Roy?"

"Safer that way, don't you think?"

"Not safe for us, no way."

"You're right. Go on back to the barn and hide out 'til this is all over. Take Annalou with you."

"I'm not leaving you, Aunt Doney." Annalou picked up the rolling pin. "And I am armed."

"Here they come, Luke. Please go, quick."

"I ain't leaving you, neither, Doney. I'll get the rifles ready. Shotgun, too."

The rattle of the Dodge truck entered Dona's body like a terrible memory. She dried her palms on her shirt and straightened her shoulders.

"I'm going to try and do this without anybody getting hurt. Luke, you stay in the kitchen and back me up through that window. I'm going out and I'll keep my rifle close."

The truck rolled into the barnyard and stopped thirty feet from the house. Dona walked onto the screen porch, wiping her hands in a dish towel, and waited.

"Luke," she said in a low voice, "only two men in the truck. Check around back."

"Got it, Sis."

"Annalou, keep the rolling pin near. Pick up a rifle and cock it like I showed you. Don't shoot unless I say."

"Got it, Aunt Doney."

"Josie, go back in with Nanna. And don't breathe a word of this to anybody. *Promesa?*"

"*Promesa.*" Josie crossed her heart.

Dona opened the screen door, her rifle alongside her leg, leaned out and said, "Howdy y'all. Can I help you?"

The passenger door creaked open and a large man stepped out. "Howdy, Dona. Remember me? It's Evan McGregor. We were in seventh grade together. Time of you and that schoolmaster. I never forgot."

"What can I do for you, Evan? You boys lost?"

"Naw, we're looking for a nigger, running from the law."

"Are you a sheriff, now, Evan?"

"Naw, we're sort of deputy sheriffs, if you know what I mean."

"What makes you think she's here?"

"She? Naw, it's a big, black man, Dona. You should be scared."

"Nobody here by that description, Evan."

"Well, we think different. And we need to look around."

"I heard your truck coming up from the river. Seems like you've already been looking around. Without permission, I might add. Who's your driver?"

"Oh, another good ole boy. This other big boy is Ross Jenkins. Remember him?"

"I do. Went to school with Ross. He knows my brother, Luke, too. Luke's not here right now to say howdy. Guess you two will be moseying on."

"Guess we won't," said Ross, getting out of the truck with a shotgun under his right arm.

"Ross, in case you couldn't hear me. There's nobody here you're looking for."

"Maybe not, but we're pretty sure you know where that big buck nigger is." Ross took a slow step toward Dona and shifted the gun barrel into his left hand.

"I do not. And I don't take kindly to threats. So, you can get on out of here now. Before I call the sheriff." She lifted her rifle and settled the butt on her hip, barrel toward the ground. "How about we put down our guns, Ross. Mine's cocked to fire, just like yours, and you know I'm a good shot."

"Yeah, I remember. You whupped me at target practice in sixth grade."

"Was it sixth? Seems like a long time ago. We've both grown up since then, right, Ross? We aren't children any more. One of us doesn't have to be better than the other, like we used to."

The kind of silence that comes before a cloud burst hung between them.

Dona cleared her throat. "Ross, I didn't know you well at school, other than the target practice. I wouldn't have recognized you for Ross Jenkins when you got out of that truck. You were one of the big boys and you didn't care to speak to little girls like me. But I remember you being kind to a friend of mine."

Ross had moved two steps closer and Dona could hear his breath. "Oh yeah," he said, "and who was that?"

"It was little Stevie Curtis. One day at school he wet his pants. All the other boys were making fun of him and he was crying and you said, leave him alone, he's my buddy. And they did leave him alone. That's how I've thought of you, Ross. Somebody who's for the underdog. Maybe you remember that time, too?"

"Tell me where that nigger is, and I'll leave you alone. And if you don't..."

From inside the house, Luke said in his quietest voice, "Doney, we found a varmint poking around the place. Right now he's tied up and got a big goose egg on his head. Name of Dinky Dwight."

"Call the sheriff right now," Dona whispered.

Raising her rifle, she said, "Ross and Evan, something tells me there's one more polecat at the party. Name of Dinky Dwight, I do believe. He's in my kitchen and seems to have tied himself up and hit his own head with a rolling pin. Wonder how he did that?"

Evan scooted into the truck, slammed the door and ducked down. Ross took one step back.

"Now, you boys have got to believe that I do not have what you're looking for. And while I've got you in my sights, my friend is calling the sheriff to come for all three of you. Threatening a helpless woman on her own porch steps; holding a gun on her. You better believe I have witnesses. You wait right there. I know you don't want to desert your buddy."

Ross jerked his shotgun to his shoulder and aimed at Dona. Her bullet caught the gunstock and went straight into Ross's shoulder. His shotgun hit the dust.

"Git those hands up, Ross. And get back in the truck. You try and move one inch toward another gun and I'll shoot again."

The sheriff better get there soon. Those were angry men, used to violent means to get their way. Anytime now they would make a run for it in the truck, probably with a gun. She'd aim for the tires, if they tried.

"Lord, don't let Annalou be an orphan again," she said aloud.

From the barnyard behind the truck, a rifle fired once. Roy yelled, "Git in the house now, Dona. I've got 'em covered."

"Hey, Roy, Welcome to the party," she hollered back.

"What about that boy, Ross," Luke hollered. "In the driver's seat. He's hurt purty bad, like as not."

"I'll take care of him. You get your selves inside right quick."

"You on our side, Roy?" Dona said under her breath.

Luke yelled, "Dona wants to know..."

"I'm on your side, Dona," Roy muttered.

Roy's voice was deeper than ordinary, calmer, and he seemed to mean it, that he was on her side. But there he was, holding two desperate men in their truck with his rifle, and there was only so much a .30-30 could do. The air amplified every sound, the breath of the man bleeding; Luke's boots rubbing ever so lightly against each other, a nervous habit he'd had since he was little; her own heart, the pounding drum of her heart. She had pulled them back from grave's edge, Luke had held them, and now Roy, at last, Roy was on her side.

"We've got another boy in here," she said, and still she could not raise her voice.

Luke repeated as loud as he could, his own voice shaking, "Roy, another boy's in here."

Roy said, "I reckoned on it, being as there was three of them and I got two right here. "Boys, get out of that truck real slow. You first, Evan."

"How'd he know there were three," Dona said.

"Dunno," Luke said. "He's pretty sharp." He stood up then and groaned.

"Is that you, Luke, groaning? You hurt?"

"Naw, just old, I guess. But that boy, Ross, we gotta get him to the house."

"I thought I got him in the shooting arm, Luke, but maybe it was worse than that. Maybe in the chest."

"Yep, I'm thinking the same thing. Wish Doc was here."

"I'll try to get a call through to him. And I'll call Mother, too. She must be sick with worry."

"What about Samuel? These boys cain't be the only ones wanting to find him, Sis. A colored boy like Samuel, you get a mob on his tail and you got a thing you can't stop."

"There is so much I haven't told you, Luke. It's not over. Not by a long shot."

"Naw, I reckon you are right about that. But Sis, maybe I can help you out a little bit better, if you tell me what's going on."

"I'll tell you all I can, I promise. But right now, we have a mess to handle."

"Luke," Roy shouted, "get some rope to tie Evan to something solid. Dona, get ready to stop this here coward from bleeding to death. Annalou, haul a cot to the porch. We'll tie Ross to it, until Doc comes."

"Roy," Luke said, "we're sure glad to see you."

An hour later, Roy stood alone with Dona in the barn's shadow. His eyes were hard as horseshoe nails, and his stare fell on her like a hammer. "You hid that nigger, that hunted, wanted nigger and you didn't tell me, your own husband? No wonder those boys were trying to shoot you, Dona."

Roy scooped up a rock and threw it hard against the live oak tree. Dona flinched.

"Roy, you saved our lives, but I didn't trust you not to turn Samuel in."

"Why shouldn't I turn him in?"

"He's not guilty of anything, that's why." Dona's voice grew tight. "And they are a mob. They are the Klan. They will kill him. They will string him up."

"Yep," Roy said. He folded his arms across his stomach and looked toward the ranch road. "I hear Doc's car. We'll try to fix your terrible mess, Dona. I'll get him to work on Ross and I'm going to follow the sheriff. Make sure those boys get to jail. When I get back, you'd better not mention that nigger ever again, to me or anybody else."

"Don't count on it, Roy."

He turned away from her and walked toward his truck; away from all she loved and believed in.

"WELL," SAID DOC STEWARD, "the boy's gonna live." Doc stood up from beside the cot Annalou had hauled to the screened porch and folded his stethoscope into his black leather bag. "He'd better not move for a day or two, to make sure the bleeding's stopped. He's already lost a lot of blood. See to it that he gets plenty of water and soup and food that goes down easy. Think you can cook supper for this boy, Dona?"

Dona thought of how Ross defended the little boy from bullies. What could make a good boy turn out to be a bad man? Could make him want to kill another man because of his skin? And she said, "I'll do my best, but can you come into the kitchen, Doc? I'll bet you'd like a cup of coffee about now."

When they were sitting at the kitchen table, hands around the blue metal cups, Dona said, "I think I can take care of him until he's strong enough to go to jail. But I don't much want to be alone with him, if you know what I mean."

"No," he said, "you won't have to. Your brother Luke's a good man—he's told me he'll keep a gun on him. And Roy, too, he'll be here as much as he can. For a day or two.

"I'll be back tomorrow and change that bandage, make sure he's not bleeding inside. Maybe he'll be strong enough to go back to town with me. Good thing that wasn't a shotgun you were toting. As it was, that .30-30 shell tore a pretty big hole in his shoulder. Missed his lungs and heart, though."

"You know, Doc, Samuel was shot in the shoulder, too, from the back. But it wasn't Ross shot him. Sure thing, it wasn't a shotgun that got him and that seems to be what Ross carries. Must have been Dinky, I'm thinking, since his arm is bandaged up, and I know Samuel hit the shooter with the pistol I gave him."

Doc cleared his throat. "Uh, Dona, I'd like to warn you not to get too involved in this. Giving a pistol to a colored man?"

"What do you mean, Doc? How could I get in any deeper than I already am?"

"I mean, is there any part of it you would be willing to overlook. For the sake of peace?"

Dona turned to the doctor, feeling like that fawn, caught in the barbed wire fence. What if Doc Steward was in the Klan? If her cousin Edward, the lofty and respected lawyer knew so much about it, why not Doc Steward? She felt her skin tingle and into the grip of her throat she swallowed gall. "Doc, please tell me. What do you know about the men who tried to lynch Samuel?"

He adjusted his glasses and peered over the rims, "I'd hate to tell you what I know. But I can tell you this: it's a dangerous business and no place for a woman."

The hairs at the back of Dona's neck tightened and she smiled, showing her teeth. "Why, Doc, don't you think I was a pretty good shot out there in the barnyard—for a woman, I mean?"

Doc Steward sat back. "I've known you all your life, Dona Willis. You've always been a fighter, but I thought you had better sense than to get yourself in the middle of the Klan's business."

"And you, Doc, where do you stand on all of this?"

Doc placed his elbows on the oilcloth and leaned toward her, "I look around me and what do I see? I see that the people who run things around here are white men. They have the power."

"You have the power," Dona interrupted.

"Yes, we have the power and that's because we have the experience and the intelligence to take care of everyone else. I take good care of my colored help, Dona. And my Mexican maids. Why, they couldn't take care of me nearly so well. I work hard, I tend to patients of every color."

"You know, Doc, my daddy did that too, and he came to believe that we are all alike under the skin. But some don't get to go to school like he did, or like you did. Some are treated like animals, working with their backs all day in the cotton and taking care of their families at night, sometimes in lean-tos or worse, with no running water. He didn't think it was fair, but you seem to. How come?"

"I guess down deep I believe that the Lord loves people like me better than people like Samuel, or I wouldn't have been allowed my success in life."

"But, Doc, why would someone like you want to kill someone like Samuel because the Lord loves you better?"

"Samuel didn't know his place, is why. He was a danger to our minister's wife, to everything we believe in. Don't you see that? There's laws against it."

"I know all about that, and I know the true story behind it. She was only helping Samuel with his reading. But if you believed Samuel was a threat to Mrs. MacMurray, why didn't you tell the sheriff? Because you didn't have proof they were having relations?"

Doc took a drink from his cup and cleared his throat. "That was why."

"And, Doc, they were not. But if they were, and believe me, I know about the law in Texas, why kill Samuel? And speaking of proof, I have proof that Reverend MacMurray goes to the chicken ranch from time to time, incognito. But nobody tries to kill him. And some of those poor women who have to sell their bodies to feed their children? Why, Doc, they are colored! The Reverend is breaking the law, sure as shooting."

"Dona, I have to go now. Thank you for the coffee." He pushed back his chair. "I'll be back tomorrow to check on Ross, and see if we can move him."

"Doc, I guess you'd better move him now. He's more than I can handle, and nobody better than you, to drive him to the jail."

"Well, I don't know. Maybe to the clinic."

"Doc, if you break the law, you could be in real big trouble. You know that Roy followed the other two boys and the sheriff to jail, don't you?"

"I'm not going to break the law, dammit, Dona." He shoved his Stetson over his white hair and stomped onto the porch.

Dona was right behind him, and she made sure Luke had heard. He nodded and handed Ross's shotgun to Dona, who put it inside the kitchen. Together, they loaded Ross, who was quiet now, from the porch into Doc's car and stood in the barnyard dust until it disappeared.

Joe Bob stood in the dust of the dooryard facing Dona who was sitting on the stoop. From the way he was shifting his weight from boot to boot, he was nervous as a new mother hen.

"Looks like Ross Jenkins's truck, settin' here empty," he said.

"Long story, Joe Bob. Where have you been?"

"Some things, Doney, you don't want to know."

"How'd you get back to the ranch?"

"One of the sheriff's boys brought me home. I've been down to the jail."

"I'm sure that was enlightening."

"Yep, I'd say it was. You been hiding a nigger up at the Sheepherder's Hut."

"A what?"

"I mean, a colored man. Name of Samuel."

"You know Samuel, Joe Bob. He's worked here at the ranch off and on. Down at the shacks."

"Yep, I guess I do. Dinky says he should be lynched. And that's what I want to tell you."

Joe Bob kicked the steps to knock the dust off of his boots and shouldered through the screen door onto the porch. He sat on one end of the porch swing and pushed it. It creaked with every turn.

"I am listening." Dona stood up and brushed the seat of her britches. "Maybe it was brave of you to go to the jail. Was it?"

"What do you mean," he said, clearing his throat and looking away from her.

"I mean, maybe you heard about how those boys tried to kill me, too, and you wanted to stop them. Maybe you were trying to help your daddy put things to rights."

"Naw, I can't claim to be no kind of hero. None at all. To tell the honest truth, I thought if they was going to string up a, uh, colored man, I'd like to be in on it."

"You'd want to murder somebody because of his color?"

"Not just the color." Joe Bob reached his long arm down and picked up his coffee. "He done something terrible."

"And what was that, Joe Bob?"

"Why, don't you know? He tried to rape the Reverend MacMurray's wife."

"And what evidence do you have?"

"Dinky told me. And some of the other boys, like Toad Trumble. He said so, too."

"And why would you believe them. Dinky and Toad?"

"Why would they lie?"

"Why wouldn't they? To try and justify their actions?"

"What do you mean?"

"I mean, would you like to hear another side of the story? Came directly from Mrs. MacMurray to your grandmother. So, it is likely true."

Joe Bob drained his cup and dropped it on the wooden floor. The sound it made was as hollow as an old bone. He studied Dona under the wide brim of his hat and turned back to the yard. "Yeah, I guess I'd like to hear it," he said.

Joe Bob was quiet as Dona talked and when she was done, he took off his hat and ran his hands through his hair. "Oh, Lordy. This is a terrible story. But if this is true, who told them Samuel raped her?"

"I think, Joe Bob, you may be just the one to find that out for us. If I were you, I'd start with the Reverend MacMurray, himself. I recall that you, uh, observed him one Saturday night, and he wasn't preparing his sermon."

"Oh, Mother, thank heavens." Dona pushed open the screen door to the back porch. She hugged Ophelia as though she hadn't seen her in years and said, "Let's go inside."

"I'm sorry it took so long. There were cars on the road from town and I was a little worried about who might be in them. But no problem that I could tell. It must have been awful here, the fight, those men, the trouble."

"It was pretty bad. I'm glad we can stay at your house for a couple of nights, to let things cool off. Is that still all right?"

"Yes, of course. I'll take Annalou with me, and Luke and Nanna can ride with you. Luke can carry Nanna, if she needs it."

"I still don't know where Luke is, but don't worry, I can lift Nanna. Would you like some coffee before we pack the cars?" Ophelia nodded and sat at the kitchen table in the seat she always chose, next to the back door.

"Annalou," Dona called down the hall, "your grandmother is here."

"Still going without sugar, Mother?"

"Well, most of the time. But maybe since this is a special occasion, I'll have some sugar."

Dona grinned. "And I know you'll have some of Mehitabel's cream."

Dona placed the cup in front of Ophelia, poured one for herself and one for Annalou, who had rushed from her room and was now halfway in her grandmother's lap.

"Oh, Mamaw, thank heavens."

"That's what your Aunt Doney said, so I feel real important right now. How are you, honey bunch?"

"I'm fine now that you are both here."

As soon as they finished their coffee, Dona gathered the cups and rinsed them in the sink. And when she joined Annalou and Ophelia on the porch, she stared out at the boys' truck for the first time since she thought she was going to die. In the late afternoon sun, it was a plain old truck, casting its shadow across the barnyard.

Chapter Nineteen

On the other side of San Angelo, the side away from her mother's white brick house where she and Annalou and Nanna had stayed last night, away from the First Presbyterian Church, the Masonic Hall, the new department store with air conditioning, Dona found Bertie at the telephone office. It was lunch time, but Bertie didn't go out — she brought her peanut butter sandwich with Miracle Whip on that soft white bread the grocery store had started selling. She was at the point of unfolding the waxed paper and setting her sandwich out on a small, square table when Dona walked in.

As often as she had heard Bertie's voice on the telephone, connecting her phone calls, asking how she was, she had not seen Bertie in ten years. But there was no mistaking the dark hair pulled into a bun, her skin, the amber of tea, the slightly hunched shoulders, the straight, white teeth or the brown eyes, wide and speckled with green.

"Hello Bertie," she said, speaking quietly. "I'm Dona Willis."

"Oh, Dona, of course you are," said Bertie, putting down her sandwich and smiling in the generous way Dona remembered. "I am so glad to see you again."

They had been together in the Presbyterian Women's Auxiliary for a short while, until Dona decided, unless she needed to hear all the town gossip, it was a waste of her time. Perhaps that had been a mistake. Gossip might have alerted her to the mob after Samuel, but meanwhile, there was Bertie, overhearing most of the conversations in town at one time or another.

"Bertie," she whispered, "is it safe to talk?"

"Would you like some of my sandwich, Dona?" Bertie said, brightly. "It's so good to see you. Whatever could bring you to our little telephone office?"

"Oh," Dona said, straightening her hat, "I was in the neighborhood and hadn't seen you in so many years, I thought I'd stop in." *Who on earth was listening*, she wondered. *Perhaps no place was safe.*

"Bertie, could you possibly find the time to have a cup of coffee with me after work? I know you are friends with my mother and I'm having a little problem I could sure use your help with."

"That would be lovely, Dona." Bertie stood up to give her a hug. "It makes me feel so good to know I can be of service to your family. Your father, you know, he saved my life."

"No, I didn't know that. Were you injured?"

"It's kind of private. Perhaps we could talk later. Girl stuff, you know."

"Oh, I see. Yes, of course. Not something we'd talk about on a lunch hour at work."

"Thank you, Dona, you have always understood me." She extended her hand to shake Dona's and Dona felt something small and hard between their palms. She closed her fingers around it.

"Very good, Bertie. Let's meet at Luby's Cafeteria at 5:15 this afternoon. For coffee."

When Dona was in her own car and had driven a few blocks away from the center of town, she pulled alongside a curb and stopped. She left the motor running and opened her hand. She was holding a tiny blue box, intricately carved with curls and triangles. It was the same as on Molly's harness, where the reins and backstrap joined at a metal circle. Was it a message from Melvar?

Dona's stomach lurched and she swallowed hard.

Blue. Melvar had told her how, in Persia, it stood for the spirit world, how it carried the power of wind and rain. Perhaps blue could save a person.

With one careful fingernail she lifted the lid and found that the box was empty. And while the outside of the box was the blue of an unclouded sky, the inside was the blue of night. Along the delicate rims, the blue was almost purple. The purple of royalty, the purple of the Divine. And the hinges were surely gold.

Dona closed the box. She made a fist around it, put her fist against her heart and closed her eyes. The box was hot in her hand. It was heavy, almost too heavy to hold. She spread her fingers away from it and looked again. The box pulsed as though her own heart beat through it. And it was changing color. It could not be crimson. That red, the color of new blood, that was a dream. That was the color of passion. And most especially, it was the color of danger.

Soft ghosts crawled up her sleeve.

"I am exhausted," she said, her voice thick with fog. And fell into sleep.

"BERTIE," DONA said, taking a sip of her coffee, "when I woke up, the motor was still running. The box was blue again. And it was time to come here and meet you."

"So, you fainted in the car?"

"I think it had something to do with the little blue box you gave me."

"Oh yes, I see." Bertie adjusted the napkin on her lap. "That was a lovely cup of coffee, thank you."

"I'll get you another." Dona pushed back her chair. She returned with two coffees and a couple of doughnuts.

"You are good. How did you know I love doughnuts?"

"Just a hunch. And besides, I do, too." They laughed and nodded their heads, like hens, their small combs shaking, feathers ruffling, making the chortling noises of contentment.

"Bertie," she said, stirring sugar into her thick white cup, "about that little box."

Bertie turned away. She pressed her handkerchief to her face. She removed her round spectacles, each gold earpiece trembling, and covered her eyes. "Dona," she said so softly it was only by watching her mouth that Dona could hear her, "that box. It is from our family. There are two of them. They are all we have left."

"Sorry, Bertie. Where is your family?" Dona had never thought of Bertie having a family; she had been a voice on a static-filled line for so long.

"Melvar is my only family. This is something you should know."

"Melvar is your family? Why should I know?"

"Because Melvar trusts you. And please do not ever tell another soul, oh, dear Dona, please do not tell."

"I promise never to tell, but tell what, Bertie?" The sweat of Dona's hands was making it difficult to hold her coffee cup.

"I am Melvar's sister."

"You are the person Melvar called his baby sister?"

"Yes, he is my big brother." Bertie lowered her head further and wiped her eyes. "And he protects me with the story that I have no family and no connections. I can do more good that way, through my job. And so can he, through his."

Dona put her cup on the table. She reached toward Bertie with one hand and with the other she felt for her napkin. "Bertie, my dear, why are you crying?"

Bertie peered through eyes still wet. "Because I am afraid."

"Of what, exactly?"

"The men who are after Samuel suspect that I'm on your side. They will soon learn that I am. But I don't think they have guessed that I am Melvar's sister. And that they could get to him through me."

"Why did he ask you to give me the blue box?"

"In Persia, in our country, blue is the color of protection. The box, it is not empty. It holds what is needed most. Melvar asked me to give it to you for your hope. But what about mine?"

"Oh, no, Bertie. What do you mean?" Dona reached for Bertie's arm.

"I did not mean to upset you. But I may not be safe. Being the telephone operator," Bertie said, as she lifted Dona's fingers off her arm, "may turn out to be dangerous." And with a shaking hand Bertie picked up her cup.

"You have been threatened? Does someone know that you told Melvar to come for Samuel? That you're in on this?"

"No. Dona, you must listen. I am not sure anyone knows about that, yet, but I got a note this morning with a scrawled message. 'Bertie, keep your mouth shut or it will be shut for you!' So, you see, somebody knows something. We do not have much time to find out. Even being here at Luby's with you..." Bertie folded her hands in front of her on the table, cleared her throat and stared with unfocused eyes toward the far wall.

There, the great, silver coffee makers stood next to thick, white cups stacked high. A Mexican worker dressed in a white coat filled coffee cups for customers at his station, chatting as though it were an ordinary day.

Bertie said nothing. She seemed far away from the clatter of plates, the clink of forks and knives, the hum of voices, dozens of people having an early supper.

"Bertie?" Dona said, putting a hand over Bertie's. "If you're in trouble, I will help you any way I can."

"You're in trouble, too."

"I know that for sure, but right now I need to know about Samuel. Is he still with Melvar?"

Bertie shook her head, "No."

"Does Samuel's family know where he is?"

"No. Not yet."

"Is he getting well? Is he safe?"

"Those are two questions. I can say yes to the first one. I must say no to the second."

"Can we move him? I could get a truck."

"They are watching you all the time."

"Then, I'll find someone else. Can you get word to Melvar?"

"Yes."

"Tell him I have a place to hide Samuel. Tell him to contact me at Ophelia's. And what about your job? Do you think you can stay?"

"Yes, I am useful to Melvar there. But I don't know for how long, and if it comes to it, I would rather lose my job than my life."

"You are a smart woman, Bertie. You'd have to be to get this far."

As she paid the bill for their coffee, Dona was troubled. She had listened closely to what Bertie said. She wanted to believe her, but something was not right. Dona gathered up her purse, put her kid gloves inside and straightened her hat. Could she really be Melvar's sister? She didn't look like Melvar, except perhaps in the bridge of the nose and that was hard to tell with her glasses. Her skin was lighter than his, but then she worked indoors all the time. And all these years, they had never told anyone that they were related?

Dona could not think about that now; it was too troubling. Could Bertie be lying about the scribbled note? And, oh no, where was the blue box?

They walked toward the car.

"Bertie, do you have the blue box? It's not in my purse."

"Yes, you returned it to me, as I asked."

"You asked?"

"Don't you remember? I told you it is the only thing we have left from our family and of course you gave it back."

"But why did you give it to me in the first place?"

"Because Melvar asked me to."

"But Bertie, after you gave it to me and I drove away in my car, strange things happened to me."

"Strange? Like what?"

"Like what I told you. The box changed color. Like I couldn't help but fall asleep and I had a bad dream that someone who was trying to protect me came and took it away. I dreamed that Melvar came to the car and woke me up and talked with me, but when I opened my eyes, no one was there. The motor was still running. The box was blue again. And then it was time to come here and meet you."

"It was a dream, Dona. Nothing to do with the box."

"It must be an important box for you or Melvar to bring it all the way from Persia. The only thing you have left, as you said."

"Can we sit for a moment, Dona? I'm tired now, in this heat."

"Will Melvar be at your house?" Dona asked as they settled onto the wooden slats of a bench, nearby.

"Melvar?" Bertie startled. "Why would...?" She stopped and covered her mouth. "Ah, well," she hesitated, "yes, it is possible, I suppose. Though he rarely visits me there."

"But you are his sister."

"Yes, but he is a busy man, and it is slow to travel everywhere by wagon and mule."

"Does he live nearby?"

"Not very near."

"I don't mean to pry, Bertie. It's just that there is so much danger right now and the more I can know, the better I can help Samuel."

"If you don't mind, Dona, please drive me home."

This must be what it's like inside the web of a powerful spider, Dona thought, driving with special care; like the spiders in the barn, their silk strong enough to capture a baby chick. She didn't want to be captured by anybody, least of all by someone she thought was her friend. It was frightening to think about that, but it was hard to think straight at all. She had so little information.

Bertie said little on the way, except to give directions. Both of them got out of the car to say goodbye at Bertie's house and as they shook hands, glove to glove, she thought she heard Molly's whinny. "Bertie, is that Molly I hear? Is Melvar perhaps waiting for us?"

"No one is here. You must go away now. Thank you for giving me a ride and for the doughnut and cup of coffee. I will not see you again for a while." She dropped Dona's hand, opened her purse, and took out the blue box.

"This is for you. I am sorry I took it." She placed the box on Dona's open palm. "Melvar said you must have it, and so you must. It is difficult for me, as you see."

"Bertie, I did not ask for the box. I am a little afraid of it."

"No, it will not hurt you, but perhaps protect you from your enemies. And there is another one, I will ask Melvar for it." Bertie turned and walked quickly from the curb toward her house. She did not turn around to wave goodbye, but unlocked the front door, entered, and closed it behind her.

Dona walked back to her car, got in, locked the doors, placed the blue box in her purse, removed her lady-gloves and drove as fast as she dared toward Ophelia's house. She searched for her own face in the rearview mirror.

Chapter Twenty

"Dona," said Ophelia, "how are you feeling this morning?" Dona sat down at the breakfast table across from her mother.

"I am tired of the cruelty of men. I never knew, growing up, what cruelty was. You sheltered us, at least when you could. I mean, we didn't know about lynchings and mobs. We didn't even hear about them at school."

"There weren't any colored children in your school. No colored families living nearby."

"Yes, but you have always had colored help. Like Mabel, who's been with you for years, like family, I've heard you say. Surely she..."

"No, for the most part, we never talk about anything except the housework. Maybe the fried chicken. Seems like we missed an opportunity."

Dona considered her mother's hands. The hands of a ranch woman come to town. They would always be thick and freckled from scrubbing work pants stained with the fluids of cows, no matter how many manicures Ruth Lily gave her at the beauty shop. They would bear the signs of hauling water from the windmill tank, from hoisting saddles onto unwilling backs, from mucking stalls, from wringing the necks of chickens for that day's dinner, and even when she had maids and gardeners and electricity in a big brick house in town, her hands were always moving. If they weren't straightening the sofa cushions, if they weren't cutting roses for the table, if they weren't playing dominoes with the nurses at the clinic, the thumbs twiddled, they rubbed the backs of the hands, they smoothed the palms and the joints of fingers. And, Dona smiled with this thought, they were the hands of a woman you could count on.

"What are you thinking about, honey?" Ophelia asked, reaching across to cover her daughter's hands with her own.

"How much I love you, Mother." She gave her mother's hands a squeeze and took hold of the table's edge. "And how much I don't understand in this life."

"Why are we all supposed to go to the ranch this afternoon? You seem so sure."

"I'd feel better if we were all there. I thought town would feel safer than the ranch, but it doesn't. And really, Mother, I am ready to go home. Juan Carlos and Roy have had to do all of my chores and their own for two days now; and Josie's kept everybody at the ranch house fed, along with the hands at the bunkhouse. Besides, I am not used to being away."

"It is dangerous to be there right now."

"It's dangerous to be anywhere at all right now."

"Are the boys who tried to shoot you, are they still in jail?"

"I don't know that, either. But I believe they are. Is there any way you could find out? I mean, don't you know the sheriff's wife pretty well?"

"Dorothy? Yes, actually I do, from women's auxiliary. You want me to call her?"

"I admit I'd feel better if I knew where they were."

Ophelia pushed back from the table and stood. "I'll call her right now, and look who's here — our favorite child. Annalou, keep your Aunt Doney company. We all need a mite cheering up."

Annalou shuffled into the kitchen in her grandmother's chenille robe, her too-large slippers whispering on the waxed linoleum floor. "Good morning, y'all," she said, and stood with her arms out for a hug. "I am so hungry."

"I'll make you some eggs, sweetie pie," said Dona, folding her close. "Your Mamaw's biscuits are on the stove. See, under the checkered cloth. She needs to make a phone call. Sunny side up or over easy?"

—

"SORRY TO SAY, my dear daughter and granddaughter," said Ophelia, hurrying into the kitchen, "but the sheriff released those boys on bail this morning."

"I feel like I've gotten lots older since all of this started about Samuel," Annalou said, scraping the last of the eggs from her plate.

"Me, too," said Dona.

"I mean," said Annalou, "I feel like I'm empty, right down to my toenails. No thinking except about Samuel. No song except "Nearer My God To Thee." Like if they lynch Samuel, or hurt him, there's nothing left for me, either."

"I heard yesterday that Samuel's getting better," Dona said, sliding another biscuit onto Annalou's plate.

"Could I have some molasses with this one?"

"Sure enough, it's right here. Melvar sent a message, saying Samuel is safe and his family soon will be."

"Did he say where they are?"

"No. He said they are out of this town."

"But they are alive?"

Dona paused, her hands to her mouth. "You know, come to think of it. I can't swear to that."

"Can we believe Melvar, Aunt Doney?"

"I think so. I sure do hope so. But, there's no way to know right now. We'll have to trust."

"That's pretty hard, when we just found out that the boys who tried to get you are loose, all over this town. Aunt Doney, I think that's why I feel so empty. Like there's nothing I can count on. Except you, of course."

"But, honey, we have to go on living like we can count on life, or we go around scared all the time."

Chapter Twenty-one

It was almost noon. Dona was waiting in her car in front of her mother's house for the others, hoping for a few more minutes by herself. It seemed like another lifetime when she was on the steps of her own house aiming through barnyard dust for Ross's shotgun.

Since her conversation with Bertie at the cafeteria, Dona was unsure about Melvar. Was he what he seemed? Was he worse or better? More to be trusted, or less? And if she was that unsure then why—and this was the hardest part—why was she about to do what he said?

Maybe when Melvar miraculously appeared at the ranch house with his mule and wagon, when she had trusted that he would keep Samuel safe and get him to a doctor, maybe he was actually part of the gang of killers.

The air seemed to thicken, and every window in Ophelia's kitchen rang as though Dona's own nerves, polished and hammered, were singing. If only the dashboard would stop jumping; if only her hands would let go of the steering wheel. Was this a breakdown? After all, hadn't her Aunt Paulina been in the insane ward since she was 14? And hadn't her great-uncle Archibald been put away for life after he tried to run himself, his wife and the horses off that butte?

She was not insane. She had every faculty she had ever had, but this awful business with Samuel getting shot, hiding him in Melvar's wagon, finding that her own mother's cousin and maybe Doc Steward were helping members of the Klan; those boys shooting at her, Ross, Dinky, Evan; and not knowing if her own husband was on her side. This was dark weather, this was a cloudburst, a tornado, this was more than a body could stand.

Dona bowed her face into her hands and moaned. Her teeth vibrated against each other. If she couldn't trust Melvar...

Dona straightened herself on the car seat, door open wide to the late morning heat and the slight shade of a live oak tree, its leaves sharp and tough against the sun.

"Luke thinks Samuel is dead, Mother. He told me so this morning before breakfast. If that's true, I would feel it," Dona said. "Wouldn't I?"

"You might, honey, but why would he say that?"

Dona and Ophelia leaned against Dona's Chevy, waiting for Annalou, Luke and Joe Bob. Nanna was staying behind at Ophelia's, under watchful Mabel's care.

"Do you think someone might say Samuel was dead to throw the Klan off the track? Might say that to Luke?"

"That's an interesting idea, but who would have the wit to do that? And who would believe him, anyway?"

"I don't know, but maybe Samuel's enemies would believe Melvar," Dona said.

"Perhaps. All the ranch wives seem to trust him, anyway, what with his rounds of peddling goods. Why is he so willing to help Samuel, Dona? Do you know?"

"I have thought about it a lot, and I think maybe it's because he's in the same boat as Samuel. I mean, Samuel's great-granddaddy was stolen from his home in West Africa and shackled and hauled like a wild horse to Louisiana and then to Texas. Melvar was stolen from his home in Persia by that crazy minister and forced to do whatever he asked, no matter how awful. Maybe Melvar thinks that if a mob would go after Samuel, it might come after him some day. Maybe he'd like to outsmart the mob."

Ophelia remembered every person who had ever wronged her, and while she had the grace not to mind, she believed in justice. She said,

"Dona, there are some smart and nasty men in that mob. They deserve to be stopped. But don't you think they deserve to have their hoods yanked off, too? I mean, shouldn't other people know who is at the heart of this?"

Dona closed her eyes and said, "Here's what I see. First is the safety of Samuel and his family. Then we must go with Mrs. MacMurray to Cousin Edward and the Judge and the other big men we know and convince them that Samuel is not guilty. After that, we must make sure Ross and Dinky and their buddy get an honest trial. And then, there will be plenty of work for you and other good women to do, to make this county a safer place for everybody."

"You can open your eyes, now, honey," Ophelia said. "You've seen real clear and you are right. It's not time to go after those pointy hoods. It makes my skin crawl to think it, but they like wearing them, and those robes, like little kids playing dress up. But they don't pretend. They are demons in those hoods."

"So, Mother, about the first thing. What would you think of Unity Ann taking in Samuel and his family?"

"Unity Ann? Oh, my..."

"Isn't she the logical one? No one would ever suspect that she'd be willing to stick her neck out."

"Well, would she?"

"I don't know. But there she is in that big house on that ranch in Comanche, no husband around, bound to need help, got lots of room, barn full of animals, farmland going untilled, and it's far enough away that the news about Samuel wouldn't mean anything around there. Plus, you know she's always loved doing outlandish things."

"That would be pretty outlandish, I guess," Ophelia said, frowning. "Well, wouldn't hurt to ask, I guess."

"I will write to her, but Mother, you absolutely must not say a word."

"Do you think it's safe to include Joe Bob?"

"You mean, can we trust him?"

"Yes, I guess that's what I mean. You know what he said back at the ranch about wishing he could be in on a lynching."

"I think he said that to shock me, but maybe you are right. How would you feel if I drove with Annalou out to the ranch in a little while, and you and Joe Bob and Luke went on ahead in your car?"

"Why, that's a right good idea. I can come on back pretty soon. I don't want to leave Nanna at my house for too long."

"Mind you, we've really got to be cautious right now."

"Who'd you hear that from?"

"From Melvar."

"He shows up a lot lately, doesn't he?"

"He does."

"Well, I'm kind of wishing I had a bulletproof vest," Ophelia chuckled. "Guess if I want to help make things better around here, this is where I start. Sure. Let's go back in the house and see what Joe Bob has to say."

"Joe Bob, Annalou, Luke?" Dona called, as she and Ophelia came through the screen door into the kitchen.

Annalou ran in from the back yard, holding her red diary. "Have you been waiting for me?"

"Well, yes," said Ophelia, "and do you know where Joe Bob and Luke are?"

"Don't know about Luke, but Joe Bob was taking a nap on the living room rug, when I looked in before."

"Joe Bob," Dona called again, and went into the hall. "Yoo-hoo, Joe Bob," her voice was friendly, light. It was so easy these days to rile him.

No one answered. Then a hush like night descended. The pendulum of her daddy's clock should have ticked as it swung from side to side, floorboards along the hall should have creaked as she walked into the living room. A deep wine carpet spread from wall to wall toward the spinet piano and her favorite overstuffed sofa, swallowing all sound. Joe Bob's long body sprawled stomach-down on the floor near the front door, his face was turned away from her into the carpet, his right arm twisted behind his back.

"Oh, dear God," Dona said, as she knelt over him, as she laid her ear against his back, her chin in his palm. And there was the beating of a heart, his heart. She said, "Joe Bob, honey, hang on."

Later, telling the story to Roy, Dona could not remember running from the living room to the kitchen. She could not remember what she said to Ophelia or Annalou, or calling for Luke, who never came, or for an ambulance, which did; but she did remember holding Joe Bob's hand, the broken arm, the twisted neck. She remembered being with him in the ambulance, walking by the stretcher along the clean white corridor of the clinic her daddy had made, and how Doc Steward appeared as though in a dream and said, "We'll take him now, Dona," and how she would not leave Joe Bob in anybody else's hands, no matter what they said. She remembered knowing the truth of that. He was still a boy, her boy, and he would not be alone.

"ARE YOU GIVING UP, AUNT DONEY?" Annalou reached across from her place in the passenger seat of the Chevy to put her hand on Dona's shoulder. They had left the hospital and were heading to the ranch.

"No, honey, no." She gripped the bottom of the steering wheel as though she held the reins of an unreliable horse. "Nothing like giving up. We needed to stop at the drug store for a few things for Joe Bob and now we have to get on home for a spell. Mamaw's taking Joe Bob on ahead of us, and your Uncle Roy drove back out in his truck. Where on earth is Luke? We all need to be at home."

"But Aunt Doney, what about Samuel? What about his family?"

"I have to try and trust Melvar. Right now, he's who we have and we've got to make sure our family is safe and nobody else is getting hurt."

"Joe Bob was pretty lucky, all told, right?"

"I'd say so. Seemed like somebody tried to bash his brains in. I wish Luke hadn't gone for a walk. I wish he'd seen who it was; but Joe Bob's like his daddy. He's hardheaded."

Annalou laughed. "Yes, he sure is. Sorry about his arm, though, his other arm is barely useful, from getting thrown off his horse."

"It will be a while before he can rope again. And your Uncle Luke, with his shaky moods, doesn't need this kind of danger. I'll feel better when he's back at the ranch, safe again."

"What makes you think the ranch is so safe, Aunt Doney?" Annalou sat back into the seat beside Dona and folded her arms.

"I can see why you don't think it is right now, honey. But if your Uncle Roy and Juan Carlos are keeping watch, and I'm there too, nobody's going to get past us to hurt you or Joe Bob, I promise. It was dangerous at the ranch right after the shooting, but now it seems more dangerous in town."

The back window shattered and Annalou yelled, "Watch out!"

"Get down on the floorboard. Now!" Dona leaned forward to press her foot harder on the gas pedal. "Bless me if that wasn't a shotgun. A ways off. Stay on the floor, and put your arms over your head."

Annalou wedged herself under the dashboard and pushed her knees up to her chin. "Aunt Doney," she said, her voice shaking, "are we going to die?"

"Don't you worry, we're nearly to the gate. Do not move, do you hear me? No matter what."

Annalou said nothing, but she whined, high and thin like a puppy in a storm. Across the fence line a cloud of dust headed toward the ranch house. With luck, that would be Roy.

Dona opened the gate, leapt back into the car, ducked her head low and rattled across the cattle guard. She pushed the Chevy as fast as it would go toward the ranch house honking on the horn, to alert all living things to the danger they were in. If she and Annalou were going to die, at least they could make a lot of noise.

"We're gonna make it, Annalou. Stay put. Take some deep breaths. When we get to the ranch house, I'll park as close to the back porch as I can, so we can run into the house. You got that?"

"Okay. But I'm really scared."

"We're all scared, honey, but it will be all right. Oh, look, thank heavens, Uncle Roy's truck and Mother's car, in the barnyard. But Annalou, we can't be too careful. Tell your Uncle Roy what happened. Go, now!"

Dona waited until Annalou disappeared inside the kitchen and turned the car to park in the shade of the barn.

The barn door opened a little. "Juan Carlos?" Dona yelled. But the man who came out of the shadows into the barnyard was Melvar, and he carried a tire iron.

"Melvar," Dona said, her hand over her mouth. She should drive away. She should get out and run into the house. She had to find Roy and Joe Bob. Melvar ran toward her, his shoulders loose and graceful as a tiger's.

"Dona, are you all right? I heard a shotgun down by the gate. Where is Annalou?"

"I sent her into the house, where the others are, for her safety. Melvar, what are you doing here? What about Samuel? How did you get here?"

"Wait, wait," he said, holding up his hands.

Dona loved to look at this man. His brown, strong hands, the way the muscles in his neck held his head, erect and proud, the creases on the sides of his generous mouth. And most of all, his eyes, gold and brown and heavy-lashed, like the eyes of her first beloved pony, seemed to understand everything she thought and felt and would ever be. But in this moment, they were as wary as a cat's.

"Don't go inside the house, Dona. No one is safe."

"What do you mean? Someone is here?"

"Your enemies have gathered."

Dona stared at the man she loved and could not love, the man she trusted and could not trust, who had brought her calico and gingham, and buttons for her dresses. And listened to her stories like no one else in her life ever had. Who had been in the barnyard when Samuel was bleeding, who seemed to be anywhere and everywhere.

Looking at him now, with her family in danger, she decided, as though it were the truth, to trust him.

"Who is in there, Melvar? Where are their trucks?"

"One car, belongs to the judge. Parked around front of the house. The ones who want Samuel. You know them. The men in charge. Please, Dona, do not go inside the house."

"I am going," Dona said. She pushed open the car door, grabbed her purse and stood. "I am not so much afraid, now," and she charged up the porch steps and into the kitchen.

"Annalou, Mother?" she called, turning her back on the door. "I'm coming."

"They're in here," said a man's voice from the living room.

Keeping her eyes on the dark hole of the living room doorway, Dona reached for her rifle. But it was not leaning against the ice box corner. She opened the purse hanging on her arm, and felt for the blue box. The heat of it led her fingers so that it nestled in her palm, and she placed the purse on its hook.

"We're okay," Roy said.

"Oh my god, Roy," said Dona, "how on earth...?" She stood in the doorway of the living room, letting her eyes adjust. This was the room of quiet, where dark shades were always drawn against the sun, severe in summer and winter these past dry West Texas years. It was the one room in the small, stone ranch house where a person could lie down for five minutes and close her eyes and no one would think to look for her there. Always the room was hushed, wearing the scent of old velvet. And yet in this late afternoon, the darkened room was close and stale with sweat. And something acrid and sharp. Fear.

As her eyes got used to the dark, Dona edged toward the oil lamp on an end table near the doorway. "I must be getting old," she said, as lightly as she could. "I can't see too well in here. I'll light the lamp."

"Leave it," someone said.

"Reverend Andrew MacMurray? I'm lighting this lamp. I like to see the faces of visitors in my home." And she lifted the glass chimney, struck a match from the box nearby, and adjusted the wick.

"Why are you here," she said, looking around at the familiar faces, and one covered with a white pointed hood. "Did anyone offer you a cup of coffee?"

"Don't get smart," said Reverend MacMurray. "You've been getting into things where you've got no business."

"Why aren't you saying anything, Roy?"

"Because," said another voice, "Roy knows I have a big gun pointed at your heart."

"One of your henchmen used a great big gun like that on my car, Judge, a while ago on the ranch road. While you boys hightailed it here like the cowards you are. Why don't you have your pointy hat on? Is that what I see, that white thing over your arm? Who is that one, under the coward's hood?"

"It is I," said another voice, "and this hood is sacred. I felt the gravity of this moment required it."

As he lifted it from his head, Dona said, "Cousin Edward, here you are, ganging up on me and my family. And you call that a sacred moment? I call it hiding. You must be so ashamed of what you've done."

"Edward," said the Judge, "tell your cousin what we need for her to do."

"What kind of small boys are you?" Dona said. "What happened to being the pillars of our county?"

"Please be quiet, Dona," said Edward. "We want to know where Samuel is, where his family is, that's all. You tell us that and we'll let you go, and all your family. You don't tell us that and tomorrow's Standard Times is going to run a real sad story."

"What story is that, Edward?"

"That some gypsy from Persia came through like he'd done lots of times, bringing little pretties to all the ranch wives; but this time, he'd gone crazy for love of one of them. Killed every member of her family in cold blood. Including her."

From her place in the doorway, Dona felt the air in the hall move against her back. Someone had opened a door.

Dona straightened her shoulders. "For heaven's sake, Cousin Edward, you can do what you like to me. You can let that hate spread all over this county, but I do not believe you have it in you to kill a little girl and her grandmother and all the family she has left in the world. Ophelia's your cousin, remember that. And her husband was your best friend. You have never been a killer, have you now?"

Edward grunted and his leather belt creaked against its buckle with the movement of his breath.

"And, Judge Angus Cameron, you are a man of the law. You would not willingly take it into your own hands, would you? You would not let your feelings run away with you. That would not be the man you know yourself to be."

The shotgun barrel dipped toward the floor.

"And Reverend MacMurray, before you decide to slaughter all of us because you can't lynch one man, I would like you to lead us in a prayer, something to sanctify this moment. You are a man of God. You believe in the words of Jesus Christ who said we are all God's children, all of us. How about this, Reverend MacMurray, how about leading us in a prayer of understanding and forgiveness, because that's all we've got left here, the grace of God."

But Reverend MacMurray was silent.

Whereupon Dona clinched the small blue box in her fist behind her back and, in what voice she had left, through trembling and dryness, recited the only psalm she knew by heart, "The Lord is my shepherd, I shall not want..." And Annalou with her sweet voice came in, "He maketh me to lie down in green pastures..." and Ophelia and Roy's, joining, "Yea, though I walk through the valley of the shadow of death, I will fear no evil...," and Joe Bob, croaking through his twisted neck, strived uncertainly to say, "He prepareth a table in the presence of mine enemies," and one by one, white hoods in hand, perhaps out of habit, perhaps out of guilt, the preacher, the lawyer, the judge, and two voices from the hall, mumbled "Surely goodness and mercy will follow me..." and made their way to "Amen."

"DONA WILLIS," Angus Cameron said, "perhaps I have wrongly used you. What you did just now, calling us all to prayer, that was a brave thing. Not that I agree with you, I do not. But, yes, that was brave."

"Yes," said Edward, "that was, well, it was like we were blessed, there with our guns and our hate. I don't know what to say, Dona, except I thank you and I thank the Lord God who was with us in this dark and crowded place."

Reverend MacMurray kept his seat when the other men had left the room. Dona turned down the kerosene lamp next to the hall door.

"Andrew MacMurray." She watched the drawn face, the hands that folded and unfolded and folded again. "Thank you for lending your voice."

He put his elbows on his knees, dropped his head into his hands and said quietly, in a tone Dona had never heard from his pulpit, "Lord, tell me what to do." His shoulders shook, and his throat constricted, and tears ran between his fingers.

Dona turned off the lamp and waited until he left the room. He wandered down the hall to the front door, and out. What sort of pact had he made with his Lord?

Roy and Joe Bob were making coffee in the kitchen when she entered. Annalou sat at her usual place at the table with a piece of stale biscuit in front of her. Melvar and Juan Carlos stood with Angus Cameron on the back screened porch. Was the judge making an apology, shaking his head like that? Cousin Edward, turning his Stetson round and round in his hands, sat with Ophelia on the back porch steps. Dona felt invisible, drained of blood, standing by mere habit in the center of the one room that all her life had been her comfort.

"I am going outside to fix the windmill," she said to no one, and walked back through the house to the front door, the side of the house they rarely used. Off the front steps Judge Cameron's car sat out of sight of the barnyard. A craggy mesquite caught the last of the sun, its long, narrow leaves shimmering, shielding the car and Reverend MacMurray, who sat in its back seat, door open wide.

"You," Dona said to the tree, "you are the only one of us who actually belongs here. You hardly need water or any kind of care, and your pods of tiny peas keep starving cows alive. I wish I had your thorns."

She walked away toward the windmill which did not need fixing at all. Each blade caught the wind with the whoosh of wings. And not for the first time, all of it was like her own body. How the blades turning sent the long steel shaft deep into the land she stood on, and how the shaft pumped the blood of the earth, rushing from far below, into the great galvanized heart of the water tank. And how their lives depended on that water, on that windmill, on the wind, on the ground to keep it safe, on someone to keep it going.

Boots crunched the dry ground behind her and Dona turned to find Melvar close by her side. "What have we done," she said.

"What you have done, perhaps, is save Samuel's life."

"How, exactly, would you say?"

"By turning those men in there. You reminded them of what is good in themselves."

"I am not sure of that. For a little while, maybe. But this hatred is so much deeper than one prayer can reach. Who do you trust?"

"I trust you."

Dona and Melvar stood like cattle, gazing off past the windmill, past the mules and wagons which should on this clear, clean day of late summer have been hauling hay from the fields, past the barbed wire fence and into the hay barn. He did not touch her; she did not touch him. But had Roy, watching from the front porch, seen what rose between them, the air shining like the first morning sun, he would have known he had lost her.

"This is not over," she said, watching the windmill.

"No," he said, scuffing the ground with his boot.

"Melvar, about Samuel, about his family..."

"They are safe for now. I promise you."

"They are alive and they are safe?" She looked to find what was in his eyes.

"They are alive and they are safe."

"And are they nearby?"

"Yes."

"At Bertie's house?"

"They are. They cannot stay for long."

"Melvar, you've saved them, but now they must be free to live their own lives."

"Yes, and so they will. This much has been hard to arrange. You can imagine."

"I can. And I'm grateful. But I'm worried about them. About Bertie, too. And about you. I wonder what you would think of taking Samuel and his family to Unity Ann's ranch out at Comanche?"

"To your sister's ranch?"

"Yes, it's over a hundred miles away, and she has a big house and barns. Plenty of space for the family; I have written to her, and she says she could use the help."

"I will speak with Samuel about this. Of course, he and his wife must make the choice and I will let you know what they say. But I see that there is more you must do, my friend, Dona."

"I know. It's not only about Samuel and his family. None of the colored people, Negroes or Mexican—nobody is safe as long as the Klan can do whatever its vigilantes want."

"What can you do about that?"

"I've got an idea, and as soon as I can get my family back to normal, and catch up on some of the chores around here, I'll go back to town. I want to meet with the women in my mother's church auxiliary. Their husbands may be Klan members and they don't know it. I mean if Judge Cameron and Reverend MacMurray and Cousin Edward are in the Klan, what upstanding man is not?"

"Dona, today...," Melvar turned toward the horizon and tried to blink away tears. "Today, in that room, in the dark, the danger was great. When the Judge's car arrived, I must have been with Juan Carlos in the barn. He had trouble with one of the horses out in the stables and we had to separate him from the others. We did not know that anyone had come to the ranch house until I walked around to this windmill for water and saw the car. I returned to the barn to get the tire iron, when I heard you honking your horn and calling."

"Why were you here?"

"Oh," said Melvar, scuffling his boots in the dust. "I heard three of them talking in town this morning at Luby's. That is one of the places where I learn things. I look like one of the Mexican cooks. You looked right at me, when you were with Bertie, and didn't see me.

"They said that Joe Bob had been hurt and one of their allies did it. He was getting out of the hospital and was going to be all right. And mainly, since the good old boys they had sent had failed, they were planning to get to you, themselves, to find out where Samuel is. So, I figured you were in danger and I came as soon as I could."

"Why were you in the hallway with Juan Carlos?"

"You had walked straight into trouble. Juan Carlos and I snuck around the front of the house to listen at the living room window. We wanted to be invisible, so when the time was right, we could help."

"It did help me to know you were there."

"But you did not need help, Dona, not from me. You were the most brave person I have ever known. And you had the blue box."

"And what does it mean to you?"

"Ah," he said, looking at the sky. "It is a blessing. It carries the spirit of my people in its colors; we think of such small boxes as borrowed, the same as perhaps you think of music of your church. It came from somewhere, it has remained, mysterious of origin, supporting the spirit, giving courage; a reminder of all that is sacred in ourselves as beings of earth and sky, but it is not owned, it is not to be kept from others who are on the path of spirit."

"I believe the minister is a monster, and I doubt the church's teachings. And you believe I am on such a path?"

"Yes, because you are. You say you see things. I believe you. I had brought two blue boxes from Persia in secret, for they would one day be of service. I did not know of course, until I heard about Samuel, that the day had come."

Dona turned away from the windmill and stared him square in the face. "Whoever are you, Melvar?"

"What do you mean?"

"I mean, really, who are you? I know you have lived off and on for many years in this county, and you have told me parts of your childhood and your return for some years to Persia. But Melvar, you seem to have powers I don't understand, and I wonder..."

"No special powers, my dear friend, but yes, a certain way of listening, perhaps, like an animal of prey," he paused. "My body, yes, my body sensing perhaps more than others."

"And how do you turn up in the most unexpected places? Do you know how to fly? Can you make yourself invisible?"

Melvar laughed, throwing back his head, the sky gleaming against his burnished skin.

"I must go inside, Melvar. The other men have gone back to town. I must make supper and talk with my family. How did you get here? I don't see Molly anywhere, or your wagon."

"They are here, but behind the barn, out of sight, out of danger. We will head back to town and see to Bertie and the others. And I will contact your Nanna."

Melvar lifted his broad hat and put it over his chest. "Dona, this has been a day I will always remember. You, the dark room of angry men, the prayer, I would not have believed it."

"Thank you, Melvar. You've made so much of it possible. And someday I hope we'll have time to talk about how that was. Right now, I'm worried about Luke, where on earth he is; and I will be in town in a day or two to speak with my mother's friends at the auxiliary. We've got some work to do together. You'll know, of course, in your magical way, where I am."

"And for now," he said with a slight tip of his hat, "I will say farewell."

"Pancakes for supper, Doney?" Joe Bob walked into the kitchen from the porch. "And sausage. Just what I'm mighty hungry for." He sat at the table, looking up at her, so much the way he had done at seven years old when she had married his daddy. "Doney, what you did this afternoon was the dangest thing. We was all fixing to be shot to death and you up and said the 23rd Psalm."

"I'm not sure I would have had the gumption to speak if you hadn't gotten hurt, Joe Bob. Somebody knocked you cold and tried to break your arm, there in your grandmother's living room, but that was the last straw for me. I was not going to be afraid of the Klan or anybody in it, ever again. They do not deserve even that much respect."

"I know who that was, beat me up." Joe Bob put his hands flat on the table. "And I think you might, too."

"Oh," Dona whispered. "It was Luke, wasn't it."

"He dang near killed me, fought like an animal, I still can't believe it. Haven't seen him since, either."

"Guess I didn't let myself think it. How awful for you."

"For him, too. I think he's done gone crazy."

"But why attack you?"

"He gets real confused about what's right and wrong, I know that much." Joe Bob's words came slowly and harsh. "Like all this about the colored. And there's something else. Luke has another life. Secret. I only found out by accident. Something happened he might be blaming on me. And I ain't quite ready to tell you."

"Thanks anyway for this. We've got to find him. And we've got to put a stop to the boys doing the bidding of the men who were in our living room today. This problem goes way beyond them."

"Can I help?"

"You sure can." She set a plate of griddle cakes and sausage and a pitcher of molasses in front of him, butter melting between the cakes.

"First thing, you can put out word for Luke's whereabouts."

"Okay, that's easy."

"And second, you can talk with the other young bucks. They're the ones most likely to join up and do hateful things out of pure boredom. I mean, you've said some pretty awful things yourself about the colored."

"Yep, and I am mighty shamed by it. It ain't the colored we ought to be worried about. It's white boys like me with too much rodeo in our blood."

"Too much rodeo?"

"Like in calf roping, the calves ain't done nothing and we rope 'em and jump on their bellies and tie their hind legs together. Why there's parts of Texas where white fellas skin colored men alive, before they string them up, and I heard about up in Jarvis, where they burned a young colored fella alive with his daddy watching. Just because a white girl claimed he'd tried to kiss her."

Joe Bob's shoulders shivered and he rubbed the back of his neck with his almost-healed arm. "I got a little taste of how it feels to nearly die for no reason whatsoever, and no chance to fight back. I didn't like it one bit, and I ain't going to do it to nobody else. Sure, Doney, I'll talk with my buddies."

"Thanks. These things have a way of coming to light. I'll go call the others."

It was full dark when they had finished supper and done the evening chores. Dona sat down on the front porch steps. Cicadas droned their songs. She tucked her hands into her apron pockets. Those insects never seemed to get tired like a body would expect them to, with all of that vibrating. And she wondered if it was the stars that kept them going. Maybe they were counting every star with each rasp of their bodies and they would never be done. Dona smiled at that. What would it mean to be done, with anything? Didn't it all go on, over and over, like it said in the Psalms, to everything there is a season and didn't the seasons always return?

Chapter Twenty-two

Dona had work to do that night, to get ready for the sheep shearing the next day. Roy, Joe Bob and Juan Carlos would be at the shearing, helping the Mexican crew who came through this time every year. Dona hated it when they sheared the sheep, pressing down on their necks with one heavy boot and pulling the poor animal's skin away from its back and hip bones, jutting out like broken limestone. She'd helped to shear a few herself, and every time the sheep bleated like children being tortured. The shearers were skilled and pulled and tugged the animals so as not to cut their skin; and sure, wool was beautiful and warm, and the animals didn't have to die to provide it. Still, she wished there were a kinder way.

But not this time; this time would be the same hot, efficient operation as usual. And she would be grateful. Wool was one of the ways the ranch stayed in the black. The Capitan owned the business and would oversee the operation. His crew would camp on-site and a cocinero would prepare breakfast, lunch and supper for the entire crew. At the end, Roy would pay the Capitan, who would disperse money based on each worker's output. Dona's job would be to haul water for the crew and feed her own bunch of family and workers.

After breakfast the next morning, when her men had gone back to the pens, Dona finished her morning chores in the barn and closed the big doors against the heat of July's last day. She started up the back porch steps to the house to find a piece of paper wedged in the screen door. A note to Joe Bob, in Spanish. The paper was dirty and had the soft feel of cloth, folded and refolded. She wanted to find Juan Carlos. She could trust him not to tell anyone what the note said, but he was out at the shearing pens and wouldn't be back to the ranch house until suppertime. Well, maybe she could translate some of it. 'Joe Bob' was written at the top of the brown paper by what was probably the stub of a pencil. Someone had pressed mighty hard into the paper; maybe they were nervous or maybe in a hurry. 'Joe Bob,' it said, 'Vienes esta noche, solo. Shacks cerca rio. 100 dólares. Tengo las noticias de Samuel. Coyote' As Dona worked it out in English, it read, 'Joe Bob, You come tonight, alone. Shacks near river. 100 dollars. I have news of Samuel. Coyote.'

"Joe Bob?" Dona said aloud. He had been talking among his friends as she asked him to, and he had been nearly killed right in his grandmother's house by his own Uncle Luke, for no reason that she could imagine. So, maybe he had found out something, or maybe this someone called "Coyote" might help. But why hadn't he said anything to her? She had to get back to the shearing pens and hope Joe Bob and Juan Carlos were still there.

Dona ran across the porch and into the kitchen. "Oh, no." And she clamped her hands over her mouth.

On the table, draped like the fox stole around her mother's shoulders, was a coyote, freshly killed, its eyes gone white, tongue lolling on oilcloth. Dona turned back to the porch and steadied herself on the door jamb. She wanted to be sick, to vomit up the poisons of the last weeks; she couldn't stand the violence, the hatred. An innocent animal, slaughtered to leave a bloody message. And she didn't believe for a minute that this "Coyote" had news of Samuel.

The news on the radio that morning, of the Negro man in Dallas, the latest in a run of horrors. A mob cut off his genitals, skinned him alive, and set his body aflame, before they strung him from a live oak tree in front of his children. What beastly creatures, these Christian citizens. What beasts the men who tried to kill Samuel. *Arise!* the earth's choir had commanded, four months ago. For the first time in her life, her whole body shuddered with the desire for vengeance. To kill them. *Was she also a beast?* She needed her mother.

DONA PARKED THE TRUCK at the back of the chute and closed her eyes. "Mother," she said, "I do not know how to continue with this."

"No," said Ophelia, opening the truck door and sliding off the seat to the ground. "I don't either, but I do know this. After I prayed for those dastardly Klan members in my very own church, we're not any one of us going to quit now."

Dona dodged her way through sheep, crowded into pens below the chutes. She got as close as she could to Roy and said, "I need to talk with you, right now."

He scowled, "Cain't you see..." But when he looked up at her, he let go of the ewe he had been holding between his knees. "Yep, I'll be right along."

The four of them gathered on the shade side of the sheep pen and went over possible meanings of the note to Joe Bob; why would it have been left in the screen door, except to get Dona's attention as the one most likely to come and go to the barnyard on this particular day? The coyote was a female, obviously healthy; and carefully arranged on the kitchen table to horrify and frighten someone. What did these things mean? And at the end, Joe Bob said that for sure he should stay away from the shacks, that he didn't have an idea in heaven who the note was from, and they all agreed that probably it was Dona who was in danger.

IT WAS DARK BY THE TIME Roy and his crew came in the ranch house for supper, hands and faces dripping water from the windmill trough. Dona had a big pot of red beans ready on the stove. Annalou poured coffee into blue tin cups loaded with sugar. There was no sign of a coyote carcass, no bloody oilcloth, no smear from a long, limp tongue.

Roy was first through the kitchen door, peered sharply around and said, "Somethin' smells mighty good tonight."

Juan Carlos, Joe Bob, the Capitan and Roy, holding their hats in both hands, circled the kitchen table, hooked their hats over chair backs and took a seat. For the next half hour, it was all Dona, Ophelia and Annalou could do to keep the bowls filled with beans, and plates laden with Josie's tortillas and fresh-chopped onions.

What a relief it was, Dona thought, to get her mind off of how the coyote lay across this very table. It felt good to feed people when they had been working hard and were hungry, and in any language, laughter was laughter.

Later, after the dishes were dried and put away, Dona, Ophelia and Annalou scrubbed the table. "The old sheet worked fine at supper," said Ophelia.

"Seems odd not to have the oilcloth," Annalou said.

"Seems odd to have had a dead coyote right here," Dona said. "Glad Roy and the boys are watching out for us."

"So, Aunt Doney, what do we do now?"

"Your Uncle Roy is talking with Juan Carlos and Josie on the back porch. Juan Carlos says no Mexican wrote that note, and that it's a phony. Not sure how he can tell, but maybe that is a sign of who could have stuck it in the screen door."

"Anybody look down at the shacks?" Ophelia asked.

"Roy and Juan Carlos were down there right after supper. They took Roy's truck. Hoped to maybe see some things in the headlights."

"Took their rifles with them?"

"Sure, but didn't see a thing," Dona said, drying the table with a worn towel. "Take a look at the chairs, will you, Mother? I didn't have time to wipe the chairs before the men came in for supper. Or mop the floor."

"I can come back and help you in the morning, what do you think, honey?" Ophelia said. "I can't see for nothin' right now."

"You want to sleep on the living room couch, Mother? Or we can move cushions into Annalou's room and you can have her bed."

"That would be right helpful, especially since Mable is taking care of Nanna at my house, now. I wouldn't want to disturb them, coming home late."

"Oh, please, sleep in my room, Mamaw? Nanna's been good company and I'd miss having a roommate."

"I think so, I think that's just the thing to do," said Ophelia. "I'll get started on making my bed right now. Annalou, why don't you come help me?"

Dona dragged the bloody oilcloth off the front porch to the water trough by the windmill and scrubbed it clean. She hung it over the clothesline to drip and went back into the house to check on Annalou and Ophelia. They were chattering away as they got ready for bed.

"Think I'll take a hot bath," Dona said, to nobody in particular.

Chapter Twenty-three

WHAT HAD HAPPENED TO THE GIRL who loved to go barefoot at the river, who padded around below the horse troughs, who squished mud between her toes and buried her feet in the soft dust of the barnyard; who popped her feet out to startle a passing hen. It was the closest she had ever come to playing.

Dona stood in the bathroom, hung her clothes on a hook, and stared down at her feet. They seemed fine. She sat on the edge of the bathtub which she had filled with water heated on the kitchen stove, and a little bit of the bubble bath from her birthday. She angled her right ankle over her left knee, and held the foot like a piglet trying to squirm out of reach. It was a perfectly good foot. The nails and between each toe were a little dirty, but the foot lay there contented, so she petted it like she would the piglet, and thought that it was good that it didn't squeal. That made her laugh, so she rubbed her toes as if they were the piglet's ears. What a fine thing to do. She put the foot into the hot water and wiggled her toes. "Ah," she said, "ah." And turned so she could move the other foot into petting position, lost her balance and slid into the bathtub like a turtle. Only with a bigger splash and a loud whoop.

"You alright?" It was Annalou at the door, sounding worried, which for reasons she could not fathom, made Dona laugh harder. "I'm fine, honey, I fell into the bathwater. But really, I'm fine."

And she was. Finer than she had been in a long time. She felt like a little girl, laying back in the water, pulling her knees to her chin, dunking her head, wiggling her toes and fingers, straightening her legs up to the ceiling; she felt like she was nine years old again, the last time she could remember being truly happy.

She lifted her left foot up out of the water and rubbed its arch. She rubbed its heel and the base of the toes. She put her fingers between the toes of both feet, she waggled them around in circles. She sat up. Was there no end to what she could do with those feet?

"Annalou, put the coffee on, will you?" she hollered, lying back in the lovely water once more and pretending that she could float. Big, grown-up body floating in a clawfoot tub. The thought made her smile, for a moment.

Dona sat up, water running from her shoulders and down her chest. She shut her eyes against the memories of the past months. "I can smile if I want to," she said. "And you can't stop me."

But it was all over, the lightness had passed, the bubbling in her chest which had played with the bubbles in the water, had withdrawn to that place where her joy had always gone. To the crucible of cruelty. The weight of the schoolmaster, branding her body for life; Samuel, guilty of being born a Negro, feared, hunted, shot in the back. Men of every color throughout the south, tortured, displayed, murdered. Women, beaten, downtrodden, used.

She pulled the rubber stopper out of the drain, lifted her body up and over the rim of the tub onto the bathmat, which, worn as it was, absorbed everything.

Chapter Twenty-four

"DEAR NANNA," DONA said, "I am happy you're back, and it's time to wake up. Here's your coffee, strong and sweet."

She straightened the covers on Nanna's bed and added a pillow to the one behind her head. "I'm sorry about what happens here sometimes, like the other night, the men who came into our living room, the danger. Were you afraid?"

"I dream so much these days, even when I am awake, that truly I heard very little. When Annalou brought my supper last evening, she told me what I needed to know. Including how much fun you had taking a bath a couple of nights ago. Staying at Ophelia's was a good break from any kind of excitement at all."

"But Nanna, I am not doing so well. It's Sunday, and I need help. Will you be, well, my priest?"

She knelt by Nanna's bed in the front room of the ranch house. It was the room Dona loved best, the way sun peeped in this early morning through two narrow windows. No matter that they were almost blind with dust. Nanna said she had not noticed, and she'd first arrived nearly two weeks before.

"A priest? What, are you, now, a Catholic, Dona?" Her eyes sparkled like a girl's, light blue sapphires, pools in a wind, rippling. "Why do you need a priest, my darling?"

Dona sat on the bed and took Nanna's hand. It was light as a dragonfly's wing. "Nanna, so much is going on right now. So much that seems evil, and I don't know if I am strong enough to face it." She lowered her chin and closed her eyes. "May I tell you?"

"Of course, my child, but I know you are strong. Why, I know about you shooting that rabid coyote leaping toward our Annalou. Shot it dead in the eye. And I heard about the praying there in the living room. And, honey, I remember the schoolmaster."

"You know about that?"

"Your mother told me. She knew I would understand. But, Dona, I can hear better sitting up," Nanna chuckled. "See better, too. Can't talk worth a squat, though, unless you give me those dentures, there." She grinned, showing not one tooth in the front of her mouth.

"Oh, Nanna," Dona laughed, and with one arm around Nanna's shoulders, brought her to sitting. She handed Nanna the dentures on a handkerchief, worn thin with washing.

"And that coffee?"

"Here you go."

"Now, how did your mother know I'd understand?" Nanna fixed her teeth and set her wire-rimmed glasses on her nose. "Because, dear Dona, the same thing happened to her."

"To my mother?"

"And to me, and I don't know how many women in our family."

"Oh, my."

"And so, I know you faced evil in that man, and that unlike so many who are terribly hurt in that way, you grew stronger for it."

"But I could never have a child."

"No, that is true. But it was not punishment for a man having his way with you, if that is what you think."

"That is what I think. I mean, I know it's not true, really. But even Mother blamed me, at first."

"I know, and she could not forgive herself for a long time. But, child, tell me about the evil you are facing now, please. I will try not to be too tired to listen."

"Yes, of course. And let me know if I should stop. It is about powerful white men in our county hating a Negro man so much, they want to hang him from a tree until he's dead."

"Samuel."

"Do you already know everything?"

"No, not at all. But your walls are thin and sometimes I hear better than I let on."

Dona smiled and kissed the translucent skin on the forehead of this grandmother she loved so much. "What else have you heard?"

"That you are trying to save his life. And that is good. And that you want to change the way we treat each other, all colors of us."

"Yes."

"And that is also good, Dona. And it is hard, one of the hardest things. I am too tired to talk long about this, but when I was a young girl, most Negroes were owned by white people, like we own the cattle and sheep. And treated like animals, worse than animals. I was an Abolitionist in my time, and spoke out against slavery, a lot like you are doing now."

"And what happened, Nanna? And why haven't I heard this before?"

"I was nearly killed by a gang of white men. They called me a nigger-lover, a whore, and other things, and took their liberty with me. It's a miracle I didn't get pregnant. Could you please take this coffee, honey. I have to rest a minute."

Dona took the cup and waited, one arm hugging her ribs, and stared out of the clouded window.

When Nanna spoke again, she motioned for Dona to move closer and whispered into her ear, "I never told you because I was ashamed, so ashamed." The fingers that wrapped Dona's arm were like claws.

"Not of my beliefs, mind you, but of being raped by those men. I never spoke of it; not to your mother, until her own problem, which I can see she has not told you about, either."

Dona put her head on Nanna's shoulder, and felt the bones. "Will it ever end, Nanna?"

"Yes," Nanna pressed Dona's hair with her cheek. "It will end if you and other brave women speak out. Raping a girl, lynching or raping a man, these are not so different, you know."

She stopped for breath, and put her hand on her chest. "There's hatred, fear, ignorance, and brute strength in both, and in war, this awful war that's about to begin. But Dona, to change anything for the better, we must have love in our hearts, and fire burning in our eyes."

Nanna lay back, murmured something Dona could not understand, and fell asleep.

DONA CARRIED NANNA'S SUPPER to her that evening, mainly so they could talk together in private. She said quietly, handing Nanna a cup of pea soup, "Remember when we talked this morning? About good and evil. You know, what those men did to you and now what's happening with Samuel. All of that. Is there any hope?"

"There is hope," Nanna said. "You are the hope. You and people like you who talk, listen, forgive." She took a sip of soup and held up her hand. She was not finished.

"People who love, and are smart and willing to help someone in trouble. Especially who see us all as equal. That is my hope. My mother, your feisty great-grandmother used to say that evil is not the opposite of good, Dona. They are kin, they slide along together. If you want to change things in this county, you'll have to see the evil ones are just like us."

Nanna handed the soup cup to Dona. "It's the old saying, hate the sin but love the sinner. When I am dying, I hope I don't have too much regret. Mainly that I haven't forgiven enough."

"And what does that have to do with making changes?"

"Change has to do with forgiveness," Nanna said, patting her bed clothes. "Putting ourselves in the shoes of the other person; feeling what they feel, afraid. And trying to understand what's at the base of it. Maybe they feel caught between two worlds."

"Sometimes you don't have time for that kind of understanding, Nanna." Dona rubbed her throat. "Sometimes the person is aiming a gun at your head. Or putting a noose around your neck."

"I know, and you have to save your own life when you can. But step back, honey. See what is really going on. See if you can find a way in."

"Where?"

"To their hearts."

"But Nanna, the heart is not designed to hold everything, is it?"

"To my way of thinking, child, it is as big as the universe. It can hold everything and the opposite of everything. Go in. See."

Dona's head, her shoulders, her chest grew lighter. "Yes," she said, "go in. I'll go where I am not expected and try to see what I have been blind to before. Maybe, some things I can forgive. Maybe that's why the 23rd Psalm came to me."

She leaned toward the white hair, parted down the middle of the small, sweet head, to place a kiss goodnight. But Nanna's eyes were closed and her mouth smiled only slightly. She had given the best she had. It was time to pass on.

Chapter Twenty-five

"Aunt Doney, I am so sad about Nanna. I was helping Josie hang out the sheets she left behind yesterday, and it made me miss her so much."

"I know, Annalou, and it helps to remember how happy she could make me, all of us, and for, well, ever so many years."

"So much to worry about. Anybody can die. Like Samuel nearly did. And do you know where Samuel is?"

Dona was mopping the linoleum floor in the kitchen, and that was the question she would not answer, even to Annalou.

She had promised Nanna to find a way into the heart of the awful troubles that threatened Samuel and every colored person in the county, and was on her way down the hall to mop the outhouse, when it came to her.

She had to find a way to talk with Eleanor MacMurray alone. Samuel was safe for now, at Unity Ann's, but the men who were after him would not quit persecuting colored men, no matter that they had prayed with her in this living room. Maybe they would slow their hunt for Samuel, maybe give it up, but there would be another Negro man who returned the smile of a white woman; another Mexican who talked back, and the mob would rise.

Eleanor would know, wouldn't she, how to persuade her husband to stop the manhunt for Samuel? And there was that story from Joe Bob, that he saw the good Reverend behind the whorehouse outside of town one Saturday night. And didn't Eleanor say he always worked on Sunday's sermon on Saturday night at his church study? What if he put the whole horrible lynching party together to hide his sins?

Dona shook her head and bent to the job of mopping the outhouse floor. How many of those men had been in that lynch mob, and who among them was hiding something he was ashamed of? Every one, was her guess, every darned one of them.

She finished the floor, pulled on her barn boots and took the string mop outside to wash it in the laundry tub. Roy, Joe Bob and a yearling colt seemed to be at a standoff in the near paddock. Joe Bob was shouting, "You dern stubborn son of a gun sorry colt." And Roy was yelling at Joe Bob, "Gotta be patient, boy, take it easy, boy."

Dona could see why the colt wasn't behaving. Who would know what to do in the middle of all that noise? She ambled over to the paddock and put a boot on the fence rail, wishing for her hat. It was nearly midday and the mesquite trees could not cast enough shade to make a difference. The heat and noise came from inside herself. She was mad as a hornet at those arrogant men in the Klan; and she was rabbit-scared by what they could do.

Chapter Twenty-six

Late that afternoon, Dona and Luke were mucking out the barn floor under the chicken roost, bandanas over their faces against the dust.

Dona said, "Luke, I am relieved that you've come home, and terrible sorry that Nanna died while you were gone. You don't have to tell me where you've been, but it's sitting in my craw to ask. How come you attacked Joe Bob at our mother's house? And how come you left him unconscious?"

"Oh," Luke said, holding the barn rake against his chest, "so he told you. I am real sorry for that. I don't know what come over me. I was purely red-hot mad."

"Mad, crazy? Or Mad, angry? And why on earth at Joe Bob?"

"Both, I reckon. And Joe Bob, he was starting to see things your way."

"About what?"

"About Samuel and other coloreds."

"Don't you, too?"

"Sometimes I see like you; sometimes I see like the devil. Cain't seem to help myself."

"No excuse, Luke. And what do you know about the dead coyote on the kitchen table?"

"I took her away, like you asked. I tied her across the back of the new gelding, like this." He held the rake across his arms. "And I hauled her to the high pasture."

"Didn't try to bury her there in all that rock, did you?"

"Nope. Laid her out flat under a cedar tree for the buzzards to find. Plenty of chicks to feed right now, I reckon."

"I reckon, too, Luke. Thank you for taking care of that. It was hard to look at her, healthy as I've ever seen a coyote. Any idea where her den was?"

"I think as how it might be over yonder to the Morton ranch."

"What makes you think that? Way over there?"

"Her color, mainly, and how big she was."

"You've been coming and going right much for a while, now, without a word. So, what were you doing over there?"

Luke grunted and bent to his raking.

"Luke, what's going on? Why don't you want to talk about it?"

"I'm about done here, if you can handle the rest."

"No, I can't handle the rest. Luke Willis, what the devil?"

"The Devil. Don't want to talk about that."

"Luke, would you please put more than ten words together at once and tell me? Somebody killed that animal and maybe it had roamed over to here, but maybe not. And maybe there is a clue there as to who did it. Luke, don't be a child. You've got to talk . . ."

Dona glanced over her shoulder at him and shut her mouth.

Luke stood with one leg out the barn door. He had pulled his bandana off and was wiping his face with it. Half of his face shone silver in the low shaft of sun.

"Can I tell you a secret, Dona? A bad secret?"

"Brother, are you crying?"

He dropped to his knees and buried his face in his hands. "I am damn sorry — for everything."

She reached for his hands, bigger than that silent boy's, the callouses tougher. And his tears splattered the barn floor.

Her throat filled to a whisper. "It was you? You shot that coyote?"

His back heaved.

"You spread it on the kitchen table?"

And from his hands came the wail of an infant.

"You wrote the note?"

He folded. His grizzled chest pushed against his knees, his head rocked back and forth. He was six years old.

"Luke, you've got to tell me."

He collapsed against the side of the barn door and onto the floor, its planks smoothed from the hooves of horses.

Dona staggered across his body to the barnyard, and vomited into the nearest mesquite brush. At the watering trough she washed her face, behind her neck, her hands, and flung her arms around in the air like the windmill.

"By god," she yelled toward the barn, "we will get to the bottom of this, now," and she turned back to the barn and Luke, her arms clenched around her heart.

Luke had moved deeper into the barn's quiet presence and sat, hunched over, on a bale of hay. Dona eased herself onto another one, and in a voice she would use for a frightened colt, she said, "Go on. I'm listening."

Luke leaned toward her. "I am under the influence, you might say."

"Of what?"

"Of Reverend MacMurray."

"But why?"

"I'm afeard of him in a big way."

"Does he have something on you?"

"You might say so."

Luke's face was dark under his hat. When he was a child, he would make a ball of himself when he was afraid, and Dona felt the place between her ribs soften.

"I don't see how anybody can help me. What I did could get me thrown in jail for the rest of my natural life. If the right folks found out."

"Tell me, please."

"I married a colored girl over to the Morton Ranch, or what passed for married."

"Okay," Dona said, "but how did MacMurray find out?"

"He's the Morton's preacher and sly like a fox. Visits ranches on Sunday, has dinner, asks the help what's going on. Like that."

"What you did is against the law of the State of Texas, but was there harm?"

"They died. My girls died."

"Which girls do you mean? Your wife?"

"I mean my wife and my baby girl." Luke folded further into himself and his sobs carried beyond Dona, the wagon, the old barn. "MacMurray says I killed them. But I never...I could never . . ."

"What kind of proof does he have, Luke?"

"No proof."

"Then, why?"

"Because he is in cahoots with the Judge, and they hate the colored and any whites who don't. And I guess, because I'm your brother."

"How did they die, your wife and daughter?"

"They was strangled. The both of them. In their bed." His voice thinned into a wail. "But don't you see? I weren't there all the time. I had to be here, helping at the ranch. I couldn't live there with them, we couldn't tell nobody we was married."

"So, anybody could have killed them?"

"I am pretty sure," Luke said, straightening up and taking out his bandana. He wiped his eyes and blew his nose. "I am pretty dern sure it was MacMurray."

"Why is that?"

"One night when she and our baby was alone, he came in the little cabin drunk as the Devil. And tried to force her, my beautiful Evangeline. And she took a knife out from under her pillow and come near to cutting off his balls. She was a cat fighter, she was, and I loved her, Dona." He pushed his face into the bandana and cried like a child.

"Oh, Luke, how sorry I am for you," and she turned toward him. "It was out of love, wasn't it. To keep a woman and your child a secret, to protect them."

"It were real. Real as this ranch. And I couldn't keep them safe. MacMurray was going to tell about us.

"The coyote. I told you. I did kill the coyote." He took a breath. "I knew her from over to the Morton Ranch when I'd be with Evangeline. That coyote had gotten after the sheep one too many times. I couldn't stop MacMurray, so, I somehow needed to stop her. What I did with her, the way I did it, the knife, that was pure meanness and I'm sorry for it. And the table. And the note. After my Evangeline and the baby girl died, I was mad at ever thing in the world. Including you, Doney."

Those were the hardest words Dona could remember Luke ever saying. Maybe all of this was a kind of relief for him, to confess his love, repent the coyote, to tell of the murder of his family, and the blackmail. She did not know who or what could help them now.

Chapter Twenty-seven

"What a savage country this is, Melvar," Dona said. And she told him Luke's story.

"It is savage. It is cruel. And I grieve for Luke. And, your grandmother. There is much sadness to be had. But, Dona, in spite of everything, what a beautiful country this is."

It was the next morning, fine and clear for early August. Roy and Luke and Joe Bob had left for the rodeo. Dona, leading Duke by the reins, had walked beside Melvar in his wagon to a mesquite grove at the river's dam. She leaned against the wagon as Melvar jumped to the ground and reached high to pluck a pod from a young tree.

"Here, open this, Dona."

"Yes, I know, it's sweet. As fresh as spring water. The cows eat them, and I've chewed on them all my life."

"But did you ever notice?"

"Notice? How a mesquite pod tastes?"

"Yes, here is another one. Open it as slowly as you can."

Dona dropped Duke's reins.

"Put your nose close."

"Yes, like new grass."

"Run your tongue along the opening, slowly."

"It's almost more than I can bear, the sweetness, the soft wet tiny peas."

"Now rub the open pod along your lips. Let your teeth barely scrape the inside."

"Oh, Melvar. I can't go on."

"And why is that, my friend?"

"I can't tell you. I am ashamed."

"Of how you are feeling?"

"Yes. I'm afraid of what you know."

"About you?"

"Yes."

Melvar took the mesquite pod from Dona's cupped hands and placed it on a root of the tree. He stood, stretching his back, and said, "You know the hill? The high pasture, as you call it?"

"Of course."

"When were you last there?"

"Yesterday. After that mighty hard talk with Luke. A line of quail chicks paraded after their mother hen. I go up there ever chance I get. Partly to make sure nobody's at the Sheepherder's Hut."

"And partly?"

"Because I feel better there, than almost anywhere."

Dona rested her back against a tree, removed her hat and shook out her hair. "I love the sounds. The world opens and you can hear the silence. I mean, not silence exactly, but more the feeling of space. It's round and whole, and leaves of the live oaks click and whisper. Everything whispers up there, in a way. I can't describe it, really. But in the quiet I can hear things I can't hear anyplace else."

"The eyes, the ears, the tongue, the nose, the tips of our fingers hold a kind of magic," Melvar said. "You can bring yourself anywhere you love through your body; or to anyone you love enough. I have brought myself to you."

"What do you mean?"

"I mean, I love you, Dona. More than this real world can understand."

He opened his arms and she stepped inside of a universe she had yearned to know. They swayed together, entwined like branches of a willow tree, until their breathing slowed and their hearts held the same rhythm.

"And what do you think of our savage country now?" Melvar's cheek rested against her hair.

"It's also beautiful. But I don't know how to love someone I cannot be with."

Melvar shook his head, his black curls falling from behind his ears onto his cheeks. "I can say only for myself, for I have loved you since we were children. I have never ceased loving you."

A small branch foundered in heavy waters against the dam. It roiled and went under, surfaced, broken end first, and again was caught in the current.

"That's how I feel," Dona said. "Like that branch, pulled from a willow, making its way after a cloudburst as best it can."

It seemed like a long time before Dona slid from her saddle and led Duke toward the tack room, but in fact on a good day, the ride from river to ranch house took less than twenty minutes. And after she had relieved Duke of the saddle, blanket and bridle, and after he had nipped the carrot pieces from her palm, and rolled in the corral's dust, and halted by the fence to whinny to Paint, she turned toward the ranch house. Her boots were as heavy as her heart.

"This will not do," she said, loudly. "Chin up, spurs on." Which made her feel a slight bit better, sounding like her granddaddy. She had gotten herself into a mess, the likes of which she could not have imagined.

Chapter Twenty-eight

Nobody answered. She had tried seven times. Her mother was usually at home now, the middle of the day growing hot. Dona wished Bertie was still the telephone operator, but ever since that day when they had coffee at Luby's, Bertie had been nowhere around. In fact, Dona was worried about her, and Samuel's family. How on earth did Melvar think Bertie could manage all of that? The whole world seemed dangerous right now.

Where was Roy? The north pasture, maybe, seeing to those new heifers. Yes, he must be there with Joe Bob and Luke; maybe Juan Carlos. Josie was cleaning the bunkhouse and Annalou was at Ophelia's, so despite their resolve as a family to keep their guns near at hand and at least two people in the ranch house and barnyard at all times, she was alone in the house; and what if someone came gunning for her again?

Why, anybody could come into the barnyard. Anybody could push open the screen door and come right on in this kitchen.

"Buck up, girl," she said, aloud, "you don't have to act like a lily-livered coward, even if you feel like one."

It was time to make chicken and dumplings. Dumplings made a person feel better. The only problem was, you had to kill a chicken to make chicken and dumplings.

Dona shoved on her barn boots, stomped off the porch and through the dust to the barrel near the barn and grabbed a handful of scratch. "Here chick, chick," she called.

It was old Muffy's time to go, and when Dona bent to catch her neck, Muffy flew a few feet away, her eyes sparkling like blackberries. "You old thing," Dona laughed. "You know, don't you." But Muffy scurried out of Dona's reach as fast as her short legs would go, the feathers of her ample rear waddling toward the mesquite tree where she flew to its highest branch.

"You are one smart chicken. You want to live forever. Well, don't we all. Remember, old girl, if you don't come to me, the chicken hawk is bound to get you."

Muffy was unmoved, her wings alert, looking as though she were about to crow.

"All right, Muffy, take your chances. We'll see how old Roy takes to dumplings and collard greens for supper, with extra pepper. I've got to get myself ready for tomorrow. It's me and Eleanor MacMurray and the Women's Auxiliary. I'll take my courage from you."

Chapter Twenty-nine

Eleanor MacMurray stood before the Southern Baptist Women's Auxiliary, not remembering one thing she had learned in elocution class in high school. She was not at home in this room. She was the wife of the Southern Presbyterian minister, and she did not know much about Southern Baptists. But right now, she judged that she was not among friends. Except for Dona and Ophelia; except for Pauline Evans, whom she had known at church camp before Pauline defected to the Baptists, Eleanor peered out at faces she saw only when she went shopping.

Dona admired the determined set of Eleanor's shoulders, her practical and polished black pumps, tied just so and lined up exactly side by side; but her eyes, the way they danced from place to place in the room, were a filly's eyes, alert and suspicious of everyone around her.

Ophelia stood close to Eleanor and took her elbow. She raised her voice to the crowd of about fifty women. "Our guest today deserves an introduction beyond what has already been said. Eleanor MacMurray is a well-educated woman with a degree in biology from Texas Tech. She's smart as a whip and has courageously led the fight to improve the schools for all children, right here in our county. If you don't already know her well, I hope you will find time to have coffee with her after this meeting. Eleanor, welcome to the Women's Auxiliary of the First Baptist Church."

Ophelia clapped her welcome and beckoned the women in the audience to join her, which Dona and some of the members did.

Eleanor glanced at the cards she held in her hands and put them on the table.

"There is little more important in making a strong and healthy community than the education of its people," she said. A murmur of agreement rippled through the crowd. Eleanor squared her shoulders.

"The more we know, the more thoughtful, the more productive, and the more useful we can be to those in our midst, whose lives are crippled by ignorance and who lack the basic ability to read. Why, did you know that in some places in this great country it is illegal for a Negro to learn to read and write?"

Hat brims shook across the room.

"What if you yourself could not read? Could not write letters to your families far from here? What if you could not read books about other lives, or papers reporting the news of the county and of the world; or magazines telling of lands where you will never travel; or what if you couldn't read a grocery bill; or what if the crumpled paper that says how many pounds of cotton you picked by the end of a week of back breaking labor was a mystery to you? Think about this." Eleanor paused for a sip of water and surveyed the room.

"You can see that reading gives you the power to decide for yourself what is fair and right for you and your family. Doesn't everyone, every human being, deserve that right?"

Eleanor MacMurray stood at her full height, turned from the speaker's table with its bouquet of gladiolus, and raised her eyes above the stolid, upright piano, to the painting that had hung on the room's front wall for as long as the oldest woman among them could recall. Eleanor gestured toward the painting, dim in its plain wooden frame.

"As you consider how whites and the colored should relate, as you consider the law, recall this parable from the Gospel of John, Chapter 4. Think of Christ's words as he stood between the angry scribes and Pharisees and the Samaritan woman at the well. It was unknown for a Jew such as Jesus to speak to a Samaritan, let alone a woman, and yet he asked her for a drink of water from the well. Pharisees condemned him for that, like our husbands have condemned Samuel Washington for saying, yes, when I suggested that I help him with his reading. I have been condemned for meeting with him after dark. Samuel was pursued by a lynch mob. But so far, I have not been persecuted. And you all know why."

Eleanor turned toward the audience. "I ask you to consider the acts of Jesus in your hearts as you ponder what you will say to your husbands about Samuel; about the Ku Klux Klan; and the education of the Negro and Mexican. Who among us does not want to read and write? Does not want our children to advance? Should it be different because of the color of our skin?"

"Yes," a voice said loudly from the back of the room. All heads turned toward the rear. It was Reverend Chester Scott, minister of this Baptist church.

"I am sorry, Reverend Scott, but Mrs. MacMurray has the floor," Ophelia said, turning to Eleanor. "Mrs. MacMurray, please continue with what you have to say."

"No," said the Reverend Scott, louder than before. "This is my church and I have the floor."

"Sir," said Pauline Evans, rising to face the minister. "Sir, this is the Lord's church; this room belongs to the work of the Lord; we are the women's auxiliary of this church; we and our guests have the floor until we are willing to give it up."

Chester Scott's face turned the red of raw beef. "Well, I'll be," he said, "I'll be..."

"You will be leaving now, Reverend Scott," said Ophelia in the firm, lilting voice she usually reserved for wayward children. "We will be glad to welcome you back for coffee and cake when we are through with our program. Go ahead, please, Eleanor."

"Thank you, Ophelia. Thank you, members of the auxiliary, for staying with us. I want you to know, straight from me, the real story of what happened between me and Samuel Washington."

Not an eye in the room strayed from Eleanor's face. Not an ear was turned away.

"Samuel worked for us for several years and I know him to be a highly intelligent, capable and reliable man, so when he told me he regretted that he had never learned to read well enough to read books, I said, I am a teacher, Samuel. I can teach you. Let me say to all of you in this room, that what I saw in that man's eyes were tears. Of gratitude. Perhaps of disbelief.

"He wanted to make sure that the lessons would be outside of his working hours, and that my husband would agree. He arranged that his family would bring his supper on the Saturday evenings when we would be at the kitchen table with a lesson book and that all blinds would be up and windows open. I was the one who was naïve; thinking, of course, that teaching someone to read is a perfectly fine thing to do."

"I do not know why, after two weeks of lessons in full knowledge of my husband, our arrangement became suspect, but over a month ago, during our lesson, Samuel got word through his family that a posse of men, masked in white hoods, was on the way to seize him because of his sinful relations with me, a white woman. It was a terrible lie, and one day we will know who started it, but for Samuel it was a death threat. He bolted immediately, but came right back to ask me to watch after his family's safety. Then he ran for his life. This is what I know from my own experience, and by the Holy Bible, it is the truth. Thank you for listening." Eleanor sat down.

Pauline Evans was the first to remove her gloves and clap; few in the room failed to remove theirs.

As the applause lessened, Pauline Evans raised her hand. "Eleanor." Her voice wavered. "Who was in that posse?"

"Samuel had run out the door, when the men in the mob burst into my kitchen. They wore their masks, so I had to judge from their voices and their clothes, but I can identify several of them."

"Would we know them?" Pauline said.

"I do believe the wives of several of them are in this room. But I am not here to accuse anyone. What I will say is that, as wives, we may lack the public standing to change things in our county, but we have a lot of influence at home. And if you know that your husband is a member of the Ku Klux Klan, and you know that the Klan is responsible for doing horrible things to Negroes and Mexicans, you do not have to stand by. In fact, you can condemn the slaughter of your fellow human beings, and know that you are in the right."

"What if we agree with them?" said a woman's voice from the back row.

"Then," said Eleanor, "you must reconcile your beliefs as a Christian with treating others as less than you. Look into the eyes of your maids, your gardeners, the men who sweep the streets. See if you find someone more like yourself than different; someone with a family, someone who works hard, and should have all of the rights we have in this country. And ask yourself why, simply because of the color of your skin, you feel you are superior. We all have a lot to learn, and we can do many things to restore peace to our county."

"Thank you, Eleanor," Ophelia said, "I think we have time for one more question. Yes, Sylvia, go ahead."

"Do you think your husband is a member of the Klan, Eleanor?"

A wave of murmurs passed through the room, and when it became quiet, Eleanor said, "Yes, Sylvia, I know he is."

"How?"

"He has handed his Klan hood to me on several occasions, to wash, starch and iron, apparently following an incident in which mud and something that appeared to be blood were involved.

"I have asked him about it, and he has always said, the Klan is protected by freedom of speech. Yes, I have said, its speech is protected, but not illegal actions. It is not only morally wrong to persecute any other person, but you can also go to jail. My husband, who as you know is a minister, has never responded to that. I, like you, have been at a loss, until now."

"What do you mean, until, now?" Sylvia said.

"I am here, speaking with you, some of the most influential women in our county, and I am asking all of us not to cooperate with the illegal acts of the Klan. In some places in this country, that would mean going to the law. But of course, in this county, members of law enforcement are apparently members also of the Klan."

"I urge each of you to go home and talk with your husband and your children about how it is illegal to lynch someone, to take the law into your own hands. Our speech is also protected by law, but it has to be protected by more than that for us to speak out. It must be protected by respect for each other, across all color lines, by forgiveness, by understanding and compassion. Perhaps, love. In the whole community. That's the only real protection."

"And what can women do," asked Ophelia, "beyond what you have said, Eleanor?"

"Speak up. So many of us, called the weaker sex, are cowed by our husbands, or our neighbors, our preachers, our own view of ourselves. Speak out and hold on to each other. A wave of women can be more powerful than anything. It took a long time for us to get the vote, but we did it here in Texas, two years before the rest of the country. We can work for equality and justice. That is all I can say today, my friends, and I thank you again for your attention and care. We all need the support of each other. You have mine."

Perhaps for the first time in their long history, members of the women's auxiliary stood from their chairs to applaud a speaker. And many came forward to shake this speaker's hand.

In her white uniform, waiting at the back of the room to serve the coffee and cake, was Mattie Hadley, wife of Samuel Washington's first cousin, Abraham, the very person who had been cleaning behind the bar at the Longhorn Saloon, and warned Samuel of the lynch mob. Mattie could not wait to spread the word of Eleanor MacMurray's speech.

"YOO-HOO, DONA!" Ophelia called from the dooryard.

Dona wiped her face with her apron and tidied her hair. "Mother," she said, opening the screen door to the porch. "Come on in. What are you doing here?"

"I tried to call," Ophelia said, breathing hard. "Something terrible has happened. Eleanor MacMurray, she's in the hospital now."

"What?"

"Last night, after she'd gone to bed, she was beaten horribly and left for dead. Nearly every bone in her face crushed, and she may be blind."

"Was MacMurray there?"

"No."

"Who found her?

"Thelma Washington. Samuel's aunt. Eleanor pays her to wash and iron the Reverend's white shirts. She picks them up from the sun porch every Saturday. There weren't any, which was unusual. She tried the back door, which was unlocked, also unusual, called out for Mrs. MacMurray and bless her, she heard Eleanor moan from back in the house."

"You think it was MacMurray did it?"

"Looks like it. Thelma found a note shoved into Eleanor's poor hands with some words scribbled from the Bible about adultery and being a whore and not obeying, and signed, 'Your Faithful Husband.' Maybe wanted to be caught?"

"Or credited," Dona said.

"I went to the hospital as soon as Doc Steward called," said Ophelia, "and Thelma was sitting in the hall outside of Eleanor's room, all hunched over, holding on to herself. We hugged each other, through many tears, and she told me what she knew."

"And Eleanor? Will she live?"

"Doc Steward didn't say much. He seemed mighty upset, though. It was my idea to ask her to talk to the women's auxiliary, and oh, my heavens, I put her in mortal danger."

"You didn't know, you couldn't know. Evil is moving through our county, a lot worse than any of us would ever suspect. But Mother, this is Sunday, and where is Reverend MacMurray?"

"Nowhere to be found."

THE WINDOWS OF HOSPITAL ROOM 214 were gray with evening light when Dona heard her friend's rusted voice.

"What name?" Eleanor's eyes, blue-black and raccoon-ringed, peered through gauze walls and inquired of Dona.

"I'm Dona Willis. I'm your friend. What is your name?'

"Don't know, Dona Willis."

"Your name is Eleanor. What do you remember?"

"Head, crash, hurt face, hurt. Know you?" Her words pushed through jaws wired together.

"Yes, Eleanor. We used to be in the same church."

Eleanor winced. "Church. Hurts."

"Yes, I can see how it would. Eleanor, do you want to know what happened to you?"

"No."

"Eleanor, you've got a long way to go. But you're a fighter and that's why you're alive at all. Keep your courage up as much as you can. We're keeping you safe. Here, try to take some water through this straw."

"Safe?"

"A policeman stands outside your room. They'll find your, uh, the person who did this to you. And he will go to jail for a long time."

"He?"

"Yes."

"Know him?"

"Yes."

"So tired."

"Of course, please take a little water and I'll sit over here for a while so you can rest."

"When I rise."

Dona turned toward the bed. "Eleanor, what did you say, dear? When you what?"

"Rise," Eleanor said, "be with me."

"Oh, I will, I will. And you will rise, I promise. With a heart like yours, yes."

"Heart of Gila."

"Heart of what, honey?"

"Gila."

"Of Gila. Gila Monster? Oh, Eleanor. Yes. The Gila Monster never lets go. Was that a joke?"

Eleanor's eyes closed over the pain of moving her head. "No choke."

"Okay, we'll have that between us. That fierce lizard and your courage. Yes?"

"Yesh."

"I will see you early tomorrow morning. The policeman is here all night long."

Dona stopped outside Eleanor's hospital room door to pull on her white gloves. She stood beside Peter Malloy, a young man she'd known when he was a boy. He was tall, now, and stood straight. He did not glance at her when she said, "Officer Malloy, it's good to see you again."

His eyes wavered only slightly as he said, "Good afternoon, Mrs. Turn."

"So, you are one of Mrs. MacMurray's guards. Thank you very much. She needs to be protected."

He said nothing. His face might well have been a photograph.

"Does she need protecting, do you think, Peter?"

Startled, he looked at Dona. "What did you say, ma'am?"

"Does Mrs. MacMurray need to be protected?"

"I," he stammered, resuming his stare at the wall across from Room 214. "I don't know."

"Do you know what happened to her?"

"I am not permitted to discuss it, Mrs. Turn," he said, his ruddy face growing redder.

"I am worried, Peter. I'm afraid that her attacker will return to kill her. Is that why you are here?"

"Yes, ma'am."

"And do you know who her attacker was?"

"I am not permitted . . ."

"Yes, I know, but do you?" The pupils of his eyes grew wide, and his breathing became shallow. "Yes, of course you do. And I understand that you are not at liberty..."

"No, not at liberty."

"All right, then, and thank you for doing your duty. I can imagine it is hard, since you've known the Reverend MacMurray since you were in my Sunday School class. And you've known Mrs. MacMurray even better. Wasn't she your reading teacher in second grade?"

"Yes, ma'am."

"Then I know you will take care of her. And that whatever you have to do, you will do. I'll be back tomorrow. May I shake your hand? And please pardon my gloves."

DONA'S SHOULDERS ACHED as though she had wrestled a steer. What had to change, in her view, was always the same thing. Men. They could be brutes and they could count on other men to stand up for them. Young Peter was afraid. Perhaps of MacMurray. Who among the men was not blaming Eleanor for what her insane husband did to her? And yet, nearly every woman she knew would take Eleanor's side. They'd all been beat up one time or another, one way or another. By a father, or a brother, or a husband.

Eleanor would live, with good medical help. She would be maimed and who knew if she would get her memory back? And if she did, would she remember who had tried to kill her? And if she remembered, would she tell the truth? There was that note, and Eleanor was brave.

NOTHING WAS AS DONA EXPECTED IT TO BE when she approached Room 214 the next morning. Instead of a policeman on duty, a woman with mop and bucket, a red bandana wrapped around her head, was swabbing the floor near the room's open door. Eleanor's bed had been moved against the back wall and the privacy curtains were tied up and out of the way. Dona excused herself to the cleaning woman and stepped across the wet linoleum to the center of the room.

"Oh, no," she said, and the walls echoed in their cold, bare voices. Dona bowed her head, pulled out the hatpin that held her cloche and put the hat over her heart. "Oh, no," she whispered, "not that."

The woman with the mop stood in the doorway and in a moment said, her voice hoarse and deep, "I am sorry, missus. She was family?"

Dona wiped the tears from her face and turned toward the woman. "She was my friend, my good friend. Do you know anything about how she died?"

"Don't know, but I heard something of it early this morning. Coming in to work, dontcha know."

"Could I ask, what did you hear?"

"Heard she fell out of bed and died."

"Fell out of bed?"

"What I heard."

"Do you know about what time?"

"Heard it was about 3:00 o'clock this early mornin'."

"And where'd they take her?"

"Down to the morgue, I reckon. Usual way. It's in the basement."

"Yes, I remember. And the policeman who was here?"

"Young Peter?"

"Yes, young Peter."

"Nice boy."

"Yes, and I wonder if you know where he might have gone?"

"He went with the body, with Mrs. MacMurray, I hear. Official business, dontcha know."

"Thank you, Mrs. And would you mind giving me your name?"

"Don't mind at all. I'm Meaghan Malloy. Peter's my cousin's son. And you are Dona Willis, married to Roy Turn."

"And how might you know that?"

"It's a little county. And now, if you will excuse me, I have to finish this room. People waiting for it, they told me."

Now, with eyes closed as when she was a girl, Dona walked the hall, knowing the hospital: its sharp scents of ether, iodine, alcohol, bleach; the tiles, smooth under her shoes; voices whispering, meant not to be heard; air moving, when a body came near. Her daddy helped to start this place, gathered the men of the county together, bankers, preachers, lawyers, ranchers, the owner of the general store, the blacksmith. They raised money in every way they could, and one brick at a time, it was built and paid for. The clinic, they called it, so as not to be grand. And the nurses who lived next door would invite her in, and she watched them starch, iron, and fold their caps, and pin them to their hair, pulled into buns. She wished she would one day be so beautiful.

Many times, when she was a child, Dona had slipped down the hospital's back stairs all the way to the basement, through the big, white swinging doors to the morgue. It fascinated her, this place of death and dismemberment, for it was where the county coroner, and sometimes her daddy, cut up bodies. And sometimes it was where murders were solved.

It was not a place that allowed people like her, these days. Her daddy was gone and rules were official and stiffly followed. But Eleanor had not rolled out of bed all by herself, that was certain. And if she was dead, her body would be there, and Dona had to know.

Except for three steel gurneys lined up like railroad cars, the small, cold room was empty. Dona pinned her hat on her head, taking comfort in the warm, familiar felt, and drew her jacket close. She had to find Emanuel Bowen, the doctor in charge.

Dona shoved and the door of the morgue closed with a thump. Eleanor dead? Where was her body, if she was dead? That young policeman, that young Malloy, maybe he'd been fed a line of bull. Where was that Dr. Bowen?

She climbed the back stairs to the main floor of the hospital, two steps at a time, grateful for chores and horses and sacks of feed over her shoulder to keep her strong. She charged through the swinging doors next to reception and peered around to see who was there. Seemed to be nobody. "Hello," she said, "who's on duty?"

"Why, hello, Dona," said a small voice from under the desk.

"Who's that?"

"It's me, I'll be right up."

Dona folded her hands together, lowered her shoulders and tried to look composed when a woman, as lithe as Annalou, emerged.

"Bertie!"

"Yes, didn't you know I was working here now? I'm the telephone operator. Had to unscramble some cords under there."

"Oh, Bertie. No, I thought you were taking care of, well, you know..."

"I do know," Bertie said, smiling. "But I am fine." She lowered her voice. "I'll have a break soon; can I meet you in the back garden?"

Dona nodded until her hat was askew. And then she said, loudly, "Good to see you again. I'm glad you are well. Bye-bye."

Not for the first time, Dona wondered, as she sat herself on the stone bench of the garden where patients and their families escaped every day from the confines of the hospital, if Bertie was a witch. Like Melvar, she showed up at the strangest times, always with some way of helping Dona out of a hard place. Once, with the little blue box that seemed to have special powers.

Apparently, she had disappeared as the county's public telephone operator to take in Samuel and his family until they could reach safety at Unity Ann's ranch. And today, she was working at the hospital.

Maybe she had heard about Eleanor. Was she alive or was she dead? If she was still alive, who was protecting her? If she was dead, where on earth was her body? And where was that good-for-nothing husband who tried to kill her? Bertie knew everything about everybody in the county, so she must have heard plenty.

Dona had a good mind to call the police station and see if Officer Peter Malloy was still on duty. She worried about the coincidence of the woman mopping the empty, echo-filled Room 214, being Officer Peter's mother's cousin. Was the county really that small? Dr. Bowen, could he be trusted to take care of Eleanor? Would he want her dead? And her husband, the Reverend, crazy as a loon, maybe he got past Peter Malloy's police guard at her door, and kidnapped her. Oh, Lord, where was Bertie?

At that, the hospital's double glass doors opened between two crepe myrtle bushes and cool air laced with disinfectant rushed out into the garden, causing the portulaca to tremble. Bertie stuck out her head, and when she spied Dona, she bent over and crept to the nearby pyracantha bush. "Don't look at me, Dona," she said in a stage whisper. "I mean, I am not here."

"Tell me what I should know, Bertie," Dona said, her own whisper harsh and insistent.

"Mrs. MacMurray is alive," Bertie said from inside the bush. "She is on her way in an ambulance to Houston, to St. Luke's Hospital. No one must know. I mean, they've got to think she is dead."

"Because they will kill her if she isn't?"

"I guess that is it."

"Who arranged it, her going to St. Luke's and all?"

"Dr. Bowen, he did it. Lots of phone calls." Bertie moved around the back of the bush, closer to Dona. She whispered, "You know about him and Eleanor, don't you?"

"No. Bertie, you don't mean they've . . ."

"Yes, for years. But he's got to act like he blames her. I understand it, don't you?"

"Oh, great heavens. Bertie, this is wonderful news. I mean that Eleanor is going to get help. I've heard about the woman at St. Luke's. The plastic surgeon. I know she'll want to help Eleanor."

"I can't talk any longer," Bertie said. "You stay right here and admire the trees, and I'll go back inside to my desk. But call me soon, if you can. There are no party lines here at the hospital, thank heavens."

Dona heard a smile in her voice and smiled back. "Thank you, Bertie, wherever you are."

But she felt the hot breath of doubt on her neck. It seemed too perfect, somehow, that Bertie would know all of that, and tell it to Dona. But maybe doubt was her nature; maybe for once she could believe. She wanted to believe, Lord knows. She would call Bertie, as she had promised. And she would make another call, too. But right now, she was going to find Meaghan Malloy.

"Sorry, Mrs. Turn," said Nurse Spence from behind the second floor's nurses' desk, "I don't know anybody by the name of Meaghan Malloy."

"She's a cleaning woman. She was in Room 214 early this morning, mopping the floor."

"Well, let me call the maintenance office."

"No, I mean, please. Tell me where the maintenance office is, and I'll go there myself."

"It's a couple of floors down. Why not call?"

"If you don't mind, I'll walk. Good exercise."

"All right, it's in the sub-basement, on the north end of the building, near the morgue."

"I know right where that is, thank you so much."

The hallway through the middle of the sub-basement grew progressively dark as she headed north. Where was everyone? Across the top of a bank of doors, a metal sign read, 'Maintenance and Service Department.' She pushed open the door on the far right.

"Come in, Mrs. Turn. We heard you were on your way."

A battalion of brooms and mops hung neatly against the far side of the windowless room. Above, waited a squadron of buckets, dust pans and cans of Bab-O, and in front, almost at attention, was Meaghan Malloy, red bandana tight around her head. On the beige linoleum floor, under one of her feet, lay Reverend Andrew MacMurray. And next to MacMurray's head stood Officer Peter Malloy.

"Meaghan, Peter! What on earth?"

"Glad you came down, Dona," Meaghan said. "Officer Malloy tells me this bastard tried to sneak into his wife's room upstairs. Guess he wanted to finish the job he started on her. Came down here looking for her body. Tried to kill me, but I knocked him out with my broom. Be careful. He could come to any minute. Help me tie his hands."

Dona dropped her purse by the door and hurried across the slick tiles. The steam of an iron on wet cloth wafted from another room, and the reassuring scent of bleach.

"I'm not here to make trouble. I've been trying to find Mrs. MacMurray, too. And now I see the Reverend right where I hoped he would be. Except there aren't any bars on these darned doors. What can we do with him?"

"Peter here," Meaghan said, gesturing toward her cousin, "he has the cutest things and he's going to give them to us. They call them handcuffs."

Dona laughed. "Yes, the right tool for the right job. Good for you, Officer Pete."

When they had secured the Reverend's hands behind his back and tied him to an old kitchen table below the mops and brooms, Peter said, "Now that things are under control, I'm calling the Chief."

"Can we trust the Chief?" said Dona.

"You bet we can. He hates the Reverend."

"Knows a bunch about him, I'll bet."

"Yep, a big ole bunch. Bad fellow, this Reverend. And that poor wife of his, all bashed in."

"She's in the ambulance on her way to Houston, I hear."

"Yes ma'am. Don't know how you heard about it, but she's going to get some good help."

"Mrs. Turn," Meaghan called from across the room, "Reverend MacMurray is waking up. Do you want to say anything to him?"

"What I want is too hateful to say out loud, even to that low-life scum of the earth. You get him settled at the jail, and I'll go upstairs and check on a couple of things. I have got to get back to the ranch this afternoon or my family will disown me."

DONA'S HEELS ECHOED down the hall of the hospital's main floor toward the reception desk. Bertie, enmeshed in earphones and wires, was speaking earnestly into her operator's mouthpiece. Dona sat her purse on the desk and Bertie said loudly, "Yes, sir, I'll give him the message. Thank you and goodbye."

"What's happening, Dona?" Bertie smiled.

"Bertie, do you know who is in that ambulance with Eleanor MacMurray?"

"Well, Dr. Bowen was going."

"Is there any way to reach the ambulance, to make sure she's safe?"

"There's the two-way radio right here."

"Do you know how to use it, and all?"

"Maybe I do. Is this an official call from you?"

"It is. Thanks, Bertie. It's official."

Bertie handled the radio like she'd used it for years, static blossoming from its voice box. She spoke, and someone spoke back, but Dona could not distinguish one word from another. She felt her ribs grow tight around her breath and she squeezed her nails into her palms until she felt the breath release.

"Bertie, please," she said, leaning over the desk. "Get the medic in charge of the ambulance. Now. We've got to know..."

"This is Dr. Bowen," said a voice that could have been his.

"Dr. Bowen," she said into the center of Bertie's hand, "this is Dona Willis Turn, tell me how Eleanor MacMurray is doing, please? And how far are you from Houston?"

The answers she got made her smile, and that was enough for Bertie, who wiped her eyes on a tattered, exquisitely embroidered handkerchief. For a moment, she was a child in Persia with someone who loved her, who cared what touched her skin.

"Bertie, call the police."

Bertie stared toward the hospital's front doors. "I already did, and here he is."

"Chief Tolland," Dona said, "thank heavens you are here. The person you want is in the maintenance room, in handcuffs."

"Perhaps the world will end today, Dona," Bertie said, her face wet with feeling. "You never know. But before it does, I want to say I love you, and all you have done for me, Melvar, and Samuel, and Eleanor. And all the people in this county, except certain white men."

"The world is not going to end and I've done nothing, not so far, anyway. And now that the Chief has Reverend MacMurray and now that Eleanor MacMurray is in St. Luke's Hospital in Houston, and Doctor Bowen is in charge, at least we can rest for the time being. Can't we?"

"You can, Dona. I'm on duty for a few more hours here at the switchboard. It's all right. It's nice and peaceful here." She chuckled at her joke and held out her hand. "I can't say it's been a pleasure to be with you today, but there's nobody else I'd rather go through hell with."

Stars floated in the black sky's sea when Dona pulled in next to the barn. She let the engine of her old car cough to a stop and stepped out onto bare ground. The ranch house was dark except for the unsteady light of the kitchen's kerosene lamp as it hung over the table.

"It can't be too late," she muttered to herself. "There's the evening star, still up. Waiting for my wish. And what do I wish? I wish for nearly dawn. I wish for chickens around my boots looking for food. I wish not to know about lynch mobs and hypocrites and liars."

She slung her purse over her shoulder and held up her hands to look at them against the sky. In the dark, even there, her skin gleamed like limestone. "Maybe white skin is a curse. Maybe it always covers hatred and cowardice. Cowardice like mine."

Annalou rushed from the porch, flung her arms around Dona's waist, and buried her face in Dona's shoulder. "Aunt Doney, where have you been so long?"

Tears choked Dona's throat and no words would be enough. They stood together, swaying and holding on until the evening star wheeled toward the west.

"I am so sorry, Annalou. I will tell you all about it when we're not so tired. Where I have been, it's not a happy place."

Buster's crowing pulled them apart, announcing that the night was half over. Dona laughed and squeezed Annalou's arm. "He's telling us to get out of his barnyard, you know."

Annalou nodded, her hair catching starlight. "I put back some beans and corn pone for you, Aunt Doney. And some buttermilk. And sliced tomatoes from the garden. You hungry?"

"I am famished, child, and you are a wonder. Let me get a few things from the car and I'll be right behind you."

"And I'm right behind you, Dona. And I'm mightily glad you're back."

"Oh, Luke." She turned toward the voice of this brother who was crazy as a peach- orchard boar. She held him by the shoulders and tried to see his face. "Are you okay?"

"I'm better now, Sister, now I hear that scum is in jail. Wished I'd put him there, myself."

"Let's go in and have a midnight supper, what do you think, Luke? How about Roy? He here?"

"Nope. Took off like a barn rat running for cover, just this afternoon."

"And Joe Bob?"

"He's on the ranch, I'm right sure. But maybe at the shacks or maybe at the Hut." Luke ducked his head into the deep shadows and said, "He wants to talk to you, I reckon. We was all glad to hear about you coming home."

"Who told you?"

"Why, Bertie. She got through on the danged party line. Said everything's better. You was coming on back."

"Bless her heart, that Bertie. I'd trust her with my life."

"Let's go eat," Luke said. "You've earned us some supper."

Chapter Thirty

"It is all here, Dona, all we need to find our way."

They sat under the mesquite tree next to the ranch house. Dona snapped the ends from green beans, Melvar worked a piece of wood with his pocket knife.

"What is all here? I've told you about Luke, how he killed that coyote, about his murdered wife and baby. You already know from Bertie about Eleanor. Is that what's all here?"

"In our hands. In anybody's hands. Like geese, like hummingbirds, we know to do these things, we know our way home."

"You mean, like instinct?"

"Something like instinct. Deeper. In my country, it is said that we are made of stars. And that we may follow the stars to find our way. My friends among the old Indians say that what you call the Milky Way, is a sacred road."

"I believe it is, myself. There are many sacred roads. And, sometimes I know things, too."

"What kinds of things?"

"Things I can't touch or see or hear, but I can feel them. Like when I am with you, now, there is something quiet, something at peace in you that speaks to me like a prayer. But I have a bad feeling when I think of how I love Luke and the trouble he has inside, and a terrible feeling when I think of Reverend MacMurray."

"What is that feeling?"

Dona turned from Melvar toward a prickly pear cactus. The cactus had shriveled and turned yellow; black smudged the bottom of its leaves.

"In May, when this cactus seemed almost as dead as it does now in summer, a single flower bloomed out of its middle, as orange as a sunset. That is what I feel about the Reverend. He sucks the juice from his family, from the congregation, from the town, and uses it to show off his learning and to seem righteous. But there's something rotten at the heart of him. Do you think I'm strange to see things this way?"

Melvar bent to the ground and picked up the shell of a snail. "You are not strange. You are also not wrong. Reverend MacMurray is as empty as this shell. His soul has dried up and withered away and in its place is his shame. There is much a man will do to hide his shame."

"Maybe bring a mob to lynch an innocent man who knows his secrets?"

"Perhaps."

"Do you have a plan, Melvar? Some way to change things for the colored, like Samuel and Juan Carlos and their families?"

"I have a plan, but Dona, it is dangerous; perhaps more dangerous than being ambushed in the barnyard by those boys."

"You know, Melvar, the danger is not the important thing anymore. I am in this so far, and I see how we white people own everything, and we hire Mexicans and Negroes to do our dirtiest work and pay them practically nothing at all. I always took that as just the way things are. But no, that is the way we whites have made them. I mean, I have tried to close my eyes again, but I can't. It's like being an owl who cannot help but see in the dark."

"Joe Bob and I have talked together," Melvar said. "He says he will speak with his friends."

"Yes, so he told me. And that may help, and should I speak again with my cousin, Edward?"

"No, I most urgently request that you not speak with him quite yet."

"Why most urgently?"

"You know that he and Judge Angus Cameron are the poison at the heart of the Klan. They bear the burden of guilt most heavily, and yet Edward is unaware of his own feelings, as surely you have seen."

"Then, who can reach him?"

"I believe I can."

"You? Why you?"

"Your cousin Edward was Reverend Sinclair's lover, Dona. I may be the only person in the world who knows."

"Because you and Mr. Sinclair . . ."

"Yes, because of that. It was often when I was 14, that he would take my body for sex, and within a day, turn to your cousin who would be waiting for him in their secret place. I received many beatings as warnings never to reveal it."

"But, Melvar, the Klan hates homosexuals as much as it does Jews and Mexicans and Negroes."

"Yes, that is the truth. And that shows the power of your cousin."

"That is not his power, that is his shame," Dona said, walking away from Melvar toward the windmill.

Melvar followed and leaned closer than before. "It is his reason for hatred," he said softly, "that is powerful. For him it is life or death that others are victims. That the Klan go after colored men and not after him. It is deep in his body, this hatred. It is hatred for himself."

"So, you are a confidante of Edward's?"

"Confidante? I suppose you could say so. Others might say I am blackmailing your cousin."

"Why didn't he get his buddies in the Klan to go after you?"

"Because I have proof of his relationship with Mr. Sinclair. It is safe. It is hidden away and if I die in an unnatural way, the proof will be released. He is aware of that."

"I don't want to guess who would release it, but of course I have an idea."

"She would protect me with her life."

"But what if you were both killed?"

"Now you know the truth and the blue box holds the key to the location."

"By giving that blue box to me, you have put me in danger."

"No more than you were, my friend." Melvar tipped his hat and turned toward the barn.

"I had hoped Edward would pull back after you and your mother met with him, and, after the awful scene in your living room, and the psalm, he has, somewhat. Perhaps now I can obtain his promise to leave Samuel alone."

Dona walked after him and caught his arm. "And all of the others? All of the other colored people in his world. Will he also leave them alone?"

"I do not know." Melvar put his hand over hers. "Perhaps I could ask something of you?"

"Of course."

"You have an understanding heart. You listen. You can forgive. Perhaps he needs someone in his family to know him, know his history, and forgive him."

"But Melvar, you may not understand. I see nothing of his relationship with Reverend Sinclair to forgive."

"You do not?"

"No. What I feel, what I believe is sinful and hard to forgive is that Reverend Sinclair forced you into sexual acts. You were a child. He stole you. He would have killed you. That to me is sin. But what he did with Edward, it seems that it was the choice of both men. Am I right?"

"Yes, you are right."

"Then, you see, I am not opposed."

"But, Dona, Reverend Sinclair believed it was a sin. Relations between men. And Edward, he believes it is a sin. It is what torments him and causes him to torment others."

"That is because of religion, and you know what I think of religion."

"So, I see now, Dona, you are the right one to talk with him, not me. Perhaps you can help to take the hate from his soul and body."

Dona bowed her head toward the water trough. She closed her eyes. The two stood together, silent, each one feeling the weight of her decision. In a few moments, Dona raised her head, offered her hand to him and said, "I don't believe I am the one to do such a large thing. But if it will in any way bring peace to our county, I am willing to try."

Chapter Thirty-one

"I want to be brave with you, Edward. This has been very difficult for both of us."

"Yes, indeed, and you can't imagine how I loathe this moment."

"Perhaps I can. I may be a ranch woman, a country woman with only a junior college education. And you may be a man of letters and reputation, but I too have thoughts about what is going on with you."

"You are suspicious of me?"

"Of you, yes, and of what you're asking others to do on your behalf, of the undercurrent of violence that eddies around you and your friends. I'm talking of Samuel."

"You are talking of the pack of thieves who pursued him and wanted to hang him from the highest oak tree in our town."

"I am."

"You are speaking of the parley among ruffians, Ross and Dinky and their ilk who took up with the pack of thieves."

"I am."

"You are not talking of me."

"I'm not? Considering what you did in my living room?"

"No. You are mixed up and I think you will never get straight."

"And are you straight, Cousin?"

"Why am I answering to you, a woman, a lover of the colored, of colored men."

"And what of your love of men, Edward? I know of you and the Reverend Sinclair, and I know you suffered mightily because of your love for each other."

Edward shot from his chair and stood, his face swelling. "What lies are you believing now, Dona? What causes you to bring such an accusation?"

"Edward, I hold nothing of the sort against you. I merely know that you've been at the mercy of another who has proof of your relationship. I know what you did in love was illegal in the extreme, said to be deserving of terrible punishment, banishment, even hanging."

Edward examined her through narrowed eyes. "If that were true, you must surely also object."

"I don't judge you. I don't object. You and the Reverend Sinclair were grown men, you agreed."

"But the church..." said Edward.

"I often object to the church. I want you to help me save Samuel. I want you to help make this county safe for everybody. And I don't give a hill of beans about you and Sinclair. I want you to see how you and Samuel are in the same spot."

Edward pushed back his chair, ignoring for once the marks his hands left on the polished surface of the desk. He glanced toward the window that reminded him every day that he was an important man. It soared with an arched flourish to the ornate ceiling and held the august courthouse, public park and the center of town in its frame. He turned his back on Dona and stood, feet planted widely, with hands clasped behind his back. He drew a breath deep into his chest and as it puffed up before him, the shoulders of his coat straightened and grew broad.

"I am a lucky man," he said. "From here I am king of all I survey, the unelected leader of this entire county, the moral center of my church. And you, my esteemed second country cousin, you demand that I make this county safe? It is already safe, Dona. It is safe for the whites, for God's chosen ones."

Dona stood. She leaned on the desk toward him. "For certain whites it is safe, perhaps, Cousin Edward. Not for men like you and Reverend Sinclair. Not for women of any color—not for Jews, not for foreigners.

Not for Negro men or Mexican men. But I believe that you're also blessed, though you can't admit publicly who you are. Do you not agree?"

"Agree? If it were true, which it is not, that Sinclair and I loved each other in that way you mean, do you think I would be blessed to be half a man? Half a man who lost his other half? And no one to weep with me?"

"You are not half a man, Edward. You're as fully present as anyone I know. I need for you to see how you are not safe, for the same kind of reason that Samuel is in danger. For reasons of birth. You were born as someone drawn to love a man; Samuel was born Black, of ancestors who were slaves. You both stand to suffer terrible punishment, prejudice, and hatred, just for coming into the world the way you are. The way the world is."

Edward turned from the window and loosened his bow tie. "I am weary unto death. Let us abide together on the sofa. Please, take a seat."

She drew off her white cotton gloves, unpinned her hat and placed it and the gloves on the low table in front of the sofa. Her yellow skirt arranged itself around her calves as she crossed her ankles and turned her shoulders toward Edward, her back straight as a window pane.

"May I get you a glass of something, Dona?"

"Just water for me, thank you."

"Do you mind if I have...?"

"Not in the least."

Edward shuffled to a cabinet set low to the floor. A wooden cross hung above it and on it a Bible lay open. Inside the wide doors, bottles of whiskey lined up like cows in a storm.

"Edward, I've changed my mind. I'll have what you're having."

Edward filled two shot glasses, folded linen squares around them and handed one to Dona.

"To our family." He held out his glass.

"To our county," she said, and clicked her glass against his.

THREE HOURS LATER, the ceilings of the room were in darkness and sheets of long yellow paper covered the table. A banker's green shade gave faint light.

Dona's pumps sprawled under the table and Edward's coat lay akimbo on the sofa's arm. He rolled his shirt sleeves to his elbows as he poured the last of the bottle into their glasses.

"And this," Edward said, "is the first proclamation ever written in our county upholding the equality of every man."

"Every person," Dona said.

"I'll drink to that," said Edward.

"I especially like how we used 'Whereas' and 'Therefore' with such confidence. Helps to write with a lawyer, such as yourself," Dona said, grinning.

"It's not as good as the Emancipation Proclamation of old Abraham Lincoln, by the way also a lawyer, but it's pretty good for country folk, I'd say. And he didn't mention homosexuals like we did."

"And what do we do now, Edward? Post it on the courthouse doors? Once we declare our position in public, will we be pilloried on the courthouse lawn?"

"Great word, pilloried. How'd you learn that word, Dona, a woman like you?"

"You really are a misogynist, you know that don't you, Edward?"

He chuckled. "Yes, I suppose I am, but I want to get over it. It is a kind of disease, I see that, and it's contagious. Or else it's in our blood, I don't know. But I am proud to be your cousin, I can confess that to you. With the help of this good Kentucky bourbon."

"And I can confess that I'm proud to be yours. I believe you have the heart for a whole lot of good in the world. And I also know that your heart, like mine, has been scarred."

"By prejudice and fear," he said.

"What does that mean to you, Edward—prejudice and fear?" She could sense his legal mind working to define and explain the terms, so she said, "I mean, how did they affect you in your life?"

"Ah, I see. You want to know more about what has made me who I am. Why I lead others to hate and persecute the colored, women—he gestured toward her with a nod of his head—and homosexuals."

"All right, yes, that will do."

"It's simple really." He smoothed his shirt sleeves and buttoned the cuffs. "It has kept me above suspicion."

"By throwing light on the behavior of other people. But I wonder how you feel about doing that."

"I feel awful. It's not true that when Sinclair died, I was alone. Your daddy and I used to talk about it when your mother was not around. He was my confessor, my guide. He would not betray me, but after he died, I had no one."

"When did Arthur Sinclair die, I can't remember."

"Almost 25 years ago, now."

"When Melvar was 18. And Melvar knew."

"Yes."

"And were you jealous of him?"

"I hated him."

"Because Sinclair loved him, too?"

"Yes. And he was young and beautiful. And . . ."

"And?"

"And he was Sinclair's slave." Edward sat down hard on the edge of his desk. He fumbled for his handkerchief and wiped his forehead. "I don't know what Melvar has told you, Dona."

Dona pushed herself up against the low table where they had been drinking and writing, and stood in front of Edward.

"Melvar told me he hated Sinclair for what he did to him."

Edward covered his face with the handkerchief, arms tight against his chest. His back stretched and spasmed with sobs.

They stood facing each other. Dona, dry-eyed and steady.

"You and my father and Sinclair were the same age?"

"Yes." Edward gasped to breathe and spoke the word again. "Yes."

"Edward, I'm sorry for all you've lost. I miss my daddy these past years. And you have missed Arthur for twenty-five. Plus, my daddy, your best friend. I'm so sorry."

They sat in the large room, dark now except for the faint shine of a street light below. Dona held her hand toward Edward. "I'm your friend, I promise. My mother is also your friend. We can trust her with anything. We have a lot of work to do to become healthy again, the two of us."

"How come I never realized how smart you are, Dona?"

"Because I am a woman, and guess what misogynist means."

They laughed. They held their hands to their mouths and laughed and took them away and laughed. They bent over and hollered like children, and Edward cried himself to sleep, his head, arms and shoulders on his desk.

DONA SAT ON THE LEATHER SOFA, with her head in her hands, looking at what the night had brought. Edward's handwriting scrawled over the sheets of yellow paper, next to two bottles of bourbon whiskey, empty. "Oh Lord," she said, reaching for the yellow sheets, "let us see what have we done here."

Across the room, an ornate brass clock ticked without mercy. It was 4:00 in the morning. Roy would be at the barn, hens running at his feet. Surely he would feed them. Pansy's snorts and chortles would remind Josie that she was hungry. And Roy would not forget the horses. He would be mad as a wet rooster that she'd stayed at her mother's.

Dona gathered the yellow paper into a stack and shoved it in her purse. This was mighty valuable, and if Edward would remember what they had written, as drunk as they were, it could save Samuel; it could save a lot of necks. But it had to be typed. Dona closed the heavy door between Edward's office and Maureen's, his secretary, and dialed her number. She was an old friend from grade school, maybe she would help, even at such an hour.

At 9:00 am, Edward stirred, his bald head shining in early sun. A white vase with its single yellow rose had fallen last night under the thrust of his arm, scattering shards of glass over the oriental carpet. Beyond his nose, a pen in a crystal holder stood upright and ready, but this was not a day for writing briefs.

"Whatcha doin', Dona," Edward drawled against the polished surface of his desk. The desk he prized for its size, its brass fittings, its price. Surely, he had been known to say that a man has such a desk only if he is loved by God.

Edward slid off the precious desk like a dead possum, one joint at a time, and sat himself in his second most prized possession, his chair. The chair's back towered above his head like a fountain of leather, pleated and tucked and buttoned. On most days, Edward towered with it, his spine straight, his hands resting lightly, somewhat elegantly, on its plush arms. But this morning, his head dropped between his knees and the chair's hand-carved legs, and he toppled onto the floor.

"Thank the Lord it's Saturday," Edward said, dragging himself back to the chair. "I really do apologize, Dona."

"Me, too, Edward. I'm as much to blame as you are. We got so excited about righting the wrongs of our county. I guess we got carried away."

"That's not like you, is it?"

"No," she said. "And it's not like you, either. But maybe it's who we really are."

"I wouldn't go that far, but I see your point." Edward got to his knees and with the aid of his chair, straightened to standing. "I think I'd best excuse myself for a moment."

"Certainly. I felt a lot better after I washed my face, too. Grab a cup of coffee from Maureen's desk. It's fresh. I made it myself."

Edward returned in a few minutes, looking brighter, and Dona said, "How about, let's go over the work we did last night?"

"You mean what we wrote, the proclamation for equality?"

"Good, you remember."

"I do, and I hope you don't take it seriously."

"I do take it seriously."

"Dona, can you imagine what would happen to my reputation in this county, if we posted that thing?"

Dona laughed. "Yes, I can. And I'd be mighty proud to be kin to you."

"Sorry, cousin. I'm not that brave, and besides I am aiming to be our next county judge."

"Which means you should be in favor of equality for all our people."

"No, which means I get paid off by some, to ignore others. That's the way it is, honey chile, and you'd best keep it in mind."

"I surely do keep it in mind. What else is there to consider, finally. It seems simple to me."

"Dona, what we wrote, the relations between the races, that is terrible complicated."

"Terrible complicated because we make it so, Edward. But when you get right down to it, who has the right to murder another person?"

"Well, in the court where I practice law, there are quite a few reasons. Here in Texas, anyway."

"So, we have to talk this all out again? Is the color of a person's skin one of them?"

Edward straightened his shirt collar. "Do you mean stringing up a Negro for cause?"

"I mean, is having dark skin a cause?"

"Not exactly. But it's what the darkies do that's cause. Like if they go after a white girl."

"If it was a white boy doing the going after, would that be cause to hang him?"

"No, of course not."

"Then, do you see that it's simple? The color of a person's skin is not supposed to matter in a court of law any more, even in Texas, am I right?"

"You are right. Except for marrying, of course."

"And killing outside the law is murder, isn't it?"

"Yes, of course, Dona, but you are being naive." He shoved the drawer into his desk. "You are forgetting what people are like."

"What are we like?"

"We are animals. We don't cotton to those who are different from us. We suspect them, especially if we are white and they are colored. Don't you know what I mean?"

"You mean it's human nature to hate people who have a different color skin from ours."

"Exactly, ma'am."

"But, if it is human nature, and I really doubt it, still we don't have to go around killing them, do we?"

"Apparently, we do."

Dona set aside her coffee cup and stood carefully. "That was some night we had, Edward. A mistake, I'm sure, but I thank you for it. I guess we all have insides that are better than our outsides."

"Or not," he said, his mouth curling up. He put his hands over his face and rubbed. "I haven't been that drunk since I was a student. But I don't regret it."

"Why not?"

"Because no one will believe you, if I say you are lying."

"No one?"

"Maybe Ophelia. Maybe Melvar." He chuckled disparagingly.

"Maybe Samuel," she said.

"So you do know where he is?"

"I do. And, Edward, if you will not go with me to post the declaration of equality, what we wrote together last night, I will do it myself."

"Are you kidding me?"

"How about if we read it together, now."

"Now?"

"I mean, we're sober now, thanks to me making coffee and your secretary coming in at five o'clock on a Saturday morning and typing it up. At least, let's see what we wrote before you throw the paper in the trash."

"I'll burn it, Dona. I don't want another soul to see it. Where is it?"

"Hmmmm, I wonder if that's what was in my purse when I went outside at seven o'clock this morning?"

"You went outside?"

"Yes, down to the street. Got in my car. Drove to Ophelia's."

"Ophelia's?"

"It's not far. I don't hide anything from her. I knew she'd worry. I was supposed to stay with her last night, so she didn't mind that I woke her up."

"And you gave her the paper we wrote?"

"I think I probably did. And I'm pretty sure it won't be a secret for long."

"Dona Willis. You are not to be trusted!"

"And you are, Edward? You, who said all last night that we would make our writings public? You, who are too afraid to go public with the truth about yourself? Don't you see? I mean, it's not just skin color that puts people in danger. You are different, too. You are afraid to let anyone know because they might tar and feather you; they might do more terrible things to you. You are in the same place as Samuel. What would be all right for a man to do with a woman could get you killed for doing it with a man. Is that fair?"

Edward sat down behind the desk and slammed the palm of his hands on the polished wood. "Get out of here, Dona. I can't stand the sight of you another minute."

"I'll tell you, again, Edward. It is not fair. It is not right. And anytime you want me to stand up for you, I will. But for now, I'll give you a chance to think about it, before I go nailing anything to any big, carved door. Toodle-oo."

Dona fastened her felt hat to her hair, collected her gloves and checked the clasp on her purse. She clicked across the parquet wood with purpose in her step, opened the door to the outer office and whispered to the black-haired woman at the desk, "Thanks so much, Maureen, for that good coffee. You were a hero to come in so early on a Saturday and type that whole thing—with carbon copies. I'll send you a dozen yellow roses; maybe make up a little for the one that's laying in its own shattered glass."

"Good luck, Dona," Maureen whispered back. "It was a pleasure. And y'all come see us again right soon."

Chapter Thirty-two

DONA PULLED THE CHEVY UP CLOSE in the shade of the barn, and creaked open the door. The rich smell of cornbread reached her before she stepped onto the dust of the barnyard. She was starving and she loved anything with cornbread, and especially fresh green onions. The dread she'd felt about coming home lifted with her eyes, and she stepped forward toward the ranch house without hesitation. Only to put her foot into a pile of fresh cow dung.

Dona stared at her shoe, one foot raised behind her. "My new shoes," was all she said. She had known not to buy light color shoes, not to consider linen, for heaven's sake, and certainly not to be proud of how they looked on her feet. Pride cometh before a fall was never truer than for a ranch woman, where no piece of clothing stayed clean, no vanity went unpunished by dirt and mud, by dung and pig slop. "It's a sign," she whispered to the shoe, its lovely beige linen buried in green slime.

For it would have been Dona's chore to milk Mehitabel this morning, to make sure she was safely in her stall and away from the bull, to keep her from the garden where she was most certainly grazing right now. *It's Roy's punishment for me, being too big for my britches*, she thought. *Or is it? Maybe it means I've stepped in a mess and now it's up to me to find a way to clean it up. It's probably a good thing I didn't post our proclamation on the courthouse door, as much as I wanted to. I've got another possibility or two up my sleeve.*

Roy fairly ran around the corner of the barn toward where Dona was bent, wiping cow dung off of her shoe and into the dust.

"What's your rush," she said, straightening up to face him.

"My rush is your trouble, sister. Where the hell have you been since yesterday?"

"Mostly at Mother's and I'm not your sister. We're married, remember? We're still married."

"Hard to tell from the way you're acting, all high and mighty. Not cooking anymore, are you? Not scrubbing the porch? Not sleeping with me? Who the hell do you think you are, going off like that?"

"I am sorry, Roy, for making you worry. You knew I was going to Mother's."

"I wasn't worried, Dona. I am mad as all tarnation."

"I'm sorry for not calling. It's a good thing I fell asleep and Mother let me stay until this morning. I was really tired." Dona gave up on the shoe and stepped onto the dust of the barnyard with a stocking foot.

"Yes, she said so."

"Oh, you've talked with her?"

"Is she going to buy you another pair of those stockings? Are you so stupid you'd step in cow shit after all these years on this ranch?"

Dona shook off the other shoe and dangled it with the first one from her finger tips.

"We didn't talk long," Roy said, "but yeah, we spoke on that damned party line, so now every busybody in our county knows you were out all night and I didn't know where. How does that make me look?"

"Why is this about you? I'm the one who stayed out."

"It's always about me, you bitch, at least in my world." Roy kicked the Chevy door with the backside of his boot. "And I'll kick in this old rattletrap, if you do that again. Next time you decide not to be a wife, you can walk the hell to town. And let me tell you something. Yes, Angus Cameron isn't just a judge, he's the boss of the Klan, like you think. And there is no way I'll let you shame him with your antics."

"And it's clear to me that you know he's a crook."

"Yep, and he holds the power not only in this county, but darn near all of West Texas; and I'll protect him as far as I can. You know, Angus Cameron and I agree on the danger of the colored learning to read and write. Why, it's an insult to hear them speak up in their own defense. We white men have to protect our women and children, our land, and most of all, we have to keep our blood pure."

"Protect your women like Andrew MacMurray protected Eleanor? Beating her within an inch of her life? So, you're in the Klan, too, Roy?" Dona stared into his eyes, hard and shining as ice, the eyes of a true believer. She shivered in the heat.

"And about Reverend Sinclair and his monkey, Melvar. I ain't allowing you to rub dirt in the good reverend's memory. Why, he's in his grave these twenty-five years." Roy turned to the barn, "I'm done with talking. You better remember what I say."

"I hear you, Roy, and I see a couple of things. Even with your back turned. You don't care about me anymore and you are against everything I believe." Dona drew her purse closer to her chest. "I'm getting hungry and Annalou's got dinner on. If you don't want to accept my apology for worrying you, okay. But I'm going to go in the kitchen now."

"Well, it's about time," Roy said in a voice Dona knew. His hands curled into fists; his neck bloomed scarlet. She ducked, held on to her shoes and ran for the porch, not letting her purse or any other part of herself fly open.

DONA WOKE BEFORE DAWN THE NEXT MORNING, spent at heart, but sound in body. She cupped her palms around her cheekbones, which remembered the times before. The jaw, too, held memory. She could be sad; she could be afraid, again; but yesterday she had done something important, even if nobody ever saw that "Proclamation." And, she escaped unharmed. This morning, with Roy sleeping it off, and the others turning over in their narrow beds, she heard the springs creak their blessings.

She was the only one in the world to know exactly this almost dawn of a summer Sunday. She and Buster, who crowed no matter what the weather. Her hands were warm and comforting, like a mother's hands might be. And she, never a mother, was blessed with Joe Bob and Annalou. Was blessed to know this land, its river, to turn over limestone rocks and find fossils, there for millions of dawns. She wrapped her hands over her mouth and whispered her thanks.

Chapter Thirty-three

"Mighty good flapjacks, Doney," Joe Bob snapped the end of a cup towel on her back.

"Thanks for helping with the dishes."

"Glad to do it. Lots easier than working those cows today. And besides, seems like we've got a snake hunt ahead of us, and I want to stay on your good side." He chuckled and went out to the porch.

Dona tried to think what was funny about trying to fool Reverend MacMurray into confessing. After he was arrested on suspicion of beating his wife near to death, even with the note signed by him, he was released by the police chief, an upstanding member of the Reverend's church. But there was the chicken ranch. He already was a fool and his weakness was colored girls. Joe Bob had seen him there once. She'd bet he'd been there lots of times. Probably spending the Sunday offering.

She found Joe Bob dozing on the porch swing, its rusty chain creaking in time with his breath. "Joe Bob." She bent close. "Sorry to wake you. I had an idea, and Ophelia is here to talk about it with us."

"There are names for men like MacMurray, Joe Bob, and you probably know all of them." Ophelia placed her coffee mug on the floor of the ranch house porch, and leaned back into the rocking chair. "To think what he put Luke through. MacMurray must have driven him mad."

"He's near driven all of us mad, Mamaw, with his infernal preaching about what's right and then going right on ahead and doing what's wrong, his own self." Joe Bob oiled his shotgun, pulling cloth through the barrels with the care of a surgeon.

"So, you think you can catch the Reverend in the act tonight, Joe Bob?"

"Yep, I believe I can. I've got a contact, a real special friend. I'm pretty sure she'll help. And Doney's idea that I could take pictures with your Brownie camera, Mamaw, if you'll let me use it." Joe Bob folded his gun rag and sealed it in its can. "I'll be in and out of there so fast he'll never know what happened."

"You're welcome to use my camera. I'll give you a lesson this afternoon. And you are right, MacMurray won't know what happened until he sees the pictures in Cousin Edward's hands," Ophelia said, smoothing her skirt over her knees. "It seems that Edward and Doney had quite a fine conversation. He's not perfect and he's sorry for the part he had in tormenting Samuel and his family, but we sat and talked in a new way yesterday, and we forgave each other. But, be sure to have extra copies of the photographs, just in case."

Joe Bob grinned and turned to Dona, who had come onto the porch from the kitchen. "Doney, I really hope this works. But even if it doesn't, you've been mighty brave."

"I'd say we've all been brave." She took a seat on the porch swing. "But, Joe Bob, this is pretty dangerous. I've learned a bit about MacMurray and none of it is good. For all we know, he might carry a gun right into Maudie's whorehouse."

"No, not likely. I've been there a few times, I'm sorry to tell you, and there is no way a man could get a gun into one of those rooms. You have to leave them at the front door, knives, too, or you don't go in. Maudie's rules."

"Your friend is one of the girls? And she'll be with the Reverend?"

"That is the plan, and Maudie's in on it. See, they don't like him. He's mean to the girls and sometimes he doesn't pay. And besides, they know Samuel. A couple of them are his kin. They will do what they can."

Roy stomped his boots on the porch steps and pulled open the screen door. "Well, the chores are done, thanks to Luke and Juan Carlos and me. What the hell are you doing, Joe Bob?"

"We've got something to talk over with you, Roy," Dona said.

Ophelia said, "Can I get you a cup of coffee? And where are the other boys?'

"They'll be in. We're plumb tuckered. Coffee sounds good, Ophelia." He hung his hat on the rack by the kitchen doorway and dusted his britches. "Can't the talk wait?"

"No, really, it can't," said Dona. "Joe Bob is about to do something very risky to help Samuel, and you should know about it."

"Hell yes, I should."

"In fact, even though you disagree, we hope you'll help."

LONG BEFORE DAYBREAK the next morning, Dona had the coffee pot perking and biscuits in the oven and wondered why the dickens wasn't everybody up? Roy had flopped onto the bed fully dressed only a couple of hours earlier, as the moon was setting. He hadn't answered her questions and now he was snoring. She had dozed off while Ophelia and Annalou were still whispering in Annalou's room, so it might be a spell before they hopped up.

But Luke and Joe Bob—they weren't in the kitchen looking for their coffee, and their horses nickered in the paddock. Where were those boys! Joe Bob going to Maudie's to trap the despicable Reverend. A dangerous business, at best. And Luke, he'd gone through hell and was acting so strange these days. What else was there to do but worry?

She slid the biscuits out of the oven, inhaled their thick, rich scent, and thought as she always did with a confusion of pride and regret, that they were on the same blackened baking sheet her grandmother had used hundreds of times—and also, was there any hope she'd ever polish it up? She finished setting the table, pulled butter from the ice box and her own peach preserves from the cupboard, and poured herself a cup of coffee. She'd sit on the porch stoop to drink it and take a minute to let its delicious aroma calm her down.

A lantern swung an arc of light in the barn door. She stood and called across the barnyard her usual "Yoo-hoo, coffee's on." The light went out. "Joe Bob? Luke?" she called.

From behind her, Roy said in a low voice, "Dona, be quiet."

Her back tingled with the heavy scent of him. Roy was afraid.

"What should I do?"

"Very slowly, do not turn around, back yourself up the stairs and get inside the kitchen. There's something out here I don't like." He ran in a crouch toward the tractor and disappeared.

Her rifle was gone from its place near the cooler. She turned out the lantern over the table and crept down the hall. "Mother, Annalou, get up and wait in the kitchen. Something's happening and I don't know what."

"Dona, come here!" It was Roy's God-voice, the one Dona would always obey. In it was command, and sorrow.

She grabbed the lantern, jerked on her boots, found her pistol and ran for the still-dark barn. The stench of blood, like hot iron, burned her nostrils.

Roy was in the back, near Luke's tool bench. "Git in here, quick. Somebody's beat Luke unconscious with his own hammer."

"HEY, LUKE, how about a cup of joe?" Roy stood beside Luke's bed, a coffee cup steaming.

Luke opened his eyes a slit and muttered, "Smells mighty good, but this... one hell of a headache." He shut his eyes and lifted his eyebrows.

"Somebody tried to open your thick skull with a hammer. Any chance you know why?"

"Nope."

"Your mother cleaned you up and wrapped your head like a mummy, but it would be good if you could stay awake, so we can see how bad you're hurt."

"Nope," said Luke.

Roy walked into the hall in time to see Joe Bob fairly run into the kitchen.

"About time, here's my son, blood and bone, and where the devil you been?"

"Sorry, Daddy, I've been in a darkroom."

"What?"

"A darkroom where the daddy of one of my buddies develops film and makes prints for the newspaper," Joe Bob said. He poured himself a cup of coffee and sat down at the table across from Dona. "I thought we needed these pictures done in a hurry. Sorry I didn't tell you first, but last evening, it was pretty rough, and I barely got out of there with my skin, let alone the film."

"Glad you're safe and back here with those pictures," Dona said. "We'll take a look at them in a minute. But, sometime last night, somebody beat up Luke real bad, and he's in his old room with no idea of why. What happened at Maudie's? And please whisper."

"I got there in good time." Joe Bob spoke fast and low. "And hid near the door to one of the rooms. My friends at Maudie's knew about MacMurray getting bailed out of jail, and figured he'd show up there. They wanted to help, like I told you. I was after a picture of the Reverend with one of the girls, so she'd have to leave the door open when they were in the room. It was going to be tricky and I was worried about the noise the shutter makes.

"I didn't want the Reverend to do anything hurtful to the girl or suspect her of being in on it. So, sure enough, he came in the house. The girl led him to the nearest room and started taking off his shirt. She didn't have on a whole lot of clothes, so as soon as he was bare-chested, she kept her back to the door, pulled off her top and put her arms around his neck. I could see his face right well. That's the picture I wanted, so I pressed the button, and I was on my way out of there.

"Only right away, MacMurray started hitting the girl, like it was her fault, and of course it weren't, so I handed the camera to a friend who works there and went back into the room and got between the Rev and the girl. That's when he really went off on me, and of course he knew who I was. I didn't have no trouble knocking him out, but I didn't want to leave him there as a problem for Maudie, so I put him over my shoulder, took him outside and dumped him under a bush next to the road. I ran back for the camera, jumped in my truck and hightailed it for the darkroom, and here are the pictures."

Joe Bob paused to catch his breath.

"But now, I worry that Luke got beat up instead of me. The Reverend gets other guys to do his dirty work, so maybe whoever did it didn't recognize Luke in the barn, near dark before dawn and all, and I'm the one who should be a wreck in that bed in yonder. That's what I suspicion, Doney. And I feel really bad about that. I hope the picture makes the Reverend look like the terrible man he is. And see, Doney, they're fresh-done and smell funny, but all the prints have a date on them, official."

Dona held the photographs in her hands, 4x4 inches square with wavy edges, as though an odd pair of pinking shears had cut each one. And there in the middle, his face in full view, was the Reverend Andrew MacMurray, caught in the act.

"Oh, Joe Bob," she whispered, "I am so proud of you. Luke took the brunt of this; but with his own reasons to hate MacMurray, he would have told you to go ahead, if it puts that devil behind bars for keeps."

LATER THAT DAY, Joe Bob and Dona were hoisting bales of hay onto the stack in the barn, jostling hens that clucked around their feet, hoping for seed. Joe Bob said, "Doney, about Eleanor, is she someplace safe?"

Dona pulled another bale off the wagon and flung it to Joe Bob. "I believe she is, but I can't rightly say any details. None of us can say anything right now."

"Got it, thanks. So, we have to be awful careful, awful quiet."

"We do. And thank heavens Melvar is helping us."

"He's a pretty mysterious fella, Doney."

"I know. He's like a magician, the way he spirited Samuel away. You are quite the magician, too. When you tricked MacMurray at the chicken ranch, got his picture."

"I'm a bit proud of that, have to say."

"As far as I'm concerned, that was evidence of his hypocritical life, and it will turn a lot of people's minds."

"Yep."

"But you know, Joe Bob, it's not only Eleanor we've had to transport to a safe place."

"Yep. Jessie. And, you know I can drive. Can I help?"

"Maybe, but turns out Samuel and Melvar are in charge. I don't want to put you in more danger than you are already."

"Aunt Doney, this is the best fun I've had in my whole life."

"Which is only eighteen years long, big boy. Let's hope you have lots more fun, but not because of women getting beat up within an inch of their lives, and men, running from a noose."

"Amen to that.

I am proud that you're looking to help. Not every boy would, you know."

"I know, but I'm kinda scared."

"So am I. MacMurray isn't going down easy. Scared or not, we got to keep our eyes open and our hearts ready."

Chapter Thirty-four

In starlight, the porch swing sat still, white paint shining in the night's shadows. Dona peered out the kitchen door to the back porch. A barn owl flew to the mesquite tree at the side of the house, like a ghost descending. The only sound was the thumping of the windmill in the steady wind.

She sniffed the air. Nothing but hay and dust. She should be asleep, peaceful in her bed. But she was breaking.

Samuel shot; gunmen at her ranch house; Ross, shot; Joe Bob hurt; Klan leaders in her own living room. Dona trembled with remembering the coyote, murdered, then Eleanor's face crushed, Luke beat up, and Andrew MacMurray yet again on the loose.

Her mother and Annalou and Roy—in their beds. Joe Bob taking care of Luke in the bunkhouse; Juan Carlos and Josie, in their cabin. Everything calm again, at least for the night. So, what was this feeling in her stomach? Premonition or terror, or both?

She dozed off and on all night on the porch swing, her hands clawed and cramped from holding her rifle across her lap. A stew of worries bubbled in her mind and she could not get past the heat of them; nor could she chop open her brain, which felt seared and charred and small.

In the gray dark of almost morning, Buster crowed. She trusted that the animals would be there. That Buster would crow; that Pansy would snuffle and chuff; that the horses would stamp and blow away the night. But for that moment she heard only the rattle and shuffle of leaves, the chug of the windmill's shaft as it pushed into the earth, as it drew itself back.

A chicken hawk screeched above the porch and something white cut through the gloom, sharp and clean as a skinning knife.

Dona stood, tiptoed into the kitchen, along the hall, out the front door, around the house, behind the machine shed, and knelt beside the trunk of the live oak tree. "Here in the last minutes of my life," Dona whispered, "let me remember what I love."

She backed into the machine shed and huddled in the corner crook between a tractor tire and a pile of barn swallow droppings, hugging her rifle to her chest.

Dona could see nothing in the dark of the barn. She heard nothing from the ranch house.

A ghost passed by the barn door, all in white. Orange light flickered and flowered from an oil lantern, held out from the white robe like a flaming shield. It was a specter of the very Devil.

But this was a man, and he called her name like she was a dog. "Here, Dona," he laughed, keeping his voice low, coaxing in a singsong voice, "bitch, bitch, here bitch, come here pretty little bitch. Nigger lover. The Lord wants you."

I am not here, she thought as she closed her eyes. But when she opened them, there it was, whirling in the gray light under the wheeling windmill like a dancer, burning alive.

"Oh, my God. Stop!" she yelled.

The fiery ghost, white robes aflame, screamed, "Help me."

That voice. She ran in the pale light to the windmill trough; found the bucket under her hands, and threw the water, green with moss, using all her strength, toward the fire, again and again, while all around, the living world was waking up.

And Reverend Andrew MacMurray was dead.

"Dona."

She tried to move, but she was weighed down to her eyelids. A low humming as from a church organ floated up her spine and trembled in her throat; it flickered and sobbed and she could not let it out.

Melvar's voice came again. "You must wake up. We all need you."

"Water." She tried to say. Frowning, she let go of the thing she was holding with jaws clenched against death. She let go and the sound came, cool and wet and blue. She took it in her throat and held it against the burning.

She awoke to Melvar, asleep in the straight chair. The dark and comforting smell of him, like the river's muddy banks, like the earth that cares for what it loves. "I didn't think you'd ever come back," she said.

He leaned forward, his elbows on his knees. "I have been here all along."

"The robe like a torch, a dream?"

"Not a dream."

"And the man? MacMurray?"

"You tried to save him. You gave all you had."

Dona stared at the ceiling of the room she passed through almost every day, where she had so often found peace in its dusk. In the musty scent of its rugs. Long ago, a leak from the faulty roof had left a stain in the rough shape of a cross on the white, pressed tin. Not the cross of the suffering Jesus, as others had seen it, but instead its arms held a promise. Sometimes it was the promise of hope, sometimes of love. Andrew MacMurray had lost his hope, his love, his way.

The cross beckoned and with all she was, she wished to fall into its arms. In her desire, the ceiling became a floor of stone. She would walk there, if only she could stand. The floor was surrounded by walls of stone, where light the color of gold flowed through small windows and a roof of limestone rose to a peak over the arched stone fireplace. Sheepherder's Hut.

"Did you speak, Dona?"

She turned her head toward Melvar and left her hand in his. "The Hut. It is a chapel."

"Ah."

"Is it possible to forgive someone who wounded you, mortally? Someone you hated?"

"Let us try, my precious friend."

And her body, feelings sharp with loss and the remains of the fire, closed her eyes. The warmth of his breath against her cheek was what she would remember. How like a rose it was, sweet and infinitely sad.

DONA LAY ON THE SOFA long after Melvar left the ranch house. She was suspended as in a cloud, unmoving. Ophelia came into the living room bearing a cup of coffee and a piece of her sweet potato pie. Still, she could not move.

Annalou came in a while later and knelt beside the sofa. "Aunt Doney, I love you and I brought you a present."

It was good to feel Annalou's hand on her wrist, her head resting like a butterfly on her shoulder. A present. Yes. But she could not stir to ask.

She awoke to Roy somewhere near. Like a newborn calf, she breathed the scent of the familiar, hard-working body, the dust of his shirt, the boots caked with mud and manure. "Roy," she said.

"Yes, it's me. I am so sorry none of us men were awake to help you. MacMurray sent himself to hell, I guess you know."

"I do. And who can forgive him for his sins? I hope I can, one day."

"The sheriff is looking into it, in case you're wondering. And it's plain to see that he set himself on fire."

"Yes," she said.

"I am also a sinner, Dona."

"Roy." Her voice faded as she spoke. "I am undefended. You may tell me now."

At that, his breath turned quick and shallow. It was like roping a mustang; he was roping something out of control.

Roy's sigh was tremulous. "You are right. I am often, in my mind, with someone else."

"And your body?"

"Yes. Her name is Rosa."

Across the room, the mantle clock, wine-red and glossy along its wood veneer, the marker of minutes and hours for years and years since it came to this rocky land in a wagon too rough for the human bodies that depended on it; in this place, resilient as ever, the clock ticked on.

"WHERE IS Annalou, Mother?"

"Why, I believe she's in her room reading a book."

Dona turned away from the back of the sofa, and tried to sit up.

"Wait a minute." Ophelia reached for Dona's shoulder and slid her arm between it and the sofa's pillows.

"Better, thank you. I'm breathing better now."

"You asked about Annalou?"

"How all of this awful business affects her."

"She was mainly worried about you. She's a really strong child, but if anything happened to you..."

"I know." Dona pulled a blanket over her knees. "I'm glad she's reading because of, well, that's what helped me when I was her age. Not to be so afraid." Dona rubbed her face. "I was afraid of nearly every man."

"Because of the schoolmaster, what he did to you?"

"Because of that. It helped to read stories about girls who went through worse than I did. Like the girls in books by Charles Dickens. Remember them?"

"I do. And Edith Wharton?"

"Yes. You gave me *House of Mirth*. I will never forget it. That poor Lily. I might have been her, Mother, in that day. Books like that made me know I wasn't alone. Was still afraid of most men, though. Maybe I still am. Roy came in to see me a while ago."

"I overheard something, maybe about another woman?"

"Have you known for long?"

"I've heard rumors."

"Did Daddy?"

"Yes."

They sat together then, two women in a small rock house on a ranch that spread over miles of cactus and rattlesnakes and black widow spiders, and put their hands together, closed their eyes and waited. Neither would have said for what, but when Annalou came from the hall into the living room, bright with feeling, it was as if she were the sun.

"Can I give you my present, now, Aunt Doney?"

"I would love a present."

Annalou handed Dona a sheet of paper, folded into the shape of the ranch house. Across the roofline it read, 'Home of Dona Willis, Queen of the Ranch.'

HER GRANDFATHER'S CLOCK called to Dona from the pale light of the living room. She leaned against the counter where a moment ago she had rolled out the pillowy dough, pressed it into rounds with her grandmother's biscuit cutter, arranged the biscuits onto her grandmother's cookie sheet and slid it into the oven, hot with coals from a mesquite fire. The tick of the old clock, the tin of her grandmother's cutter, biscuits that smelled as they baked exactly as when she was a little girl, in this moment Dona thought, no matter what you do, you cannot hold on to anything.

It was a kind of relief. Maybe she could let go on purpose. She was still a little weak from the fire, and was so mad at Roy she thought she might shoot him dead; but, maybe she could leave that behind. He'd told her more about this Rosa, about how he loved her, and how he loved Dona, too, and would it be okay with Dona. What? she had yelled. You've got another woman and you've got the nerve to ask permission? And he had nodded into his shirt buttons. What a clown. Imagine him trying to run this whole ranch without her? And with a hussy, besides. And who was Rosa, anyway?

After she told him to get out of her sight, she had gone on and on about it in her mind until she blamed herself. Blamed herself! What a typical womanish thing to do. Well, she, Dona Willis, did not want to be typical. She wanted to keep this ranch, she needed help to run it, she wanted to live in a house of family and friends who loved each other. Was that asking too much? Apparently. But now. Yes, that was the point. Now. This minute. How was she doing?

The oven door squawked as usual when she pulled it open. The biscuits peaked, high and golden. Fresh-churned butter waited, cool and sweet in the icebox. On the kitchen table, peach preserves glowed like small suns in a bowl like summer's sky. How was she doing? This very minute, she was doing just fine. And land sakes, there was nothing and nobody worth getting her guts in an uproar over. She sighed.

Except of course, Samuel. And the lynch mob. And nearly getting killed out there in the barnyard. And Eleanor. And Joe Bob. The litany again. But even that, she thought as she walked to the back porch to ring the breakfast bell, even that. Maybe she could get to the bottom of the awfulness better, if she didn't carry around old feelings about Edward, Esquire, or the Reverend, or the Judge. If she could think brand-new thoughts, if she wasn't afraid, if she didn't feel like a green-broke filly around them, maybe she'd find a new way to help Samuel and his family. And how about the other people in the county whose skin and eyes were dark and beautiful?

Like Melvar's.

Dona felt heat surge to her face, having nothing to do with biscuits from the oven. *Rosa,* she thought, *how different is she to Roy than Melvar could be to me?*

As they walked side by side from the barn to the ranch house, later that afternoon, Dona said, "Roy, I've been thinking about this business with Rosa. If she is the woman who works for the MacGregor's, I've met her. And I want to make a deal."

"A deal?"

"I'm not going to stand in the way of you and Rosa, but I need you."

Roy stopped in the shadow of the barn and turned away from her.

"Just listen, okay?" Dona shuffled her boots to face him and stood as tall as she could.

"Here's the idea. You and Rosa can live here at the ranch, in exchange for helping me out. We'll have to get a divorce so you two can get married, if you want to. But if you stay here, Joe Bob will have a home, Annalou will have an uncle, and I'll have enough help to keep the ranch going."

"You wouldn't mind? About Rosa, I mean?"

"I'm sure I would mind sometimes; but you and I haven't been happy together for a long time. And I know I'd never be happy being married to you, with you loving somebody else."

Roy pulled the bandana from around his neck and wiped his face. "Dona, you sure do know how to surprise a fella."

"You're not my enemy, and neither is Rosa. Maybe we still need each other. What do you think? Could we make it work?"

"I see how it could, between you and me, and I'd be mighty glad to stay on this ranch, but it's hard to think that Rosa will agree. Rosa is Mexican."

"Yes, I remember that from when I saw her, and I guess I am a little surprised, prejudiced as you are against anybody dark-skinned, that she's the one you want to be with. What will your buddies in the Klan say to that? Lots of them say terrible things about 'Meskins,' as they call them like they are dirty, lazy, thieving . . ."

"Well, all I know is, Juan Carlos is my best friend, more like my brother," Roy said, taking off his Stetson to wipe the sweat from his forehead. "And I couldn't trust anybody more than Josie, when you're not around to take care of us and the ranch house. Cowhands from Mexico are the best I've ever known. We couldn't run this ranch without 'em."

"It's a mess, for sure, here in Texas, for Mexicans and Negroes. Lots of distrust of us, and for good reason," Dona said.

"I don't know these answers, but I'm ready to stand up for her, and me being with her, if you agree."

"How about if I talk with her, myself? We met a couple of times at the MacGregor Ranch. Would you ask her?"

"Yep, I'll ask her tonight. But Dona, is there someone else for you, too?"

"Maybe there is, and maybe there isn't. I don't know. But, Roy, old and tough as I am, I'm fine either way, I promise. How about you and Rosa come by on Sunday morning and we'll have a talk down by the river."

"Maybe she'd like it if I fixed up those shacks for us, you think?"

"Maybe she would. Maybe she'd like to make them beautiful."

Chapter Thirty-five

"I love mornings on this ranch," said Annalou.

"Me, too. Especially now that September's come. Here's a cup towel. Want to help dry these dishes?"

"Sure enough. I was out real early, Aunt Doney, is why I missed breakfast, and I walked clear down to the river dam."

"Good thing to do. Wish Josie and I hadn't had so many men to feed today."

"They were drenching the sheep and goats?"

"Yep. Seven big appetites. Glad you got to miss it. But you can help me in a little while with dinner. It's mostly all cooked."

"Aunt Doney, you know how the fog rises sometimes over the river?"

"It's beautiful, isn't it?"

"I was watching a momma raccoon, she was swimming with her babies from one side to the other. It was kind of mysterious, with the fog and all. And, maybe it was my imagination, but I saw, across the oat field, there was a woman. Kind of near the shacks. Seemed to be working, like hoeing weeds, maybe."

"What did she look like?"

"Her hair was black like Josie's, but real long, in a braid, and she was wearing some kind of dress or maybe a skirt. I couldn't see real good. So, who could it be?"

Dona hauled the iron skillet from the stove, scoured it clean of bacon grease, hung it on its wall hook and untied her apron.

"Tell you what, let's make our way down to the oat field and see what we can see. I have a hunch it could be our new neighbor."

By the time they had walked their horses to the edge of the oat field, the woman was on the steps of the nearest shack, sweeping. They could make out the orange and yellow of her head scarf, her black braid gleaming over her shoulder.

"So that's Rosa?" whispered Annalou.

"That's Rosa. And isn't she lovely. I sat with her and Roy for a spell yesterday morning."

"You aren't a little bit jealous?"

"Course I am, honey. But I'll get over it. My being jealous isn't going to help a thing. Let's make her welcome."

"*Hola!*" she said, as loudly as she could without yelling.

Rosa shied and whirled around like a colt with its first taste of the whip. She held the broom like a shield and straightened her shoulders to face them. "Oh, Señora Dona," she said, lowering the broom, "it is you."

"Good to see you again, Rosa. This is my niece, Annalou." She smiled and walked closer, holding Annalou's hand.

"We've come to say hello, and see what we can do to help you get settled in."

Rosa set the broom against the screened porch. She lifted the front of her skirt and wiped her face. "*Lo siento, Señora Dona.* I am glad to see you, *y mucho gusto, Señorita Annalou.*"

"You have been crying, Rosa?" Dona said, edging toward her.

Rosa sank to the wooden step, her skirt hovering over her sandals, tears welling in her enormous brown eyes. "*Sí.*" She smoothed her skirt and pushed her scarf further back over her hair. "I must be brave, *Señora.*"

"What are you afraid of, Señorita? Me? Or Annalou?"

"No, not of you. Not after the talk."

"Can you tell us?"

"*Mí familia, Señora. Mí papa.* He no like Señor Roy. He no like me to talk to ranchers. White and brown, *no es bueno. Muy peligrosa.*"

"I see," Dona said, "I hope you and your papa can work it out. It sounds like he loves you very much."

"*Sí, mucho*."

Dona made room on the porch steps for herself and Annalou. "So, it will be a while before you and Roy will move in here. Time to make it really nice, Rosa. Let's sit here a while, together. *Está bien*?"

Rosa cut her eyes at Dona and smiled. "*Bien*."

In the silence between them came the river's song, its gurgles and whispers joining twitters and chirps of tiny birds in the willows.

"Rosa, may Annalou and I help you with these chores?" Dona gestured widely with her arms. "So much to do to make the shacks a home."

"*Muchas gracias, Señora*."

"You've already begun, by hoeing a little garden, I see."

"*Sí*, for the chiles and yerbas."

"And water for the garden?"

"At the river I filled the bowl," she said, pointing to a metal rimmed bucket.

"*Muy fuerte*," Annalou said, grinning.

"*Ah, hablas español*, Annalou."

"*Un poco*," Annalou said in a soft voice. "You can teach me?"

Rosa smiled as she looked into Annalou's face, and her eyes shone. "*Sí, claro*," she said.

"All right," Dona said to Annalou, "let's start with the outhouse and the kitchen. Rosa, maybe you will sweep out the bedroom and living room? No telling what's under the furniture. I am really sorry for what a mess it is. Some bad hombres came and tore it up a few weeks ago."

It was late morning when Dona looked up from mopping the kitchen linoleum.

"Oh, great heavens, the men will be coming back in less than an hour."

"Sounds like you're the one needing help, Aunt Doney."

"Josie's got dinner all cooked, so I just have to heat it up and set the big table outside the ranch house. You can stay here and help Rosa."

"No," Rosa said. "I will help."

And so it was that dinner was served that day in the shade of the barnyard's largest live oak tree. While six cowboys ate their fill of chili and beans, corn tortillas, home-canned tomatoes, hot peach cobbler and coffee, Roy, their boss, picked at his food. And from the ranch house kitchen, throughout the meal, came the laughter of two women and a girl, washing pots and pans, and banging loudly.

Chapter Thirty-six

THE SUN HAD SET, EXTRAVAGANTLY, the next evening, when Roy and Joe Bob stomped onto the porch.

"Dona, you terrible woman," Roy hollered toward the kitchen, "we're back from huntin' and we're mighty hungry."

Dona turned from the stove, her brown and white checkered apron hanging around her neck, and yelled, "Well what's keepin' y'all from the trough?" She grinned toward the iron skillet, ham steaks sizzling, toward the bubbling cauldron of red beans, the pan of cornbread, golden as a late sun, and tied her apron tight.

"You washed up, boys? And where's Luke?"

Joe Bob nodded and spread his hands.

Roy said, "Luke'll be here in a minute. Had to get those hounds locked up and fed. Sorry it's after dark, but we had a mighty fine jack-rabbit hunt."

"Smells awful good, Doney," Joe Bob said.

Dona chose her favorite blue bowl to dish up the red beans, forked a ham steak onto four yellow plates and put them on the table. "Hope Luke's food doesn't get cold." She poured coffee into the blue metal cups.

When she'd taken her accustomed seat, Roy said, "Dear Lord, bless this supper, Amen, and pass the cornbread, please."

"Here comes Luke," Joe Bob said, peering across the porch to the barnyard. "A mite put out, from the looks of it. I'd best be careful around him tonight."

"You still wary of him, after he blindsided you at Ophelia's?"

"Naw, we done cleared that up. I'm just kidding," and Joe Bob grinned.

Water gushed from the windmill pump into the trough. They smelled the lye soap as Luke washed up, and they stiffened their backs, waiting for whatever was wrong tonight.

"Dadgum dogs," Luke muttered as he came into the kitchen and pulled out his chair. "Cain't for the life of me think why I don't shoot ever one of 'em. Stooo-pid animals." He picked up his fork and knife and cut into the ham. "Why the tarnation do I spend all my money on them useless critters?" He cut a piece of cornbread in half, splayed it on his plate and covered it in a slurry of red beans and pot liquor. "Gotta git rid of them ungrateful cusses. Pass the milk pitcher, Roy?"

"Sorry for your bad dogs," Roy said, handing Luke the pitcher. "Could I have some more beans, Joe Bob?"

Not one looked at Luke and not one could quite hide a smile.

"H'it's not a bit funny," Luke said presently, sitting back in his chair and holding his coffee between his hands.

"They's a nigger, I mean a Negro; a fella. Out by those hounds. Saw him with my own two eyes."

Dona stiffened. "Who was it, Luke?"

"Cain't tell one of them darkies from the other. Specially not in the dark. But it weren't Samuel. I'd a knowed him. I saw a man's eyes, and those hounds, they bayed like the dickens. They know a stranger."

"Better not be," said Roy, glaring at Dona.

"The hounds would know Samuel. He's worked here enough. But even if it is Samuel, he's my friend and I've been looking for news of him for weeks. As you know." She pushed back her chair and carried her dishes to the sink. "Joe Bob, I'd take it kindly if you'd do up these dishes tonight. I'm going for a little walk."

"In the dark?" Roy stood from his chair, knocking it to the floor. "No wife of mine is going out in the dark tonight. Not with some goddam, uh, man lurking around."

"Nope, you can't go with me this time. Can't trust your temper. I'll be safe enough with my rifle and a lantern." And she disappeared.

—

"WHAT DOES IT MEAN that a man has come," Dona muttered to herself. "Is he hiding near, folded into night? Is it Samuel, or is it someone else in trouble, running for his life?" She held her lantern high, its light a terra cotta glow on the chicken coop, a flicker across a rusted wagon wheel, and at her side, the long steel barrel of her rifle. She stomped her boots across the gravel road, the crunch and stagger purposeful to warn the man, the stranger or the friend.

She was not mad to go out alone in the dark, though her reason was shaken and she was a little strange. She thought of Samuel, his strength, his gentle ways, the way he held his pain, his shoulder smashed from the back, a rifle's bullet at close range; his willingness to lie in Melvar's wagon under bolts of calico and, as she had trusted, to ride to safety. He was a man she would risk her life for, again.

She had reached nearly to the dog pens where Luke had seen him and all around were the mournful calls of whippoorwills and the crackling of armadillo hide against stalks of maize. The hounds had grown quiet. She flinched at the curdling cry of a screech owl. And there, against the faint light of sky, was a man.

"Who's there?" she called in her strongest voice.

The man did not move. "Name of Daniel."

"What is your last name, Daniel?"

"Washington, Ma'am. Brother to Samuel."

"You have news?"

"Yes'm."

"Thank heavens. Please come with me to the barn, Daniel. We'll make you a safe place to stay the night." She led the way with the lantern, its light steadier than before, illuminating here and there the eyes of owls and possums.

"I would invite you into the ranch house, but my husband is not so friendly right now. Best we should be careful."

"Yes'm."

The barn door grated open and Dona gestured to one of the horse stalls, empty for some time. "Please take hay from this stack and make yourself a comfortable place to lie down. I'll bring blankets and food and some water. If anyone else comes besides me, keep yourself hidden. It will be black as coal in here until I get back. Can you manage?"

"Yes'm, I'm mighty grateful to you."

"No need. You have come with news of your brother and that means a lot to me. We'll talk when I come back. But I'd like to know one thing. How come the hounds weren't baying when I found you tonight?"

"Oh, Missus, that is an old way our momma done taught, to calm the fears of animals. Didn't work with the other man around, 'cause they's his dogs. But when he left. Well, comes in mighty handy at times. I cain't tell you how it is; but my brother, Samuel, he has it, too."

Dona blew out the lantern, closed the barn door as quietly as she could and felt her way to the ranch house steps. The kitchen was dark and she could see no lights anywhere in the house. As she came through the screened door onto the porch she whispered, "Is anyone here?"

The swing creaked and Annalou said, "I am here. I was waiting for you."

"Samuel's brother is here, Annalou. He's in the barn. We need to help him like we did Samuel. Water, can you get that in the dark?"

"Yes. But what about Samuel?"

"I don't know yet. I am afraid to find out. But the brother, he is hungry and he has walked a long way. I'll wrap up some cornbread and ham from supper, and get blankets from the hall closet. Why are the lights out? Did Uncle Roy and them go to bed already?"

"No, they went down to the shacks."

"The shacks? Roy and Rosa have been fixing them up, but it's going to be a while before they move in. Why would they go down there now?

"Uncle Luke thought the man would run from the hounds and hide down there. They want to find him, too."

"Did they want to find him to help, or to hurt him?"

"I don't think they wanted to help. Seemed pretty upset when you left. Took the truck."

"Uncle Roy, did he take a bottle of whiskey?"

"He tucked something in his pocket, could have been whiskey."

"They're down there drinking. I'd bet my bottom dollar."

"You'd lose, pretty wife." Roy pulled open the screen door, kicked his boots against the steps and said, "Cain't anybody get a light going in this dern place?"

"Go right ahead, Roy, there's matches in the kitchen. Annalou and I, we're having a heart to heart. Don't need a light."

Roy slammed the kitchen door back to its hinges and a chair screeched across the linoleum floor. "Goddam it, woman, where's the lantern?"

"You didn't ask about that, Roy. It's right out here by me. But, there's another one in our bedroom. I thought it was matches you were after. They're on the kitchen table. Help yourself."

She reached for Annalou's hand and whispered. "He's been drinking for sure. Stay out of the way, and I mean it."

Dona stood from the swing, took the lantern into the kitchen, lit it, and called out, "Roy, here's the lantern from the porch. What are you looking for? Maybe I can help."

"Cain't help me with nothin', that's for sure."

"Where are Luke and Joe Bob?"

"Out in the dark looking for that Ni— that man, your friend."

"Nobody's there. Best call them in, it's a wild goose chase. Let's get some sleep, it'll be easier in the morning."

"You worried about what we'll do if we find him?"

"You won't find him. And even if you did, I wouldn't let you hurt him. You know that already."

"Don't fool me, girl, you've hid him, like you did Samuel, or maybe that is Samuel."

"Luke is the one who saw him. I can't see anything in this dark."

Roy stumbled against the kitchen table. "I gotta go to the barn. Got to get something for the boys."

"Whiskey? I know you hide it out there."

"None of your business."

"Everything is my business on this ranch, Roy. But if you have to know, I found your bottle in the barn and I hid it here in the house."

"You damn sneaky bitch, get me that bottle or I'll hog-tie you like the last time."

"I learned my lesson. I'll get you the bottle, but I wish you wouldn't take it to the shacks. Joe Bob, he's too young for that kind of drinking; and Luke, well, he never could hold his liquor. We've got lots of work tomorrow, remember?"

"Don't you never tell me, never, what to do. Fetch that bottle now and I'll be on my way."

"How'd you get here?"

"Truck."

"But there weren't any headlights."

"Nope, I parked down by the cattle guard and walked up."

"Wanted to catch me?"

"Yep."

"Well, there wasn't anything to catch me at. I took that lantern out to the dog pens and sure enough, whoever Luke saw there was long gone."

Dona felt her way down the hall to the linen closet. She rummaged through the towels and pulled out a bottle. "Here it is, Roy, right where I hid it. Take it and go, and don't come griping to me tomorrow about how you feel. Work is work and it has to get done."

"Just shut up," Roy growled, grabbing the bottle in one hand and the lantern in the other. He kicked open the screen door.

In a few minutes, the truck engine turned over and when it was out of ear shot, she gathered together food and the blanket, unhooked a lantern from above the kitchen table, grabbed the box of matches, her rifle and went to the porch.

"Annalou, we'd best hurry."

By now the old crescent moon was raising its light in the east and without the lantern Dona could see the faint outline of the barn. Buster crowed. Dona sniffed the air, cool and fragrant with the scent of new hay. The barn owl hooted, once, twice, and in the moon's light it flapped from under the barn's roof. Nothing was amiss—and everything.

"Annalou, hold onto my shirt, I'm going to crack the barn door a little. Daniel," she called in a low voice through the narrow opening. "It's Dona. Are you there?"

"I'm here."

"I don't know where to hide you, Daniel."

"I've got a place to go. I'm come to tell you Samuel is all right. Melvar took care of him ever since they left here in the wagon. He gave me this, to give to you. Hold out your hands, please?"

Daniel's hands wrapped around Dona's felt like Samuel's had, comforting and sure. He dropped something familiar into the basket of her palms. And there lay the twin of the box Bertie had given to her on a day that felt like years ago, and was only weeks.

"I see that it is from Melvar. Thank you for bringing it to me."

Dona leaned on Annalou's shoulder. "Let me sit down, please. Seeing you and hearing this, it's almost," she drew her breath, "too much good news . . ." Annalou helped her into the horse stall where Daniel had been hiding and she hunkered down on the hay.

There they gathered, eating the food left from supper; the three of them, shoulder to shoulder, huddled on the floor until Dona regained herself and said, "Where will you go, Daniel? Where is Samuel's family?"

"The family, all safe. Melvar has seen to it. And I'm going back to your sister's ranch, where Samuel and I have been these past weeks."

"To Unity Ann's. Thank heavens."

"She's a mighty generous friend, like you. A doctor friend of hers helped Samuel, and with his lung and shoulder healing he's had easy work with the cattle out where nobody could see him. We're pretty fair carpenters and we've worked up an idea or two for how to help her and some other folks. We're aiming to bring our whole family there."

"How'd you get here?"

"Unity Ann. Back of her truck in a load of cotton. Left me off by your main gate and aims to pick me up there before daylight. She's gone see your momma and said to say she loves you. Says it ain't safe to use the telephone."

Dona shook her head, "Unity Ann. That girl has surprised me all her life. Well, I love her, too."

Daniel raised on his haunches and whispered, "Shush, there's somebody coming."

"Close the barn door all the way, quick," Dona said. But there wasn't time enough as the headlights of the old truck swept through the door and onto the barn's back wall. The engine shook to a stop.

"Maybe they're drunk enough to ignore the door," Dona said.

They sat as still as the harnesses slung across saw horses, waiting to be mended. This was Luke's territory. He softened leather here, he sharpened hoes and knives and plow blades; he would come inside. Maybe he would think he'd forgotten to shut the door.

Luke kicked the barn door open wider and hollered, "Anybody in here?" Hens clucked and grumbled from the roost. Luke waited until they settled down; he was listening; they were all listening. Something plopped to the wooden floor in front of the horse stall. It meowed. Luke's voice was hoarse and low, and close.

"Dadgummit, Bronco, you stupid cat. Scared me out of my wits. Git back to work and catch me some rats." He chuckled to himself, stomped out of the barn, and pushed the door shut.

They crouched against the stall's sides, not moving, not speaking until Roy yelled from the ranch house, "What the dickens you been doing, Luke? Those girls, where the hell are they? What's going on around here?"

"Annalou," Dona whispered, "we've got to get out of here. Daniel, take the rest of that food and you give my undying love to that sister of mine. I will find a way to get there real soon. You have given me so many gifts tonight. Y'all take good care and if there are angels, I know they'll be with you."

Dona stood up from the hay, drawing into herself the scent of horses and leather and feed. "Come on, Annalou, let's go out the chicken coop door and make those fellas believe we've had a beautiful walk with the rising moon, tonight. Get that storytelling mind of yours going; thank heavens for whiskey."

Chapter Thirty-seven

Annalou had felt inside every nesting box; she had lifted floorboards, broken by one heavy hoof or another; she had searched in the rabbit brush off to the north side of the red barn, but nowhere could she find an egg. There were always eggs in the early morning, lots of them. The hens were happy hens, they ate grass seeds blowing in barnyard dust, they scratched for beetles and tiny stones, they snapped up flies and ticks and ate a goodly manner of chicken scratch from Aunt Doney's own apron every day. So why hadn't they laid? And on this of all days, when Mamaw was coming for Sunday evening pancakes.

"Silly," said a voice, "can't you guess what happened to your dern ole eggs?"

Annalou whirled around. "Who's there?"

And of all the people she would hope to see in the world, that very one came running toward her, arms stretched out, mouth wide with laughter. Merrybelles. Merrybelles had come back, like she promised weeks ago; like Annalou had wished for every day since then. Merrybelles, her new friend, maybe down the road her best friend; who was not afraid of nobody, not even Joe Bob.

Annalou ran to Marybelles and hugged her round and round, hens flying in alarm all about.

The girls could hardly speak for laughing, and when they could be still enough, they collapsed in the barn's doorway and lay back in the scattered hay, panting.

"You, you gathered all those eggs! I was worried something terrible."

"Oh," Merrybelles said, "it was a grand trick. It was so funny to see you searching under the floorboards. Some pretty odd hens you'd have, to lay there."

"I know, but I was desperate. I thought a weasel had stormed in here, or a big milk snake and sucked them all up. Aunt Doney would have been so upset."

"Well, they are all fine, not a one cracked, and I'll get them for you in the shake..."

"...of a lamb's tail," Annalou finished, laughing again. "And, by the way, where is your fine mare?"

"I took the liberty of watering her at your windmill trough, and right now, she's out there saying hello to your good-looking gelding, Paint."

"We're both lucky today. So, I have to ask. Merrybelles, where did you go when you and Sheba left here?

"Like I said I would, Sheba and me, we made our way to Brownwood, to my aunt and uncle. Not my real aunt and uncle, mind, but somewhat family. Took quite a many days, as you would suppose, with Sheba and me, following the river best we could. We had to stop ever night at ranch houses or farms or lean-to shacks to ask for our supper and a place in the barn for shelter."

"Were people nice to you? Did they ask questions?"

"Most were nice. But where there was fellas who had bad business on their minds, I'd put myself back on Sheba and off we'd go. Don't cotton to no bad boys. Which makes me wonder, weren't you having some bad business with a boy right here at the ranch?"

"Uh huh, I was, but things are better now. I talked with Aunt Doney and my grandmother about it, and they talked with Joe Bob and he's been okay with me ever since. But my Uncle Roy, he's still mad at me for making a fuss. Didn't believe Joe Bob tried to get in my room, and he said, if it did happen, it was my fault for being a pretty girl."

"Don't that just tan your britches. Not a bit of it was your fault and I sure do hope you know it."

"It's better for now, and a lot of worse things have happened since you left. I've been hoping you'd come back. I know for sure if you share my bedroom, Joe Bob won't ever try to get in there again."

"I can stay for a spell, if you'd like me to. And it would be grand, if I can go back to school. But I have to tell you that I got into some trouble in Brownwood, and I feel a real big need to say it. The problem was me, not liking to be their servant."

"Their servant?"

"You know I like to work hard, you'll remember that about me—-helping out in the kitchen when I was here before, right?"

"You're a really good worker. And you can gather eggs real good, too."

Merrybelles grinned. "Yep, a good egg stealer, that's me. Well, I didn't steal no eggs in Brownwood, but I wasn't about to do ever lick of work around that place while they sat around and drank their bourbon straight."

"What's bourbon straight?"

"Oh, sorry. Bourbon is whiskey and straight means it ain't got no water, no nothing added. Makes it stronger."

"My momma and daddy only drank beer, lots of beer," Annalou said.

"Well, anyway, my aunt and uncle started trying to punish me if all the chores wasn't perfect, which was impossible for one person."

"Punish you?"

"Yep, they tried to lock me in a closet, but I picked the lock. Then they pushed me down the basement stairs in the dark and padlocked the door from the outside. It was too thick to break, so I had myself one big grief cry and dug my way out through an old window."

"That is horrible. They must be crazy or something."

"Crazy is a nice word for it. So as soon as I could, when they was drunk as skunks, I snuck out, saddled Sheba, stuffed my things in my saddle bags and took off. Didn't hardly stop until I got back here." Merrybelles face shone.

"You must be exhausted—and starved. That's why you stole those eggs!"

Merrybelles laughed. "Sure, that's it. And don't never tell that tale, Annalou, it's gotta be in a book sealed with seven veils. Like in far off Arabia." She stood and swiped the hay from her britches. "And now, you got an idea about how a gal might panhandle some breakfast around these parts?"

Chapter Thirty-eight

"My heart is plumb cluttered, Luke," Dona said. Supper was over and the others had gone to do the evening chores. "So much, I don't know what I feel or think or what to do."

She stretched the damp cup towel on the drainboard, wiped her hands on her apron and sat at the table. "I never on God's green earth believed until lately, with Samuel coming here and all, that you could ever be in favor of the Klan." She spread her hands on the oilcloth in the kerosene lamp's circle of light. "It's like, all of a sudden, I see my hands like they were somebody else's. You know what I mean?"

Luke nodded and opened his hands into the light. "I do. Times are, when I don't know my own self. Lots of times, lately."

"I wish I'd known about your feelings, you know, about Samuel. At first, you were mad about him being here, but then, you seemed to want to help him get to safety."

"Thought I did, but after you shot Ross in the shoulder, and I helped, and you are my best sister, something happened. I couldn't see saving a colored man and shooting a white one. Something in me went kind of haywire."

"I'm wanting to understand, you know? Doesn't fit with you, being with Evangeline and the baby and all. That day when you nearly broke Joe Bob's neck, there in Mother's house? Was it because he was catching on to something?"

"Nope. Joe Bob was starting to stick up for that ni—, I mean Samuel. We had a fight about it, real quiet like, there in Mother's living room. Joe Bob got the worst of it, I guess."

"But he never blamed you."

"Yep. I didn't mean to hurt him. That's these hands." He turned them, palms up. "Like they have their own minds."

"They don't. They have yours. And what about MacMurray? "

"What about him?"

"Was he at the center of all of this?"

"Sort of."

"Just sort of? If he's not, who is?"

Luke pushed back his chair, "I don't think I can..."

"Yes, Luke, you can. I do not want to hurt you, Lord knows. But I have to have the truth."

Luke shut his eyes and slapped his hands over his mouth and said, "The Judge."

Old Buster crowed somewhere in the barnyard; the great-granddaddy's clock ticked in the living room; the windmill whined and walloped the air, but the foundation of the old rock house held fast.

"Oh my god, Luke, I've known Angus almost all of my life. I admit that I am afraid of him, and I saw his white hood that awful afternoon in our living room. Roy told me as much, too, but I guess I couldn't believe it. If he's the main man, he's got to be stopped. In a bit, we'll decide what to do, but right now, I need to know if you still plan to kill somebody—like you meant to kill Joe Bob, and like MacMurray was meaning to kill Eleanor."

"No, Sis, I do not. Not now. Lest the Devil come in again. I'll stick around and help you with the ranch."

"Okay." Dona stood from the table and turned to the stove. "If you can put the Devil behind you, I guess I'll need your help right much."

Luke pushed his hat over his slick head and shuffled to Dona's side. "And you, you cain't stay out of trouble, but you gotta keep your head down a mite better."

He put his arm over her shoulder and squeezed.

CHAPTER THIRTY-NINE

THE DOVE TWISTED A TWIG from the old willow and whistled off. Dona perched on a low branch curving over the Kelly Hole, her favorite place along the river's grassy edge, water green and murky from the heat. Above the willow, and toward the field of maize, past ready for harvesting, pecan trees climbed as high as the new buildings in San Angelo. A ripple below the willow caught her eye and she drew back. But this was not a water moccasin or a snapping turtle.

A rare river otter slithered onto the bank and glared at her. Neither one spoke, though Dona could not help but chuckle. The otter sat still for a moment and started to dance. It wasn't a "grab your partner and do-si-do" dance, the kind Dona had done all her life, but graceful. The otter shimmied and slid, it rolled and shook, it kept inside its own circle as though a line had been drawn.

"Are you reminding me to dance?"

The otter stopped, mid-twirl. Not a hair vibrated. Its berry-black eyes caught Dona's and might have held them for all eternity had not Duke snorted and nickered a message they both understood. The otter vanished. Someone was coming.

The wagon clanged and clattered over ruts and rocks along the river road. Dona craned toward the sound, embarrassed that her heart splintered and her hands trembled on the branch. "Get a hold of yourself, old girl. He's come to find you after so many days."

"Dona," Melvar called. And she clambered up the stony riverbank and crouched, as still as the otter had been only minutes before, until her heart slowed in its ribs. She pushed against a tree and stood.

"Melvar," she called out.

"Yes, Melvar. The one who loves you."

"And I have missed you for so long," she said.

Dona felt she could live forever in the warm circle of his arms, but in a moment, she drew back. She had to tell him of Luke's troubles.

Light from the kitchen window met them as they rode into the barnyard. Melvar pulled Molly to a halt beside the animal barn and jumped from the wagon. "Please stay here, Dona, for a few minutes. I need to talk with Luke."

He called out toward the house, "Hello, it's Melvar. Is anyone at home?" The shadow of a figure appeared in the kitchen doorway.

"Whatcha want?"

"I hope to talk with you, Luke."

"What about?" He shuffled onto the porch and pushed open the screen door.

"Oh, a few things. Please."

"Did Dona tell you anything?"

"About the coyote and something of your little family."

"Okay. We can talk right here."

Dona waited on the wagon's seat.

Melvar cleared his throat. "I have taken some care to protect Samuel and his family. And Dona, I would give my life to save hers. Do you know that?"

"I suspicioned as much."

"When Dona told me about the coyote, about the note, hard to think you were the one." He reached for a mesquite twig laying propped against the steps and broke it between his thumbs, feeling the pinch of thorns. "Anything you want to tell me? I can perhaps be of help."

"I love my sister. But..." Luke pushed his hat back and rubbed his scalp. "Can't rightly understand, myself. Sometimes I do things and it's like some other cuss is doing them."

A crow flew up from the maize field, hovered, and dove into the dry stalks. "Like that there crow. Part of me is in the sky and part of me is pecking at the ground. Cain't depend on which one I am."

Melvar took off his hat and turned it upside down in his hand. "Like this, Luke? Like this way I've got a bowl. Many times at midday, I have dipped it into a river and poured water over my head." He put the hat on his head. "And like this I have a tent for shade."

"Yep," said Luke, waving his own hat in the air, "and sometimes a prod for them stubborn cows."

"You have it. Hardly anything is just one thing. And for sure a man is not."

"Melvar, I am a sinner."

"So am I."

"I mean I am a big sinner."

"Because you loved a colored woman?"

"No." Luke straightened his back and turned toward Melvar. "Because I weren't brave enough to bring her and the baby home with me. I didn't stand up to nobody. I didn't save 'em. I didn't even try."

Dona left the wagon and came to where the men stood. "Melvar, would you go in the front door and telephone Ophelia? Ask her if she would bring Annalou back and stay for supper."

Melvar tipped his hat and started around the house.

"And," she called, "Roy and the other boys are out in the West Lee pasture. Ought to be home for supper pretty soon. Could I ask you to get the molasses out of the can in the shed and fetch me a side of bacon from the smokehouse? We're having pancakes and bacon."

She waited until Melvar was out of sight and put her hand on Luke's arm. "Look at me, Luke." He faced instead toward the river pasture. "I heard what you said to Melvar. I know you are ashamed." Luke nodded. "And crazy as a coot."

Luke shot a glance at her out of the side of his eyes.

"And who wouldn't be. But this critter in your mind is going to get wilder, if we don't grab it by the neck."

"How do you hang on to a rattlesnake? It ain't got no neck."

"You get a forked stick and a burlap sack, that's how."

Luke nodded. "But, Sis, you cain't never go after rattlers alone; they always got company in their den."

"You're not alone either, Luke."

He pulled his hat off of his head and turned his face to the sky. "I guess not. It's not just me and those clouds in front of the stars and whatever comes out of them, not anymore."

Melvar moved across the porch, eased out the screen door and sat next to Luke on the stoop. "You have more than a few friends now, and you can count me for one."

"Thank you, kindly. I don't deserve nothin' good. But I'm mightily grateful."

"LUKE, Molly and I have to get back to town. As you'd say, we've got a heap of work to do before bedtime. Dona, would you take a walk with me?"

They stood together in the shadow of the barn, face to face; Melvar with one hand on Molly's neck.

"I need to say, Dona, and I hope you will forgive me if it's improper. But this is what I have learned from you. How important the small things are. How the eyes of a girl of nine can light a whole life. How the wrong word can bring a lynch mob; how a woman can get an answer from a mother snake; and, here's another little thing, how your eyes, so many years later, can shut down my breath."

"Melvar, I have doubted you, and that is no small thing."

"No." He pulled his Stetson from his dark curls and clamped it over his heart. "But I gave you reason. Do you trust me, now?"

"I do. And do you trust me?"

"Yes."

"Will you be back this way pretty soon?"

"Pretty soon? I'm like that lizard on the barn door. I'm waiting for the next fly to come along."

"And I'm the fly?"

Melvar threw his head back, and laughed. "Not hardly. I meant the fly was like a chance; I wait for the chance to see you, your eyes, green as that lizard."

"My brother, Lon, he never trusted anybody with green eyes. How come you do?"

"It's not the color, Dona, it's the lightning."

"In my eyes?"

"Yes, ma'am. In your eyes."

They stood so close that each could feel the heat of the other's body, but there, in the barnyard where any manner of being might be watching, they did not touch.

Dona whispered, "What do you really want?"

"To be with you for the rest of my life."

"Why?"

"I have loved you since we met that morning after church. When all the world seemed evil and doomed, when I was a slave boy to Reverend Sinclair. And you did not laugh at my accent. You did not make fun of my name. But, Dona. I must ask this. What of Roy?"

"He does not love me. No. He respects me, he counts on me, and perhaps he loved me when we were children. But after all these years, he finds he loves another. Her name is Rosa Cruz, and she is, as he says, as beautiful as a sunrise."

"Yes, I have seen her."

"And I, I have come to know her a little. She is a match for him. She is lovely, she is ambitious, and she knows hard work."

"You have said this much to him?"

"I have. And that if he must be with her, they can stay at the ranch, build up the shacks to any kind of home they want, and take care of the livestock."

"You are very generous."

"I care about Joe Bob. And if Roy stays here, Joe Bob can stay here."

"Do you think always of everyone else?"

"Sometimes I do. But in this instance, I am thinking of myself."

Dona wrapped her arms about her ribs. "Above all, please remember, that I know the real, the natural you." Her words pushed out. "The one with room in his feelings for the real me, under my worry and the know-it-all. How can I thank you for loving me, still?"

She touched the softness of his shirt sleeve, felt the muscle above his elbow tense and relax. His hand opened toward her, and when she placed her own hand in his, it was for only the time it takes for a bird to hunch its wings and fly away.

Chapter Forty

Next morning, after she'd cleared away the breakfast things, Dona saddled Duke. The first tap of her spurs set him at a trot along the River Road and west toward High Pasture.

Dona leaned over the saddle horn and said, "Did you hear about Bertie, arriving here last night, with her troubles?" Dona clapped the reins and Duke broke into a gallop, headed for the first cattle guard and, without hesitating, jumped over it.

The situation with Bertie was not going to be easy. Last night, whispering to Dona in the quiet of the living room, she had confessed at last that it was Judge Cameron, or one of his henchmen, after her. Like he'd been after who knows how many others. And now, he had gotten her fired from her job at the hospital and someone had put a note in her car saying 'Leave town now, or die.'"

And what Bertie had, the reason the Judge wanted her dead, was evidence that would damn him to hell. The string of beatings and lies, how he exhorted the men to clear the county of those "uppity niggers and dirty lowlife Meskins" who were after their jobs and their women. Bertie knew about all of that. She had been the county's telephone operator, after all, and the lines had buzzed for years from the Judge's chambers, reaching out to this farm and that ranch, to this feed store and that machine shop.

In the beginning, Bertie had helped, thinking she was doing her job. She knew pretty much where every person in the county could be reached. Apparently, since she spoke English with a slight foreign accent, the Judge had thought Bertie was stupid. But because she was good at her "little job," as he called it, the Judge appreciated her help and rewarded her well.

"Perhaps Dona had wondered how she could afford her nice, big house on a telephone operator's salary?" Bertie asked.

Dona said she had not.

But of course, Bertie said, she had listened in. And, being brilliant, not stupid, she had kept records of his calls and made detailed notes of the conversations, thinking she might someday need them.

She wasn't sure how the Judge found out about the records. But one day, the letter came, the letter she had shown Dona in the coffee shop, and she had lied and said it was from Dona's cousin, Edward, threatening her life if she did not leave town. But really it was from the Judge, which she didn't say because she hoped to use her notes against him. And from then on, as she knew Dona knew, her life had been miserable.

"Right," said Dona, leaning closer, "I've heard that the Judge is at the heart of the troubles, but not the details. Is there a woman or a colored person in this whole county who's safe from persecution, these days?"

They sat without speaking for a while, until Dona said, "Bertie, you may have Annalou's room for tonight. I don't want you driving home right now."

"Thank you," Bertie said, and Dona, in the dim light of the room, saw the tears, bright in her eyes.

She led Bertie into the bedroom, and fluffed the pillows. "Bertie, dear, I want you to know that this home is your home for as long as you need it, okay?"

Bertie lay back on the pillows, folded her hands over her chest and took a deep breath. She coughed. "Would you mind, that little coverlet over my legs?" And in moments, she was asleep.

Dona closed the bedroom door and tiptoed back to the kitchen. She wished she had a bigger house. Luke and Joe Bob were living in the bunkhouse. Eleanor had only last week been moved by Dr. Bowen from the smallest bedroom to Unity Ann's, to finish her recovery. She supposed she could leave Bertie in that room, where she seemed so comfortable right now. But it was Annalou's room, and she and Merrybelles couldn't stay at Ophelia's forever. And school would start soon.

For the next couple of days, Bertie seemed as lost as a needle under a porch, and was so altogether mad, she pitched the white enameled pan and its unshelled peas out of her lap into the dusty dead grass of the barnyard. She was sick of this business of being afraid. She wanted to get on with it.

All of this she told Dona the next night at supper. She thanked Dona for her kindness, for her patience, for her bravery and on and on, but enough was enough. She was good and tired of feeling like a sack of potatoes on the back of a mule, like a horse gone lame at the rodeo, like a barnyard cat with no teeth.

"You're well, Bertie, your spirit's back. You've made it."

Bertie sat down at the table. "I have, Dona. And now I aim to go back home. Thank you for saving my life, I think."

"But, Bertie, what will keep the Judge from trying to kill you there?"

"Could we make him think that I died?"

"Roy might have told somebody you are here, or Luke, or Mother."

"Could we say that I died today? And then I could hide out someplace safe."

"Do you have a place in mind?"

"How about where Samuel is?"

"I'm worried you might endanger each other. How about a trip to Austin or Houston? Do you know anybody there?"

"Not really, not well enough to ask a favor like that."

"What about Edward, Bertie? Would he give you a safe haven?"

Bertie blushed a deep scarlet and stared at the floor.

"Why, Bertie, what is it between you and Edward?"

"Oh, Dona, there is something. I have always liked Edward, difficult as he can be, he reminds me of my blessed father. I miss him so much.

And these days, Melvar's gone, lots of the time on your business." She frowned into Dona's eyes. "I am lonely. I told you at Luby's that we, Melvar and I, that we were lonely. But I'm the one. And Edward, I always wished, and I know better, I know his preference for men, but that we could, you know, be companions; family, you might say."

"Bertie, that is a wonderful idea. I think Edward is lonely, too, and the two of you would have such amazing conversations. Please ask him to give you a hand."

"Maybe," Bertie said. "But you need to tell everyone else about my untimely, unexpected death. Right away."

"I'll think about it, Bertie."

Chapter Forty-one

Standing in the middle of the kitchen, staring at the cracks in the oilcloth covering the table, Dona turned to put the kettle on for tea, for comfort. She had waved goodbye to Bertie, and hoped to feel better. But she might well have been in the middle of the Gulf of Mexico—which was the only salt water she'd ever seen in her life—with sharks and jellyfish on every side and no boat in sight. She shuddered and shook herself and wandered to the back porch. She peered through the screen, across the barnyard toward the main gate. The way out.

She put her hands on her hips and said to the hot, dry afternoon, "No, sir. You sharks might come, but I am not giving up on Samuel, or Bertie, or Eleanor—and I'm not giving up on this ranch."

That said, she sat on the porch swing and made her own breeze. And perhaps it was a breeze that was stirring up dust out there, along the ranch road. She hoped it wasn't a vehicle, but it was moving right along. A Ford sedan, gleaming like a ruby in the sun, was barreling toward her at ridiculous speed.

Perhaps the last person Dona expected as a visitor stepped out of the car, her dress and hat a matching peach, her shoes the latest style, high-heeled pumps from the shoe store in town. Dona took off her apron and shook out her skirt as she squared her shoulders. It was Mrs. Margaret Cameron, wife of Judge Angus Cameron. Why on earth?

"Hello, Dona," Mrs. Cameron said, holding out a gloved hand.

"Why, hello, Margaret," Dona said, taking the hand in her own brown, calloused one. "And what brings you to these far distant parts?"

"Might we go inside? I am tired and hot from driving that noisy thing all the way here."

"Of course, please do come right on in. I just put the kettle on for tea."

"Tea? Might you have a little brandy?"

"I'll see what I can find. Let's go sit on the porch, out of the sun."

"Thank you for your welcome, Dona. I am long overdue for a visit."

Dona thought this was an odd thing to say. When had she and Margaret Cameron ever had a visit?

In a few minutes, Margaret was pushing herself on the porch swing, her stockinged feet dancing against the wooden planks of the floor as though butterflies flitted under them, and holding a small glass of whiskey to her lips. "Ah, this is what the doctor ordered," and she smiled into the glass.

"If I may ask," Dona said, glancing at Margaret's feet out of the sides of her eyes, "what brings you here today?"

"Oh, I was born rude as a mule and to barge in on you like this; well, I didn't know what else to do, who else to turn to."

"And here we are, and I have long ears—like a mule, you might say."

Margaret laughed, threw the whiskey back in her throat and put the glass on the porch's wooden floor.

"First, I want you to know that I come empty-handed. Like when I was born. Had nothing then, have nothing now."

"All right, that makes two of us. But Margaret..."

"Yes, you thought I was rich like my husband, didn't you?"

"You might say so. And I mean, look at you. You dress like a million dollars."

"You are kind. But didn't anybody tell you that looking like this could be a way to show off a cripple?"

"What may I do to help, Margaret?"

"Oh, Lordy, you are already helping. Shaking my hand, shoving whiskey toward me, letting me talk to you, woman to woman. Believe me, you are helping."

Dona put her hands over her stomach. This place, this edge. It was dangerous. Margaret Cameron, the Judge's fancy wife, driving in her fancy car, in her fancy clothes, to the ranch, as plain and dusty as all get out, and asking Dona to help her. The barnyard opened a crack, and edges crumbled. Did the Judge ask Margaret to confide in Dona to get her trust, and find out what was going on with Samuel?

"Margaret," Dona said, leaning over her crossed arms, "why did you come to me?"

Margaret clasped her fingers with their polished nails around Dona's arms. "I see you don't trust me, and why should you?"

"Yes, why should I? Please tell me why."

"Because," Margaret loosened her grip and sat back in the swing. "Because I need for you to. And because I don't have another place in the world to turn." Black tears rolled from her eyes, spreading mascara on her rouged cheeks. She pulled a handkerchief from her dress sleeve and patted her face. Her mouth wobbled. "How can I convince you, Dona, that the Judge does not know why I am here?"

Dona took the handkerchief from Margaret's hand and wiped the dark stains from her face. "I don't know what to tell you. I am no friend of your husband's, that's for sure. It's my guess that he is one of the big men behind the Klan who wants to lynch Samuel."

"You are right about that," said Margaret, retrieving her handkerchief and shoving it under her cuff. She leaned toward Dona's ear. "He is the one, and I know who they all are."

"Does he know you are here, at all?"

"Yes, I told him, but I said it was to get you to come to women's auxiliary next month."

"Why?"

"You were a champion barrel racer and we're having a program on rodeos and religion."

Dona chuckled. "Well, to imagine that barrel racing would connect with religion is a little far-fetched. But it's a good story."

"Dona," Margaret said, looking into her lap at her hands, twisting and turning as though they might get away. "They'd rather die, those men, than let a woman get the better of them. Really, they are suspicious scaredy-cats and they hate power in anybody but another white man."

"Before you go on," Dona said, her palm open toward Margaret, "let me tell you that those "men," as you call them, came close to sapping the juice out of me when they got Samuel shot. I mean, it was like being in the middle of a dream where the quirks and hateful habits of a bunch of white boys grew into a nightmare. And it was madness that wasn't momentary in the least. I was on these steps right here when one of those boys threatened to blast a hole in my head. Now, that's a pretty strong reaction to a powerful woman, wouldn't you say?"

"I do say so, and it is one reason to despise my husband. He sent those men to get you."

"But why?"

Margaret shifted in the swing and pushed the porch floor with her foot. "You've always been a troublemaker, Dona. Like my foot, here. You push one way and the swing moves the other; you push back again and so does the swing."

"You mean, I started the whole thing?"

"Why, you invited a Negro family and a Mexican family to your own wedding, when there'd never been anybody but white folks in that church. Or since, may I say."

"Or any other white church in our county, for that matter, Margaret. Which I think is altogether unchristian. But why was that such a big thing for your husband? Those families were, I mean they are, my friends. Samuel and Juan Carlos and their families. It was my wedding, mine and Roy's, and he said he didn't mind too much. At the time."

"Could you spare another whiskey? Maybe a bigger glass?"

"Yes of course, I need a cup of tea, myself. Want to come in the kitchen?"

"I'll sit here in the swing. Some birds out there on the big mesquite next to the barn, I don't know them. Got any looking glasses?"

"Whiskey and binoculars, coming right up. And then please excuse me for a minute. I have to put a pot roast in the oven."

Margaret lowered the binoculars, shoved her feet into her shoes and lurched into the kitchen. "Those birds are as foreign to that mesquite tree as, well, as your friend, Melvar, is to this county."

"And are they as helpful?" Dona said, turning from the oven. She could see Margaret's outline against the glare of the afternoon, and hoped she was smiling.

"I think they are painted buntings, and they do eat right many bugs." Margaret leaned against the kitchen table.

"Have a seat, and I'll slice us some cornbread to go with our tea. You've got to drive home, right?"

"Oh, don't worry about me. I'm used to driving half-crocked. Only way I can stand going home, half the time."

"What's it like at home?"

"Like a bacon, lettuce and tomato sandwich."

Dona laughed. "Margaret, you are a funny one. What do you mean?"

"I'm the bacon in the middle, fried to a crisp; hemmed in by lettuce and tomatoes on all sides, greased up by Miracle Whip and fairly suffocated by bread."

"I see you've given this some thought. And I get the bacon, but what's the lettuce and tomato?"

"Money and his girlfriends. Don't be dense." She blew on the tea Dona handed her and took a sip. "Oh, yes, that's just right."

"And Miracle Whip?"

"That's the hardest one for me. It's what people think. Very good cornbread, by the way, especially with that molasses from the general store. Made over in Louisiana."

"Is that why you can't refuse? What people would think, if you left the money behind and ignored his girlfriends?"

"I'd get eaten up, that's why. Chewed and swallowed and flushed down the toilet. There'd be nothing left but the painted fingernails I'd buried in my husband's eyes."

"So, you have no choice and your husband gets to do whatever he wants?"

"That's about it."

"Margaret, do you have children?"

"Not at home. A girl and a boy. Girl married, up in Dallas. Boy working those new oil rigs down near Galveston."

"And you have a maid? A gardener?"

"Yes, of course." Margaret flicked a crumb of Dona's cornbread from the oilcloth table cover with her fingernail. "Everything happens there without me, except the part about being my husband's wife, which means his property. Or maybe it's more like his hunting trophy, the once-beautiful head he hangs above the fireplace."

"Have you ever thought of going to college? Maybe learning to do something for pay?"

"So I could get out of there, you mean? Yes, I have thought of it, but what would I do?"

"What did you used to love to do, as a girl, I mean?"

Margaret chuckled. "I wanted more than anything to be a doctor when I grew up. But you see what happened."

"And of course, it is too late only if you think it is. A woman standing will get off the mark faster than a woman sitting down. Why not explore what's available at our junior college?"

"I feel like a chicken who's been too long in the cage. I don't know how to scratch for my own food." She pushed back her chair from the table.

"That's what I'm saying. Maybe you can learn. Stand up, get over there, look at the course catalogue, see what sends a little thrill through your middle. Maybe they have courses for future doctors. You are a smart woman. You've figured out how to live with a tyrant for how many years?"

"Too many," said Margaret, smoothing her skirt over her knees and rising. She held the edge of the table for a moment and steadied herself.

"Margaret," Dona laughed. "You're darned near as tall as I am. Did you slump when you were a girl, to be shorter than the boys?"

Margaret giggled and put her hands to her mouth. "I did. Did you?"

"Sure did. For a while. And then I said to hell with it. Let them get to liking tall women."

"Oh, you are so good for me, Dona. And now that I'm standing up, maybe I should drive on home. I'll look into that college thing tomorrow." She wobbled on her high-heeled shoes to the porch and held on to the door jamb. "Thank you for listening to me. It's been a long time."

"Margaret, maybe you can spend the night here? I'm a little worried about your safety, driving all the way back to town. It will be dark before you get there and you are so welcome."

"I can make it, and if I'm not there to serve supper to the Judge, there will be hell to pay."

"Shall I send some food home with you?"

"Oh no, Jessie will have it ready."

"Who's Jessie?"

"Our live-in help. Jessie Washington."

"Do I know her?"

"Well, she's young, a Negro."

"Is she by chance a cousin of Samuel Washington's? She's got the same last name."

"Why, I believe she is."

"And does the Judge treat her well?"

"The Judge does not treat any female well, Dona."

"Oh, my. I am so sorry. For her and for you."

"Why for her? I try not to pay attention, but she seems to get what she wants — a nice house to keep clean, plenty of her own cooking, a room in the back."

"It sounds pretty unhappy for you."

"It's miserable, but she's a good cook." Margaret walked to the porch swing, gathered her purse and hat and pushed open the screen door. "Well, I will see you soon."

"Margaret, what did you really come here for?"

Margaret peered toward the red of her new Ford sedan, shining next to a Model T truck, its fenders and running board bright with rust. She hesitated before she spoke.

"I was sent by the Judge, Dona. He wants me to convince you to give up Samuel."

She looked toward the barn, straightened the feather on her hat and said, "But, right away—maybe it was the old truck, maybe it was the gray weathered barn, or maybe it was you, inviting me in the way you did—I knew that wasn't why I was here."

Dona's hens had gathered by the foot of the steps, squawking and shoving to be close.

"I have to feed these girls, as you can see. I wish you'd stay, truly. But if not, could you come on back soon?"

"I will, I promise. I'll try to call first."

Chapter Forty-two

Two days later, Dona was in the barn pitching hay for Dolly, the sorrel mare with a foal, when a car banged over the cattle guard at the edge of the maize field. "Somebody's in a hurry," she said to Dolly.

It was Margaret. Her car came to a halt just short of hitting Luke's truck.

They had seated themselves on the swing, Margaret's whiskey glass from home in her hand, when she whispered, "There's something I need to show you."

She pulled from her purse a small photograph. "Dona, this is Jessie."

In the middle of the frame, a child peered out from eyes swollen almost shut. Patches shone on her dark cheekbones and her mouth had distorted into a grimace.

"This child has been beaten, horribly. This is Jessie?"

"Yes, she is sixteen years old. This is what the Judge did to her while I was here. She let me take the picture with my new camera after I told her I would show it to you."

"Oh, my god. And where is this child now?"

"In my car."

"She's here? Why didn't you tell me right away?"

"I wasn't sure if I was still welcome, given why I came last time. She's in the back seat. Still pretty laid up, maybe running a fever. I made a bed for her so I could bring her here."

"Yes, of course, let's get her inside."

"I lied and said I was going to visit my mother in Waco, to show her my new car. I've hired a temporary cook and housekeeper. Angus knows

I'm upset about Jessie, but I told him that her family came for her. I have five days."

"The two of you will stay in Annalou's room. She's with a friend, visiting her grandmother in town, and I'm sure she won't mind. Do you think Jessie was raped as well as beaten?"

"Probably. Or attempted. The Judge is not the young bull he thinks he is."

"Thank heavens."

Margaret knocked on the back door of the Ford and drew it open. Jessie lay splayed on a patchwork quilt, her eyes rolled back in her head. Sweat beaded on her face and neck, her skin shone like copper.

There are a lot of words for rage, but Dona pushed with her breath and held them between her ribs.

"Jessie, dear," Margaret said, poking Jessie's shoulder, "Dona is here."

Jessie's eyes fluttered open and closed, a moth trapped by a window.

Dona reached in and felt her cheek. "So hot. Jessie, can you sit?"

She took Jessie's hand and the child pulled herself up, her lips clamped against the pain.

"Let's go, sugar."

They staggered, the three of them, to the shade of the screened porch. "Maybe this is far enough for now," Dona said. "Let's make a pallet here on the swing. I'll draw a glass of water."

In ten minutes, Jessie was lying on a quilt, resting her elbow on a pillow, and swallowing water as best she could. Margaret wiped up what dripped to her chest.

"Thank you, missus Dona," Jessie mumbled as she let her frail body collapse onto the swing. "Thank you, missus Judge."

"Margaret, let's go into the kitchen and let Jessie rest. I'll make us some coffee."

"I have a feeling," Margaret said, holding her glass with both hands, "that we should take her to the river."

"The river? Well, we could do that when she wakes up, I suppose. What makes you think of the river?"

"Are your folks coming home for supper?"

"They are, but it will be late today, what with the rodeo and all."

"Seems like we might want to get Jessie to a private spot. Don't you have a couple of shacks down there?"

"We do, but how on earth do you know that?" Dona set a cup of coffee and a plate of molasses cookies on the oilcloth in front of Margaret.

"Honey, the Judge, he tells me things, and he knows everything there is to know about you."

"That's pure comfort," Dona said, grinning. "It's a wonder he's let me live at all."

"He tried to get you killed." Margaret dipped a half-eaten cookie in her coffee and peered over it to look at Dona.

"Well, I know that."

"But you were too smart for his boys. And, from what I gather, too sharp a shooter."

"But why did he stop? Why not try again?"

"People started hearing about Samuel, about what you had done to hide him. Your mother speaking up at the church women's auxiliary, and Eleanor turning nearly everybody's heart and getting beaten so horribly. After that it would not have been popular to have you killed, and the Judge, he cares what folks think. I'm pretty sure there's somebody in your family who reports to him."

"It's my husband."

"You know? Well, then, you know why I think Jessie'd better be someplace else at suppertime."

"He knows that I know. And I can handle him, I think, but maybe you are right. A friend has been fixing up those shacks, so let's see if Jessie is strong enough to take a bumpy ride."

IN THE AFTERNOON SUN, as Dona, Margaret and Jessie rumbled up in the car, the river was as green as the turtles that slid off their rocks. Near the dam, shafts of sun reached clear to the bottom where, except for their long whiskers which waved in the slight current, catfish hung motionless. Blue jays gave no screech of warning; no buzzards circled the sky.

"It seems pretty safe here right now," Dona said, "but for how long, I can't say."

They helped Jessie to a cot on the screened porch of the shack nearest the river, and in a little while, her arms around her chest, eyes closed, she sang, over and over, as softly as a dove murmurs, *I'm gonna lay down my sword and shield, down by the riverside, down by the riverside, ain't gonna suffer war no more.*

"Bless her," Margaret said. "Let us pray that she is right."

"WHAT IS THE SHADOW that follows that child?" Dona said. She and Margaret leaned together against the trunk of the nearest pecan tree, and whispered. "I mean, how can it be that she is thin and brittle as barbed wire and only sixteen? And why would she be the one your husband beat and raped and beat again?"

"My husband would beat and rape any colored girl who stayed still long enough, and Jessie was our maid, for heaven's sake."

"But why. What kind of sickness sets up inside of him?"

"Huh," Margaret patted her hair into place. "About the beating and raping? He is a good ole boy. He's a judge. He's rich. He's a bully and he would shoot horses if he could get away with it. About why Jessie's so thin, I have my guess. You noticed when you bandaged her, she's emaciated, really."

"Yes, I was horrified by her wounds and almost more by her skeleton."

"After he beat her the first time, for resisting him, she stopped eating. She tried running away, but you know how it is around here."

"How do you mean?"

"The so-called leaders of our town, they help each other. When Jessie escaped it was the Reverend MacMurray who spotted her and brought her back to our house. She kept cooking for us, but not eating, I guess."

"Wasn't there anything you could do?"

"Not right then. You see how much makeup I wear."

"Oh, I see."

"Usually, he hits me where it doesn't show, but that time he was really mad. When I got on him about how he treated Jessie, none of my business, he said. You keep your hunting dogs better than you keep her, I said. Shut up, woman, he said, or I'll sic my hunting dogs on your fancy ass. And, he would have, too. I'm deathly afraid of those dogs."

"I don't mean it's your fault, Margaret. But what can we do, now, to keep her safe?"

"First, we've got to help her get well, and fatten her up a bit. She can't live long like that."

"She can't stay here at the shacks. And besides, we'll be using them again pretty soon. She won't be safe anywhere on this ranch. Could you possibly take her with you to your mother's?"

"My mother's?"

"Yes, didn't you tell the Judge that you were going to visit her?"

"I did, but remember? That was a lie. I was coming here with Jessie. My mother's a drunk and in no shape to help anybody."

"Then where can she go?"

"How about back to her home, with her mother?"

"But, her whole family is in danger now, too. What with Samuel gone, we'd better believe that the Klan is looking for Samuel's wife and little boys and watching every aunt, uncle and cousin."

"Their every move," Margaret said.

"And you have no money?"

"Hardly. Only what the Judge gives me and that is precious little."

"You know, Margaret, we can't let this drive us crazy. We are the ones who have to keep ourselves together. We have to take care of this child, and we have to figure out how to keep this from happening in our county ever again."

"But Dona, this is a shoot 'em first and ask questions later land."

"Lord, don't I know it. But I'm thinking of something. Can I tell you, and you'll promise to keep it a secret?"

"I swear on our little Jessie's mangled face."

Chapter Forty-three

"Okay, let's see." Dona put her hands behind her back and walked up and down in front of the mesquite tree beside the screened porch. She hummed and cleared her throat. She stared at the mesquite tree's thorns.

"Look here, Margaret. See how these thorns stick out all over the branch?"

"Sure, it's a mesquite tree. So?"

"Bear with me a minute. See what they're protecting?"

Margaret peered more closely at the twig Dona held toward her.

"They protect the branch, I guess." She put one hand to her throat. "No. They protect the whole tree."

"Right," Dona said, touching a thorn with care. "This is a beautiful tree, and it grows in harsh conditions, a lot like Jessie. And she's not the only one we've got to take care of. There's Eleanor, beaten almost to death by that jackass, thankfully deceased, preacher husband of hers, and dear Bertie, another prey of that husband of yours. How can we gather enough thorns to protect all of them?"

"I can't imagine. The Judge has an awful lot of friends and some of them are mighty mean cowboys."

"How about the cowgirls?"

"Who?"

"The women. It has to come from here." Dona clasped Margaret's shoulder and struck her own chest. "From us. From us and our friends. They know about what happened to Eleanor, they know about Samuel and that I was nearly killed protecting him. There are a lot of strong women of every color in our county, who know lots more than we do, and most of them have women's groups in their churches. And as you know, from when we met with them about Samuel, my mother is president of the Baptist Women's Auxiliary."

Margaret peered into the screened porch to check on Jessie. "She's still asleep, and looking like a bruised little angel."

She glanced up the dirt road toward the ranch house and whispered, "You are right, most of us don't like our husbands being in the Klan. We're not supposed to know. But from the ladies I've talked with, we all do know, but nobody knows what to do about it."

"Let's give the ladies something to do, then."

"Meaning what?"

"Meaning, protecting Jessie and Eleanor and Bertie, and other people in trouble, like Samuel. With their powerful thorns."

"Thorns?"

"Margaret, every woman you know has ways to get around her husband. Even if he gets drunk and beats her up. Or if he's stingy. You can still find husbands who have a conscience and might offer to help. But most men are teenage boys at heart, and they all want two things from their wives, food and sex. Give them those and you can have the car anytime you want it."

"Car?" Margaret laughed.

"Yep. We need a way to get these women out of here. We need money to rent a safe place for them to be. We need women to take care of them until they can be on their own again. We need a story to tell the husbands and preachers so they'll leave us alone while we do the work."

"Dona, you are a wild woman." Margaret paced up and down the porch, clapping her hands. "I am getting revved up for the first time in years. And I have an idea."

"Shoot. Sorry," Dona laughed. "I mean, go ahead."

"How about we say we want to make a place of holy contemplation, just for women, down around Del Rio, maybe, or over in Comanche. Say that women will be better wives for having a time to pray and rest and think about our blessings — for example, our fine husbands."

"And it wouldn't matter what color a woman is," Dona said, "she is welcome to spend time there. We wouldn't exactly mention color, but we'd accept every woman in need of protection — and men who are hunted by the Klan."

"I've thought of another reason the husbands might go for this. They'd reckon that they'd have more time with their mistresses."

"Good thinking!"

"And, Dona, we've got to ask the colored women, too, you know, to help. Negroes and Mexicans in our town and the farms and ranches. They are some mighty strong human beings, if you ask me, and they are in danger all the time, sometimes from their own men, and especially from us white folks."

"Look at Jessie," Dona said, slapping her hands around the tree and avoiding the thorns. "She's as powerful as they come, given the breath of a chance. It has to come from here, from us, from Jessie, and you, Margaret, and Thelma Washington and me. Whatever we can do to make things better right this minute will make a difference for a long time." Dona felt goose bumps rising in excitement.

"But where? Where can we set up a safe place?"

"I'm thinking of my sister's ranch. Unity Ann's, over in Comanche, a little over a hundred miles from here. She's got extra room over there and she's already helping certain people. She had a terrible bad husband who thank heavens, drove off in a fancy automobile and left her and the ranch for good. And she's got more gumption than is usually healthy for her. I'm pretty sure she'll be eager to use it to help the other women and men being persecuted."

An hour later, bringing her mouth close to the child's ear, Dona whispered, "Jessie."

Jessie struggled to wake, her eyelids quivering.

"Jessie, we need to take you to a safer place tonight. I know you're feeling poorly, but do you think you can stand to get back in Margaret's car?"

"Going where?"

"To my sister's house, honey. There are a couple of people there who will be mighty glad to see you. But I can't tell you, yet."

"Safe?"

"It's as safe as anywhere we can think of. Margaret will be back real soon. She's gone to find your mother and let her know you are all right. She must have been crazy with worry."

"Not my momma."

"No? Why not?"

"She says nobody's safe, so don't worry about it. Do your best, child, is what she says."

"That hasn't worked so well, has it."

"No ma'am. But my momma, she has nine, so no time to worry over just one. Specially one in the middle."

"But you know, I suspect your momma says that so you won't worry about her. Worrying about you, I mean."

For the first time that day, Jessie smiled. "Ow," she said, covering her mouth. Her hand came away with a spot of blood.

"Your wounds are too fresh to smile. But I must say it was lovely to see a twinkle in those eyes. And Margaret will get you to that safe place quick as she can. In fact, thank heavens, here she is. I'd love to go with you, but I've got to go see the boss."

Chapter Forty-four

THE CLERKS HAD LEFT THE COURTHOUSE in late afternoon, when Dona slipped into Judge Angus Cameron's office, shut the door behind her, and said, "Hello, Angus."

"Dona Willis Turn." He rose from his desk. "What on earth do you want?"

"An answer to this question, Judge. What right do you have to go above the law?"

"You have no right to bust in here, and you sure don't have the right to question me. I am the judge of our county's court, duly elected by a landslide."

"You are Angus Cameron to me," Dona said, taking the chair across from him. She clasped her hands in her lap, white gloves glinting against her coat, black as a buzzard's eye. "I mean no disrespect to your office, but you, Angus, you are disgusting."

Judge Cameron sat back down in his big, leather chair and laughed. "Disgusting? Me? How am I the one in this august office who is disgusting, when you are the one who is hiding a nigger running from the law?"

"The law? A lynch mob is now the law? Tell me how that can be?" She shook her shoulders, uncrossed her legs and sat with her back straight as a yard stick.

"Let me remind you of something, Dona. Do you remember when we were children? I was ahead of you in school, of course, being older, but I always thought highly of you. That is, until we all found out that our schoolmaster had his way with you on the schoolroom floor. And after that, I felt you were soiled and that you had lured the schoolmaster to lose his senses."

Dona sat forward, her lips trembling, and said, "And how does this lie relate to the lynch mob, Angus?"

"I have known all along that you have something of the Devil in you. Something that attracts trouble. You of all people would come to the aid of that nigger because you agree with what he did."

"And what was that?" Dona's stomach wedged against her backbone.

"You, being sullied yourself, understood how he could convince Mrs. Eleanor MacMurray to go beyond the bounds of decency. And I, having seen the consequences of depraved behaviors from my position as judge, could understand how decent men might want to punish Samuel Washington as quickly as possible. Before he could destroy another innocent white woman's life."

"Is it true, Angus, that you raped and beat Jessie Washington? Is it true that you locked her in a room in the back of your house because she would not agree to your further advances?"

The Judge sprang from his chair and glared at Dona. "You may leave now. This conversation is ended. I don't know where you got such slanderous information, but wherever it came from, and who brought it to you, will be punished as well."

Dona marched toward the door in the Judge's chambers, her heels snapping on the marble floor. She reached for the brass door knob, embossed with the seal of their county, and halted. She turned to face him, and shook her head.

"Angus. How did we come to this? Little Dona, young Angus, children of innocence and occasional happiness. When did we split so far apart? I have to leave now, but I'll be back before long. We are not done."

"A WOMAN STANDING CAN GET A MOVE ON QUICKER...," Margaret said. "Thank you for saying that, Dona. Meant a lot. And I heard about you busting into the Judge's chambers. No sittin' around for you."

They settled in the swing of the ranch house's back porch with their coffee cups, the cool early morning air around their ankles.

"So, I am not sitting around any longer, either," Margaret said. "I am resting my heels, right this minute, but honey, something has fallen away. My old way of seeing things, you know, and I hope it doesn't ever come back. But you can't imagine what it took to get myself out here this morning, in secret. The Judge has gotten wind of our friendship and he wants none of it."

"Does he know about Jessie? That you took her away?"

"I don't think so. I drove part of the way from here like I was going to my mother's and then changed course. Had to stop a time or two to take care of her."

"You were a hero for doing that. And now that Jessie and Eleanor are at Unity Ann's, I guess I'm impatient about others in danger."

"That's what I'm here to tell you, if you'll hold up a mite. Everything's ready at Unity Ann's. Samuel and his family have a cabin all to themselves, and he and Daniel built a few snug little rooms real quick in Unity Ann's barn for Eleanor, and whoever else needs a safe place. And they are working on a kitchen and a bathroom with running water and a flush toilet, and did you know Unity Ann has electricity?"

"No, I didn't know that, but they can't have done it so fast. Who helped?"

"Unity Ann's wetbacks and their families pitched right in."

"Margaret," Dona lowered her voice and leaned toward her friend, "we mustn't call them wetbacks any longer. Like we should never say nigger. Same thing to them."

"Same thing to us, too, I guess," Margaret said, finishing her coffee. "Seeing them as different, lower, you might say, than we are. Which of course they are not." She grinned. "See, Mrs. Turn, you're not the only one who can whistle a new tune."

Dona took her friend's hands in her own. "I will not tell your husband about our plan, but I must go to see him again in a couple of days. He is the hub of a mighty dangerous wheel, and we've known each other nearly all our lives. I hope you will understand."

"Hard as it is to say, I believe you are the one to talk with him, and I trust you not to betray me."

Chapter Forty-five

"THANK YOU, ANGUS, for taking this time. I know it's late." Dona walked close to his desk and waited.

Judge Cameron stood, his eyes lowered and his arms crossed over the pleats of his robe. Wood paneling on the walls held the silence.

"Have a seat. I have something to say."

Dona slid into the chair opposite his.

"I don't remember." His voice was low and rough with feeling. "I have tried not to think about it. I have become what I am." Out the window toward the town's park, emerald water glided past children playing on the river's banks.

"Maybe it had to do with what happened to you. You were so young. The schoolmaster was crazy, we all knew it, and he was strong. You didn't have a chance. I heard about it from his own mouth, Dona, did you know that? Did you know that he bragged about it to my father, in my presence?"

Dona said nothing. Her gloved fingers gripped each other on her lap.

"And I do remember that something changed in me, right then. I was fifteen, older than you, but I was afraid. So afraid, I went to the back shed and folded myself into the pile of horse blankets and cried myself to sleep. When I woke up, I knew I could never let something like that happen to me. I would not be weak, not in any way."

He cleared his throat. He was crying now. She nodded slowly.

"And so, I grew mean. It helped that I was big for my age, tall and brawny; and you may remember how I beat up smaller boys. I can't say I was proud of it, but it worked. The grown men seemed to like it, my being a bully." Angus chuckled and shook his head. "And some of the other children came to look to me as their leader, perhaps in fear. I took it as a sign of respect, and found ways to reward them. At least, I left them alone."

Angus sat back heavily into his leather chair. "And so, I learned how to get my way. And how to turn people against each other. Especially to turn other whites against the Negroes and the Mexicans. Easiest thing in the world, really. Easiest thing in the world."

He drew a handkerchief from inside of his robe and wiped his eyes. "Doney, would you pray for me?"

She swallowed her satisfaction at watching this man-child abjectly place himself in her hands, but she could not pray for him. Who would hear her prayer? He must make his own appeal, his own confession, to whatever power he served. But something was not making sense.

She spoke slowly. "When you were in the back shed, Angus, on the horse blankets, what really happened?"

He squinted, alarmed. "What do you mean? Didn't I tell you? Haven't I told you too much?"

"You have trusted me with a lot, and I will keep my silence, but you have omitted something. Something that happened to turn you to darkness."

She handed him her handkerchief, smaller than his, more delicate, but bearing the strength of her grandmother's embroidery. "There, take your time. And tell me what you are able."

He removed his robe, its weight. He loosened his black tie and the first button of his shirt, white with starch, held Dona's handkerchief to his face, and sat back in his chair.

"I can't say anything else right now."

"Perhaps you have forgotten. But Angus, your body holds everything, all that has happened to you, all you love and all you fear. Listen to it."

Angus closed his eyes and it seemed to Dona that he had left the room, though he was large before her. Presently, he spoke.

"My body has been wounded, almost to the point of death. It is hard to understand, but when I ask it to speak, I see something like a red ball with an arrow through its middle. Like the heart children carve into trees. Only this is carved into my belly. And the scar goes clean through to my back. And there is a sound, like the beating of a huge drum, and I am . . ."

With that, Angus pulled the metal wastebasket from under his desk and threw up into it, retching again and again. Dona gazed out the window at a live oak tree that had stood for over two hundred years in that place.

"*Fragile*," she thought, waiting for Angus to right himself. "*We are all fragile, every one of us. And this man, this child I knew, is among the most tender*."

As she sat there, her eyes closed, Dona returned to the time when she was thirteen and Angus was fifteen. To the day when Angus pushed over his desk, rushed from their one-room schoolhouse, and vomited into the cactus grove under the big mesquite tree. Everyone heard him, and some of the children covered their mouths. But when he came back to the classroom, no one said a word, not the students, not the teacher. It was as if he, the biggest boy in school, had never left. She wondered about it, then; but it must have been after she was raped. For it was a teacher, not the schoolmaster, who was in the classroom; Angus must have known by then what had happened to her.

"Angus, dear Angus. I am so sorry. You had no one to tell, no one had any idea what you were feeling. You were, you are, a sensitive person. It must have been awful to keep silent, to hold the knowledge of what the schoolmaster did to me."

"It wasn't just that," Angus said after a while. "It was not only what he did to you." He rubbed his neck as though it pained him, spread his hands on the desk blotter and said, "You guessed. How I don't know. But after I heard him boast to my father, and after I ran to the darkness of the shed for comfort, the schoolmaster jerked open the shed door and found me huddled on the horse blankets. He had a wildness about him that terrified me, and you of course remember how large and strong he was." Angus paused to glance at Dona.

"Yes, I remember," and she felt her lips draw between her teeth. "Please go on, Angus. This is so hard, but it is up to us."

"I don't remember all of it, but I know he didn't give me time to defend myself. He straddled me like I was a horse and put his huge hands over my mouth, and pushed my head into the corner." Angus gasped and crossed his arms high against his chest. Tears dripped from his chin, and as he moaned through his open mouth, his fear and grief were presences in the room.

"I fought as hard as I could, but his weight, his bulk, his fist against my chin forcing my head back. It was too much, and whether I felt it or knew it or dreamed it, when it was over, my belt was gone, my pants were around my feet, and my buttocks were on fire. When I sat up, I could see that my thighs were smeared with what appeared to be my blood, already drying. And I suppose you, of all the children in our little school, could know how I felt."

"Yes," she said, rubbing her eyes with her coat sleeve. "I do know. And now I understand so much better. Let us sit for a while without speaking, if you have the time."

"I have the time," he said.

Chapter Forty-six

Luke's woodworking shed was a smoldering ruin, when Dona returned to the ranch that late afternoon.

Roy and Juan Carlos were away, shipping cattle to Fort Worth. And where was Luke?

Dona searched and hollered and found him at last in the skinning shed, standing, facing the far corner. He flinched but didn't turn around.

"Luke, thank heavens I found you. Your shed. Who would do such a thing?"

"Don't you know Dona start fresh start fresh our mommy used to say doubt you remember." He turned toward her and his eyes burned through the gloom.

"I remember." Dona sidled closer. "Gently now. I am your sister and I love you. Can you tell me about the fire?"

"I cain't tell you nothin' you don't know, Doney. Ever thing is what you know." He turned and moved quickly toward her, brushing past ropes and heavy chains.

Dona edged back toward the open doorway. "Luke, my darling brother, I can see how sad you are and I want to help." The air behind her changed.

"Who's coming?" Luke said, his hand closing around a meat hook from the wall.

"You gonna protect me, are you Luke?"

"Naw, all my easy days is gone." He held her eyes and shifted his shoulders toward the corral.

"Nobody out there, Lukey." Her voice was smooth as cream. "Think it's the wind. Maybe what spread the fire today, don't you think?"

"I'm gonna use this here hook to hang myself like a slaughtered steer. And don't you try to stop me one bit."

"Luke, my only brother. I love you. You can be happy again."

"Murderin' that momma coyote." Sweat darkened the collar of his denim shirt. "It weren't the beginning." Tears ran down the furrows in his cheeks and into the corners of his mouth. "That snake preacher, murdering my wife and baby girl, were the start. Weren't nothin good after that. Hurtin' Joe Bob, and this here fire to my own shed, them's the end, Sis I ain't nothin' but trouble to you or nobody in the world."

"Lukey," Dona said, opening her arms to him, "put the hook away and let's take a walk to the big barn. It's cool in there; it helps us to be around the hens. Remember when we were little, how they'd make us laugh?"

Luke jabbed the point of the hook into his arm and pulled it out. "This don't hurt, Doney. You wanna try it?"

Dona stepped back, feeling the edge of the doorway with her shoulder. No one was out there, no one. "I can't, Luke. And I don't want you to. Stop it now, or I'll tell Mother on you."

Luke's eyes grew as wide as a child's. "Oh, no. I'm kidding, Sis, just kidding. Don't tell." And he gouged the hook deep into his chest.

"You're bleeding, Lukey," she said, swallowing hard. "Let's fix you up, ok? You'll be all right and I promise not to tell."

She reached for him, for the hook, but he stepped back like a dancer.

He grinned, "You wouldn't, Doney. You love me." Red blossomed along the left front panel of his work shirt.

"You know I do. You are my big brother. We take care of each other, don't we?"

"I cain't take care of nobody." He jerked the hook out of his chest and thrust it in again. Blood rushed from the wounds.

"Luke, stop right now. Think of your heart. Don't hit that artery. How would you save a horse? Save yourself. Luke!"

She turned, shrieking, pushed out of the skinning room and ran, blinded, across the corral and the barnyard to the smoldering ruins of the shed. She screamed for help, but no one answered. She jerked open the door to the barn and went to the rifle rack. It was empty. If a gunshot, Juan Carlos would come. Someone would hear. In her mind, Luke's heart writhed and spasmed and grew pale. A blue jay screeched and screeched. Her mother's car banged across the cattle guard, carrying Annalou and Merrybelles, heading her way.

"My darling boy, why did you do it?" Ophelia's face was stiff with anger and grief. "You tried to destroy your own self. Are you mad?"

"Mother," Dona said. "Be gentle."

Luke peered through eyes made of dust. Where was the dance of light on blue water? Where was the glint of mischief?

Ophelia lay her head on the hospital bed, next to Luke's wrapped and tortured body.

"I heard the voice, Momma," Luke whispered through lips dry and harsh as straw. "It said punish." His throat clinched and he faltered, "it ... it said, kill."

Luke's eyes closed over eyeballs rolling like storm-driven waves. He gasped for air and arched his neck as though trying to break from bonds. Blood burst free of his heart through shredded chest muscles and layers of gauze, soaking sheets, pillows and Dona's hands, as she tried to staunch the flow.

"No!" Ophelia's cry, as it hit the walls, was like a wild bird, trying to escape.

Dona said, her voice like a trumpet's call, "Get the nurse. Now."

But, as Ophelia ran toward the door, the whisper of Luke's clothes hushed. His eyes stilled. He had obeyed his mind, and it had stopped tormenting him.

It was an hour before she and their mother consented to leave his side, to clean his blood from their hands, to weep together in the corner of the room.

The rest of the family, arms entwined and heads bowed, kept watch outside the door, until Luke's body was taken away.

That night the coyotes moved, while silver shadows blossomed under cactus pears. It was the hour when coyotes sniffed the river, hoping catfish would whisper through their whiskers the secret to breathing underwater. Dona walked her horse along the river bank where cows chewed their cuds and turkeys flapped their way to tops of trees. This night dropped heavy on the ranch.

Her shoulders bowed with the weight of dread; regret, like a needle, pierced and pried her chest until her saddle horn was slicked with tears. She wished the foxes would speak out, she begged the coyotes to snap her thoughts in their big jaws and sing them to the sky, this blackest night. "Please, won't you help me now," she said to catfish and jackrabbits. "My brother died today. He massacred his body. Survive, you say?"

Chapter Forty-seven

The straw hat hung on its peg at the back of Luke's closet, next to his best Stetson, which was felted and broad-brimmed. The sort of hat that every proper cowboy wore on Sundays and to funerals. Dona had not been eager to fetch the straw hat, so much a part of Luke that the smell of the bandana tied around its crown seemed to bring him bodily into the room. It was the one hat he could never throw away, even after the rim unraveled, even after Joe Bob put a hole in it with his BB gun, all those years ago. Dona imagined Luke's fingers, long-boned and calloused, pushing the hat up and off his forehead, so he could scratch his head when he had a problem to solve.

And Luke was good at solving problems, mechanical ones. He could fix the tines on a harrow, the carburetor in the old truck, a broken wheel on the hay wagon, and sharpen anything with a blade — or a point. But, and here she took down the hat and pressed it to her chest, Luke was awful at fixing problems of the heart. Always had been.

And when he fell in love with Evangeline at the brothel, a woman beautiful and kind and who loved him back, and when they had their baby daughter, all in secret on pain of death, and when Reverend MacMurray murdered Evangeline and the baby in their sleep, poor, poor, darling Luke; was that when he went mad? Was he crazy when they were growing up?

There were his moods, how he wouldn't speak to anyone, including to her, his favorite sister, for days; and then how, for another few days, though he never said much, he would be bright and ready to sit with anyone over a cup of coffee at their kitchen table. You never knew, with Luke. Something would tip him over the edge and it was as though another being had taken over. How else would he come to torture himself with regret and blame; how else would he come to gouge his chest with a meat hook until his tender heart stopped altogether?

The straw hat comforted Dona now, as though the brother she loved and feared and worried about and loved again was somehow not dead, would never die. They would bury him in his Sunday Stetson; but this one, she would keep.

Chapter Forty-eight

Luke was to be buried by the river near his catfish trot lines. The family figured the creatures knew him there, and others who loved him could come often to pay their respects.

Choosing a preacher had been hard, as they couldn't trust their own, from the Baptist or Presbyterian churches in town. They asked Unity Ann's minister from Comanche, a tall, rangy fellow with an untamed shock of red hair, named Gabriel Steele, who seemed to have eyes for Unity Ann. And Dona wondered if he had also learned about Samuel and the others, and if he did, would he say something to Roy or Joe Bob? Or, worse, to Judge Cameron, who had not been expected, but showed up anyway with his wife, Margaret, who kept close to Dona.

Cousin Edward raised dust on the river road when he drove up in his new yellow roadster, bearing Bertie in the front seat. For that moment, given the occasion, they stopped smiling.

Joe Bob and Roy had made the coffin out of pecan boards left over from the tiny box Luke had built for Nanna, buried in her pink dress. They sanded and rubbed the wood's grain until it shone like fine furniture and, with Melvar's help, loaded it into his wagon, which Bertie had cleaned and draped with black cotton fabric from Melvar's special supply. Molly had pulled the wagon with the dignity only a good mule can manage on a cattle ranch and was now standing at the front steps of the ranch house waiting.

Roy, Joe Bob and Juan Carlos bore the shrouded body across the porch and laid it in the coffin. The brown and white quilt Nanna made for Luke when he turned twelve, with its patches depicting bucking broncos, cowboy hats, fishing poles, and knives, draped in folds from his head to his feet, and was tied by his favorite lasso. Annalou and Merrybelles placed a cup and spoon Luke had carved out of live oak wood, in case an angel offered him coffee. Before the lid was nailed on, Dona climbed onto the wagon and placed Luke's Sunday Stetson over his heart for protection. It was time to gather at the river.

ON EITHER SIDE OF THE BURIAL HOLE, near a pecan tree between the maize field and the river bank, Melvar, Juan Carlos, Roy and Joe Bob stood ready for when the time would come to lower the coffin into the hole.

Josie, her Sunday hat tipped forward, lingered near the food tables, which she and her new friend, Rosa, had worked since dawn to prepare, until Dona waved them into the circle around the grave.

"The family is all here," she said to the Reverend Steele. "Friends are gathering. We will be ready when you say." But she did not feel ready. Angus Cameron loomed like a specter, capable of anything, and she would have to speak with him after the burial.

EARLY THAT LATE-SUMMER EVENING, when the river glowed pink and green in the low rays of sun, its banks seemed to fold and curl in time to the fiddle. Melvar sat on the seat of his black-draped wagon, circled with sheaves of hay and the purple-black blossoms of nightshade. He played for his friend, Luke, tunes from Persia, from Scotland, from Ireland and America. He played as though speaking what the others, seated on wooden benches, bending over campfires to stoke the flames, or leaning against trunks of pecan trees, hats over their chests, wanted to say. Dona knelt in the dirt by her brother's newly covered grave, smoothing the rough sod as though comforting a child.

She was aware and thankful that Unity Ann and their mother, Ophelia, were at her side so that they, Luke's remaining family, might be of comfort to each other. And that Annalou and Merrybelles, Joe Bob, Roy, and Juan Carlos stayed close. She counted on the presence of Edward, Bertie, Margaret Cameron and Eleanor MacMurray, whose broad hat hid the scars that remained from her injuries. But she was most aware of Angus Cameron. Throughout the graveside service and the meal that spread on long tables, and now, as the music moved people to sway and to dance, Angus kept to the edges. Like a body's shadow, he sat now among the trees. It was time to talk.

She closed her eyes and whispered, "Oh, for the strength of a small bird."

Perhaps it was this thought or perhaps it was her own stubbornness. She dropped her shoulders, wiped her hands on her sleeves, and went to his side.

Angus removed his hat and stood to give Dona his seat. She said, "Take a stroll with me, Angus?" He replaced his hat, nodded, and waited for her to lead the way.

"You have something on your mind," she said, as quietly as she could.

They turned toward the dirt road that had brought them to the river and walked toward the west. When they were out of earshot, he said, "I have so much on my mind, it's hard to know where to start."

"I am not in a hurry."

"I have thought hard about our conversations," he said. "And first I need to thank you. I've held some terrible things inside myself for a long time, and I've done some equally terrible things because of that. Dona, you are the first person who knows, and now I have spoken with Margaret."

"Yes?"

"I have hurt her in ways I never understood before. I have hurt so many women, and girls like little Jessie. I can't expect Margaret ever to forgive me."

"What does she say?"

"She says she has to talk with you."

"And why hasn't she?"

"This is all so new, and then Luke dying, and now the funeral here at the river, no time."

"Forgiveness is sometimes slow, Angus." Dona paused on the road and faced the craggy, handsome man she had feared for so long. The sun was at the horizon and his skin glowed in its crimson light.

"But if you're sincere, when you ask for Margaret's forgiveness, and if you're truthful in your humility, perhaps there's a chance. I'll talk with her about anything she wishes. And, Angus, what about Samuel?"

"I know that it is hideous to pursue another human being with the intent of crucifying him. And especially when he has no chance to defend himself in court."

"It's not so different from the schoolmaster assaulting you, is it, Angus? That was a kind of crucifixion, too, of a completely innocent person."

Angus halted and took in the sky. "I'm always surprised at how fast darkness comes on these plains. And look, stars are beginning to show themselves." His sigh was long and ragged. "What shall I do about Samuel?"

"What about the others, Angus? All of the colored, the Negroes, the Mexicans, the Jews, who are persecuted for not being white Christians. And what about the way we see anybody who is different from us. The way you see women. Thinking or acting like you are better, that you have the right to punish and control, when really you and the other Klan members are bullies and sissies, afraid for yourselves. It's all of that, we need to consider; what we need to change. There is so much for all of us to take in. Like, what gives white men the right to persecute colored men and rape a woman of any color at all?"

They were at the place in the river below the dam, where streams of water laced together around rocks, separated, wove again together. She moved closer to Angus and said in a low voice, "Why can't white and colored children go to the same school? Why can't white and colored families live in the same neighborhood? Why on earth can't anyone marry anyone else, no matter what color, or even what sex?"

"Whoa, Dona. That is a lot, what you ask. Those questions are dangerous. But you know me now, and you are kind." He pulled off his Stetson, drew his fingers through his hair and replaced the hat. "Not easy, but it's kind of like I've seen the light, you know? It shines on a world that's really different from what I thought it was. So, at least I am willing to try."

"Maybe we can begin to answer one or two of those questions," Dona said, quietly. "Do you know where Samuel is?"

"I do. And his wife and sons, and his brother, Daniel, and Jessie. And I know that Eleanor has been there, too. It's good to see her here, today. I know about the refuge for mistreated women and innocent men hunted like animals. The Reverend Steele may be sweet on Unity Ann, but maybe you won't be surprised that he answers to me."

"No, I am not surprised. And you have done nothing to harm anyone at Unity Ann's?"

"Nothing. And I won't. And I want to do whatever I can to help make that place safer, larger, and whatever else Samuel and Unity Ann want it to be." He hesitated and turned toward the river. "It's a start."

Dona stayed with him, walking slowly. "And the members of the Klan, the ones you lead?"

"I think I can persuade them to cease and desist at least some of their criminal behavior. I can't ask them to disband, as they have the legal right to exist. You understand that, right?"

"I do."

"But I can turn in my own hood and robe and membership, as Edward has already done. And Dinky and Toad and Ross and others I've thought of as "my boys." You may not know they were in the Klan. Or perhaps you do?"

"I know more than most, I believe. Many in our county, as supposedly upstanding as The Reverend Andrew MacMurray, are Klansmen."

"Andrew was as deadly as the flames that got him," Angus said, "and plumb crazy."

"Angus, there are those who believe you must be punished, even killed, for what you have done to so many others. What do you think of that?"

"I am praying every day for forgiveness, for compassion, which I know I do not deserve. What do you think should happen to me?"

"I think by tormenting others you have punished yourself, to an extent that has been almost beyond redemption; and yet, I believe you when you say you have gone through a deep conversion, a true change in the way you see, well, almost everything. I hope with all my heart that it will last."

She looked directly for a long moment into Angus's eyes.

"Angus, you have the ability to accomplish great evil or great good, and we will see which you actually choose. I believe in the power of forgiveness, and when they see the results of your own compassion in action, many will forgive you. But because you have entrusted me with the deepest wounds and sorrows of your life, I choose, now, to forgive you for what you have done to me and my family."

Angus said, "Thank you, Dona," and bowed his head into his hands. Tears ran between his fingers.

Dona did not reach for him. She did not say, 'There, there.' She thrust her hands into her skirt pockets and squared her shoulders. She said, "But, Angus, you will have to ask Samuel and Jessie and Bertie, and everyone else you have tried to destroy, for their forgiveness. I cannot give you that."

"You are right," he said, and dried his eyes with the palms of his hands. "The list will be long, but if you think they might talk with me, I will seek their blessings."

As they approached the campfire and Luke's grave, the lilting melody from Melvar's fiddle changed to the prayerful strains Jessie Washington had sung when she was near to death, and little by little the voices raised whatever words they knew: *I'm gonna lay down my sword and shield, down by the riverside, down by the riverside, gonna study war no more...*

Angus stood for a moment close to the fire and drew from his coat pocket the white cloth of his Klan hood. He held up the pointed shape with its holes for eyes, ghostly with emptiness, tossed it into the flames, and watched as they brightened.

Margaret wept into her handkerchief and moved to Dona's side where they were joined in a circle around the fire by all of the other relatives and friends of Luke's who had scattered along the river bank after his burial.

Amazing Grace, they sang to the fiddle's strings, *how sweet the sound that saves a wretch like me. I once was lost, but now am found, was blind but now can see.*

They sang the verses, again and again, until every person had dried the tears they had not expected ever to shed, until the fiddle grew quiet. Dona rubbed Molly's ears, and climbed into the wagon beside Melvar.

"You are all invited to the ranch house," Dona said, opening her arms, "for coffee, and sweet potato pie. Let us go together."

Epilogue

SAMUEL CHUCKLED, "THIS Sheepherder's Hut, Dona. Lordy, lordy it sure does feel different from the first time I was here. Not running from nobody, at least right this minute." His face crinkled around his eyes.

It was the late edge of afternoon, a year after Luke's funeral. A strong north wind had swept down through the Panhandle, bringing the crisp, cool air of October. They sat together on the great, flat stone outside the Hut, and Dona turned toward him.

"Is it enough, this minute of rest?"

"I'd say it's what we got." He looked to the sky and spread his arms. "It's like I've grown wings. Long feathers, like the scissor-tailed birds; like I could fly from the butte, a golden eagle. The terribleness of that night when the Klan came after me, I guess I'll remember it 'til I die. But since then, you taking me in like I was your other brother; Melvar, carting me off to that doctor, saving a black man's worthless life, as that boy said, the one who shot me; and on to Unity Ann's place–what we named Unity Ranch — and maybe I made a difference there. Sure helped me. Did you know that Eleanor MacMurray and I still read together? I got my own books.

"Judge Cameron helped, too, that's for sure, but it's not just that. We got some hope. Something big changed for us dark-skinned folks. Not everything, not nearly everything, but a good bit, to get 'em off our backs. And I pray that one day, we'll grab onto our own...," and he cleared his throat, raised his eyes to the tops of the live oak trees and said, as loudly as he could, "Our own power."

Samuel shifted his shoulders toward the bluff where his boys were hunting for fossils, shouting back and forth with Annalou and Joe Bob, home from college that day. "Dona, just listen to that. My wife, my boys, what it's done for us. And the whole county."

"Samuel, I hope you believe me. All of this, the good things, helping the women and girls in trouble, protecting the colored folk who are treated like animals, those things are happening because of you. Your courage, your hard work, and because so many people trust you and whatever you say."

He propped his elbows on his knees and pressed the palms of his hands together, his long fingers entwined. "Makes me feel like praying for it to continue. But, to tell the truth, we've got a mighty long road of danger ahead of us. I heard about a new group in Texas for the rights of the Negro and other colored folks. Name of NAACP. It scares me, what it will take to really change things. But Maisie agrees, and we're joining up."

They rested there, in the late afternoon sun. Down the bluff, Melvar's deep laughter mixed with the murmurs of mourning doves and the drone of crickets. Anyone watching would wonder at the peace of such a place, filled as it was with wild things.

The Beginning.

Acknowledgements

As every writer knows, writing a book can be lonesome and scary work. In my experience, it's essential to our sanity and happiness to be part of a community of writers who encourage us, celebrate even our teeniest successes, and love us without judgment when we falter. I am deeply grateful to so many who have helped me along the dusty roads of this novel—and my life.

My deepest thanks go to my brilliant friends, the writers Jacqueline Sheehan, Diana Gordon and Celia Jeffries, for never losing faith in me and this book, and for being there at the hardest times. A special bow of thanks to Jane Mortifee, gifted yogini, brave writer, song-filled fellow-traveler, and to acclaimed artist, Susan Sensemann, whose generosity and artistic eye always inspires. I am indebted to the other incredibly helpful readers and comrades through the process, who steadfastly slogged through full, ragged drafts and kept me going with their invaluable insights: Becky Jones, Cathy Roth, CD Nelsen, Julia Mines, Martha Olver, and Gina Ayvazian. And my enduring gratitude to Robert Marstall, whose artwork graces my books.

To all the writers in my workshops, manuscript groups, and retreats: thank you. For fifteen years, you listened to parts of this book as it grew into its present self, offered astute suggestions for improvement, and wanted to hear more. Your enthusiasm kept the story alive. To Robin Glenn, colleague and guide through years of the work that goes into offering workshops and retreats all over the world, and to Ellen Meeropol for her generous and sage advice, my forever thanks and admiration.

My heart is full of gratitude for my beloved children, John Sackrey and Ponteir Sackrey, who not only read the manuscript, they made it (as they make my life, every day) a whole lot better. My niece, Cari Clark, deserves special thanks for faithfully keeping our family's West Texas history alive, and insightfully interviewing Texas authors. And I am beholden to the memory of Blake Lewis (Skipper) Duncan, my bigger-than-life cousin, who imparted what it took to run a ranch in West Texas in the "old days."

To the Great Darkness Writers, Pat Riggs, Marianne Banks, Jacqueline Sheehan, Marion VanArsdell, Jennifer Jacobson, Melenie Flynn, Morgan Sheehan, Alan Lipp and Edie Lipp--that faithful, talented bunch of writers and dear friends who've kept me and each other writing on Wednesday evenings for decades; to the memory of Pat Schneider and Amherst Writers & Artists, where I began; and to Straw Dog Writers Guild, which offers writers every day the irreplaceable gift of community, and of which I am so proud to be a part, my special gratitude.

Thank you to my oldest friend, Ann Jones, courageous writer and my hero for sixty years, and to the generous Mary O'Neil and her cottage on Cape Cod, where I've found unfailing refuge for so long, and finally finished the manuscript. A big hug to Ginny Sullivan, for her poems, her gardens and our friendship. My great thanks to the esteemed folks at Levellers Press, Randy Zucco, Ashley Taylor, Caleb Wetmore and Steve Strimer, who shepherded me and the details of this book with patience and skill until we were as good as we could be.

And to the writers who ventured to Patchwork Farm Retreat and those beautiful and exotic places where we wrote together, thank you for your creative minds, your adventurous hearts, and most of all, for entrusting me with your words.

About our Audiobook: Thorns of the Mesquite is available in print, thanks to the wonderful Levellers Press, and as an audiobook, due to the labor of love by a team of gifted, generous artists to whom I will be in debt for my life time: Judith Fine, talented reader; Craig Eastman, producer and master fiddler; Matt Chartsonis, audiobook guide; and Len Berkman, dramaturge, cheerleader and academic sponsor at Smith College, which provided us a rare recording room

It is the intention of the author that all profits from this book be shared between organizations that protect the civil rights of all people, and those that serve and support victims of domestic violence.

Source Notes

EPIGRAPH
Bertolt Brecht's poem "Motto," serves as the epigraph (or motto) to his collection Svendborg Poems. The Svendborg Poems collection itself was published in 1939. Brecht worked on compiling this collection primarily during the winter of 1937-1938 while living in exile in Denmark. The work was largely completed by July 1938—the time of this story.

PAGE 23
How 'Ya Gonna Keep 'Em Down on the Farm? (After They've Seen Paree) was written by Joe Young and Sam M. Lewis with music by Walter Donaldson, and published in 1918.

PAGE 26
Fiddle tune, "Turkey in the Straw," is an American folk song that first gained popularity in the 19th century. The song is related to a number of tunes of the 19th century and the origin of these songs has been widely debated. Links to older Irish/Scottish/English ballads have been proposed, such as "The Old Rose Tree".

PAGE 26
"Leave the familiar for a while." is the first line of "All the Hemispheres," a poem by Hafiz. From 'The Subject Tonight is Love', translated by Daniel Ladinsky. Hafiz, whose given name was Shamsuddin Muhammad, lived in the 14th century in Shiraz and is the most beloved poet of the Persians.

Page 61
Twinkle, Twinkle, Little Star" originated from an English poem, "The Star," by Jane Taylor, published in 1806, and the French folk melody, "Ah! vous diary-je, Maman," first published in 1761.

PAGES 296 & 321
From the traditional African-American spiritual "Down By The Riverside," also known as "Ain't Gonna Study War No More". The song's origins are traced to before the Civil War and likely drew on biblical

imagery from Isaiah 2:4, envisioning a future of peace where swords are beaten into ploughshares. It evolved through oral tradition, with the Fisk Jubilee Singers making the first recording in 1920.

PAGE 322

"Amazing Grace" originated as a poem written in 1772 by John Newton, an English clergyman and former slave trader.

EPILOGUE

NAACP: The first branch of the National Association for the Advancement of Colored People in Texas was established in El Paso in 1915 and by 1919 four branches, including Dallas and Austin, called Texas home. But Texas did not provide a welcome to the new Texas branches that were met with bitter racial animus often fostered by white supremacy organizations like the Ku Klux Klan, and many faltered. The organization in Texas experienced a significant resurgence after World War II, with membership increasing dramatically.

Patricia Lee Lewis (aka Pat Sackrey) was born and raised in Austin, Texas. After she moved north with her family, she lived for forty-three years on a little mountain at Patchwork Farm Retreat in Westhampton, MA, where she led hundreds of creative writing workshops and retreats, and seventy writing & yoga retreats in ten countries.

Patricia has dedicated much of her life to advocating for women, civil rights, peace and democracy, a healthy environment, small farms, rural communities, and the arts. She holds an MFA in Creative Writing from Vermont College of Fine Arts and a BA from Smith College (Phi Beta Kappa). She is the author of two acclaimed books of poems: *A Kind of Yellow*, which won first prize in poetry from Writers Digest International, and *High Lonesome*, published by Hedgerow Books.

Currently residing in Northampton, MA, Patricia serves on the advisory council of Straw Dog Writers Guild, where she was also the founding president. At age 88, *Thorns of the Mesquite* is her first novel, a work fifteen years in the making, and is a testament to her heritage and lifelong dedication to storytelling.

www.ingramcontent.com/pod-product-compliance
Lightning Source LLC
LaVergne TN
LVHW041112080826
845145LV00007B/1782

* 9 7 8 1 9 6 5 6 6 4 2 3 0 *